IN THE
RAVENOUS
DARK

ALSO BY
A.M. STRICKLAND

Beyond the Black Door

IN THE
RAVENOUS
DARK

A.M. STRICKLAND

{Imprint}
MAKE YOUR MARK

NEW YORK

{Imprint}
MAKE YOUR MARK

A part of Macmillan Publishing Group, LLC
120 Broadway, New York, NY 10271

IN THE RAVENOUS DARK. Copyright © 2021 by AdriAnne Strickland.
All rights reserved. Printed in the United States of America.

Library of Congress Cataloging-in-Publication Data is available.

ISBN 978-1-250-77660-0 (hardcover) / ISBN 978-1-250-77661-7 (ebook)

Our books may be purchased in bulk for promotional, educational, or business use.
Please contact your local bookseller or the Macmillan Corporate and Premium
Sales Department at (800) 221-7945 ext. 5442 or by email at
MacmillanSpecialMarkets@macmillan.com.

Book design by Elynn Cohen

Imprint logo designed by Amanda Spielman

First edition, 2021

1   3   5   7   9   10   8   6   4   2

fiercereads.com

There are spirits who lie in wait
For would-be literary crooks,
Ready to drag them to Hades
And bury their souls in books.
So steal not this tome, dear reader,
Lest you the book demons offend
With piracy or sleight of hand,
And thus cursed by this verse, you end.

To Lukas, for everything

ROYAL FAMILY TREE

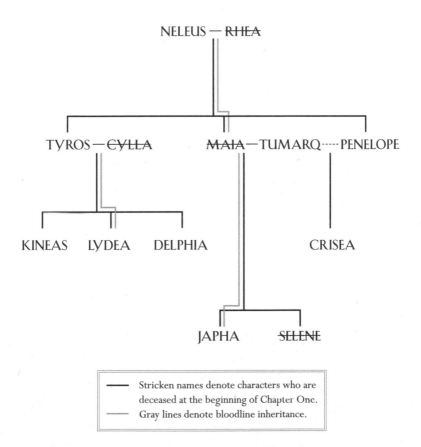

NELEUS — ~~RHEA~~

TYROS — ~~CYLLA~~   ~~MAIA~~ — TUMARQ ----- PENELOPE

KINEAS   LYDEA   DELPHIA   CRISEA

JAPHA   ~~SELENE~~

—— Stricken names denote characters who are
    deceased at the beginning of Chapter One.
—— Gray lines denote bloodline inheritance.

BEFORE

There wasn't much warning the day they came for Rovan's father.

Rovan was playing the hiding game with her straw doll in the front room of their house, which lay on one of the main avenues leading to the agora. There were stacks of cloth to tuck herself behind, since her mother didn't put all her weaving outside on display in the morning. The bolts surrounding Rovan revealed glimpses of leaves and flowers twining in intricate patterns, with butterflies and skulls so cleverly layered you couldn't tell where an eye socket ended and a wing began.

Rovan could see her mother outside through the wooden slats of the shutters, shaking out fabrics in myriad bright colors and ornate patterns, letting the warm breeze catch them and draw the eyes of early shoppers. At the echoing clatter of many hooves, Rovan drew closer to the window. A feeling of sick anticipation twisted in her stomach.

The bloodmages came riding down the stone-paved street. Cloaking their left shoulders were deep red chlamyses with a woven black shield in the center, leaving their right arms free. Familiar crimson marks streaked their skin down their single bare arms and what Rovan could see of their calves. Maybe the symbols twined everywhere, like her father's, which even came up to his neck.

The bloodmages were so vivid, their intricate silver helms glinting in the morning air, and yet they were accompanied by dark shadows lurking in the air behind them—silent smudges against the brightness of the day. Except these shadows weren't cast by the sun. They seemed to sap the light and liveliness, even the joy, from their surroundings. *Guardians*, they were called.

Rovan didn't know how the bright riders could pay so little attention to their so-called guardians. Those eerie, unnatural shadows were nearly all she could look at, as if they were windows into another, darker world.

The *under*world.

Rovan couldn't make out any features in the darkness, even though she felt she should've been able to. The guardians were people, after all.

Dead people, watching over the bloodmages.

The bloodmages, two men and two women of varying heights and builds and skin tones, drew in their horses a few buildings away from her mother's shop. Wards, her father called them— different from him even though he was also a bloodmage with the same red markings, because they had their shadowy guardians watching over them. Rovan was never to draw their attention.

Which meant she probably wasn't supposed to be staring at them, but she couldn't help it. Lurking guardians or not, these warded bloodmages rode beautiful horses, wore well-woven and dyed clothes, and more importantly, never had to hide. They sat tall, proud.

Sometimes Rovan wondered why her father was hiding from them—why he hadn't *begged* to become one of them. She sometimes fantasized that he had, and he would carry her and her mother away from their house on a prancing horse in broad daylight, his blue hair streaming like water in the sun, and she would have a new dress billowing out behind her. She wished her father could ignore a strange, shadowy guardian for that. But he hated them.

A hand dropped on her shoulder, nearly making her yelp. She turned to find her father standing behind her, his eyes—usually

2

gold at home but magicked now to look brown—fixed on the figures on horseback. His blue hair and metallic irises were familiar to her, but uncommon anywhere else in the polis.

"Bastards," he muttered under his breath. "Stay quiet, love."

At seven years old, she already knew to keep her voice down. "Dolon says he wants to be a guardian when he grows up."

Her father's eyebrows shot up. "Who is Dolon?" He wouldn't have known, because he rarely went outside during the day. While the color of his hair and eyes could be altered, hidden, the marks on his skin couldn't. They proved he was a powerful bloodmage and made up what he called his *bloodline*—long strings of red symbols known as sigils weaving over his skin.

"He's the boy who lives down the street," Rovan said.

Her father cursed under his breath. "This death-obsessed city. What an abomination to let children think . . . Look, love, I know what they say: that anyone, if they train hard in life and do great things, can become a hero in the afterlife. Maybe even a guardian to a living ward. But it's not that simple or nice."

"Why are the guardians so bad?" she asked, even though she could sense that they were. *Feel* it in her gut. And yet she couldn't stop staring. The guardians were like dark flames. Fascinating. Dangerous. Begging to be touched, even at her own peril.

Her father frowned at the approaching riders. "Because they don't belong in our world."

Being one of their *wards* didn't look all that bad, at least. Rovan said as much.

Her father sighed. "It *is* bad, love. It can only be bad."

"Why?"

"Because dealing with the dead comes at a price, and the cost to the living is higher than we—"

With a sharp squeeze on her shoulder, he cut off.

Because the bloodmages did what they'd never done before:

3

They stopped in front of the shop instead of passing by on some important business. Her mother grew still outside, and her father ducked behind a stack of cloth, dragging Rovan down with him. For a second, she was terrified the riders had seen them, but that was impossible with the shutters mostly closed. Still, the blood-mages spread their horses out in front of the house, sun glinting off their silver helms, coming close enough now for Rovan to see that the intricate metalwork included skulls and blooming flowers.

"Good morning, my lords and ladies," her mother managed with relative calm. "Can I interest you in some weaving?"

The riders didn't even acknowledge her. A warded bloodmage rode to the forefront. She spoke in a level tone, and yet her voice came out amplified, as if she were shouting. Louder than shouting. Rovan could feel it vibrating in her bones.

"Silvean Ballacra, we know you are in there. Come out, and we can resolve this without blood."

Rovan's heart stuttered in her chest. Silvean Ballacra was her father.

Her mother's eyes darted to the house and away. "There's no one by that name here."

The bloodmage ignored her again. "There are ten more of us out back, so don't try to sneak off. If you don't come out now, we will set fire to the place."

Rovan glanced at her father, her breath held.

His eyes were squeezed tightly closed. "She's telling the truth," he said. When his eyes snapped open, they were golden again. "Quick, hide like we taught you. And if they search the house and find you, do like we practiced."

"But—"

"*Do it*, love, for me. Remember what you promised me."

She tried to grab his chiton as he stood, but it tore from her grasp. And then he was outside, standing tall in the sunlight, his feet bare, the crimson marks of his bloodline blazing on his skin for all to see, revealing himself to be an unwarded bloodmage, at the very least. And maybe something else. The brown of his hair lifted away, leaving only deep blue. His shoulders were squared. He wasn't hiding anymore.

She had wanted this, hadn't she? But it felt all wrong.

"There you are, our long-lost Skyllean," the lead bloodmage said. "Some were beginning to doubt you even existed." She raised an eyebrow, her sharp gaze tracing Rovan's father from head to foot. "That's a long bloodline you have there. Longer even than rumor had it. Certainly longer than mine." She shrugged her marking-covered shoulder. "But there are far more of us."

Her father was one man against four warded bloodmages. But he didn't look afraid.

Cold dread rose in Rovan's chest. Her breath came too fast, making her dizzy.

"I'll leave quietly as long as all of you leave with me," her father said.

The lead bloodmage's sharp eyes found Rovan's mother. "Who is she, that you would want to protect her?"

"No one of consequence. I paid her, if that's what you mean. For my bed and hers, on occasion."

The lead bloodmage frowned. "She's still a woman who sheltered a foreign spy and unregistered bloodline without reporting him."

"She didn't know I was Skyllean." He gestured at his hair. "I was disguising myself. And she didn't know I was unregistered. I wouldn't want to get her killed in a fight simply for her ignorance." He raised his hands, as if in surrender. "I'd say that's a fair trade. You get me, and nobody dies. *You* don't die."

The lead bloodmage stared at him for a few seconds. Then she turned to a man standing nearby in a threadbare chiton—Dolon's father, a shopkeeper a few doors down. "Who else lives here?"

5

"There's a child," Dolon's father said hesitantly. "She plays with my boy."

Rovan's fear spiked in her stomach like she'd swallowed a dagger.

Outside, the ward's eyes lit up, and Rovan's mother turned on the shopkeeper, staring at him with a hatred Rovan had never seen.

"Search the hou—" the lead bloodmage started, but then suddenly her neck erupted in a spray of red.

It took Rovan a second to realize that the liquid hadn't come from anywhere outside the woman. It was coming from *inside* her. It was her blood, a fountain of it. And it took Rovan another second to realize her father had done it.

His fingers were splayed. The woman's blood spiraled toward him like a snake in water. He threw his hand out, casting her gathered life force in an arcing spray, and then there was fire.

So much fire. A wall of it, shooting up in a half circle in front of their house and tearing through the four wards and the shopkeeper. Horses screamed and reared. Their neighbor shrieked, his hair and clothes alight. He tried to run toward Rovan's mother, but she hefted a wooden pole, usually used to display draped cloth, and smashed him in the face. He went down in a burning, thrashing heap.

Other figures, cloaked in the warded bloodmages' red and black chlamyses and helmed in their same silver skulls and flowers, emerged from the alleys all around. Balls of fire and vicious-looking wooden stakes were suddenly flying for her father. He batted them away like a cloud of flies. The stakes went spinning, the balls of flame guttering. Only *his* fire continued to burn, even expanding to the other wards with a red sweep of his hand. But her father wasn't just waving about. His fingers were twitching, *writing*. Spelling out destruction. Though the sigils he wrote were invisible, their effects weren't. Rovan had never seen him do anything like this, and it was both awful and amazing.

He even turned the warded bloodmages' own weapons against them. The wooden stakes rose as if by their own accord and launched for the necks and eyes of their wards. Another chorus of screams rose.

For a second, it looked like her father might win. Rovan felt like she was choking on terror and hope all at once.

But in the chaos, she had forgotten the guardians. Those shadows came awake—*alive* wasn't the right word—and she saw them as they truly were.

One guardian especially: a man with curly dark hair and flat black eyes—cold, cold eyes—who seemed to draw the light from around him as he materialized. The lead bloodmage, whose throat her father had opened, now lying on the ground half-pinned under her charred horse, suddenly arched her back and let loose a gurgling cry at the exact moment the guardian solidified. It was as if his appearance had caused her more pain.

The shadow-man didn't even glance at the dying woman. He only had eyes—dead eyes—for Rovan's father. Raising a gleaming sword, he charged. The guardian moved like smoke, impossibly twisting and weaving around the streaks of fire her father launched at him. And yet her father ducked the blade as quickly as the guardian moved, and he blocked whatever he couldn't avoid with fiery, sparking shapes he pulled from nowhere. At the same time, an inferno flared right under the guardian's black boots, and all the flying wooden stakes spun in the air and spitted him like a pincushion. He went up as if made of straw, leaving nothing behind but wisps of shadow and stakes that clattered to the ground.

"Die again, dead man," her father snarled.

If only that guardian had been the only one. Three more appeared around Rovan's father. Three swords glinted in the sunlight.

It was her father's turn to cry out in agony as one took him in the shoulder, one in the back, and one in the thigh. It didn't matter that the guardians and their swords vanished immediately after. The damage was done. All her father's magic evaporated in swirls of smoke, and he collapsed in a flood of his own blood.

Rovan couldn't help it—she screamed. Her mother did, too, when Rovan came charging outside, her hiding forgotten. Rovan didn't know what to do, only that she had to do *something*.

She didn't get far. Two wards caught her arms in invisible sigils, ignoring her thrashing and kicking, and hauled her forward as if she were a puppet on strings. The sight of her father made her sob. He was trying to gather his own blood before him to launch another attack, though he looked ready to faint, his face paler than pale. He stopped when he saw his daughter. The blood hovering before him spattered to the paving stones like rain, and he slumped over.

A ward marched up to Rovan, his cloak singed. The woman who'd been in command was now staring sightlessly at the sky.

"Who are you?" he barked.

Rovan was weeping too hard to answer. She was pretty sure she wasn't supposed to tell the truth, anyway.

"That's my daughter!" her mother cried. "She's only seven. Please spare her, I'll do anything!"

"Silence, woman," the ward snapped. He turned on Rovan's father. "Silvean, is she yours?"

Her father shook his head drunkenly. Blood dribbled from his mouth.

"Why all this, then?" The ward threw his arm out to encompass the destruction, the death. His eyes were wide, nearly wild. "Why attack bloodmages like yourself?"

Her father spat red at the ward, though it didn't reach him. "I'm nothing like you, you death-tainted fools. I'm free."

The man shook his head. "You're mad. You freaks always have been."

8

"It's far madder to make compacts with the dead," her father said. His voice had gone weak, and his eyes slid to the side as he slumped lower.

"His kind isn't warded!" someone shouted in the crowd. "They're trying to take over our polis, just like the blight wants to! They have no one to stop them!"

"Get rid of all Skylleans, I say!" cried another.

"Fool, don't you know the crown prince is supposedly married to a Skyllean witch?" someone hissed.

"Mad," was all the ward said, still staring at Rovan's father, and then he turned back to Rovan. "Bring her here." He tore off his gloves, fumbled at his belt pouch, and withdrew a gleaming silver pin as long as her hand. It had an ornate silver skull at the top.

Rovan knew what was coming. Her mother always had a needle stuck into her sleeve for this exact purpose. Her mother would prick her own finger, draw blood that had no magic in it, and then Rovan would be able to do her trick. Fool them all, swapping her mother's blood for her own. She'd done it before, but never with this much of an audience.

Rovan glanced around, but neighbors who'd patted her head or given her treats with indulgent smiles now looked on with hard eyes as the ward seized her wrist. There was hatred in their expressions, she realized. For her blue-haired father, and what he was—which was *not* one of them. And maybe hatred for her, if she proved to be like him.

Why they didn't hate the guardians in their midst was beyond her. She had seen their true faces now, with their dead eyes and their wicked swords, and knew beyond a doubt that her father was right. They were evil. *Wrong*.

Rovan was relieved when the ward pricked her finger carefully with the frightful needle. Blood blossomed around the tip—just not Rovan's. It was a simple matter to keep her own hidden deep

9

under her skin, and move her mother's to that spot instead. The ward swiped away the drop with his own finger, held it up, and examined it with a frown.

"I told you," her father slurred, blood bubbling from his mouth. "Just an ignorant slut and her brat."

The ward spun away from Rovan, losing interest in her as quickly as that. "To do all this for nothing . . ."

Slut. Brat. Nothing. The words hit Rovan like stones, winding her, leaving pain in their wake.

"I wouldn't say *nothing*," her father said. "I took some of you down with me." He slumped entirely to the ground, his head thumping the cobbles, without another look at his daughter or her mother.

A scream was building in Rovan, one that felt too big for her small body. Her mother only looked on in glazed shock.

One of the wards stepped carefully up to her father, knelt, and put fingers to his neck. "He's dead."

The ward who'd pricked her finger glared and spat on the ground. "What a loss," he said. "If we can't gain anything from him, we at least need his corpse to prove we found him. Bring him."

Two more wards dragged her father's body to one of the remaining horses and slung it over the saddle. Rovan tried to reach for him, but hands dragged her back. Her father's head dangled, blue hair drifting, and he left a trail of blood behind on the cobbles that looked like strewn poppies.

1

I awake outside, staring up at the bright midday sky, with no clear idea how I've gotten wherever I am. The fact that I'm wretchedly hungover is a clue to my curious lapse of memory, but my head hurts too much to puzzle over it. I can hear the bustle of people as the aromas of food and horse dung waft over me in a light breeze. The front side of me, at least, is warm from the sun, but my backside rests on something hard and tilted, as smooth as glass. I groan and roll over.

And nearly fall off a rooftop. I catch myself at the last second, gasping. I sling my leg back onto a marble lip, scraping my knee, before my weight can drag me off. The gentle slope of the slippery roof—which is indeed glass—is still threatening to help me over the edge, and the mosaic-whorled ground is a dizzying distance from my down-turned face, about the height of six people standing on top of one another.

"Shit," I breathe. Then I throw up.

The vomit—as red as the wine I must have guzzled the night before—vividly splatters a pile of oranges stacked in a neat pyramid on a vendor's cart down below. There are lots of carts ringing me, because this is the agora, I realize. At the center of the square is a huge gazebo.

I know precisely where I am, at least: I'm spread-eagled on the edge of the gazebo's dome, a rippling blue and green glass replica of the veil that protects the entire polis from the blight. This replica "veil" only shelters a fountain of the first king of Thanopolis, Athan-atos, though he symbolizes the city itself, of course. Ringing the fountain and supporting the dome are three statues of the goddess, sculpted in white marble: the maiden, the mother, the crone. The maiden holds a chicken and a knife, hinting at blood soon to be spilled; the mother cradles—what else?—a baby; and a dog sits at the crone's heels, mascot of the dying en route to the underworld, since dogs are supposedly the guardians of thresholds. I more often see them eating trash.

I'm certainly not shaping up to be immortalized. My vomit has narrowly missed the outstretched chicken in the maiden's arms and hit the oranges instead. Better to have infuriated a fruit vendor than the goddess, I suppose.

The fruit vendor is indisputably furious. He's shouting at me. "Rovan, you drunk of a girl, what are you doing up there?"

Oh no. He knows me. Luck is not on my side today.

"Ugh, who's shouting?" moans a voice, quite nearby.

I carefully lever myself up to look. *Yes, right.* Bethea is up here with me. Her lips and eyes are swollen, but she's nonetheless lovely as she props herself up on her elbows, blond hair and warm skin glowing. A crown of brightly wilting flowers sits askew on her head, and the disorderly folds of her peplos reveal too many voluptuous curves for decency. And yet I bet the two of us have thoroughly dispensed with decency already.

Don't get attached, I remind myself. *You're leaving soon enough.*

Bethea smacks her lips. "Where are we? Oh, the agora. On top of the statuary. And it's market day. Lucky for us."

"Do you remember what we were doing yesterday?"

She ponders for a moment. "Oh!" she exclaims, making us both grimace at her volume. Rubbing her temple, she finishes, "There was the pageant."

I vaguely recall people parading through the streets, wearing gossamer death shrouds and cheap clay masks molded to look like skulls, colorful ribbons streaming from their wrists and wreaths of flowers in their hair. That's where Bethea's wilting crown must have come from. It all had something to do with the king—the current king, Neleus—though I didn't care enough to discover exactly what. Pageants are often held to honor the famous and wealthy deceased, as if to put in a final good word before their arrival in the afterlife. But King Neleus isn't dead, as far as I know. He is apparently old and sickly, has a middle-aged son ready to take over, and also has nearly grown grandchildren, but I've never seen any of them. The business of the royal family, other than that of the king, is mostly kept secret outside of the palace, away from the prying eyes of the populace. I'm fine with knowing next to nothing about them.

What I *do* know is there was plenty of free-flowing wine.

"Yes, the pageant," I say. "That explains it. Somewhat."

The two of us must have stolen across the dark and empty square last night after the festivities, climbed up the gazebo on a whim—though the goddess knows how we managed without breaking our necks—and then . . . Vaguely tantalizing memories of the two of us entwined surface in my mind. I remember more of *that* than how we got up here, especially the part where I was too drunk to achieve satisfaction.

"Lovely. Rather, *you're* lovely," Bethea adds, her eyes growing heavier lidded. She pinches a loose lock of my wavy hair—burnt umber in the daylight. "I'm sorry I wasn't successful at persuading you to surrender." Wincing, she pokes at her mouth. "I think my lips are numb."

"That's *my* fault and shame," I assure her. "I was utterly wine wrecked."

"Shame?" She arches an eyebrow.

"No, I . . . not about anything *we* did."

"Are you sure? Your mother hasn't convinced you?"

My mother doesn't approve of my wine drinking *or* Bethea, never mind that I'm nineteen years of age and can do whatever and *whomever* I please. At least her disapproval has nothing to do with the fact that Bethea's and my potential pairing can never result in natural children. Both of us are fine with that, even if some people might tut in reproach. No one much cares what you do in the bedroom, and yet having children is deemed a sacred duty to the polis, especially if you're a bloodmage or a royal. But I'm definitely not a royal, and by all appearances I'm not a bloodmage. My dalliances are, as I've made clear, not exclusive to anyone and temporary, besides. No, my mother's issue is with Bethea's social standing. She fits into the category of "the less fortunate" as the poor daughter of a husbandless medium who communes with spirits in a back alley.

I shake my head. "My mother doesn't have a peg leg to perch on. Everyone knows *she's* ruined goods." Ever since my father was hauled away when I was seven years old, and killed for being a fugitive, an unwarded bloodmage from an enemy island kingdom, suitors haven't exactly been lining up at my mother's door.

The memory still makes my stomach clench. Even now, I can smell the fear in the air, the blood. I try to shove it away.

At least, whatever my mother's reputation, no one can resist her weaving—*my* weaving. My mother doesn't have to lift a finger anymore, while my patterns are widely thought to be the most beautiful outside of the royal quarter. My scrolling vines and blossoms look as if they've grown from thread, my butterflies and birds ready to flap their wings. Since my mother takes credit for all my work, I view my drinking and dalliances as a fair trade.

And soon, so soon I can almost taste it, my mother won't have to worry about me at all, because I'll weave enough for her to retire on and leave all of this behind.

What I *can* taste now isn't so pleasant. I roll my dry, vomit-flavored tongue around in my mouth and glance down at the still-shouting vendor. "I think we've been discovered."

Bethea giggles. "Oh no. At least I didn't fall off the roof and split like a melon. That would have been a real scene from some horribly dull tragedy. How did we get up here?"

"I was wondering the same thing. I'm also wondering how we get down."

Bethea peers over the edge and shudders. "I better not have to be drunk to make the return journey, because we're out of wine." She flops back. "At least the view is lovely."

I lean back on my elbows as well. Temples and official buildings, creamy and orderly, rise among verdant gardens and cobbled streets lined in blooming trellises until they reach the royal palace at the polis's center. The palace is built of white marble in the smooth, swirling shape of a seashell, its perfectly round, columned tiers climbing to a point that nearly touches the shimmering magical barrier that surrounds the polis like an overturned bowl. I've never seen the sky without the veil, though my father told me it merely lends what is plain blue more of a green iridescence. The city itself rests atop a plateau that faces inland with jagged cliffs and slopes gently to a seaport on the other side, with just enough space for its populace and the farmlands that feed us. Beyond that, past the veil that protects us, is the blight. The blight is even less visible than the veil, but its effects on the land are obvious. The blight is *everywhere*, killing the land either through drought or a deep freeze. Depending on the direction you look from the polis, you might see the vast ocean to the east, billowing white snow around inhospitable mountain peaks to the northwest, or the dusty gray brown of the southwest desert. Any way you look, the blighted wasteland surrounding us is nearly devoid of life. The blight has consumed the entire continent aside from Thanopolis, half burying the skeletons of old towns and cities under either sand or ice.

And yet, somewhere beyond that great, desolate expanse is the island kingdom of Skyllea, which the blight hasn't yet swallowed. My father's homeland. Another memory: one of his strong, red-lined hands overlaying mine, directing my finger on a tattered map to find Skyllea. The warm rumble of his voice against my back, his stubble scratching at my cheek. His excitement, his pride. My urge, nearly overpowering, to go wherever he wanted, to *be* whatever he wanted. I thought I might explode with it.

There's a hole in my chest, long walled off—except for the siren call of Skyllea, echoing in the empty dark.

It's only as solid as a dream to me, but one I will reach out and touch someday—someday soon. As a child, my father warned me away from getting too close to the veil and the blight's edge, but if merchants can cross it, I can, too. I've woven and saved, saved and woven. I've spoken to a Skyllean trader who says he'll be taking his family's caravan across the wasteland and I can buy passage. The journey is treacherous, and you need blood magic to protect you from the blight's slow poison, which is why no one can leave without the king's approval. All bloodmages—wards, with their guardians—serve him, and none would use their magic for such a thing without permission.

Maybe there, in Skyllea, I can escape that final memory of my father, the one that wine can never permanently wash away. His blood on the cobbles. A dead man's eyes. My own guilt for ever secretly wishing he would join those who ended up killing him.

Under other circumstances, I might appreciate the opportunity to get a view of the wastes I'll soon be traversing. But as curious as I am, right now my goal isn't climbing *higher* atop the fountain's precarious and potentially fragile glass dome.

"Anyone have a rope?" I call, after scooting myself to the marble edge. There are some good-natured chuckles. At first, all they seem to do is laugh at me, until a rope comes flying up from a rather handsome sandal vendor with muscular arms and a wide grin.

"Your wish is my command," he says with a flourish of his hand.

The loop makes it only as far as the chicken in the maiden's arms. Luckily the goddess is raising it in a sacrificial manner. But Bethea and I will still have to climb down roughly the height of an outstretched body to reach it.

"Let me go first," I say.

My knees tingle as I grip the vine-carved marble lip and slide my feet over the edge. I'm barefoot and have no clue where my sandals have gone. I try not to think of all the nothing between me and the market square far below as my toes catch what feels like a flower crowning the maiden's head. Gaining a foothold is a little tricky, making my breath come short as I cling to the edge, but after that it's easy going until I reach the chicken. I pause for a quick apology to the goddess when I use the maiden's nose for purchase. Dangling from the rope makes my stomach plummet. As if to catch up with it, I slide down too quickly, burning my palms badly. But I don't mind once I'm back on level ground, the mosaic tiles warm and reassuring under my bare feet.

A crowd of onlookers clap and cheer. I give a bow, and then immediately regret inverting my head. The fruit vendor doesn't need a reminder of what I've done; he's rinsing oranges in a wooden bucket and glaring at me.

"Would have served you right to break your neck," he growls.

I smile as sweetly as possible, given breath as sour as mine. After a flirtatious wink for the helpful shoe vendor—which changes to a wince at the fierce stinging in my palms—I turn to call encouragement up to Bethea.

Just in time to see my friend slip.

And fall.

It all happens too fast. My thoughts freeze, but my hand doesn't. I don't think. I don't consider the consequences. I only *move*.

Move, move, move—the one sigil that I've used over and over again almost every day, manipulating my mother's wooden loom and natural fibers in fantastic patterns far faster than anyone without magic could have.

I throw out a hand toward Bethea, sketching as I do that simple symbol I know better than any other. Except it isn't thread I feel running every which way through her body, but a tangled network of veins. I don't try to move *those*, only to lift all the blood in her body at once, preferably without tearing it out of her. Already knowing that won't be enough, I reach my other hand toward the fountain of King Athanatos with the same sigil, but in a complex layering like I would create for a weave—a *shape* in my mind, then in the air. Every drop of water roars toward Bethea like a river's current, forming a massive sphere for her to land in. It explodes shortly after impact. I can't hold it, or Bethea, for much longer. The displaced water floods one entire quadrant of the square.

And it leaves my friend soaked, alive, and entirely intact upon the ground. For a second, I'm too giddy with relief to realize the cost of what I've done.

Bethea turns to me on hands and knees, sputtering, wet strands of hair clinging to her face, her flower wreath long gone. "What just happened? Where did this water . . . How am I not . . . ?"

I'm not even sure. I had no idea I was powerful enough to do such a thing. I stare wide-eyed at my own palms. There's blood beaded on them from where I skinned them on the rope—the blood that powers all living magic. It must have made my sigils vastly more potent.

I remember the moment my father took my small shoulders, stared intently down at me with his golden eyes, and said, "You can never show them, Rovan. I love you, and if you love me, and you love your mother, *no one* can know what you can do. Promise me."

I promised him with all the fervency of a child who would do anything for her father.

Now, I quickly fold my arms and glance around. If I'd hoped to slip away, it's impossible. The handsome shoe vendor retreats from me with his hands raised like I'm a wild dog about to attack. The fruit vendor's mouth no longer spits curses or grumbles, but gapes, his oranges scattered all around.

A woman points and screams, "It was her! I saw her hands move! She did it, and she's not warded!"

More people begin pointing and shouting. "An unregistered bloodmage!"

A man starts tugging at the rope still looped about the maiden's statue. Never mind that I saved someone's life; they'll truss me up like a pig. My breath starts to come faster. I can smell the blood again, the smoke from the last memory of my father. Taste the fear.

Even Bethea stares at me with something like horror. "You did that? You can . . . You're a . . ."

"*Witch!*" someone cries.

The more timid onlookers sidle away as if I carry the plague, leaving behind the harder sort. But there are plenty of those. An angry crowd closes in on me. They're only a few steps away from becoming a mob.

And then Bethea steps between me and them, holding her arms out as a barrier. Her short frame and wet peplos aren't very intimidating, but she's doing her best. She glances back, her eyes wild. "Run," she gasps.

Just as with my blood magic, I don't even think. I run.

2

I dodge through the market crowd, ducking under arms that grab for me. They come so close that body odor fills my nostrils and a pin on a sleeve snags my hair. Some other people run *away* from me, but too many are following. Far too many for Bethea to possibly halt.

One thought pounds through me in time with my beating heart: *home*. I have to get home. I can race back, gather what savings I have, maybe hide with the Skyllean merchant until he can smuggle me out of the city. My dream is still within reach. It's just all the more urgent.

I can keep my promise to my father—the only part of his memory I haven't betrayed.

I try to tuck into an alley that will wind its way to my mother's humble storefront, but someone beats me there: a man with frightened, frightening eyes.

I want to hurl him aside with a sigil. As easy as it would be, using more blood magic will only incriminate me further. Instead, I snatch up the first thing to come to hand, lying on a nearby food stand: a wooden ladle the size of a club, meant to stir vats of who knows what. Before the man can duck, I bash him over the head with it, the force of the blow vibrating up my arm. He flies aside, crashing into a stall—but a few angry vendors take his place, probably thinking their goods are at risk. I drop the ladle and run in a different direction . . . only to find myself pinned between two stalls and a wall too smooth to even dream of climbing. I whip back around, my skinned palms pressing into the stone behind me.

I barely notice the pain. My throat feels like it already has a noose around it as I face my pursuers.

A half-dozen men, one with the rope from the fountain, have cornered me. I'm trapped.

"Stand aside!" a voice cries, and the crowd begins to part. I hear the clatter of hooves.

I nearly sob in relief . . . until I see who is coming.

They tower above the crowd on their horses, their left shoulders cloaked in blood-red and black-shielded chlamyses, their heads glinting in silver helms wrought of skulls and flowers. Crimson marks run down their bare right arms and what I can see of their calves under their chitons. They look the same as the day they came for my father. And those strange, terrible shadows like living death flow in their wake.

Wards and their guardians. At least a half dozen of each. They often watch the agora on market days—to keep the peace, supposedly, but also to keep an eye out for any unsanctioned magic.

I haven't drawn this close to them since the day they killed my father. I raise my hands in surrender, because that's all I can do until I can try to convince them I'm not a bloodmage.

But then someone screams, "She's going to cast her magic again!"

The horses pull up short, and the warded man in the lead slashes his arm through the air at me.

My world goes dark.

A light slap on the cheek brings me to semiconsciousness. I groan. The ground I lie on has the chilly smoothness of marble, and my hands are bound tightly behind my back. There's a hush around me, but I can hear the scuffing of quite a few pairs of boots, the clop of shifting hooves, and the thrum of the city in the distance, muted as if by tall buildings, taller than I'm used to.

I open my eyes to see the blue-green, veil-covered sky shimmering alongside an inexplicable explosion of flowers. But then someone looms over me and shoves something between my lips, pinching my jaw open in a firm grip. It's a skin of wine. I never object to wine, and so I take a pull without protesting. But when I try to stop there, they hold it against my mouth, tipping it back, until I choke and sputter and drink a good deal more than even *I* would want to.

I cough as soon as I'm freed. "I'm going to be sick."

"Not sick," a man says. "Just too muddled to do much of anything. Can't be too careful, now can we?"

"I'm already muddled after what I had last night." But then I taste it in the back of my throat: a sweetness too overpowering for any wine alone. The dizziness hits me a moment later.

"Why wake me up just to drug me?" I mutter. Rough hands haul me to my feet. For a moment, the world is too bright and fuzzy to make out.

"Because you need to walk now that the horses have gone as far as they can. You also need to answer questions—a lot of questions—but not use magic," the man says, and I realize I'm speaking to the leader of the wards who found me, the one who knocked me out with a sigil in the market.

The market. Where I used blood magic. And now I'm under arrest and surrounded by wards. It's almost too much to take in, and my wool-stuffed brain isn't helping. I still have the presence of mind to look for *them*. I can only spot those horrible shadows now if I squint; they mostly blur into my strange surroundings. Nevertheless, to be near so many guardians makes me shiver.

Even if I can barely see straight, I still vividly remember how those shadows coalesced into men the day my father died. I can picture their cold, dead eyes. Hear the screams. Feel the wrongness of death walking among the living—*killing* the living.

Despite my fogginess, a different kind of clarity begins to sharpen inside me:

I'm fucked.

"Where am I?" I ask. White buildings swoop in the background, marble everywhere, intricate whorls of it comprising a massive trellis that arches gracefully over the square we stand in. Trellises are usually made of wood, and something about the many-branched shape of this one disturbs me. I realize it looks like a sun-bleached rib cage, and its blossoms like lichen growths. Creepy or not, I'm in a much nicer part of the polis than I usually frequent. Horses and red-cloaked people ring me in a dizzying circle.

And then my eyes snag on the swirling white spike of the palace towering over me.

"You're in the royal agora, about to enter the Hall of the Wards," the man answers me. "I am Captain Marklos, and you are . . . ?"

My heart kicks like a horse in my chest, cutting briefly though my haze. "Why are we here? I didn't do anything wrong."

"I didn't say you did. But you *are* a bloodmage like me, so we just need to sort a few things out first." He says it casually, trying to sell the friendly act, but I'm not buying.

With my fingers, I make the slicing motion of the sigil for *sever*, which I usually use to cut yarn. I hope I hit the ropes binding me and not my wrists. Instead, I hit . . . nothing. Because the sigil doesn't do anything. When I try to feel the shape of it, the true form that's a mold for the world, forcing reality to fit and summoning the sigil into being, it simply slips away from me. And then my feet are trying to slip out from under my body.

"Steady now, I've got you," the captain says—as if *he* wasn't the one who drugged me—his grip on my arm like an iron band. He launches into motion, hauling me with him. "Isn't this exciting?"

I can barely breathe, and not from excitement.

A wide stone building lined in white marble pillars rises up before us. Unlike the rest of the city, where stone goes mostly unadorned outside of public gardens, these columns are twined in scarlet vines in a pattern too regular and intricate to be natural. They must have been grown with magic. The decorative tops of the columns are difficult to make out through the foliage, but one with sparser growth leaves no doubt in my mind: It's meant to look like the knobby end of a bone.

Bones, all around me, covered in blossoms. A *death-obsessed city*, my father called it. But this is the opposite of yesterday's pageantry, where the living masqueraded as the dead. This is death dressed up as life, and it's far more frightening.

I try to halt before we enter the building. I feel like if I go in there, I will never come back out.

"I'm not a bloodmage," I insist, but the words slip and slur on my tongue.

"Of course you are. I pricked your finger while you were unconscious." The captain glances back at me warily, without letting me stop. "I've never felt such raw power in someone's blood before. The question is how, and more importantly *why*, you've hidden from us for so long. You are a citizen of this polis, and as such, you have a duty to it like everyone. Your duty is just . . . different. More important than most."

"Wait." I try to pull away on pure reflex. I'm not sure where I could run, even if my hands weren't tied behind my back. Bound like I am, unable to use sigils, it's hopeless.

"Rovan, don't! Just go with them, and it'll be okay." Bethea's voice.

I turn in surprise, nearly tripping. My friend is among the group just behind me and the captain. I didn't see her before. She isn't bound, but her face is drawn beneath her still-damp hair. I

25

hope she's more afraid *for* me than she is *of* me. But then I remember how she stood in front of the mob for me, and my attention catches on her pale lips.

"She's cold. The least you assholes could do is offer her one of your fancy cloaks."

Most of them stare at me in shock, for my language or audacity, I'm not sure. And I don't care, because a ward actually unpins her chlamys and drapes it over Bethea's shoulders.

"You were the one who tried to drown her in the fountain," Captain Marklos said. "Rovan, is it?"

He frowns when I only glower at him, then tugs me back into motion, heading between the columns into the massive entry hall. The polished marble is cool under my bare feet, smoother than anything I've felt before. More unnatural red vines climb the walls and pillars, enough to drape the ceiling high overhead in a leafy canopy.

I struggle to get my breath under control. I need to focus.

"What is she doing here, anyway?" I ask, tossing my head back at Bethea. "She doesn't have anything to do with this."

"Witnesses said she was the one caught by your magic, so we took her for questioning just in case." *In case* you *don't want to answer our questions*, is the unspoken threat. "Are you friends?"

I don't respond. The less involved Bethea is, the better. Maybe she's thinking the same thing, because she doesn't answer, either. That's wise on her part, even if it stings a little.

It shouldn't sting. I'm the one who has chosen to never get too attached. I've been planning to leave Thanopolis, after all. And besides, terrible things happen to people who get too close to you, at least in this city.

And at least if you're a bloodmage.

"You have nothing to fear, Rovan," the captain says. "We just need to list your name in the Registry to establish your future

26

bloodline and assign you a guardian for your protection. It's all for the best. Think how much good you can do for your fellow citizens, your king, once you're able to use your magic in service of the polis."

Guardian. My feet stutter to a halt before a column-lined hallway that cuts a wide swath into the center of the building. My father died to keep himself—to keep *me*—from the guardians. I've despised and dodged them every day since.

"Excuse me, I'm really going to be sick," I say.

"I highly doubt—"

I double over and throw up on his boots. Red to match the vines splatters the pale marble of the floor with truly stunning range.

"Goddess," Marklos hisses, abandoning his grip on me to back away. "I didn't give you that much wine!"

"I told you"—I gag—"I was already hungover." I spit up even more, hunching over between my knees, arms twisted painfully behind my back.

"She's telling the truth," Bethea murmurs somewhere behind me. "She had . . . a lot to drink last night."

When I finally glance up with teary eyes and sticky lips, the man gives me a look that rests confidently between disgusted and disappointed. I'm fine with that. Used to it, frankly. And at least he isn't trying to force more drugged wine down my throat. With any luck, there was only time for a partial dose to kick in.

"You," he declares, "are disgraceful."

"I know," I blurt. "You've made a mistake. I want to be retested. I'm not a bloodmage, and I can prove it."

The captain's understanding smile isn't comforting. "Of course. I was just about to have you tested again in front of the Ward Council to show them what I found. There's your opportunity to prove me wrong."

27

I try not to let anything show on my face as he drags me to my feet. Because I can fool him if I have another chance at the test . . . but I'll need someone else's blood to swap in place of my own. I've only ever used my mother's. And yet I once saw my father rip a stranger's life force out through her neck. Maybe I can borrow a little blood from someone else even if their finger isn't pricked. But, without such easy access as a needle gives, it would take a subtle touch not to alert anyone, and I'm not sure I can manage subtlety in my drugged state.

If only . . .

There's a cry behind me. "*Rovan!*"

It can't be. That's *my mother's* voice.

I try to tear away from my captor. "Mother!"

I shouldn't be so glad to see her. I should want my mother far away from all of this. But I want to fall into her arms as if I were nine instead of nineteen.

"Let me go," my mother shouts at the two wards who've seized her with invisible sigils in the middle of the entry hall. "That's my daughter!"

Marklos eyes her curiously. "Let her through. Perhaps we've found another unregistered bloodmage."

"I am *not*," my mother spits, swatting a chunk of her frizzy, gray-streaked dark hair out of her face. She pushes through the crowd to me. The fact that she doesn't comment on my appearance proves more than anything how worried she is. She must have sprinted here, by the sweat on her face. "Release my daughter."

Captain Marklos smiles his unconvincing smile. "I will in just a moment, after she's answered a few questions. Would you care to join us?"

My mother huffs and straightens her chiton. "Of course." She meets my eyes. "You can test her, you can test me, and then you can leave us be."

The captain cocks his head. "Do I know you?"

My mother draws herself up to her full, meager height. "No. Why would you? I have nothing to do with you lot. I mind my own business, keep my head down. I'm a simple craftswoman, a weaver, as is my daughter."

He casts a disdainful glance down at the spray of my vomit. "A veritable artist, it seems." He continues down the hall, dragging me after him. "We'll see for certain."

I have no choice but to stumble onward. "How did you know they took me?" I ask my mother out of the corner of my mouth. She's by my side.

Her voice is tight, and her eyes dart around at our ostentatious, magic-infused surroundings. She's clearly more frightened than she seemed a moment ago. "The man who sells fruit came to the house and told me. He saw . . . what happened."

So even after the fruit vendor discovered I can wield blood magic, even after I *vomited* on his oranges, he still warned my mother. At least one person in the market doesn't hate me—the one who has the most right to—and hopefully that means I can convince the rest of them that their eyes deceived them. At least long enough for me to depart for Skyllea and leave my mother in peace.

Maybe there's still a chance I can get my life back. Never mind my dreams. The thought feels fragile, as if even considering it too much might break it.

And first, I have to pass a test.

3

Our party soon reaches a wide, high-ceilinged chamber, all of it twined in scarlet vines as if we're standing inside a beating heart. Tall windows cast huge slants of light onto a half circle of red marble tiers like an amphitheater's. But now *I'm* down on the stage, with the audience arrayed above me. Luckily the seating isn't full. This meeting has obviously been called on short notice.

"My lords and ladies of the council," the captain calls, hauling me forward by my still-bound arms. "This is the girl I've summoned you here to see, and these are her witnesses." He nods at my mother and Bethea.

Several dozen people quit their murmuring to look up. Just like Captain Marklos and the other wards I've seen, they all have red marks decorating their skin. *Bloodlines.* I still don't entirely know what they mean. Whenever I ask my mother about my father's, she says it was his history written on his skin, but then she'll inevitably go on to grumble about handsome blue-haired mages with grand pasts and future plans who sweep you off your feet and then get killed, leaving you to raise a child all alone in an uncaring world. Honestly, I don't think she knows much more about bloodlines than I do. All I know is those marks are sigils, only in numbers far greater than the few simple ones I know, and a bloodmage is much more powerful with them than without.

"And what do you say, Marklos?" a severe woman at the center of the first tier demands. "Who is she?"

"Lady Acantha," he addresses her with a brief bow of his

head—she's obviously noble—and then he gestures at me. "This is an unregistered bloodmage caught this very morning working a sigil of great strength. She kept this young woman from falling off the king's gazebo in the agora, most notably drawing all the water from the fountain to break her fall."

The king's gazebo, not *the goddess's gazebo.* It's an odd thing to notice, especially at a time like this, but I do. Perhaps they honor the first king of the polis, Athanatos, before the goddess?

Acantha's eyes widen. "That would be utterly unprecedented from someone without the strength of a bloodline behind their magic. Did you see it?"

"No," Marklos says, dragging Bethea forward, "but she did, as did many others."

Acantha turns to Bethea. "What happened? How do you know this supposed bloodmage?"

Bethea quivers in fear, nearly in tears. "She . . . we . . ."

"Start somewhere. What were you doing on top of the gazebo?"

"Drinking wine and k-kissing."

I can't help giving her a sidelong look. *Dear goddess.* She doesn't need to tell the woman *everything.*

The councilwoman's eyebrows rise. "And then?"

"I f-fell. Something caught me."

"What *thing*?"

Bethea shoots me a terrified glance. "I felt a tug on my body. *All over* my body, from the inside. And then I landed in water."

"Water that wasn't there to begin with," Marklos adds.

"Yes, thank you, I realize that," Acantha says drily. She turns back to Bethea. "What is it you do?"

"Do?"

"Yes, *do*, for a living, you or your family."

"My mother tells fortunes and communes with the dead."

31

"Oh?" I don't like the tone of the woman's voice. "How interesting. Maybe the aptitude runs in your family. We can always use more acolytes in the necropolis."

Bethea lets out a frightened squeak.

The necropolis is where the city's dead are washed and interred while their shades journey to the underworld, but also where shadow priests, those who study the magic of death, dwell along with their acolytes. To understand death, shadow priests must stay close to it, even live like the dead, separate from the things that make life worthwhile, in my opinion: light, music, laughter, wine, and sex.

Shadow priests' abilities are learned rather than innate. *Anyone* other than a bloodmage can study death magic—the pneumatic arts, as they're called—as long as they're willing to act like corpses for long enough, and provided they live long enough. Shadow priests tend to become so enamored with death that they die quickly. Honestly, death magic seems more like a terrible disease to me.

It's shadow priests who perform the rite to bind guardian shades to their wards, since blood magic and death magic can never be wielded by the same person—at least not without killing them immediately, I've been told. I don't know what the binding process involves and hope never to find out.

And I certainly don't want Bethea to join the shadow priests as punishment simply for knowing me—to be cursed with a fate almost worse than death and then die sooner rather than later, anyway.

"Whatever she claims I did, it's not her fault," I declare, drawing all eyes to me. "She's just a silly, airheaded girl who will spread her legs for anyone, and her mother is a poppy-addled charlatan."

The words are out of my mouth before I can even think of recalling them. They have to think Bethea isn't worth anything, even if she's worth something to me.

Never mind that I've hardly shown it before today.

Anger sparks in me, for myself, for these people holding us here . . . and maybe for my father, for what he said about me and my mother long ago:

Slut. Brat. Nothing.

Lady Acantha only regards us both with a level gaze. "We'll see."

"*No*," I snap, "you'll tell us what you want with us *now,* and then let us get back to our lives. We're citizens of this polis as much as you. We have rights." My temper is burning away the fog in my head.

She blinks, affronted. "By right of the law, you're here to be tested, you insolent girl, though Marklos has already insisted you are a bloodmage and a *uniquely* powerful one at that."

"Then give me the test and you'll see that I'm not."

"If you'll pardon my asking, why are you trying to prove you aren't?" Acantha assesses me from her high perch. "Wouldn't you *want* to be a ward? Keeping citizens safe is a duty that shouldn't be frowned upon, but that isn't all we do. Some of us maintain the farms that feed the polis, the gardens that make it beautiful, or the veil that keeps out the blight. Some are celebrated craftspeople or liaisons to the palace. Why, some of us are even royals. You should be so lucky."

I don't shrink under the councilwoman's gaze, but draw my shoulders back and stand taller. My hands are bound, my feet are dirty and bare, and I probably have vomit on my chiton, but I don't care. This is my chance to give voice to what I should have all those years ago, *before* my father was taken. Before I betrayed him in my thoughts.

Without the use of my arms to gesture, I jerk my head at the smudge near Marklos. "I don't want one of *them*."

Acantha glances over her own shoulder, as if surprised to find a faint shadow there. "A guardian? They're heroic citizens who have proved themselves in this life and after, and they are here to protect us. It might not be as clear nowadays, but it is a protection we need. Those without magic don't always understand us. They used to be a danger to us."

They still might be, given the chance. I keep hearing the screech of the woman in the market: *Witch!* And yet . . .

I arch a brow. "Are you sure guardians aren't meant to put the *people* at ease more than they are you?"

Acantha's shrewd gaze narrows. "Does it matter, if the effect is the same? Indeed, there is old-rooted fear on both sides. We have a power that shouldn't go unchecked, that should serve the state, but that also shouldn't shrivel in fear of the masses. Both sides rest easier with guardians in between. I assure you, they're quite unobtrusive. Most of the time, one forgets their presence."

I scoff. "Even when you're in bed with someone? Maybe you get excited at the thought of a dead stranger watching, but—"

"*Rovan*," my mother snaps, scandalized.

Acantha tilts her head at me. "Why do shades among the living offend you so? The goddess herself is the guardian of the threshold, straddling both life and death."

I toss my hair. "Yeah, but she didn't give us *these* guardians."

"The first king did. Will you disrespect Athanatos now? He rebuilt our great Thanopolis from the ashes of chaos, brought many different peoples together under the safety of the veil, and created a paradise. It was he who first introduced the hematic arts into the royal family by marrying a bloodmage, who established bloodlines to make us stronger *and* used the pneumatic arts to bind guardians to us for our protection. The king respected blood magic and death magic equally, and found a way for them to work hand in hand. Why would you scorn such a gift?"

"Because those things are *dead* and *wrong* and—"

"I *have* heard such pointless rhetoric before," she interrupts, her tone still more curious than offended, "and let me tell you, it leads nowhere you wish to follow."

I shrug. "If I'm not a bloodmage, then it doesn't matter."

Acantha turns to my mother. "And what about you? Are you the source of this pernicious . . . and dare I say *treasonous* . . . prejudice, or did it come from, say, her father? You see, Marklos has a theory, implausible as it may be. He sent word of it as soon as your daughter arrived, which is why we're all here."

"I don't know what you mean——" my mother starts.

"Ah, here he is. You'll have to excuse him. He's not moving as quickly these days."

A man enters the hall. He has a limp, his cane clacking on the marble tile, and a richly embroidered green himation covering his arms and head. But I can see bits of bright silver-streaked dark *blue* hair peeking out from the hood. And despite the deep lines in his face that weren't there before, I would recognize those features and that voice anywhere.

"I don't see why I need to——" He breaks off at the sight of me and my mother.

"*Silvean?*" My mother's cry is disbelieving, desperate, and . . . betrayed. She takes a few staggering steps toward him and then lurches to a stop. "You're alive?" she gasps, and then covers her mouth in horror. Maybe because she realizes what *she* just betrayed.

Marklos's face splits with a grin. "Silvean, do you know this woman? Or perhaps her *daughter*? Don't you think she might look a little like you?"

My father's gaze shoots to me, and it feels like an arrow piercing my chest. He didn't recognize me at first, but now he can't look away. His golden eyes pore over my face like it's the lines of a book he desperately needs to read.

Look away, I beg silently.

He manages, but I feel a tearing sensation as he does.

35

He turns back to Marklos, sounding only slightly shaken. "Let's not dance around each other. I've never seen this woman or this girl in my life."

"*She's* seen *you*," Marklos says, gesturing at my mother. "She knows your name, and yet you haven't left the confines of the palace in . . . what . . . thirteen years?"

Twelve and a half. It's been twelve and a half years since my mother and I watched my father get hauled away, seemingly dead. Not *that* dead, apparently. Bloodmages make for miraculous healers, and the king would have the best serving at the palace, then and now, so my father must have been revived after his captors brought him to the brink of death.

Twelve and a half years doesn't explain how worn he looks, but there are more pressing things to worry about.

"You see," Marklos says, "I was there thirteen years ago, when we found you, the infamous Silvean Ballacra, rogue bloodmage of Skyllea. I was guarding the back of your house, so I didn't get a good look at the woman or the child you were hiding with. Perhaps that was for the best, since I survived while many of my fellows did not."

I certainly didn't recognize the captain, but that's no surprise. I was so young when I would have last seen him, and there was such chaos.

My father shrugs, more ease coming back into his shoulders and his voice. "If this is her, I honestly don't remember. That woman meant nothing to me, and her child wasn't mine. It was proven."

"Then you won't mind if we test this woman and her daughter for blood magic right here before the council?"

"Of course not."

"Of course not," Marklos echoes. "After all, you're so *happily* married to Princess Penelope and ensconced in the palace, though still no luck on a child yet, am I right? Ten years you've tried now? You *have* been trying?"

A pit opens up inside me. I feel like I'm falling. My father is married to a . . .

"Princess?" my mother says faintly. She's trying to bear all of this quietly, but I can see the strain is nearly too much for her. It breaks my heart.

I would give anything to get my mother out of here. Funny, since we both, just a day ago, would have given anything to see my father again. That was before discovering that he'd joined the royal family.

We couldn't have known. Outside of the palace, the affairs of the king's children or his children's children are kept private, at times down to their betrothals—kept especially private, apparently, in the case of a once-fugitive bloodmage from an enemy kingdom marrying into the family. That, and I've avoided hearing about royals my entire life because I hate them. But Marklos obviously knows the details.

My father's stony expression cracks once again, and heat escapes in his words. "That's none of your fucking business, Marklos, and I'd thank you to keep your mouth closed before I shut it for you."

"Still fire in there, eh? I figured you were just pretending to be asleep," the captain says, seeming to enjoy himself. "Which is all the more reason your bloodline should be preserved. It would be a shame for the polis to lose it simply for lack of a blood heir."

Without further delay, he seizes my mother's hand, withdrawing one of the long silver needles topped with a skull that I remember from all those years ago. He probably wants to discount my mother as a source of magic first.

Which is fine by me. My mother won't even have to discreetly prick her own finger this way with the hidden needle she's no doubt carrying. I feel eyes on me, and not just those of the other council members. I glance up and catch a flash of my father's golden gaze before he looks away.

37

It was only for a second, but his expression brings back memories with a fierce potency. He's telling me to do as he taught me.

I'm already planning on it. I've gone this long without his guidance, haven't I? I don't need it now.

My mother's test is over in a heartbeat. "No magic," Marklos declares. "The girl didn't get it from her mother."

"You're assuming a lot," I snap, turning to expose my bound arms. At a nod from the captain, a warded man nearby cuts my ropes with a swipe of his fingers. I want to rub my wrists, but I hold out my hands before Marklos can try to take them. I want him touching me as little as possible. Luckily there's no more blood on my burned palms, just tight, raw-looking skin.

The captain moves slowly, holding my eyes and then studying my hands as he lowers the needle toward one of my fingers, making sure I'm not sketching any sigils. He likely thinks I can't because of the drug, but he's being thorough.

He doesn't know I can sketch this one—if only this one—without twitching a finger, picture it as clearly in my mind as if drawn in blood, or call it forward even in my sleep.

Move.

Blood wells on my fingertip around the needle's point. Marklos carefully dabs it up and examines it. The entire hall is silent.

"Well?" Acantha demands.

"*Damn it*," Marklos growls. Because, of course, my mother's blood—which I borrowed both twelve and a half years ago *and* just a moment ago, moving it from her finger to my own in droplets too small to spot—doesn't have any power in it.

"See?" I say, unable to rein in my grin. "I told you I'm not a—"

Marklos backhands me, snapping my head sideways and causing black stars to explode in my vision. Before I know what's happening, he unsheathes his dagger and draws it across my palm in a burning slash. I cry out, trying to wrench my hand away, but he doesn't let me. There's no way I can withhold the flood of blood, not with how deep the cut is and how badly my skull is ringing.

The captain jerks my wrist, whipping a red splatter across the marble in front of us. At his gesture, it turns to fire that burns brighter, hotter, and more violently than if fueled by a barrel of pitch. Anyone nearby has to back away from the inferno.

"*Now* do you see?" Marklos cries.

That's all he manages to say before he's lifted off his feet and thrown across the hall. He slams into a marble pillar with a sickening wet smack.

I see my father's arm outstretched before him. It's shaking.

"Never touch her," he snarls, and his fingers twitch to sketch more sigils. But before he can, he doubles over as if in pain, then collapses to his knees. He's immediately surrounded by wards, and I can't see what's happening no matter how I try.

Marklos peels himself off the pillar, clutching his head and leaving a misty red outline of his body behind on the white marble. My father moved the captain using his blood, just how I slowed Bethea's fall, except so forcefully that some sprayed out the back of him, never mind what's now oozing through his fingers from his cracked skull.

That doesn't stop him from finally saying what he's wanted to all along. "*This*," the captain snarls, pointing a bloody finger at me, "is Silvean Ballacra's daughter, and probably the most powerful bloodmage in the city, second to him."

For a moment, there's silence. And then shouting as I'm swarmed by wards, my arms seized. I can't spot my mother in the writhing chaos, but I hear her scream my name and then—agony in her voice—my father's name. Struggling against my captors, I catch a glimpse of my father dragging himself to his feet with his cane. Between the sound of my mother and the sight of him, I feel like I'm tearing in half.

None of the wards try to hold my father, either to help him up or to restrain him. And then I see it: the pale hand resting on his arm that's attached to nothing but air. No, not nothing. It comes from the shadow at my father's side.

His guardian. My father has been warded. Of course he has, if he's now part of this world and living in the palace. I just hadn't had the chance to realize it yet, to spot the smudge of darkness behind him. Now it's all I can see, even after the ghostly hand vanishes back into shadow.

A deep stillness settles over the dark blur. It almost seems to be looking right back at me.

Feeling drains from my body, leaving me numb. I shudder involuntarily.

Lady Acantha calls for order until everyone falls quiet. She sits in a pillar of sunlight. "While most unexpected," she begins in a normal voice, clearing her throat, "this is most fortuitous." She turns to my father, who leans heavily on his cane for balance. "You desperately need to pass on your bloodline, don't you, Silvean? It looks like we finally have an heir of your blood to allow it. Though, by the sound of it, she's not turning out to be any more biddable or loyal to her polis than you."

"This is not my polis," he hisses, panting with effort.

"But it is hers," Acantha says with a brisk nod toward me. "And perhaps she will be made fit to serve it with the right guidance. And with a guardian, of course."

A guardian. I will be warded, just like my father. This is everything we wanted to stop. I'm not sure what the councilwoman means about my father passing on his bloodline, but I know it can't be good, not with that look on his face.

40

He meets my eyes. There are tears in his. "I'm so sorry, love," he says.

And then he collapses.

I let out a wild cry, a terrible emotion sweeping me up on its crest. Before I can lunge for him, Marklos makes another one of those twisting, slashing motions with his hand—plenty of blood on his fingers to aid him—and I join my father on the floor.

4

I'm having a curious dream. At least, I hope it's a dream. I'm laid out on a cold stone slab in a dark room, naked save for a white sheet draping my body up to the shoulders. A few candles surround me, illuminating a haze of incense drifting in the air like a low fog and casting faint light on my too-pale skin. I look dead, and someone is chanting something that sounds suspiciously like funeral rights nearby.

I can see all of this, because I'm not really *in* my body, but floating above and looking down, as insubstantial as the incense. Am I a spirit, cut loose from my flesh? Am I *actually* dead—a shade? With the weight of my physical form has gone all my earthly cares. I really don't mind that I might be gone.

"You're not dead," says a calm, deep voice.

I turn—though *turn* isn't really the right word. Rather, I redirect my focus, and suddenly I'm in a black stone chamber with no doors or windows. The room with the stone slab, the chanting, the candles, and the incense have all vanished. I'm somehow standing on two feet in a body that isn't quite substantial. Thank the goddess I'm clothed in a simple white chiton and not naked, because I'm not alone.

A man stands in the chamber with me, in the shadows opposite. When he sees he has my attention, he shifts forward into better lighting—which is still minimal but enough for me to make out his features.

Black hair falls in curls to his shoulders, tucked behind his ears by a dull silver circlet. His face is beardless except for a slight shadow of stubble on his pale skin, and he appears to be in his early twenties. He almost looks normal—though abnormally striking—except he wears a strange knee-length chiton all in black, layered with a breastplate, sword belt, and skirt of featherlike strips that I've seen warriors wear—pteryges, I recall—all in black leather. Bracers of the same material, with silver studs, adorn his forearms, studded black leather greaves his legs, and black sandals his feet. His eyes are no color I can detect, like his pupils have swallowed the irises.

"While you're not hard on the eyes, you're also kind of creepy," I say.

"But you're not afraid," he says. It isn't a question.

"Maybe I would be if I weren't dying."

He shakes his head gently. "You're not dying, either."

"Then what is this?"

"You're somewhere in between the living world and the underworld. Your spirit has been guided here after your body was placed into a near-death state. But you're still alive." His voice is so flat, so calm, my first impulse is to disturb it, like throwing rocks into a still pond.

Caution, I tell myself. Aloud, I say, "Why was I brought here?"

"Because I wanted to introduce myself. My name is Ivrilos." He holds out his hand.

I eye it, remaining on the other side of the chamber. "I'm not sure I want to meet anyone who requires all *this* for an introduction." I hesitate. "Especially someone who doesn't know that colors exist in the world."

He smiles slightly. "There aren't many colors where I come from."

43

"Where do you come from?"

"Originally from Thanopolis, like you."

"And now?"

He cocks his head. "I think you know. You just don't *want* to know."

I scoff. "Right. Thanks for the insight, whatever it means." But something scratches at my thoughts, an unpleasant suspicion. I take a step back.

He takes a step forward.

"What do you want from me?" I ask, my voice climbing higher.

"Like I said, to meet you. You and I are going to be companions . . . for a while."

And then I remember where I've seen such strange eyes before: on the guardians, the dead men. These eyes are the same. Cold and dark and flat. *Dead.*

He's one of *them.*

"Oh shit," I say. I take another step back and meet the wall of the chamber with my heel.

He cocks his head to the other side, looking almost catlike. Predatory. "I must admit, it surprises me to hear you say that."

I force a laugh, and it comes out like a bark. "Ladies don't curse where you come from, either? No colors, no cursing . . . it must be terribly dull."

"There aren't as many ladies as men, truth be told. But no, most of them don't curse much."

That doesn't make sense. The underworld should hold the shades of as many women as men. But now isn't the time to ask about that. As he's spoken, he's taken another step toward me.

"They can't talk, then, these dead ladies?" I ask, trying to sound calm.

The dead man's mouth quirks up at one corner. "So you *do* understand where I come from. And no, it's more that they are well bred. Manners prohibit vulgarity."

"Do you live in a palace in the afterlife?" I ask as if trying to piece together a puzzle, when in reality I only want to keep him talking until I find a route of escape.

"Something like that."

"Well, I'm not well bred, so why the surprise?"

"Perhaps because the shape of your mouth doesn't match a word so crude."

I blink. Is he saying my mouth looks nice? While at the same time trying to sneak up on me and do . . . *something* . . . bad to me? My caution evaporates like water thrown on a blazing fire. "Go stick your head in a chamber pot until you drown. Oh wait, you're already dead. Can you go die again?"

"I must decline," he says with a slight bow of his head.

He takes another step toward me. I don't have space to flee backward, so I edge sideways. How the hell does one leave a room with no doors or windows?

"Don't ever expect politeness from me," I spit as I move away blindly, my gaze locked on him. "If you come near me I'll scratch your weird black eyes out."

He purses his lips. "That will make it difficult for me to kiss you."

I nearly trip to a halt. "Excuse me?"

"Ah, now, that *was* polite," he says. "My lips, rather regrettably it seems, have to touch you. Not necessarily *your* lips. A hand would do. I was planning on kissing the back of yours when I took it."

I resume circling. "Over my dead body."

He pivots in time with me, though for the moment he doesn't come any closer. "I'm afraid we can't fight to the death. As you

45

know, I'm already dead, and your spirit is trapped here, so this has to end sooner rather than later and in only one way." He sighs. "I don't usually have to force this. They often come willingly."

"Because you're *so* charming?" I snarl.

"No, because they're usually younger than you. Less distrustful."

My mouth falls open. "And you kiss them, too? That's disgusting."

"Did you not hear me say a kiss on the hand suffices? Trust me, it's not passionate. It's all just part of the bond." His tone is infuriatingly patient. *Polite.*

"Why are they younger?" I keep moving, keep talking, trying not to let my eyes dart around too obviously as they search for some crack in the perfect black walls. "I'm not *that* old."

"I didn't say you were. Most bloodmages simply get their guardians as adolescents, when their abilities are first confirmed." He hesitates. "Although your father was older than you when I was bound to him."

I freeze. "My father . . . wait. You're his guardian, too?"

"I am."

"But how can you guard two people? Isn't that . . . too much?"

"I believe I can manage the both of you," he says with a slight smile. He doesn't sound overly confident, only matter-of-fact. "That's why I was chosen for you, because I was able to contend with your father so well. He was . . . resistant."

"Ever hear the saying, 'Like father like daughter'?" I squint at him. "If you've been his guardian for nearly thirteen years, and you've warded others before him . . . How old are you?"

His smile slants into something crooked. "I'm twenty-three."

"Like hell you are. How long have you been *dead*?"

The dead man's gaze slips away for a brief moment. "Not as long as some. But let us say I have experience. Besides, I won't have to guard both of you for long. Once he passes you his bloodline, which will be imminent . . ." He trails off at what he sees on my face.

"Then what?" I whisper. When he doesn't say anything, I scream, my nails trying to dig into the wall, "*Then what?*"

"I'm sorry." He sounds sincere, which makes me want to sink to my knees. Because that means what has gone unspoken is the truth.

My father will die when he gives me his bloodline.

"I thought you knew," he murmurs.

I don't crumple to the ground like I want to. I straighten my spine and hold up my fists. Blood magic won't work here; I can sense that. So I'll just have to use my hands.

He arches a black eyebrow. "Are you going to fight me?"

"Did my father fight you?"

The dead man regards me. "Like a wildcat. But he lost. And you don't strike me as—"

With a feral screech, I throw myself at him.

It doesn't go well. He traps one arm as soon as I claw at him, followed promptly by the other, and then he holds me pinned as I thrash and scream. He cinches me tight against his hard chest with one arm while he cups my head with the other to keep me from biting him—which of course I try to do as soon as he's close enough. Our stance could almost look intimate.

How is the man so strong, so solid? It isn't fair. He's a shade, and I'm supposedly alive, and yet he's subdued me as easily as if I were a child.

He brings his lips to my ear, and his breath stirs my hair. "I truly am sorry," he says in a gentle ghost of a voice.

And then he kisses my cheek, which is wet with tears and stuck with strands of my hair. His lips are cool and soft, and yet, for a brief moment, I feel like they're stealing something vital from me. But then I don't feel anything anymore, because the dead man is gone from the chamber, and so am I.

5

I awake in dimness. For a moment, I'm wildly afraid I've come to on the stone slab, and someone will be washing my body, and I'll be dead . . .

But I'm only in a room with heavy curtains drawn. A ridiculously opulent room, I realize as my eyes adjust. My bed has posts like twining trees with real leaves and flowers laced in a canopy overhead, and nearby sits a wooden desk shaped like a blooming rose.

I sit up, and a wave of dizziness hits me. Where on earth am I? And *who* has put me in a night shift, the quality of which is too good for me to have ever afforded? Also, I can't be positive, but I'm pretty sure I've been washed, hair and all—hair that once again possesses its natural blue tint, which I haven't seen in years of magicking it into something more normal. I take a whiff of my arm. I've been perfumed, too.

"Do you often sniff yourself?"

I jump nearly a foot off the bed and barely swallow a shriek. It wasn't a dream, or a nightmare, or even a poppy hallucination. Because there he stands, near the window, as solid as if he were made of living flesh: the dead man. He's wearing the same dark attire as before, black cloth and leather. He looks just as young and infuriatingly handsome. It's as if he's walked straight out of that tomblike chamber and into the real world. *My* world.

"Get out!" I shout at him, drawing the bedcovers to my shoulders.

"I'm afraid you'll have to get used to this," he says, nodding down at himself. "I'm here to stay."

"Why can I see you now? Aren't you supposed to be, I don't know"—I flap my hand at him, as if waving away a bad smell—"a shadow or something?"

"Now that I'm bound to your spirit, you can see me as if I were truly alive."

I pick up a brass candlestick shaped like a woman with the wings of a dragonfly. "Can I hit you as if you were truly alive?"

His tone is as patient as ever. "You can try."

I fling it at him. My aim, miraculously, is true. Except the winged woman flies *beyond* his leather breastplate, passing right through him, and clangs violently against the wall.

"You said—!"

"I said you could *try*."

For a minute, I only seethe at him from across the room. "Where is my father?"

"You'll see him soon enough."

My words are clipped, boiling. "What if I really, *really* want you to go away?"

"That's at my discretion. But since you so politely asked . . ." He nods at me and vanishes into the shadows.

"And don't come back!" I shout.

A knock sounds at the bedroom door.

Ignoring it for the moment, I slide out from under the heavy covers and stand, bracing myself on a bedpost until I find my balance. Then I stumble over to the window's thick curtains and whip them aside.

I stare down over the polis from a higher vantage than I've ever seen before. I must be in the wealthy sector, atop the hill in the center. Maybe I'm in a manor or . . . no, I can't think about the alternative. The spread of buildings and streets beneath me is nearly impressive enough to distract me from anything else, but it's what lies *beyond* that makes me gasp.

It looks as if there's merely a shimmering glass pane between the outer farmlands of the city's plateau, which are sunny and verdant, and the blowing expanse of ice and rock that sprawls across the horizon. The entire world outside is white, endless white, with huge clouds billowing up where the wind parts around the jagged black claws of boulders raking the blanket of snow. I'm facing north, then, not south toward the desert. I can see better than ever what the blight has done. It's too much nothing. Too much death, especially with the jumbled ruins of old towns and cities poking up like broken teeth in a few places. The veil suddenly seems both incredibly frail and immensely powerful.

For a brief moment, I wish the veil would fall and the blight would bury Thanopolis. I wonder, too, for the first time, if my father has ever wished for the city's demise after how its people have treated him.

My father is alive. I have to find him.

Casting around, I discover a length of cloth, deep green like the one my father wore, and heavily embroidered with twining vines. I throw it over my shoulders, partially covering my thin night shift, and push open the bedroom door.

I'm in a sun-drenched marble hallway, lined in arches as delicate as spiderweb and spiraling windows of cut glass that also look out over the city.

"Oh, mistress!" a voice squeaks behind me. I spin to find a girl, younger than me, in the simple tunic of a servant. "I knocked because I heard a noise . . . If you had told me you were awake I would have . . . Shall I help you dress and put up your hair? That cloth is meant to be pinned as a peplos . . ."

Wearing it as such would be far more elegant, but I don't care about that *or* my hair, which is already more brushed than usual. I've never had a servant try to serve me, besides. This is all too much, too overwhelming, and I need to keep moving.

51

I half trip on a rug too plush for my feet, and hurry down the hallway, trying to ignore the dizzying wealth around me. I have to find . . .

Him.

I practically burst into a marble dining room lined in graceful columns, intricate tapestries, and verdant plants growing in elaborate shapes. He's seated at the opposite end of a long, polished wooden table that looks like a vertical slice of a massive tree trunk, with a strange woman and a girl about my age on either side of him, both dressed in practical, short, and yet finely-woven chitons, hardened leather bracers on their wrists and leather headbands strapping down their hair. The woman has a long dark braid tossed over one shoulder, showing the first signs of gray, and sun-bronzed light skin; the girl's hair is almost black, her skin warm brown, and yet there's an obvious resemblance between them, likely mother and daughter. Neither has a bloodline. There's a pair of wooden swords leaning against one wall, as if the women have just come in from a training session.

There's something so familial about all of them seated here like this that for a moment I think perhaps my father *does* have another child. But it doesn't seem likely that this girl is his, not with the woman and my father being so light skinned. Besides, the girl would have been born about when I was, and my father lived with my mother and me for another seven years after that. And why else would everyone be so excited to discover my existence, if he already has a blood child?

"Rovan," my father says, sounding slightly breathless. His cane is propped near his chair, a fine green himation draped around his shoulders. Time has marked his face as surely as the bloodline his skin. He looks *so* much older. He leaps up, as fast as he's able with his cane, and takes a few quick, lurching steps toward me.

I take a step back, and he stops. My mouth works. "What . . . ?" I'm not sure where to begin.

52

His own mouth seems incapable of forming words. His eyes hold too much to decipher. There's pain in them, despair even, but he also looks at me as if he's thought he would never see me again.

My stomach is churning. I fold my arms across my chest, wrapping myself in the cloth like a protective blanket, and stare back at him, my throat almost too tight to breathe, let alone speak.

"We weren't sure when you would wake up," he finally says. "Are you hungry?"

A strangled laugh escapes me. Food is the last thing on my mind. "What have they done to you? What do they want with me? And who are *they*?" I ask finally, waving at the other two at the table. The woman and the girl stare at me like I'm an animal on parade, and not a very special one at that. Neither of them has gotten up.

"Who are *we*?" the girl says. "More like, who are *you*? This is *our* home."

My father turns to them distractedly. "This is Princess Penelope, the youngest sister of the crown prince, and her daughter, Crisea." He doesn't call the princess his wife, even though I know she is, nor Crisea his child. "Penelope, Crisea, this is Rovan . . . my daughter." He gestures to a chair. "Please, Rovan, sit. You've been asleep since yesterday. I know the process can be draining."

"The process," I repeat, without moving for the chair. "You mean when I was bound to a dead man against my will? The same dead man who is your guardian, apparently?"

My father's half smile doesn't crease his eyes. "There's not much of me left for him to guard, I'm afraid."

"Silvean, sit down if she won't, before you fall down." Penelope's tone is stern, impatient, and wholly practical. No love lost between them, then. The princess turns the same coolly assessing gaze on me. "Carrying the weight of a bloodline, especially one as heavy as his, wears on a body. The more powerful the bloodline, the worse it is. He should conserve his strength."

"That's it, my dear," her father says with a bitter twist to his mouth. "It's only my bloodline that's using me up."

She rolls her eyes. "Don't start with your theories again, Silvean. No one wants to hear them."

Goddess. They sound like an old married couple. They *are* an old married couple, and I can't stand to hear it.

"I want to know," I say, my voice rising. "*What's* using you up, and how do we stop it?"

My father's expression seems to soften at my concern, but Penelope speaks over him.

"As for what my family wants with *you*, other than to see all rogue bloodmages warded . . . You're the only one who can receive Silvean's bloodline, which is becoming too heavy for him to carry. It's a bloodline they can't stand to lose, which they will if he collapses under its weight. You're their best hope." She says *best* as if I'm not very promising at all.

"But I don't want it!" I cry. "I don't want *any* of this!"

"Believe me when I say this is the last thing I ever wanted for you, too," my father murmurs. "But you may not have a choice."

"Help me, then," I say desperately. "We can help each other, somehow."

The dead man appears, his back against a pillar at the edge of the room, arms folded across the black armor of his chest. "She's resistant enough as it is, Silvean. Don't continue in this vein. You know it will only be harder for her."

I spin on him. "Who invited *you* here?"

Penelope looks back and forth between me and my father, before her eyes settle in the dead man's general direction. "Oh, is that Ivrilos? How is he today?"

She must only be able to detect a vague shadow without making out the details or hearing his voice. *Lucky her*, I think.

"*How is he?*" I say incredulously. "Who cares! I despise his very essence."

"Fine choice of words," my father says. "Essence is exactly what he is, as a shade. Or pneuma, or breath, or whatever people have called it throughout the ages—it's all the same, the intangible substance that composes the spirit."

I glare at the dead man. "If he's all air, can he blow away and let us get back to our conversation? Better yet, why aren't we burning this place to the ground and leaving?"

My father looks at me with a level expression. A practiced cover, I realize, for eyes that are deep wells of pain. "They have your mother. She's safe, but they're holding her to ensure our cooperation, both yours and mine. And of course they hold *you* over me as well. They've never had this kind of leverage before. I can't put one toe out of line."

My heart turns into a cold and painful lump in my chest. *My mother*. This is all my fault. But at least I want to do something, anything, unlike the man in front of me. "Why didn't you *already* burn this place down, long before they had her or me? I've seen what you can do! It's been almost thirteen years, and you've just been *sitting here*, eating at the same table as these people?" I sneer unabashedly at the two women, ignoring the deepening scowl on Crisea's face. "Why didn't you come *back?*"

Here it is: the accusation. It bubbles to the surface like pus from an old wound. Because I *was* wounded that day my father was taken. And now I'm realizing he could have healed me.

It isn't just that I lost my father. I've blamed *myself* bitterly for what happened, for once wishing he would join the wards. I know it's not entirely logical, but I've felt like that wish brought them down on his head. I've nearly drowned myself in wine trying to forget. I've wanted to escape the past so desperately that I planned to leave everything and everyone I've ever known behind.

And yet my father has been here, living in the palace all this time.

"You don't understand, Rovan. I——" He grimaces. "I can't say much, but know that I am little more than a glorified prisoner here. You'll find out soon enough that guardians watch over their wards in more than one way."

"Silvean," the dead man warns.

"So they're our captors as much as our protectors," I say. "Do they hurt their wards?"

My father doesn't respond, only stares at the dead man with a tight expression.

After a second, the dead man sighs and answers me. "Only those who resist. I don't advise making a habit of it."

For a moment, I consider using my favorite sigil to throw the entire table at the dead man to show him how I feel about *that*, but then a wave of dizziness overtakes me. I stumble over to a chair and sit down hard. I can't remember when I last ate or had a drink of water. The most recent thing to have passed my lips was on its way *out*, sometime yesterday morning.

My voice cracks. "So that's it? We just give up, roll over like dogs, and have breakfast?"

"Lunch," Crisea corrects.

"Who cares which meal it is?" I erupt. "I don't even know where I am, I don't know where my mother is"——I toss my head at my father——"and I don't even know *you*. Not anymore."

He flinches. "I know."

"You're in the palace, silly child," Penelope says in her no-nonsense tone that makes me want to scream. "There are worse places to be, such as the dungeons, so I don't see why you're complaining. And you have a busy day ahead of you, so I recommend you conserve your strength and eat something."

Goddess. So I *am* in the palace, that spiraling white structure rising like a seashell to dominate the center of the city. I'm about to tell the princess where she can shove her recommendation when my attention snags on two words. "Busy day?"

"Didn't you hear about my dear father, King Neleus?" Penelope asks. It doesn't sound like he's very dear to her at all.

I shake my head. I don't give a flying fig about the king right now.

"How could you *not* have?" Crisea scoffs.

"Cris," my father begins.

As much as my father and Penelope don't seem to like each other, he still has a pet name for her daughter. Fury burns through me again.

"No, I hear nothing down among the plebeian rabble," I snap. "We're too busy putting food on the table or looking out for our families to care whether or not the king's morning shit went well." Although there *was* that pageant the day before I was caught, where everyone dressed up in clay skull masks and flower wreaths . . .

"King Neleus is ill," my father supplies quickly. "Too ill to live much longer, but at least he's in his seventy-somethingeth year, so excuse me if I lack sympathy for his plight." He drags himself over to a chair next to me. He's in his early forties—too young to look like this, to talk like this, to move like this. "As with all the kings, he has the choice of falling on his sword or drinking hemlock before he becomes unfit to rule. That . . . event . . . will happen within the week, and will only be attended by Crown Prince Tyros in the necropolis, whose duty it is to perform the final rites and inter his body. I know you wouldn't have heard much about the rest of the royal family, but the king, especially his passing, is another matter. There are celebrations in honor of him across the polis, most notably a commemorative banquet this evening here in the palace. Our presence has been . . . requested."

I seize a pitcher and a goblet, fill the latter with water, and begin gulping. It's only after I slam down the empty vessel that I say, "I must decline."

"I don't think it's optional," my father says gently.

"Why, will *he* force me to go?" I don't look in the dead man's direction.

"Your presence could be assured in many ways," my father says. "You're expected to meet the rest of the royal family. It would be best to play along at this point, for your mother's sake."

In response, I tear into a loaf of bread with my bare hands. I alternate bites with stuffing grapes and chunks of melon into my mouth, chewing it all indiscriminately and ignoring the fact that it's delicious. Penelope and Crisea both watch with marked distaste. I couldn't care less. They want me to eat to regain my strength? Fine. The better to find my mother, wherever she is, fight whomever I have to, and get out of here, with or without my father's help.

My father waits for a few minutes, not touching any food, while Penelope and Crisea finish their own meal. I relish the awkward silence. *Let them choke on it*, I think.

"Rovan," he says eventually. "Would you accompany me on a walk? I can show you some of the palace, such that I can, and there are important matters we must discuss."

"Don't be gone too long," Penelope says before I can open my mouth. "The royal tailor is coming in soon. He'll alter one of Crisea's dresses to fit the girl for tonight."

"Will there even be enough material to cover her?" Crisea mutters, raising an eyebrow in my direction.

"*Must* we do this?" I burst out, spinning on her. "Are you worried I'm going to take him from you? Since your *real* father doesn't seem to be around anymore, you must be desperate not to lose this poor substitute."

Hurt cuts across Crisea's face.

"Rovan—" my father starts, but Crisea interrupts.

"He's been my father for all these years, not yours," she spits. "*I* actually care about him. He was supposed to have been safe, but then you had to show up and start all of this. You should have kept your nose down in the mud, you worthless pig."

Penelope sighs. "Crisea. No need to insult her breeding. She *is* technically your stepsister, and a part of this family now."

I gape. "You people are *nothing* to me. You're not my family. And you conniving royals are the ones who did this to my father in the first place, so it's your fault if he's in danger. And you know what? You can keep him, if you both want each other's company so badly. And you can keep your damned dress." For good measure, I add, "At least I *have* breasts."

Never mind that Crisea is perfectly fine, if thin and muscular like she's boiled all her fat off in martial exercises—and if also a bitch.

The girl twitches like she wants to go for a sword. "I should gut you for speaking to me like that."

I stand abruptly, causing them all to jump. "Try it. I am a blood-mage, and I will *throw* the next person who—"

I feel a hand on my arm and fling myself around, alarmed that I might find the cold, pale skin of the dead man's against mine. But it's only my father, reaching out from his chair, and I realize he's done it more to warn me than to restrain me.

Because the dead man *is* standing right behind me, a looming black figure that looks entirely too substantial, as if he was *about* to do something to me. I jump an involuntary step back and bump into the table, knocking over a glass. I hear it shatter. I don't take my eyes off the shade. I glare at him as if daring him to come closer, and he gazes implacably back.

Apparently he doesn't approve of threats to the royal family.

"I need to get out of here," I say into the tense silence that follows. "And I need answers."

"How about that tour?" my father reminds me quickly.

"Sure. As long as *he* stays behind," I say, raising my chin at the dead man.

"I'll be just out of sight," the shade says, as calm as ever. "You won't even know I'm there."

My hand gropes behind my back, seeking a knife or a plate or something else to throw at him, but he vanishes before I have the chance.

My father stands slowly. "Let's go. I'll be back, don't worry," he adds to Crisea, who sits with her arms folded, giving me a deadly stare.

I tug my shawl tightly around my shoulders and follow him out into this strange new world.

"Keep it quick," Penelope says.

I slam the door behind us.

6

I follow my father out into a pale marble hallway lined in columns and lush tapestries depicting scenes of hunting, dancing, and other recreational activities of the wealthy. Two guards—normal flesh-and-blood humans, not guardians or their wards—stand outside. They don't attempt to stop us or even look at us, although one frowns when I slam the door.

Nonetheless, my father pulls his himation over his gray-streaked blue hair and waits until we're out of earshot before saying, "This is the royal family's wing. King Neleus's children live here and their children as well, along with their spouses if they have them. The king has an entire wing to himself, which the likes of me has never been allowed to enter."

He says it as though trying to distance himself from all of this. Never mind that this is where he lives, he's married to the king's daughter, and I've never seen three paces' worth of this hallway's wealth in my entire life. Lines of what look like real gold thread the creamy marble all around us. Flowers and vines grow entwined around each towering column, blossoming in a profusion of color and perfume. The tapestries are no less alive—*actually moving*, I realize as I look closer at the tiny figures and scrolling leaves. I've always been forced to hide my magic when weaving, to make it look as though it has come from hands and loom alone, no matter how skillfully done. These palace artisans certainly have no such restrictions.

"I'd prefer other accommodations, of course," my father

continues. "To live in the palace, you still need some drop of royal blood in you or association by marriage. But an arcade and a lovely garden connect this wing of the palace to the Hall of the Wards, where every bloodmage is allowed, even if they're common— though warded and registered of course. I keep my office within view of it, but I'm not allowed to fraternize. It makes me feel a little less of an impostor to be near there, if no less a prisoner." He's speaking too quickly, nervously.

I don't have the time or the inclination to put him at ease. "I don't actually want the grand tour. I want to talk about what the hell is happening with you and me and my mother, and what this bloodline business is that everyone keeps going on about." I eye him sideways for any hint in his expression of what I fear—what will happen if he gives his bloodline to me.

But all he says is, "Consider a bloodline a store of magical knowledge, recorded within the very body of a bloodmage. It can be passed on, but only to an heir of their blood who possesses magical ability. It's common enough for a bloodmage to have a child— but only one—with a gift of any potency, although they could hand it down to a grandchild of similar or greater strength."

My brow furrows. "But wouldn't that make them extremely rare?"

"Smart girl. Yes, bloodlines are always at risk of being lost through death or lack of an heir. Especially in Skyllea. There, bloodlines are only passed down to the strongest mages within the strongest families, preserving the most potent magic. We're much rarer and highly valued." He smiles slightly, with pride that shines like light through broken glass. "Which is why the creation of new bloodlines is encouraged if a mage without one is deemed strong enough. Think of it like being raised to magical nobility." He frowns. "Here, however, establishing new bloodlines is more than encouraged. Four hundred years ago, the first king, Athanatos, made it mandatory for anyone discovered to have magical ability to start a bloodline. That's why you see so many short bloodlines here, with only a few sigils marking the skin. The long ones are still rare and considered precious."

"How do they get longer?"

"Before turning over the bloodline, each bloodmage adds sigils they have discovered or used in a new way, making them effortlessly accessible to their successor, and not requiring the use of fresh blood to access their potency—though of course blood never hurts. That way, each life is like a chapter in a growing magical record that's handed down through the generations."

"So then that's . . . actual blood?" I ask, pointing at his red-lined forearm. The symbols, as always, mean nothing to me.

"Yes," he says, "the red actually comes from blood, the blood of my ancestors. My own blood will add to it." He mutters, "Sooner rather than later, I believe."

"Penelope said it was a heavy thing to carry," I say, prodding. "And maybe to pass on?"

He scoffs, clacking his cane more forcefully against the marble floor. "She wouldn't know. She inherited neither her mother's magical gift nor her bloodline, which is why she was still unmarried by the time I met her—but I can return to that unfortunate topic later. Many here don't truly understand bloodlines. My people, on the island of Skyllea, started the tradition millennia past. I know they say the first king, Athanatos, did," he says, heading me off as I open my mouth, "but actually he borrowed the idea four centuries ago. More like *stole* a sacred ritual, along with our sigil-based writing system, and bent them to his own ends. Not only did he make it mandatory to start a bloodline if you don't have one to inherit, but you *must* pass it on to the child of yours with the most magical ability by the time that child is twenty."

Twenty. That's coming soon for me, but I still have time to figure out a plan before my father has to give me his burden. Maybe I only take his gift for blood magic, and he can retire in peace with my mother and weave cloth.

"Why so young as twenty?" I ask, still too afraid to press him about the other thing.

"There's less risk of losing a bloodline to the perils of age, and the mind and body are still sharp and strong, able to train without flagging. I suppose the king wanted his bloodmages to be in their prime, of maximum use."

"He wanted a magical army."

My father gives me a knowing look. "Athanatos claimed it was to strengthen blood magic in general, for the sake of the polis and its future generations. The magical gift was and is still as rare as ever before, but now *all* of it would gradually build on itself over time, rather than within a select few families and individuals. Seems egalitarian, but yes, as you say, I suspect it was to increase Thanopolis's magical power—in quantity if not quality. It also made it easier to keep track of all bloodmages in the city, since bloodlines were recorded in the Register from then on, their children closely monitored for the gift, and anyone with magic warded—to protect their bloodlines, supposedly, as if they were treasure troves belonging to the polis."

"Or to keep them in line," I finish bitterly. "They want to use our power, not have it used against them. But why not have normal guards watch over us, like the ones I see around this place?" I gesture behind me, at a pair we'd just passed. "You know, *alive?*"

"A shade can easily follow where many could not, and watch and listen without being intrusive. Those are the usual reasons given, anyway. They can also stop us more efficiently than any number of living guards could, and without violence. I also have other suspicions."

"Silvean." The name comes from nowhere, rising as if from

the columns around us. The dead man. He's indeed watching and listening, even if we can't see him. It's frankly creepy.

"Stay out of this," I hiss.

But my father says, "He's right to warn us. I'm not sure if he'll let me tell you everything, but at this point, we should get behind closed doors."

I frown. "Can't he just float through them?"

"Yes, of course," my father replies. And yet his tone isn't concerned. It makes me curious enough to follow without question.

It gives me time to take in the palace, despite myself. It's impossible not to, with the sheer amount of riches splattered on every surface. The hallway curves and slopes gently downward along the spiral structure. Gold-threaded pale marble gives way to dark gray veined with red, and life-sized statues stand between the columns like sentinels, with wreaths of living laurels and flowers growing atop their heads and twining their feet.

"Are these royals?" I ask, nodding at the statues.

"Famous wards. The royal gallery is restricted."

Also curious. I've certainly seen plenty of statues of the first king, Athanatos, but perhaps the rest of the family isn't supposed to compete with the city's founder. *He* seems only to be in competition with the goddess for status. I remember how the wards called the fountain *his* instead of *hers*. Athanatos has definitely achieved something like godhood in the eyes of the people. Even his name—which I somehow doubt he was born with—means "immortal," and Thanopolis was named after him.

"Why is the royal gallery restricted?"

"Now that's a very good question. One worth asking, I daresay. But later."

Before I can press him, the walls of the palace lift away, exposing the hallway to the open air. We've reached the base of the palace. Through the columns lay a lush garden of trees shimmering in a warm breeze, bushes trimmed or magicked into the intricate, twining shapes of galloping horses and winged beings, and a riot of beautiful flowers. But it's the wards more than the paradise around me that make me freeze, and those flickers of darkness in the bright sunlight behind them. They're mostly gathered on the other side of the garden's extensive grounds, toward the Hall of the Wards, I assume, identifiable by their red chlamyses with the black shields, talking in groups or strolling about. It's the first time I could draw near them without fear of discovery, because I *have* been discovered. I'm one of them now: a ward, with a guardian. That doesn't make me feel any better, and the urge to duck and hide is still strong.

My father must sense my tension. "We'll stay over here, on the palace side. Most of them can't enter without invitation. My office is just this way."

I wait until we reach a wooden door carved with looping scrollwork, over which my father sketches a quick sigil to open it, before I ask, "Why did you ever come to this city from Skyllea if you knew it was like this?"

"Another good question," he says, and holds the door open for me.

His office is huge, overflowing with scrolls and books and loose stacks of paper on every surface, even the floor. There's *so* much paper, which has always been too expensive for me to purchase. I don't know how to write other than the few sigils I've memorized and traced in my mind or in the dirt of our courtyard. I'm only slightly better off with reading, but most of what I know is what my father taught me when I was seven. My mother is fully illiterate and couldn't help grow my meager knowledge.

"For a long while, my people didn't know it was like this here," my father says after resealing the door, oblivious to the wealth around him. He moves a pile of books off a chair for me, and then shoves some papers aside to lean heavily against a near-buried desk. "Skyllea refused to follow Athanatos all those centuries ago in the founding of the polis, so we remained isolated on our island."

He points to a map on the wall, outlining a mostly bare continent, aside from Thanopolis on its plateau near the coast, with a large, oblong island to the west. He, or someone, has shaded in the frozen peaks and desert plains with smears of dark charcoal, which cover most everything other than the city's plateau and the island of Skyllea. The blight. Within that shadow, scattered Xs mark what must be old city ruins.

"We were only aware of the blight's coming, not its beginning—a gradual change stealing over the mainland, like winter and drought, except spring rains never came. And yet it's worse than endless winter and drought. It's a poison that seeps into the heart of everything that touches it, slowly at first, so that you might escape if you leave quickly. But if you linger, even to cross the mainland between Skyllea's coast and Thanopolis without a magical shield that few know how to master, then you'll be forever touched by it, and eventually die. All the more reason for us to stay isolated on our island, even though we heard disturbing rumors escaping this city about mandatory imposition and registration of bloodlines and strange rituals binding them to the dead. For years we ignored it, following our own path . . . until the blight reached the shores of Skyllea and began to affect our own lands. We are holding it off now with a shield of our own, but the entire island is still at risk. Mayhap the entire world."

I glance at the map nervously. Lightly sketched shapes hint at other landmasses beyond our continent's borders and oceans. "It's continuing to spread?"

"Yes, it's even starting to cover the sea with ice in the north, and the oceans are toxic in the south. There is an immense magical imbalance in the world, Rovan, but no one here cares because we—*they're* safe behind the veil," he corrects with a grimace. "My people actually suspect the source of the imbalance is *here*, in this city. We weren't sure how or why, which is why a delegation from Skyllea came to Thanopolis a couple of years before you were born. Aside from the usual diplomats, there were two bloodlines, some of the strongest on our island: myself, and a woman named Cylla. We volunteered because we were young and foolhardy and ambitious. We weren't utterly incautious, though. Only Cylla presented herself at the palace with a small armed escort, while I laid low. She was acting as emissary of our people, but also hoped to uncover the truth of what was happening here. She went without me, because we thought they would see her as less of a threat and reveal more to her, even though she was as strong as I. We never thought they would—*could*—do to her what they did, or else we would have never let her go alone." He pauses, staring off as if into the past. "We would all have run."

"What did they do to her?"

His hand clenches atop his cane. "She was bound to a guardian and married to the crown prince within the month. Pregnant within two, with the twins. The royal family wanted the strength of her bloodline for their own, and they certainly never wanted her returning to Skyllea with whatever she learned. Our delegation was quietly slain, and I was trapped in the city alone, hunted. Cylla didn't betray me. But the veil"—he shoots a glance upward, as if he can see it through the cloud-carved wooden ceiling—"detects the presence of magic in whoever passes through it. I warned you and your mother about it ages ago. So the wards knew another powerful bloodmage had entered the city with Cylla."

I thought he'd warned me away from it because the blight was dangerous without a bloodmage's shield. Not because it would betray me. I was foolish to think I could ever simply cross through the veil with a Skyllean merchant caravan.

"That's why you were hiding with my mother," I say.

68

"Not at first. At the start, I was by myself in a city still foreign to me. I managed to sneak word of what had happened through the veil with a Skyllean merchant, warning them not to send any bloodmages after us. But I couldn't leave and just abandon Cylla." He smiles wistfully. "Then I met your mother. I didn't plan for you, Rovan. You became the source of both my greatest joy and then my greatest fear, once I realized how powerful you were."

"You were afraid they would find me." I choke on a laugh that's half sob.

"It was why I never tried to return to you, after they found me. I *couldn't*. I was soon warded myself, by Ivrilos, and forced to marry Penelope, the crown prince's youngest and most stubborn sister. They wanted my power for their future generations just as they did Cylla's. And since your mother and I were never married, not officially, I was in that sense a 'free' man." He spits the words with bitter irony.

"How did they force you? Did the dead man somehow . . . He can't *actually* control our bodies, right?"

My father shakes his head. "Other than the usual threats of pain, Crown Prince Tyros promised to make Cylla's life easier and to never touch her again, since he had his three children already—the twins and his and Cylla's younger daughter." He sighs. "So I married Penelope, even if I didn't want to. But she was just as unwilling in the marriage as I, and nothing ever came of our match. No child."

I can't halt the words on my lips. "But you raised Crisea like a daughter."

"Do you begrudge the girl any kindness I might have shown her?" He scrubs a hand over his face before I can answer. "Believe me, I feel guilty about it. Every single day. Every time I embraced her and remembered she wasn't you. Every bite of food I took from a silver fork that I knew you and your mother would never be able to eat. Every night I lay in a soft bed next to a woman who wasn't your mother—when the princess deigned to sleep there and not with her lover. Guilt has been my closest companion."

I flinch at the self-hatred in his voice. "Did you never try to run?" I whisper. "I don't mean back to us. But to Skyllea."

I can't tell him, not yet, that journeying there has been my greatest dream. It's too precious, too fragile.

"Oh, I tried. Several times. But I never quite mastered the trick of shielding against the blight. We have mages in Skyllea who specialize in that, but of course I could never ask the help of one of Thanopolis's mages. Perhaps it was good that Ivrilos was too great a deterrent for me to escape." His lips twist. "Though I'm not supposed to talk about that, so as not to sour your relationship."

"It is most thoroughly and completely sour already," I snap, standing abruptly from my chair to pace. And yet there's not much room to move, with all the clutter. Nowhere to escape. I turn back to my father. "And Cylla?"

"Several months ago, she passed her bloodline on to her eldest daughter, Princess Lydea, twin of Prince Kineas, who will very soon be declared the crown prince once his father, Tyros, becomes king."

"Then is Cylla . . . ?" I begin hesitantly, and then trail off at the look on my father's face.

"Dead, yes, before she could ever become queen consort instead of princess consort . . . all titles she never wanted in the first place. The process of passing on a bloodline kills the bearer," he adds, as if it's an afterthought and not the worst of it. "It takes a life to transfer it."

I have to put a steadying hand on the chair back, because my eyes flood with tears. "So I'm here," I choke. "I got caught, like a great imbecile, and they now possess a child of yours, which you never meant for them to have." I look up at him. "What happens to you?"

He approaches me slowly, and I feel his hand cup my face. His thumb brushes a tear off my cheek. This time, I don't pull away. I lean into him.

"Rovan . . ."

I squeeze out the words. "How soon?"

"Likely not until you are twenty. My time is running out in any case."

"Why?" I throw up my arms, forcing him to withdraw. I want his comfort, want to fall into his arms and cry, but more than that I want to be moving. *Doing* something. "Is it really so heavy to bear, the bloodline? Can't you hold on a while yet? We can figure something out, plan our escape!"

"The bloodline shouldn't be doing this to me, or to anyone—" My father cuts off, hissing and slapping a palm to his forehead, fingers clenching his blue hair. "*Stop it.*"

"What is it? Is *he* hurting you?" The dead man must be. He seems to be able to sap my father's strength in an instant or cause him pain. I don't see how it happens this time, but I still spin in a circle, fists raised as if I can fight off the dead man. "Where are you, you dusty coward?"

My father holds up his other hand to forestall me. "Maybe I'll only speak of what I can—the bloodline—and see how far that gets me. It shouldn't be a secret that my own parents didn't give this to me, but my grandfather, because in Skyllea bearers of the bloodline don't wish to end their own lives before their time."

My father's lips press together, either in pain or because he's worried he's said too much. But I consider his words . . . and their significance. It's enough for me to understand: Bloodmages live full lives in Skyllea until they're ready to pass their bloodlines on. Meaning that something *else* is prematurely aging my father. Or perhaps something has changed the nature of bloodlines within Thanopolis, to make them sap their bearers of vitality.

"The veil," I say suddenly. "Is it somehow drawing from the bloodlines—from you?" I gasp. "Or is it . . . *them*? The dead?"

He grimaces again. "Rovan, I can't. He really doesn't want me to say."

I grit my teeth, biting back more curses. "Okay, then don't. I'll figure it out myself, without the dead bastard's permission."

My father sighs wearily, seeming older by the minute. "There is a lot I haven't told you, and much of it I pieced together on my own, like you will have to." He glances meaningfully at the papers strewn about, and then at the wall near the map, where another scrap of parchment hangs. This one shows a red sigil that nearly looks as if it's written in blood. "You might just have to follow in my footsteps. Follow your eye." He holds my gaze, the look heavier than the gold of his irises.

He's obviously trying to tell me something, something he doesn't want the shade to know, but I'm not sure what. I have no idea what the sigil means.

"I don't know how to read very well," I say hesitantly. "And I know only the few sigils you taught me as a child. *Move*, *sever*, *seek*, that sort of thing."

My father blinks in surprise. "And they caught you based on that? I taught you those only as a means of channeling your urges toward magic, and to help your mother. What did you do to draw their attention?"

I'm indignant. "Just because I know only a few sigils doesn't mean I can do nothing with them. I learned to get creative."

He squints at me, as if trying to see me better. "Show me."

I should feel indignant at *that*, but I don't. I want to show him. To impress him. I glance around the room, my eyes bouncing from surface to surface, book to book, as if establishing the warp and weft, marking the invisible sigils as I go, weaving the pattern with

72

my mind. When I'm done, I nod. I don't even raise a hand to make the motions. Maybe I'm showing off, just a little.

Scrolls, books, and papers fly across the room, clearing the floor and chairs and realigning in neat stacks on shelves and desktops. The office transforms from complete chaos to tidily overfilled.

My father starts in shock, nearly falling over, and then gapes. "How did you do that?" he asks. "You didn't even sketch a sigil in the air."

"I did. Just with my mind and not my hands. Nothing you could see."

"Which sigils?"

"Just one," I say, feeling suddenly bashful. "*Move*. Only I used a lot of them, layered just so. It's the only one I can do that with."

He shakes his head in wonder. "Despite the seeming simplicity of what you did . . . the control alone . . . and your ability to hold it all in your mind . . . Rovan, many far more experienced bloodmages with an entire bloodline at their disposal couldn't do what you just did, not without sketching in the air at the very least, and likely with their own blood as ink, to map it all out."

"I did sketch the sigils out at first, in charcoal on a rock, or in the dirt. And when I could manage, I sketched them in the air. I didn't know I could use blood, so I had to know them perfectly. I used *move* the most. Eventually, after years of practice, I could form a whole picture in my mind of whatever I wanted to weave, however complicated. Except it was more than a picture by then, it had . . ."

"Depth. Like a sculpture," my father says knowingly. "You're an *artist*, Rovan, except your tool isn't a chisel or a brush or even a loom. It's sigils."

"Just *one* sigil, mostly."

"You'll learn more. And with them, you can make almost anything, you realize, not just a weaving."

I remember the ball of water I summoned for Bethea and feel a flush of pride, but then focus on the ground as sinking shame takes its place. "I still got caught. And I couldn't do anything to save myself, or my mother, or you. And now I don't know how I'm supposed to follow in your footsteps."

"I'll help you. I promise. I'll teach you. For the moment"—he sags back against the desk—"I think I need to rest before tonight's banquet. And you have an appointment with the tailor."

"I don't want to see a tailor or go to any pompous banquet," I hiss. "These people are vultures!"

"Do it, Rovan, for your mother's sake. For me. Please." He holds my eyes again, but this time I can tell he's so, so tired.

"Ugh," I say, and he smiles slightly, knowing I've relented.

But then his smile drops. "Rovan, I'm begging you . . . keep your head down. Try not to ask too many questions, at least for tonight. Be on your guard. Don't think to find sympathy or succor." His mouth thins to a grim line. "Not from any of these *vultures*."

7

I hate my gown, I hate the grand banquet hall, and I hate the people around me. Most especially I hate my guardian, standing all too visibly behind my father and me as the guests mill and mingle before serving starts.

Even *he*, the dead man, has dressed for the occasion. A bright silver circlet binds his dark hair, and he wears a long black robe, embroidered in ghostly silver thread around the collar and sleeves, though his black sword belt still cinches his trim waist. This time, two half-moon blades, gleaming wicked and sharp, hang on either hip. He looks like a king who has stepped out of legend. Or rather, the underworld.

Despite hating the sight of him, I'm jealous of his strange blades. I would feel more confident with a weapon facing all these people. My gown isn't nearly protection enough. While the sapphire-blue creation has *plenty* of material, contrary to what Crisea implied, it's terribly thin, draping in gossamer folds from gold feather pins at the tops of my bare arms to the floor, and belted tightly across my breasts and down around my waist and hips with a twining strophion in cloth of gold. My dark, blue-tinted waves of hair have been piled atop my head with a heap of red poppies and coiled with thin gold chain, which matches the spiraling gold cuffs around my upper arms and wrists. Other than the chains and cuffs, I feel naked . . . which is perhaps fitting.

I'm unarmed, unarmored, and in the den of my enemy. A feeling of helplessness threatens to consume me, but I need to stay alert, look for any way to help my mother and escape. Still, my predicament makes me want to do something, anything, even throw a table across the room, merely for something to do.

The dead man is a shadowy warning at my shoulder.

My father and I trail behind Penelope and Crisea, who seem far more at home than we do in this strange place. The palace's grand banquet hall is as opulent as one would expect. There are golden chandeliers shaped like antlers so entwined with blooming flowers that they look like hanging baskets bigger than carriages, dangling from a sky-high ceiling painted in blue and gilt-lined clouds.

"My wedding feast was held here," my father murmurs. "I haven't been back since, and I can't say as I've missed it."

Penelope either doesn't hear him or pretends not to have as she threads her way through the crowded tables. The bejeweled guests part around her and Crisea, leaving plenty of room for us in her wake.

I feel as if I'm stepping into a gilded trap that will close around me at any moment. I should be screaming, at the very least. Instead, I'm supposed to smile and greet people.

Penelope steadily makes her way toward a table near the central dais where a tall, dark-skinned man stands. He's older than my father, perhaps in his later forties, though he looks younger. His black braids are streaked with silver, but his arms are powerful, his back straight. He's handsome in a hard-cut way. I don't need the sword at his hip or the ceremonial bronze breastplate and gold-tipped pteryges over his red chiton to tell me he's a warrior, and a high-ranking one at that.

"Princess," he says to Penelope with a bow of his head. His eyes are warmer than the formality sounds on his lips. He gives Crisea a crease-eyed smile.

"You know I prefer my military title," Penelope says. She's come in armor herself, though Crisea wears a lavender peplos, which I have to admit looks great on her. "Rovan, this is my late sister Princess Maia's husband and the leader of Thanopolis's armies,

General Tumarq. Tumarq, allow me to introduce my stepdaughter, Rovan Ballacra, only recently reunited with her father. It was a joyous occasion." Her tone communicates anything but joy.

Nonetheless, the general gives me a respectful nod. "Greetings, Rovan."

I don't know what else to do, so I nod ever so slightly back, swallowing my emotions with questionable success. The man is being polite enough, and at least he isn't a ward. Still, he's another obstacle in the path of my escape. Although . . . I wonder if he knows where my mother is being held, and if I can somehow ferret the information out of him.

If the general has noticed my tepid response, he's unperturbed. "You have a name that sounds unfamiliar in these halls, like my own. My ancestors originally heralded from a kingdom north of Thanopolis, but my parents, their last rulers, were driven here by the blight. Even if the wards and their guardians try to make us soldiers obsolete, it is now my greatest honor in life to protect this city's walls." He lifts a strong, calloused hand. "But I remember what it was like to feel the stranger, as I'm sure your father once did and you do now."

"My mother, too, no doubt," I say before I can think better of it. "She's supposedly a guest behind these walls, as well."

My father clears his throat. He sounds slightly strangled.

Tumarq remains impassive. "Indeed, the palace is unparalleled, and it can be disorienting. But you might find something in common with my offspring, Japha, as a ward."

Word of me has already spread, then, if he knows I'm a newly warded bloodmage. I reluctantly turn my attention to the person lounging in a chair next to the general—the only one yet seated, as far as I can tell.

"I do not call them either my son or my daughter, since they insist they are neither." The general smiles.

Japha languidly stands to take my hand in greeting. They're in their late twenties, with slightly lighter skin than General Tumarq. A bloodline patterns their warm brown arms. They're taller than me, flat chested and slim limbed under a deep purple, green, and silver chiton that falls to the floor, artfully woven with peacocks. Their short-cropped hair is near black, and kohl lines their dark eyes. A perfect wreath of angular twigs and iridescent green feathers crowns their head, like a bird's nest but less messy. Somehow, they pull it off exquisitely.

"Then they *are* neither," I say.

Japha gives me a surprised—and appraising—look.

It's not a strange concept to me, but I'm impressed the royal family allows Japha to be who they are when there's such an emphasis on gender roles here in the palace. In the wider polis, no one would complain much. Just as men sleep with men and women with women without creating an uproar, so long as they're not shirking any childbearing duties, there are men and women who were not called such at birth—as well as those who are called neither. I once knew a street actor so skilled at playing either man or woman that I wasn't the least bit shocked to find that offstage they were in fact sometimes a man, sometimes a woman, and often neither, like Japha.

"I don't fault Japha for that, either," Penelope says, surprising me. "Goddess knows I would be a man if I could."

"So declare yourself a man," Japha says without hesitation, in a smooth, cultured voice that doesn't sound particularly masculine or feminine.

The princess blinks. "My father would never accept that."

Tumarq smiles fondly at her. "I would . . . *Lieutenant*."

She rolls her eyes but can't help sparing him a smile in return. "I know, just as you accept Japha. But my father expects us *all* to do our duty." She gives Japha a look as she says this.

"Ah, yes, my grandfather likes people in their *very* particular places," Japha leans toward me to say confidentially, though everyone can hear. "Until it suits him otherwise."

I'm only partially paying attention because, with everyone grouped together, I can suddenly see the similarities: Crisea looks a lot like General Tumarq and Japha. Crisea must be Tumarq's daughter, Japha her half sibling. Penelope's lover is the man who was married to her sister, Maia. That sister is now dead, having passed on her bloodline to her child Japha, but Crisea was born while Maia was still alive. That strikes me as awkward, never mind that Penelope is still married to my father, if only in words. But neither he nor Penelope nor the general seem bothered.

Japha smiles at me, their eyes sharp, as if they know what I've realized. How *they* feel about what lies between their aunt and father I can't begin to guess . . . and I don't really care. All I want to do is get out of here.

"That makes you something like my cousin," Japha continues. "We have other *dear* cousins in attendance. Tonight's feast is in their father's honor nearly as much as our grandfather Neleus's. Crown Prince Tyros is to be king, after all." They mean Tyros's children, then—and Cylla's. The children that are the result of their mother's capture and abuse. Japha sweeps forward and loops their arm through mine before I can protest. "I have been tasked with introducing you, so we can leave those who think and speak as unsubtly as clashing swords to have their own little chat. Are you coming, Silvean?"

My father looks tired and reluctant, but he says, "Of course. That's the point of dragging Rovan here. I'll be right behind you."

And beside *him*, I see the dead man.

"No one needs to drag me anywhere," I say. "Let's get this over with. Who knows, I might even enjoy it." I glare for a moment at the silver embroidery on the shade's right shoulder, refusing to meet his steady gaze, before facing forward.

Japha's clever eyes don't miss it. "Still not used to him yet? I'm not, either." They toss their twig-and-feather-wreathed head. "Mine is right next to me. Even less of an entertaining conversationalist than my father or aunt, that one."

I peer over their shoulder, unable to see much of anything in the soft light of the banquet hall. But then I blink at Japha. "Wait. How could you not be used to your guardian? Didn't you get your guardian long before your bloodline, when your gift was first . . . you know . . . discovered?" I'm still not used to openly talking about such things.

"My dear, I got my bloodline only three years ago at twenty-four and my guardian at the same time, because I wasn't meant to have either. My sister, Selene, was."

I nearly stumble over the long folds of my peplos. "How were you not meant . . . ?"

"I was supposed to be a warrior," Japha says, with a conspiratorial wink. "So they assumed I was until I proved otherwise."

I still must look confused, because my father asks me, "Do you know the mandate of threes, as it applies to the noble families of this city?"

I shake my head. I only know three is an important number because of the tripartite goddess.

"If you're born noble or royal in this city, then you don't have the burden of manual labor. Therefore you must do *something* with yourself, because goddess forbid you indulge in idleness and excess." My father scoffs at the absurd crowd around us, drinking and lounging before the no-doubt extravagant meal about to take place. "And if your parent has a bloodline, then there are only three proper paths for you: a bloodmage, a warrior, or a priest or priestess in the necropolis." My father says the latter with marked distaste. "It's a practice that echoes the maiden with her blood sacrifice, the mother who will defend the flesh of her flesh at all cost, and the crone who has grown acquainted with death. Those are the three faces of the goddess, symbolizing the three parts of us: blood, body, and spirit. That's why three is the number of noble children said to be most pleasing to the goddess, to serve all forms of her with either sigils, sword, or death magic."

"I'm impressed, Silvean!" Japha crows. "You know the doctrine better than I do, and I was born here."

My father measures his breath with the tap of his cane as he continues. "In the royal family, the eldest boy—the heir—most often trains in combat, the eldest girl is often the future bloodline, and the third child, of whatever gender, is for the shadow. Unlike where I come from or within the lower classes here, where the chance to possess the gift is equally distributed, royal women usually inherit the bloodline. Someone in this family, somewhere along the line, decided they made better bloodmages."

Japha snorts.

"Yes, well, Japha and I prove the lie there," my father adds.

"For that reason, many of us nobles stop at two children," Japha says, waggling a pair of bejeweled fingers, "when a bloodmage has probably been born, if indeed the parents are capable of turning one out. If they aren't, they'll still have one child to train as a soldier for the polis. Even if the second child only amounts to spouting poetry or whatever frivolity, their parents will still rejoice they don't have another child. Because who wants their offspring to live among the dead?"

Japha's mother must have stopped at two—even if their father continued with Crisea.

My father says, disapproval still plain, "The problem is—which isn't a problem to anyone *here*—the necropolis is then forced to recruit from the lower classes."

Bethea, I think, with a stab of pain. I haven't known Bethea for long, but I still hope that the threat to send her to the necropolis

81

was an empty attempt to scare us both into confessing, and that the wards simply let her go after they found what they wanted in me.

"The royal family sometimes flouts tradition even further," Japha says. "Case in point: my lovely aunt Penelope. My mother, Princess Maia, received *her* mother Rhea's bloodline at twenty, and so Penelope was supposed to have served in the necropolis as the third runt of the king. But as a child she was allowed to train in combat alongside her brother, Crown Prince Tyros. Then Penelope became pregnant at eighteen to avoid her fate. Rather than strip her child, Crisea, of her mother, King Neleus allowed Penelope to continue her martial studies. She's now a high-ranking military officer. The mother is the warrior indeed, in her case."

"Which was why the princess was as yet unwed when I was brought to the palace," my father mutters.

"Good for her," I snap, and then turn back to Japha. "So what happened with you and your sister?" They've been cleverly steering us away from the original topic of conversation.

"That is a story for another day," Japha says, and then they announce theatrically, "For we have arrived!"

I look up and nearly gasp.

The three who stand before us are beautiful. Beyond beautiful. The crowd gives them a wide berth out of respect—or perhaps fear—where they stand before the dais. They all wear white shrouds in differing materials, and crowns of black roses with tiny skulls set in the center of each.

The twins are obvious, but only because of their age and the shape of their faces. Otherwise they're like night and day. The young man has hair like glinting pewter, his skin tanned and lightly freckled from the sun, and silver-gray eyes as sharp as gleaming knives. His broad shoulders and muscular build, as well as the gold-sheathed sword at his hip, tell me exactly who received the warrior's training . . . and who's to be the next crown prince. His twin, and the one who received Cylla's blood-line, is equally stunning, but she has hair like a raven's wing, skin as luminous and pale as the moon, and countless blood-red symbols tracing the lines of a lithe body barely concealed under white gossamer even thinner than mine. The third child of Cylla's, a girl a little younger than me, has a mass of curly hair as white as snow, complete with a light blue sheen as if reflecting the sky, pure silver eyes that nearly glow, and a smile as sweet as a songbird's trill. Somehow, I know she's the spitting image of her mother. Her looks are simply too Skyllean.

As striking as she is, it's the elder, dark-haired sister who is undeniably the most beautiful woman I've ever seen. I distantly hope I'm not staring.

"My dear cousins," Japha continues, "may I present Rovan Bal-lacra, the newest addition to our most esteemed family. Rovan, this is Kineas, Lydea, and Delphia."

Lydea. The name sinks into me like claws.

"*Prince* Kineas," Kineas corrects, squaring his muscular shoul-ders in a subtly aggressive stance. His cold steely eyes carve me as if I'm a slab of meat at the butcher's. Not in a lecherous way, more methodical and categorizing. Breasts—*slice*—stomach—*slice*—thighs . . . I try not to squirm. "So you're the one we've all been waiting for," he says in an exaggerated drawl, as if I'm not living up to anyone's expectations, let alone his.

I suddenly wonder if Japha is being supportive, introducing me like this, or feeding me to the lions for sport.

Lydea's dark gaze hasn't left me, either, but the look in her eyes is very different from her twin's. One corner of her red-tinted lips curves upward. "Oh, Kinny, I think she's rather magnificent."

So, I think, *Kineas is the sword, attacking from the front, while Lydea is the dagger from behind.*

Delphia smiles at me timidly. She looks as fragile as ice crystals under her cloud of white hair, as if one harsh word will scatter her. "It's a pleasure to meet you, Rovan."

And she, the runt of this litter, must be hopelessly kind—a trait born of desperation. If she pleases the others, maybe they won't eat her alive.

I'm *not* going to try the same tactic. If I'm in the lions' den, I might as well bare steel.

"I see only one of you got your mother's hair and eyes." I give Delphia a genuine smile, then I turn that smile on Lydea, twisting it like a blade. "You must take after your father. In temperament, as well as looks, I wonder?" I eye Kineas speculatively, tapping my lip with a finger. He can't help but stare at my mouth, which has been painted especially full. I don't mind his attention if *I'm* the one directing it. Besides, he's not going to be appreciative for long. "And you . . . you're somewhere in between, like me. A little muddied."

Kineas sputters. "I am *nothing* like—"

"Indeed, your gray hair makes you look a lot older."

"I beg your—"

Lydea's bark of laughter cuts him off. "I *really* like you," she says, looking at me as if sizing up a competitor. And yet something in her gaze once again makes me flush.

"Isn't she wonderful?" Japha nearly sings. "I can't *wait* for us to become better acquainted."

"Indeed," says a disembodied voice to my left. I jump, turning, and there's the dead man. I meet his eyes unintentionally, but then I can't look away. It's like staring down the bottom of a well, the black depths of his gaze. "Crown Prince Tyros is coming. Silvean is already aware of this fact, but the man can be . . . unpleasant. Please don't do anything rash."

The dead man retreats. Japha has noticed me twitch and watches me carefully as another man steps into view, taking the shade's place.

Everyone bows, even my father, and I belatedly follow their lead. When I lift my head, I'm facing the crown prince. Tyros is a man in his fifties, perhaps, his hair gray and black in equal measure. His stony face is lined, but less with age and more like his unyielding expression has simply . . . settled. Whereas Kineas's eyes are like sharpened daggers, his father's are the blunt iron of chisels.

"So you're the girl," Tyros states more than asks. "At least you're something to look at."

My lips part in shock, and my mouth nearly falls all the way open when Lydea says, "Now, Father, surely she's more than *something*, but let's not be crude."

His lips twist the slightest bit. "It's not for you to say. Come, Kineas, what do you think?"

"I haven't thought much of anything about her," Kineas says, not even looking my way.

"And why would he?" my father says at my side, his voice deadly quiet.

Crown Prince Tyros turns on him with patient relish, like the blight's ice freezing the oceans. "Only that Kineas is a good judge of flesh—horseflesh, at least. He always knows where to match a good broodmare. We must decide what to do with the girl."

Kineas smirks, Lydea gazes coolly at her father, and Delphia faces the floor as if trying to melt into it. I wonder if she learned that tactic from her mother. Japha, on the other hand, has a gleam in their eyes that I would almost call dangerous . . . but it's nothing compared to the sound of my father's voice:

"You will decide no such thing."

"Oh?" Tyros says, utterly unconcerned.

"No."

"That's unfortunate. You see, I might already have plans for her."

The words make me boil, both nauseating and infuriating. The

85

dead man warned me against *doing* anything rash, but not necessarily against speaking.

"Those might conflict with *my* plans," I say cheerfully, "which involve you choking at your earliest convenience."

"Rovan!" my father croaks.

Lydea sounds as if *she's* choking for a moment. Delphia actually gasps, while Kineas gapes like a fish, making him look far less attractive than he is, which I take a moment to appreciate. The crown prince, with his cracked-marble face, simply stares at me. I stare right back.

My father places a protective hand on my arm. "Your Highness, she didn't mean it."

Tyros exhales a slow breath out his nose. "I see she is uncivilized, untrained. She will learn. I would strike her myself if it wouldn't soil my person on this blessed occasion. And ordering one of my men to strike her would create too much of a vulgar stir at a feast honoring my father's descent into twilight. Fortunately, it seems, he's too ill to be here tonight. So," he adds, almost lightly, "Ivrilos. Hurt her. Quietly."

My guardian appears at my side before I can blink. His eyes are sharp, heated.

"Ivrilos—" my father begins, pleading, but the dead man cuts him off.

"That was your idea of restraint?" he snaps at me. "I would tell you to remind the crown prince that I don't answer to him, but that would only challenge him to get more creative with your punishment. You leave me no choice."

Before I can wonder to *whom* the dead man answers, he bends far too quickly for me to dodge, dipping his mouth alongside my ear. His words, quieter than a whisper, keep me from jerking away. "This is where you gasp as if you're in pain." A heartbeat passes as I'm too stunned to react. "Do it!"

And then I feel it: a pinch on the back of my arm, hard enough to make me jump and elicit the gasp he wants, but not hard enough to really hurt.

The dead man can hurt his wards in ways I don't yet understand—some of which I witnessed with my father—and yet he just *pinched* me? I was expecting something much worse. Icy hands of death chilling me to the bone, gouging into my flesh, sucking the life out of me, or . . . *anything* else.

Before I can burst into hysterical giggles, my brain finally catches up. He's trying to help me. To *avoid* hurting me. I won't argue with that, even if I won't thank him for it. I add a low moan and a near swoon on the heels of my gasp, though I don't have to reach far for the swoon. I'm suddenly dizzy, and have no idea why. Maybe even from a touch so light as a pinch? My father steadies me.

He, himself, doesn't know I've mostly faked my reaction. He looks furious. But he doesn't say anything.

"You and Ivrilos both must teach her to behave," the crown prince says to him. "The sooner the better. After all, think of her future. Think of her mother."

The threat is barely veiled, as practiced as a fighter resting a hand on their sword. The base of my spine grows cold. Still, we can't just stand here and do nothing while this man does whatever he wishes with us. At the very least, we can talk back to him. I turn to my father, practically begging him with a look.

But he bows his head, eyes downcast. "Yes, Your Highness."

I can't believe it. *This* is the man who nearly died to protect me, now allowing me to be punished with barely a protest? Accepting a threat to my mother? Bowing his head to the family that had destroyed our lives, and the lives of so many he loved?

Tyros moves away without another word, turning his back on us. Something churns in the pit of my stomach. It's the knowledge that while my father once fought for me, he has *also* lived in this palace for nearly thirteen years. He's been taught to behave. To bow.

He's a man who no longer fights. Out of fear for me and my mother, yes. But his fear has made him weak.

My father turns away from me, too, as if he can see the judgment written in my face, a sigil spelling out my shame. He thumps his way down the dais steps, leaving me. Again. I can only stare after him and hope that tears aren't forming in my eyes. Kineas smirks at me.

I won't cry. Not in front of *them*.

The dead man is still standing nearby, watching me. "Rovan, I—"

Lydea walks right through him without knowing. "Now that that's over," she says briskly, "I need a drink. How about you?"

I do. Goddess, but I do. It's probably a terrible idea to go with her, but I don't care. If anything, I have to get away from Kineas before I smack the smug look off his face. I let the stunningly beautiful princess take my hand and drag me away from the dais. I throw one last glance back at where Japha and the dead man have been standing, but they've both already vanished, one into the crowd and the other into thin air.

It's just me and Lydea.

8

I don't know how many hours later, how many plates of food listlessly picked at, how many glasses of wine guzzled, or how many falsely polite guests mocked by either me or the princess—knowing looks exchanged between the two of us—that I find myself in a dim hallway outside the banquet hall, perhaps a servants' passageway, with Lydea still leading me by the hand. Everything blurs behind a pleasant, alcoholic haze. The princess's tinkling laugh, as musical and sharp as breaking glass, fills my ears, and her pale face burns like a lantern.

She might be drawing me away to murder me, for all I know. And still, I can't help but think, *Goddess, she's beautiful.*

I glance over at Lydea, see another one of her sparking looks, and decide *to hell with it.* Murder plan or not, I push her up against the wall. Wonderingly, she lets me with a short gasp. In the breathless moment that follows, the princess's dark gaze swallows mine. Her hand trails down my arm.

A caress, with pointed nails.

"You know," she murmurs, "they say that Kineas and I were a lot alike. We were inseparable as children."

"What changed?" I ask. I don't know for sure they're so different now, but somehow I can feel it. Even if she's still just as dangerous, she is *not* like her brother.

My response seems to ignite the sparks in her eyes. "I amend what I said—I really, *really* like you."

I can't help it. I kiss her. Something inside me mutters of caution, and so I only brush Lydea's mouth with the lightest of feather-light touches. Her lips are as soft as silk, and as red as blood.

I can't believe what I've done. Or *why* I've done it. Maybe because the crown prince won't like it. Maybe because it's akin to hurling a table across a room for something to do. Or maybe because the princess is jaw-droppingly gorgeous, and I'm always one to kiss as many beautiful girls as will let me.

And maybe because I'm incredibly drunk. I've done less intelligent things under these conditions.

Before I can wrench myself away, maybe even run, Lydea spins *me* around, presses *me* against the wall, and kisses *me* with far less hesitancy.

Her tongue is like intoxicating, overpowering wine in my mouth, but I freeze. The princess must sense it, because she pulls away a hand's breadth.

"If you don't want to give me this," she murmurs, "I'll not take it from you. I'm not my father. Not my brother." A hectic flush lights her cheeks as she meets my eyes. It seems important to her that I understand this. Or maybe she's scared to admit it, in this place. "Though you *did* give me some indication that such advances were wanted," she adds with a wry twist to her red lips, the color now slightly smudged.

Her breath is warm against my face, sending tingles from my scalp to the tops of my feet. I struggle to parse the situation, but my brain isn't working. There's only Lydea, filling my vision, delicious and decadent, like a forbidden dessert that I want so badly to devour.

"Don't . . . ," I begin, and her expression falls a fraction. "Don't *stop*."

Her wicked smile returns. As do her lips to mine. And just like before, it's not a tentative kiss. It's a kiss that curls my toes and sends my senses buzzing. I forget for a moment that I'm somewhere I don't want to be, with someone I shouldn't want to be with. My head threatens to float away from my shoulders.

"Is this flying?" I gasp, when my mouth is finally free enough to do so.

Lydea's delighted laugh makes me want to kiss her again. Before I can, the wall suddenly slides out from behind me. Rather, I suppose, I'm sliding down the wall.

My first thought is *Poison!* And then my next is *Oh right, I'm drunk.*

The princess catches me with surprising strength.

"Oh dear." She sighs into my hair. I think she might sniff it, like a bouquet of flowers—which I find terribly charming—before she asks, "Are you utterly wine wrecked, Rovan Ballacra?"

"You sound like my mother," I mutter into her shoulder, which smells quite nice. And then I remember my mother, imprisoned. My father, cowed like a whipped dog. The crown prince and Kineas, eyeing me like a piece of meat at market. I groan in a mixture of despair and disgust. Belatedly, I realize Lydea might think I'm disgusted with *her* when she doesn't ease me to the ground so much as let me drop the rest of the way. At least it's not far.

"Let me fetch some servants to take you to your apartments," Lydea says somewhere above me, and then her voice fades down the hall. "We can continue this conversation later, when you're in a more fit state."

Before I know it, I'm hoisted to my feet by impersonal hands.

The trek back to my father and Penelope's apartments, with my spiraling thoughts and dawning mortification, is sobering enough that I'm able to walk on my own by the time I arrive. I awkwardly dismiss the servants before I reach the outer doors, and fortunately the common rooms beyond are empty and barely lit. Penelope and Crisea left the banquet hall well before I did, and I haven't seen my father since he walked away from me. They're all likely asleep.

Perfect. Once I change out of my wretched dress, there will be no one to bother me if I go in search of another carafe of wine.

Except my guardian, of course. "I'd advise you to go to bed." His voice comes out of the darkness as soon as I'm alone in my oversized, overdecorated bedroom.

Already, he knows me too well.

Any thought of the strange protection he provided during my meeting with the royal family, of my wonder at it, evaporates in the heat of my sudden anger. He has a horrible hold on me, he's keeping me trapped here, and now he wants to give me *advice*? I spin toward his voice in the candlelit dimness, and he's there, standing in the shadows, black-robed arms folded, as if waiting for my tirade.

I'm more than happy to give it to him.

"*Don't* advise me. *Don't* talk. Just, just"—I shove a finger at his nose and carefully emphasize—"fuck you"—I stab again—"in the face."

He raises a dark eyebrow. "I don't think you could manage that."

I goggle at him. "That wasn't a proposition!" I wave a hand and almost lose my balance. "And how typical to think such a thing could only be done by a man. I feel sorry for your lady friends, if you have any."

"I don't mean it's impossible for you as a *woman*," he says, the slightest bit of exasperation entering his tone for the first time I can remember. "I mean it's impossible for you due to *my* state, which is immaterial, and yours, because you can't see straight." He narrows his eyes and mutters, "I can't believe we're discussing this."

Of course *this* is what makes him react. It never fails—the best way to goad a man is to insult his prowess in bed. Even a dead man, apparently.

"I can too see straight," I say, and then squint. My rose-shaped

92

desk appears to be actively blooming, even though I'm nearly positive it isn't. "Maybe not. But believe me when I say you're the last person whose face I would want to sit on, unless I was trying to suffocate you."

"Also impossible."

"I *meant*," I say as if he hasn't spoken, "fuck *yourself* in the face."

"Now that's most assuredly infeasible," he says with a too-flat expression.

"Because you can't bend like that or because you're dead?"

For all the world, it looks like the dead man is trying not to smile. Is he *laughing* at me? The thought enrages me further, as does his sigh. "You're very drunk, Rovan. Please just go to—"

"Don't call me Rovan!" I burst. "You don't get to call me that."

"What should I call you, then?" His tone is patient, which makes me want to take an ax to it.

"You can call me Mis"—I hiccup—"Mistress Rovana-la-la-laaa"—that part I extend into a cracking, wavering song—"the Most Excellent."

The dead man, circlet glinting on his dark crown of hair, drops his face into his hand, as if taking a break from our conversation.

I widen my eyes in a parody of remorse. "Am I embarrassing you? Making you mad?"

"There's a distinct chance of both." Maybe it's my imagination, but it still sounds like he's trying not to smile. I can't see his lips to be sure.

I suddenly *want* to see his lips, and the thought makes me flush for some reason. Maybe that's the wine.

I sweep an arm out as if rejecting him. "Then I need to try harder."

"In any event," he says into his hand, "as fittingly unique as that name is, I can't even repeat it—"

"Can't or won't?"

He carries on, head still bowed, "So I will persist in using your given name, Rovan, until you provide me with a better option."

I sneer at him. "That's all you get, my friend. No, not my friend. My *enemy*."

He drops his hand to stare directly at me. "I'm not your enemy."

I can't hold his dark gaze anymore, so I twirl away instead. "That's right, you're my *guardian*. So guard me. Hey, guardian, look, I'm falling. Save me!" I teeter toward the bed and let myself tip over backward. But my aim is poor. My shoulder cracks into the treelike corner post hard enough to shiver the leafy canopy, my hip bounces off the edge of the mattress, and I crash to the floor in a rush of sapphire silk. I rub my bottom, belatedly discovering my elbow hurts. "Ouch! Hey, where *were* you? You're supposed to catch me! You're a terrible guardian. I hate you." And then I'm crying.

Where have these idiotic tears come from? I suppose I'm still very drunk and very tired. And I'm a prisoner in the palace, bound to a dead spirit, and I've just embarrassed myself in front of a viper of a princess I had the foolish audacity to kiss. Besides, my elbow hurts *a lot*. Maybe a few tears are allowed.

I assume the dead man will only stare imperiously down at me, or maybe vanish, fleeing. But suddenly his eyes are level with mine, close—close enough to startle me. I choke on a sob, swallowing hard.

"You can hate me," he says quietly, "but I *can't* touch you for anything other than true peril, because the costs are too high."

I stare, tears forgotten. "The cost for you . . . or for me?" I remember that even his *pinch*, as soft and as brief as it was, left me dizzy. I remember that I still have questions about *how* he can affect me, all the ways he might be able to hurt me, but my mind is able to focus about as well as my eyes.

He ignores me. "I would've liked to have caught you. It's a shame to see you in this state."

I spit at him. It passes right through his cheek and spatters the floor beyond him. "Fuck your shame! I don't need it, and fuck you—"

"—in the face, yes. Rovan, get into bed."

I thump my head obstinately down—at least there's a rug underneath me—and close my eyes, sniffing wetly. "I'm tired. All the time. But especially at the moment. I think I'll just stay here."

"Suit yourself." He stands then, vanishing from the narrow view between my cracked eyelids. I think he's gone, but then I hear his voice from somewhere above me. "I can't lift you, but I suppose I can do this."

The soft, comforting weight of a blanket settles over me. I would like to have seen what his hand looks like when it's more material, but I can't feel much of anything because I'm suddenly asleep.

9

When I open my eyes, I think that a fitting name for hangovers would be *morning regrets*. Kissing Lydea was probably a terrible idea. And just what exactly *did* I say to the dead man? And did I really sleep on the floor out of sheer stubbornness? I definitely regret the vicious crick in my shoulder and neck, which only amplifies the ache in my skull.

I smack my lips and croak, "Dead man?"

"I have a name," comes his voice from the shadows.

When I turn my head, the shaft of sunlight from the window hits me like a spear in my brain. Another regret: not shutting the curtains. "I don't need it. But I do need some water. I don't suppose you can get me some?"

His voice is nearly as flat as before, but it's somehow lighter. Somehow *gloating*. "I don't suppose *you* remember what we discussed last night?"

"Unfortunately, I remember too much." I sit up, resisting the urge to vomit on the rug I used as my bed—that would be a poor way to repay it. "It's not too much to hope that you were somehow drunk as well and don't remember any of it?"

"Unfortunately," he echoes, "I'm incapable of getting drunk."

"Pity for you."

I'm suddenly staring at his studded leather greaves as he stands over me. He's back in his usual fighting attire.

"I would offer you a hand as well as water . . . but as I mentioned—"

"Not another word!" I shout, and then hunch over, assaulted by my own volume. "Ugh."

There's a soft knock at the door, followed by a voice—my father's. "Rovan? May I come in?"

I almost prefer the dead man's company, but he's already vanished. While my mother has seen me like this plenty of times, my father hasn't. But then, the state I saw him in yesterday is worse, in my opinion.

We may as well get to know each other as we are now.

"Yes," I moan, not bothering to drag myself off the floor.

My father slips into the bedroom. He leaves the door cracked, as if to allow a hasty retreat if need be. He won't meet my eyes. "You came home late last night."

"This isn't home, and last I checked I could go to bed whenever I wished."

"It's just that you don't want to draw attention to yourself. I've already gotten word from Penelope, who was only too happy to share that you were drinking heavily and in *close* proximity to Princess Lydea."

I fold my arms and turn away from him and the too-bright sunlight. "So *now* you want to act like my father. Too late, I'm afraid. And after the help you offered me last night, I'm definitely better off taking care of myself."

"That's unfair," he says quietly, and the hurt in his voice stabs at me. "You know they have your mother. They have *you*. I can't—"

"Can't step out of line, can't fight back, can't do anything, I know."

He's silent for a few heartbeats. "What would you have me do?"

"I don't know. *Something!*"

"*Something* isn't always wise, Rovan," he says. "You don't understand—"

"I understand that you're *not* the man who was taken from

97

Mother and me years ago." He stares at me in shock, but I hold his gaze as I add, "That man is dead. That little girl is dead, too, so it's best we just get used to it."

He flinches.

Finally, he says, "Maybe you're right. In any case, you won't like what I've come here to say, so I'll just be out with it. You are expected to attend lessons, social engagements, that sort of thing. You've already missed an appointment this morning."

My mouth drops open. "Goddess forbid I miss my *social engagements*. You know what, the crown prince can roll up the schedule he's made for me and eat it. I hope he chokes."

"Yes, you've made your preferences on that quite clear. But you should know that after last night the crown prince is no longer—"

"*Crown prince* this, *crown prince* that. Even if you're not one of them, you do like to go on about them. I plan to ignore the lot as much as possible, like normal." I haul myself upright, but instead of moving for the washroom or anything more useful, I fall back on the bed. "You know, sometimes doing nothing *can* be effective. I'm going back to sleep."

"Rovan," my father says a little desperately, "you can't just stay in here."

"What, are they going to torture me for skipping lessons? And if I can thwart even their smallest plan for me, or even make their day slightly less pleasant, then I will. It's the *least* I can do," I add, before dragging a pillow over my face to block out the light. "Close the curtains on the way out."

A few moments later, I hear the swish of heavy fabric and the soft thud of the door. I don't bother to check that he's left.

I can swear my father hasn't been gone longer than a few minutes before I hear the door open again and another voice in the room, startling me.

"Are you awake?" The source of the voice moves to part the curtains with a flourish.

"Japha?" I groan, sitting up so fast my head swims. I throw up a hand to shade my eyes.

Japha stands in a shaft of sunlight, wearing a lovely floor-length peplos of bright orange woven with red and white poppies, the same orange painting the lids of their eyes along with a dark line of kohl. They've belted the garment with a leather pteryges, like a male warrior would wear over a shorter chiton.

"Hello, my dear." There's a pause, and then Japha fans a hand in front of their face. "One thing's for sure, you need a bath. It reeks of booze in here. Are you ready to wash and get on with your day yet?"

"No," I say, dropping back onto the bed.

"Fine, I will entertain you in the meantime." Japha sits in the chair near the rose desk. "Let's see, what news do I have . . . Well, the old king, Neleus, is dead. My uncle, former crown prince Tyros, is the new king, so long live the king and all of that."

"Hurrah," I rasp, staring at the leafy canopy as my hands clench at my sides. That's probably what my father was trying to tell me. In the wake of everything else, the death of one king doesn't mean much to me, only that a man I hate is now even more powerful.

"My thoughts exactly. The old codger chose to fall on his sword instead of drink hemlock or let sickness take him. Hard as nails until the end—though only Uncle Tyros witnessed *that* in the necropolis, so maybe he's putting a valiant spin on it. Can't say as I'm sorry to see the old man go, other than it means my cousin Kineas is the new crown prince. The evil squid."

I snort with enough force to jerk my shoulders against the bed. "Squid?" Although the sea ice is freezing along the coast from the blight, there's still one channel out from the port and under the veil to the deeper ocean for traders and fishing boats. I've seen plenty of squid in the market: sad, pale, limp little creatures when out of their element. Imagining a squid with Kineas's face makes me laugh despite myself.

Japha says, "He's a slippery one, quick to strike with those tentacles of his, whether it's to stab someone with a sword or snare some poor unsuspecting girl. *Slimy* might be the better word." They give an audible shudder. "I've heard more than rumors. Accusations of violent treatment in his bed and even word of some commoner girls gone missing, all of which are quickly silenced with heavy purses and likely heavier threats."

I sit up, squinting at them, or maybe wincing from the pain. "Do you really dislike your cousin, or is this all some sick game to win my trust?"

Japha meets my gaze. "I *would* like to win your trust . . . but with the truth, if I can. And what you need to understand now is that everyone here is playing some sort of game, sick or otherwise, and you want to be on the winning end as much as possible. I think we would make fine teammates."

I scowl as my hands twist in the blankets alongside me. "This is my life, and it was just *ruined*, my mother has been taken captive, and . . . my father . . ."

I don't know what to say about my father, really. I should be thrilled he's alive, but it's all so much more complicated than that. I still want my father, but the father who was taken from me nearly thirteen years ago.

"What do you think happened to me three years ago?" Japha rejoins. "My mother wasn't spared, either. She was a princess, and yet she died all the same to give me this *thing*." They lift their red-patterned arm. "I also lost my little sister in that particular game—Selene. She was supposed to inherit the bloodline at twenty."

Here's the story I wanted to hear last evening. Now I'm not so eager, but I make myself ask, "What happened?"

"She killed herself," Japha says bluntly, "to avoid the bloodline, or because she felt she wasn't a good enough bloodmage, or maybe she was just sad—we'll never know. With no one else to inherit my mother's bloodline, they turned to me. They'd ignored the potential in my blood because I trained as a warrior. I failed magnificently at that, so after my sister died, they tested me again and found I was actually a much stronger bloodmage than she had been. Suddenly I made sense, because they found a purpose for me, some way for me to fit into their plan . . . twisting who I am against me." Japha scoffs.

I open my mouth, and then close it. "I'm sorry." The words seem inadequate.

Japha plucks at their armored, flowery gown. "No matter. I'm still here, still me, despite what my skin looks like. *Red*." They tsk, glancing at their arm in disdain. "It clashes with so much of what I wear."

I wish I could just make the best of my situation, but I can't just sit back and *hope*. "The crown prince—"

"You mean the king?"

"Him, yes. Tyros. He said he had plans for me, and mentioned something like *broodmare* in the same breath, the shit-eater."

Japha chortles. "I don't believe I've ever heard a king referred to in quite such terms." They hesitate. "I'll help you, however I can."

I hold their orange-and-kohl-lined eyes. "Why?"

Japha shrugs. "Because you need help. Your father, frankly, doesn't have the strength to do it."

I suppress a wince, even though I know it's true. "Why *you*, though?"

"You're a wildflower in a garden of rose-covered thorns. And maybe because I get daily reminders, even now, that I don't belong, either."

"That doesn't mean I can trust you. You might just be out for yourself. And *you* led me into that lions' den."

Japha cocks their head. "At the banquet, you mean? Delphia is harmless. Lydea less so, but she actually likes you."

I can't help my flush, and I wonder if Japha knows about the kissing.

They don't seem to notice, continuing, "Kineas . . . just forget about Kineas for now. Forever, if you can." They stand from the chair in a rustle of orange linen and leather skirting and busy themself straightening their attire in the rose desk's mirror. "I hate him, but he's now our crown prince, and there are some things we must suffer with grace. Or at least with excellent clothes and makeup and underhanded insults." They spin back around, hands on their hips. "So get out of bed and help me suffer in the best way possible, and I will do whatever is in my power to help you do the same."

"Ah," I say with a short, bitter laugh. "You just want me to attend all my lessons and social engagements and whatever other horror awaits me, just like everyone else."

Japha throws up their hands. "I can't win with you, it seems. I truly want your company, but I'll tell you a different truth: If you cooperate, your mother will be released after a time deemed suitable proof of your dedication and given a monthly stipend to support herself in peaceful retirement."

I gape. "Why didn't you tell me that in the first place?"

Japha shrugs innocently. "Maybe I thought you would want a friendly face that came without bribes or threats."

Cooperating may well be worth it if it means at least one of us—my mother—can be free. That will be worth sacrificing my own freedom.

At least until I find a way to escape.

Still, I shake my head slowly, not willing to give in so soon. To seem weak. "I have no friends here. My father has made that clear enough."

"Are you sure?" Japha bats their lashes, and I can't help but roll my eyes and smile. Their expression grows serious. "Your father has never trusted anyone in the palace enough to make a friend. Or maybe he felt too guilty."

Guilt has been my closest companion, my father told me.

"But I want to be your friend, Rovan," Japha continues. "Which means I won't lie—whatever is coming for both of us isn't going to be pleasant or easy. But I'd rather face it with someone than alone. Anything shy of a death sentence, we'll deal with."

They hold out their hand. Despite my reservations, I feel hope for the first time since getting dragged into the Hall of the Wards.

As I reach out, my eyes catch on Japha's bloodline. I dare ask in the lowest possible voice, "Is there some way to . . . escape this? Maybe—"

Japha seizes my hand and hauls me up from the bed so hard I fall into them. They wrap their other arm around my waist to steady me and bend their head to my ear in the same motion, whispering, "Not out loud. They're always listening. Write it."

Great, I think. I can't write.

Maybe *some* lessons are a good idea.

"Whatever comes, we'll survive," Japha says louder, clapping me on the back before releasing me. They add with a hard, little smile, "Well, until my bloodline kills me. At least you don't have to worry about that. Yet."

Which makes me remember: My father has said it's not his bloodline that's killing him. Bloodmages in Skyllea aren't suffering the same fate. Something is wrong with Thanopolis, and it stinks of death. Maybe while I'm trying to survive life in the palace and find a way to escape both its walls and my guardian, I can *also* try to discover what's happening, so my father can survive his bloodline, too.

And then perhaps we can *all* escape Thanopolis—my father, my mother, and even Bethea or Japha if they want.

103

First and foremost, I need to at least pretend I'm cooperating until I know my mother is safe and comfortable. And as much as I hate my guardian, I can't entirely ignore him anymore, not if I want to learn as much about him as possible: where he comes from, how he's bound to me, how he holds such power over his wards . . .

And then I need to lose him.

I also need to talk to Japha. They may know things I don't, and what's more, they may actually tell me.

"Is your guardian here?" I ask, my tone merely curious. "I'm still not used to mine."

Japha tosses their head. "Damios is over there, sulking in the corner."

I squint. I can't see much more than heavy shadows that might already be there. "I'm not sure where mine went. Dead man?"

He appears in the opposite corner, arms folded. "I'm here."

He looks wary. He also seems oddly aware of the other guardian's presence without actually acknowledging it. Interesting. Maybe guardians are so used to working alone that they're territorial and prickly in another's presence, like cats.

"Just checking," I say. "I knew it was too much to hope that you might have gone for good. Anyway, carry on being dead."

Japha laughs merrily. "Do you know, I make mine help me pick out the day's outfit? Damios hates it, which is half the reason I take so long. But if he doesn't give me his opinions, then it never ends. I must make warding me an actual chore so he feels pride in doing his duty."

"That's an idea," I say, smiling sweetly at the dead man as I head for the washroom. Japha's right. I *do* stink of booze.

The dead man merely stares back at me over folded arms as I pass. But then I hear his low murmur behind me: "Rest assured, warding you is chore enough already."

I spin around only to find his expression as smooth as glass. I toss a rude gesture at him.

"Ooh, you have a spicy one, do you?" Japha says, intrigued. "What's his name?"

"You know, I never caught it," I lie, turning back to the wash-room. "And since I can't be bothered to ask, I think I'll just keep calling him 'dead man.'"

"Is he handsome?" At my horrified look, Japha demands, "*What?*"

"He's *dead*."

"If we have to stare at them all the time, they might as well be good-looking. Think of him like a vase or tapestry or some other bit of decoration." Japha waits precisely half a heartbeat. "So, is he?"

"I hadn't noticed that, either," I say, meeting the dead man's dark eyes. He's absurdly handsome, but I'm not about to admit that.

His brow climbs ever so slightly. The look isn't arrogant, like I imagine Kineas's would be, or flirtatiously teasing like Japha's. He's just politely doubting my claim.

Japha sighs. "Mine is somewhat tolerable. Very regal cheek-bones."

"*Barely* tolerable is the most that can be said of mine," I declare. I march the rest of the way into the washroom, banishing the dead man's utterly perfect cheekbones from my mind.

10

Only a few days later, I'm cursing the hope that got me out of bed and made me willing to suffer. Because that hope has led me here, to this room—the dining room—with this woman, my new etiquette instructor. The gleaming marble columns and tree-trunk table, the plush rugs and intricately entwined plants don't make her company more tolerable. At least Penelope and Crisea are blissfully away at their martial training, and my father in his office.

I'm no closer to discovering anything about guardians or blood-lines, or a path of escape. The dead man is avoiding me, as if he knows what I'm up to. I can't write Japha. My other source of reluctant knowledge is my father, and he and I have barely spoken since the banquet. Perhaps he's trying to give me space, or perhaps I've driven him away. If only I could be as effective at that with *other* people.

I've already endured a parade of endless servants arriving to clean and serve me, as well as tailors sent to me without invitation and who don't leave as demanded. They're apparently plaguing me by order of the new king, to make sure I'm properly outfitted in my new environment.

Broodmare, I keep hearing in my mind. And then Tyros's worse threat: *Think of her mother.*

I can't stop thinking about her. If I can't make progress any-where else, at least I've been pretending to cooperate, for her sake. Never mind that the woman sitting across from me makes me want to tear out my hair.

"In writing," she declares, "you address the king's second cousin with the third honorific I mentioned——"

"I told you, I can't *write*." There are gold-whorled plates and glass goblets shaped like opening blossoms laid out in front of us, but without food or drink. They're for demonstration of proper usage only . . . except for my orange-streaked goblet shaped like a lily, which I don't allow to go dry for long.

"That should soon be remedied," the woman says, scribbling on a piece of paper in front of her. I don't know her name. I've made a point of not remembering, since it's *bad etiquette* and it piques her. It's the same tactic I'm using with the dead man. "You've already been appointed tutors in reading and writing, have you not?"

Oh, I have, and they're almost as insufferable as her.

"You should *really* stop drinking so much," my etiquette instructor says. "It's unbecoming."

My mother. Think of my mother. It's a chant that keeps me going. I drain my cup, and then barely stifle a burp with my hand. "Excuse me. You were saying?"

I can almost swear I hear a dry chuckle from among the columns behind me. Have I amused the dead man?

The woman's lips pinch even tighter, which is a feat. "I am quite sure you heard me."

Without even a twitch of a finger, I weave my favorite sigil, *move*, into a pattern that I force into reality. A stream of wine rises from the half-full pitcher, curls prettily through the air, and refills my goblet. I lift my cup.

"The one benefit to this whole mess is that I have an endless supply of wine, thanks to the royal cellars, and I'm not about to give that up. It's the only thing that makes your presence bearable. So, cheers."

"How *dare* you?" the woman says. "After all the king has done for you, this is how you respond to his favor? As much as I'd like to leave you to drown in ignorance *and* in your cup, it is my duty to fulfill the task assigned to me. You must be ready."

"Ready for what?" I ask, nervousness churning in my belly with *perhaps* too much wine.

"About that," Japha answers, sweeping into the dining room unannounced—a common occurrence of late, but one I appreciate. At their arrival, in a bright yellow peplos patterned in golden sunbursts and paired with a wide belt of bronze disks and matching bracers, I think, *Thank the goddess*, until they continue, "There is a grand ball tonight that everyone but me and my royal cousins were made aware of ages ago. It's a surprise party for us, apparently. I've only just received word." They sound none too pleased.

"It's not the good kind of surprise?" I guess, my stomach dipping further.

Japha plants hands on hips as they come to a halt before me, utterly ignoring my etiquette tutor. "Not only do I have no time to plan my outfit, but no, I can't imagine it's the good kind of surprise. I'd guess, given my age and the lack of warning, it's the sort that ends up with me betrothed to someone I detest. The same fate likely awaits Kineas and Lydea, since they've been equally kept in the dark."

"Betrothed? All of you? *Now?*" It's hard to imagine Japha and Lydea married off, just like that, especially against their will. I couldn't care less about Kineas, but if I'm about to be deprived of Japha's company, I'm not sure how I'll manage. And Lydea . . . I want to think less about why I'd rather *she* remain unengaged.

"I don't know for certain," Japha says, "but my hunches are usually right. Lydea suspects the same. I haven't bothered to ask Kineas what he thinks."

It strikes me as odd to be so secretive about an arranged marriage. "If you don't have any say in the matter, why do they care if you have warning?"

Japha waves a hand. "Oh, there have been dramatic protests in the past. Locking oneself in one's room, swallowing hemlock, running away in the dead of night with a lover, that sort of thing. The latter would only work in dear Kineas's case, since he's the only one of us without a guardian shadowing him. If our guardians didn't report our whereabouts at a time like that, then *they* would be in trouble with whatever underworld authority they answer to."

I should be focused on the horror of their imminent betrothal, but I can't help asking, "Who *do* they answer to?"

Japha shrugs. "I'm not sure. I would guess a king or something like we have. I don't see why the pattern would change just because they're dead."

The dead man *did* say he lived in something like a palace in the underworld, so that would make sense. Especially if this king of his was once a living king . . .

I remember my father mentioning that the royal gallery is forbidden, and that the question as to *why* was a good one. Maybe there's some clue there to how the whole guardian system works. I make a mental note to investigate.

Maybe even try to break in.

"I see," I say, pondering. "But why announce your betrothals now, of all times? Seems like a rush after Old King Neleus was only just interred in the necropolis."

Japha shrugs. "The time is right for Kineas and Lydea and overdue for me. They're twenty. I likely would have been betrothed by twenty under normal circumstances, but no one thought I was worth marrying off until I received the bloodline. And then, since my sister's death, I've been stalling. We're allowed a few years to mourn in extreme cases, but I think King Tyros has decided my time is up. I hear it's common with new leadership for a few things to change in a hurry."

I don't like the sound of that, especially considering the type of man the king is. But at least the focus isn't on me for once. Not that I want Japha to be in that position.

They frown. "It is odd, though. Tyros *did* seem to tolerate my . . . status . . . as neither niece nor nephew when he was the crown prince, whereas it was *his* father, Neleus, who disapproved of both me and the unusual situation with his two daughters and my father." It's the first time Japha has come close to admitting the affair aloud, and yet they say the words without hesitation. "I thought the only thing standing between me and a sudden betrothal, or a worse decree from my grandfather, was my uncle. But maybe this is a prime example of a new king trying to appease the old."

"Or maybe tonight has nothing to do with you?" I say.

"One can hope," Japha says, sighing, though they don't sound convinced.

"Do you have any ideas who you might be matched with, if your betrothal is to be announced?"

My etiquette instructor, nearly forgotten at the table, nods sharply. "*Is to be.* Now that was proper grammar for that situation. You're already improving."

Both Japha and I turn on her. She seems to shrink.

"Do please get out," Japha says cheerily. The woman leaves in a hurry, and Japha settles into the vacant seat. "I'm not sure who they'll stick me with in marriage. Poor woman, whomever she is." I open my mouth to object, but Japha continues, pouring some wine and meeting my eyes with their dark, kohl-lined gaze, "Not because I'm not excellent. I *know* I am. But the chances that a woman will be happy with someone like me are . . . slight, I imagine."

"Why a woman?" I ask.

Japha rolls their eyes. "The same reason Lydea will no doubt be matched with a man even though she's uninterested in them—tradition, heirs, blah blah." They raise their glass.

110

I smile, and then admit, somewhat sheepishly, "I've begun to wonder if they'll stick *you* with me."

Japha chokes on a mouthful of wine, sputtering.

"Would *I* be that bad?" I demand. "It's just that I'm supposed to be a 'broodmare' for *someone*, and they married my father to the princess because of his bloodline, but maybe that's not enough for *me*, the peasant . . ."

Japha shakes their head quickly, wiping their mouth. "I've already been assured that this night holds nothing unfortunate for you. Besides the fact that we're two loose ends who'd be conveniently tied up in such a pairing, we don't make sense together because I have a bloodline and you *will* have one." They smile slightly. "Anyone would be lucky to get you, but, alas, it's not to be me."

I'm touched, but at the same time I feel an odd pang. I don't want to be married to Japha against either of our wishes, but of all the combinations, it's the least horrible. "I know two bloodlines can't combine, but couldn't we pass on both separately? Not that I'd want to pass one on to anyone, let alone my child. Or to even *receive* one myself."

"Me either, which is yet another reason they won't put two rebels like us together. Especially after what happened with your father and my aunt—or rather, what *didn't* happen. The main reason is that there's generally only one child whose blood is worth anything, magically speaking. Two paired bloodlines mean one might die out, unless you're interested in dalliances outside of marriage." They shrug. "No one is willing to bet on that and risk losing a bloodline. Besides, bastards are harder to use, politically speaking," Japha adds, taking another sip of wine and eyeing the table.

I hear a strange noise over my shoulder and can't help turning. The dead man stands there, leaning against a column, an odd look on his face before he wipes it clean.

"Why is there no food?" Japha demands. They haven't heard the dead man, of course.

"The plates are for demonstration only, though I *rebelled* when it came to wine," I say, facing forward. "Do you know who the match might be for Lydea . . . and for Kineas?" I mention him only so I don't sound overly interested in his twin sister.

Japha is busy glaring at the empty plates. "Lydea, no, though she's as important and precisely placed as my mother, as both a bloodline and sister to the crown prince, and my mother married a famous warrior and heir to a kingdom. It was admittedly an abandoned kingdom, thanks to the blight, but one that still had plenty of displaced people who needed ruling. So whoever is chosen for Lydea will be equally grand, though I have no idea who it will be. Kineas, though . . . there might be someone more obvious for him."

It's their tone that makes me ask, "Who?"

Japha toys with their glass. "It's only speculation, of course. Helena is her name. Her line was once the ruling family's, spun away a few generations ago. She's still royalty, but distant enough that a match could be made. Well positioned, well bred, due to inherit a decently long bloodline in two years, and . . ."

So she's eighteen, a year younger than me. *Poor girl.* I wait. "And what?"

Japha has an odd expression on their face as they stare over the long table, into the distance. "Helena's beautiful. Even Kineas talks about how they would be suitably matched." They frown. "Though he doesn't deserve her."

I grimace. "And you like her? Or at least you respect her?"

"She's . . . innocent," Japha says softly, "but there isn't much to be done for her if she's chosen for Kineas."

Poor girl, indeed. This has all reminded me that as much as Japha wants to help me, they only have so much power. *Whatever comes,*

Japha had said, except we don't have any choice about what that is, only how we can deal with the aftermath.

As long as my mother is safe, I can survive anything, I hope. At least there's always wine. I take another drink.

Japha's eyes follow me. "There's no food, but there's paper." They slide the sheet my instructor was using closer, along with an inkwell and pen. "I've helped you with a couple sigils, so I can help you practice writing, too. Here, we can send each other notes about the worst outfits we see in a given day."

They scratch at the paper for a moment and then quickly wave it in the air to dry—much harder to read that way, if anyone is spying. They fold it and pass it to me.

"Thanks," I say, and tuck the paper against a plate. "Though I can't write much yet."

Japha winks. "I'm patient."

I'm not. I need to learn how to read better and write quickly, or else figure out another way to communicate with Japha.

"Anyway, what do you plan to wear?" they ask.

"Hmm?" I say, tearing myself away from my conspiratorial thoughts.

"You're of course invited to the ball. And if not, I invite you." Japha stands, straightening their sunny yellow peplos. "I, myself, am going to go get into something more fitting for the occasion. *Darker*."

"Good idea," I say.

I'm not going to hide. I *am* going to ensure my mother is safe, but I'm also going to look people in the eye as I plot to escape them.

Japha moves for the door, but as they reach for the gilded handle, it suddenly opens. My father steps in. He lurches to the side after he nearly bumps into Japha, giving them a wide berth and a suspicious nod. Japha merely rolls their eyes and leaves.

"What was Japha doing here?" he demands as soon as the door closes.

"I'm not allowed to have visitors?" I ask. "Our mutual shadow didn't prevent it, so I figured it was safe."

"*Safe?* This isn't about what Ivrilos thinks is good for you, it's . . ."

When he trails off, I arch an eyebrow. "It's about what you think?" I stand from the table. "Japha is doing more to help me than you are, so think again."

"They're not your friend, Rovan—"

"Excuse me," I say, brushing by him to head for my rooms. "I apparently have a ball to get ready for."

"I—you're going?" He sounds genuinely surprised.

"Why not?"

"My presence specifically *wasn't* requested. I'm to stay here. To rest, apparently."

I glance back at him. He *does* seem tired. Or, hell, maybe Penelope just wants to enjoy General Tumarq's company without her husband around, and so she pulled some strings.

And maybe without my father hovering, warning me to keep my head down, I can discover more answers. I hoped he would be the source of some, but other than his cryptic advice to follow in his footsteps, he's nearly been as tight-lipped as the dead man.

"Good," I say, making my voice hard. "You won't even have to go anywhere to do nothing, this time."

I leave him standing over the table, looking somewhat lost even though he's supposedly home.

Home. This will never be my home. Because I'll never let it become that.

11

The ball is taking place in a different room from the banquet that honored the old king. The space I step into now, arm in arm with Japha, is less like a traditional ballroom and more like the Hall of the Wards, except attendees arrive as if in a proper amphitheater, entering onto marble tiers that drop down to a central dais where some of the royal family stands for all to see, with huge windows as a backdrop. The white-wood window framing isn't regular but like the branches of a tree against the sky, clear glass invisible in between. The ceiling is made of branching windows, as well. But since it's an overcast night outside, the white wood and marble expanse feel cavernlike in the surrounding darkness.

Unlike much of the palace, there isn't any living greenery here. I shiver. It's like a tomb. The only color is in the white marble under my feet, blue veined like exposed, pale wrists.

"A bit much, isn't it?" Japha murmurs.

The two of us have arrived with Penelope and Crisea, but I've exchanged next to no words with anyone but Japha. Penelope and Crisea immediately seek out General Tumarq. I'm grateful that Japha sticks by me, otherwise I would have no one. And Japha seems grateful to have me. I can tell they're on edge by how tight their fingers are on my arm.

At least I have my own dress this time: black silk, twined in a blood-red strophion dripping with strands of rubies. A ruby-studded net catches up my blue-gleaming hair, all of it draped in black and red poppies. I'm still appreciating the blank look the dead man gave me as I was leaving my quarters. It spoke of disbelief. Now he's being especially discreet, perhaps not wanting to set off my temper. I can't decide if I'm relieved or frustrated, and then I settle on frustrated. He'll no doubt appear in a hurry if I decide to toss someone across the ballroom.

Japha stops, drawing me to a halt as well. "Brace yourself, but we should go pay our respects to King Tyros. It's expected."

I follow Japha's gaze down along the thronging tiers to the lowest level, where the new king stands on a raised marble dais carved like an open clamshell, and at his side, Kineas, the new crown prince. Both are dressed in extravagant blue himations, golden laurel wreaths on their heads—triumphant instead of mourning now. Lydea and poor Delphia are nowhere to be seen. The younger girl is probably hiding. As for Lydea, she's probably off sharpening her daggers.

I snatch the first goblet of wine I see from a passing silver tray and down it. I've frankly tried to forget about the princess *and* our kiss. I still can't help but wonder how she's dealing with the likely possibility of her betrothal . . . and then tell myself I shouldn't care. I have enough on my plate.

Handing off my empty glass to someone I'm not even entirely sure is a servant, I turn away from the dais. "Damn expectations and damn the king. I don't care."

"I agree."

I nearly choke in surprise as Lydea slides up alongside me as silently as a shade, mirth and something more dangerous glittering in her dark eyes. Real-looking raven's wings and thorny branches wrought in silver crown her black hair. A stole of black feathers lines her shoulders, from which falls a dress made of silver links, woven loosely enough that I can catch glimpses of the bloodline and pale skin underneath. Not that I'm looking—much. Lydea's own gaze travels the length of my body, tracing black silk and ruby strands and leaving heat in its wake.

116

"Mm, so you have a dark side as well, do you?" she asks.

I struggle to recover from the sight of her, never mind the suddenly irresistible memory of our kissing. Lydea is flawless. Beautiful and deadly, she reminds me of the perfect, shining coils of a waiting snake. As with the dead man, I want to disturb her perfection. I summon a sardonic tone. "My life did just get upended."

Lydea's smirk fades. "Indeed. I'm sorry about that."

"Are you?"

She shrugs, uninterested in meeting my challenge. "As far as I'm capable."

My fists tighten involuntarily.

Japha edges closer, between me and the princess, smiling brightly—an obvious diversion. "If you refuse to pay your respects to the king, Rovan, shall we dance?"

Lydea squeezes Japha's arm lightly. "I believe my rank surpasses yours, and so it is *my* right to ask Rovan for a dance."

My eyes widen in alarm.

Japha laughs, but there's an edge of nervousness in it. "You, dancing with a woman *tonight*, of all nights? People will talk, dear cousin."

"As if you were one to care about *that*," she says, running admiring fingertips over Japha's latest inspiration in formal attire: a dark teal strophion meant to define the female figure, crisscrossing over a copper breastplate shaped for a man, with a long wine-colored chiton underneath. A crown of teal flowers slowly blooms and refolds, over and over, atop their close-cropped hair—magic, of course, literally and figuratively. Lydea smiles wickedly. "Anyway, let them talk. If it is a question of who will lead . . . I will."

My heart speeds up. I don't trust Lydea . . . and maybe I don't trust myself.

"Please, Rovan," Lydea says, her voice low and husky. "It is

117

likely my last night to be free. Fly with me." She holds out a pale, slender hand, traced in red sigils.

Is this flying? I remember asking her in a drunken haze.

Like Japha, Lydea must feel the bars of a cage about to come down around her this evening. I see the princess's headpiece—the branches tangling the raven's wings, thorns pinning them down—in a new light.

I take Lydea's hand. As the princess leads me down along the tiers toward the ebb and flow of dancing couples in the low center of the room, I shoot a panicked glance back at Japha. They merely shrug, as if to say, *You got yourself into this mess.*

Lydea turns about, liquid smooth, entwining the fingers of one hand with mine and putting the other at my hip. Her fingernails graze my skin through my gown. I suddenly wish I had a lot more wine, but then we're dancing.

I've never been a skilled dancer, despite my recent lessons. But with Lydea leading, I don't need to be. She dances well enough for the both of us.

"Why do you want to dance with me?" I ask bluntly. "Is this some attempt to humiliate me further?"

"Does it look like I'm humiliating you?" she asks with a delicate arch of her black eyebrow. We glide and twirl across the blue-veined marble in a shimmer of rubies and silver links.

"I can't say this is humiliating, no," I say, trying to pull myself together, "but I can't fail to remember the last function like this. Your family punished me and shamed my father."

"Do you forget what happened *after*, or were you too drunk? Or maybe you just want to forget, because of my family?" Lydea's hand tightens on mine. "Remember, it wasn't *me* who forced your father to bow. That was *my* father." No amount of warm honey can hide the bitterness in her tone.

I'm surprised. "You really don't like him." It's not a question, and I should be more careful than that. Not only are others close enough to eavesdrop, but our ever-present, if currently invisible guardians can likely hear everything.

"Ah-ah," Lydea says, leaning forward to breathe the admonishment into my ear, sending shivers down my neck. "Don't expect me to spill my guts when you haven't even stabbed me yet." She draws back, red lips pouting. "You haven't even tried to *kiss* me again."

Blood blossoms in my cheeks in a rush, and the princess laughs, damn her.

"So you *do* remember what happened last time." She sounds delighted.

Kiss, I suddenly think. If there's one way to whisper in someone's ear that won't draw attention, that's probably it.

I don't give myself time to reconsider, because then I'll be too terrified to ever do it. I bring my mouth to Lydea's jawline only somewhat discreetly, unable to resist planting a kiss there—purely for appearances' sake, of course—before I reach her ear.

She smells *so* good.

"Can I trust you?" I murmur as low as I can. My words could be sweet nothings for all anyone knows. Or I could be nibbling her ear. I try that out, just in case.

"Yes," Lydea breathes. "Japha and me both. But leave Delphia out of anything risky, and beware of Kineas and my father."

"Will you help me," I say, barely audible, "find a way to escape them?"

"Depends," Lydea says, "on—"

The sharp blare of a trumpet cuts her off. A burst of white doves takes flight from the clamshell dais, dissolving into a rain of red rose petals that fall as if from the white branches high overhead. Before I have time to do much more than bat a petal away from my nose, King Tyros is speaking over the crowd, his voice magically amplified.

"We have celebrated the passing of the crown from my glorious father to us, and now today, we celebrate our glorious future. I have some announcements to be made regarding my children and my sisters' children."

Lydea's face has gone hard. I search for Japha in the crowd and catch their rueful gaze.

"First," the king continues, "may my youngest daughter, Princess Delphia of the line of Athanatos, and my niece, Princess Crisea, daughter of Penelope of the line of Athanatos, come forward."

I blink at the same time as Lydea, her icy facade cracking. Murmurs rise in the crowd. These aren't the names anyone has been expecting. The two girls, one with a crown of dark hair, one wreathed in the snowy curls of her Skyllean mother, step onto the dais.

"Too long have we gone without respecting the goddess," the king booms. "My sisters had three children together, even if they came from two mothers."

But only one father, I think, before I realize with a jolt where this is headed.

"The third child should always serve that third and final aspect of the goddess: the crone. Let it not be said that I, myself, refuse to lead by example. So it is with great pride that I declare that my youngest daughter, Delphia, will accompany my niece, Crisea, to begin apprenticeships in the necropolis. They will bring honor to our family by devoting themselves to the goddess in this regard."

The room falls absolutely silent. Lydea is crushing my hand in her own. Her eyes are fixed on the dais, her face paler than ever before. Yet it's nothing, *nothing*, compared to Delphia's expression. The girl is nearly as white as her hair, terror in her eyes. Crisea—*perfect little warrior*, Japha called her—looks ready to vomit.

And yet, neither of them protest. The king hasn't left any room for argument. They stand silent, motionless, staring out over the heads of those assembled as if already separate and striving for life-lessness. I can't help but pity the both of them, even Crisea.

"Your Majesty—brother . . . ," comes a choked voice from the crowd. Penelope takes several hesitant steps toward the dais, rais-ing a pleading hand. "Please—"

The king's voice cracks like a whip. "You shirked your duty to the necropolis as my third sibling, but I begged our father to allow you to care for your daughter and follow your own path as a war-rior, against his better judgment. Perhaps *that* is why the goddess didn't see fit to grant you another child." His lips twist in obvious disapproval. I figured the royal family had seen my sudden arrival as a blessing, but perhaps the king views me as more of a curse that could have been avoided. "Now that your daughter is grown, allow her to carry your burden with grace, dear sister, and to make amends with the goddess on your behalf."

After such a public reprimand, Penelope can't do much else, even if her daughter has just been as good as sentenced to a slow death. Penelope falls silent, head bowed, shoulders shuddering. Tumarq stands next to her, his face a carefully blank mask, but I can see tendons standing out on his arms, his fists clenched.

Tyros waves a hand, and two black-swathed figures sweep for-ward to escort Delphia and Crisea from the dais. I haven't spotted shadow priests outside of the necropolis often, only at the most important public ceremonies. They aren't supposed to be enjoying life, after all, instead embacing death. The sight of them makes me want to take a step back. Or maybe run.

It isn't their death shrouds, the likes of which are often worn by lay people in honor of the dead, but their masks. Just as blood magic most powerfully controls fire, water, and living or once-living material—flesh, bone, fiber, and wood alike—death magic holds dominion over air, earth, and metal—the inert, the never living, the void. Death magic, I'm learning, is responsible not only for the shades wandering about, but for most of the stone- and metal-work in the palace. The black-shrouded figures before me wear masks made of elaborate strips of dark iron winding around their necks and faces, leaving gaps only to breathe and see by. The ends of the strips rise in spikes around their heads, forming jagged, disturbing fans. They're utterly terrifying.

King Tyros doesn't even look at his own daughter as she's taken away by them. He's colder, crueler than I guessed him to be—even crueler than *Lydea* guessed him to be, based on her stunned expression.

"I don't understand," she murmurs. "He loves her more than any of us."

"Onto other matters," the king says, smiling and clasping his hands before him as if this were a celebration and not something more like a funeral rite. "Japha nu Tumarq, my first sister's child and inheritor of her powerful bloodline, we must announce your betrothal."

My stomach plummets.

Japha strides forward through the crowd, not hesitant in the least, their flower-wreathed head held high. *There are some things we must suffer with grace. Or at least with excellent clothes . . .* Japha is living up to their own words with the highest standards.

"Japha," the king continues, "I am pleased to present your future wife, Helena of Radeus." He spreads his arms, and a young woman with a curtain of wheat-colored hair and a gold-embroidered cream peplos steps forward to meet Japha. She's lovely and . . . shockingly sweet-looking, for a royal.

Now Japha's jaw nearly drops.

Helena, I think. *Helena was meant for Kineas.*

But Lydea appears unsurprised. She doesn't clap when the ballroom explodes with applause. "And now we cheer and forget that my father just condemned my sister and cousin to a tomb until they die from lack of light and living."

I'm not clapping or cheering, despite Japha's turn of good fortune. And yet I don't know what I can say about Delphia that will sound sincere enough. "I thought two bloodlines shouldn't marry. Isn't Helena due to inherit her own in a couple years?"

"No." Lydea's voice is flat. "You wouldn't have heard; it was an embarrassment kept quiet. Helena doesn't have a drop of power in her blood. She was never even warded. Her parents finally had to admit it. They're trying for another child, or so they say. My guess is they never wanted Helena or any child of theirs to carry the burden of a bloodline . . . let alone to face the necropolis." She flinches, cursing under her breath. "*Delphia*. And I thought *I* would bear the heavier burden."

I retake her hand and squeeze gently. "For what it's worth, I'm sorry."

Something flashes in Lydea's eyes, and I can't tell if it's gratitude or pain. She opens her mouth to say something, but the king's voice rises instead.

"Princess Lydea of the line of Athanatos, my elder daughter."

Lydea drops my hand as if it burns her, her face glassing over like a frozen lake. She comes forward on silk-smooth steps, without hesitation. Meeting her fate like a queen instead of a princess.

The king's smile looks staged as he peers down on her from the dais. "You, my daughter, are hereby betrothed to Alldan Cannar, prince of Skyllea, third in line for their throne."

I nearly gasp in shock as a man steps up from behind the dais. His forest green hair is crowned in golden stag horns and wreathed in vines and white flowers—more than a match for any of the headpieces here, and that's saying something. His tunic, so deep green it's almost black, is embroidered head to foot in thorny gold branches and cut in an unfamiliar style, though perhaps my father might recognize it. His dark coppery skin gleams with a metallic sheen, and his eyes are a brilliant violet. I can't help staring.

A Skyllean prince? From what my father has said, Skyllea and Thanopolis are enemies, especially after what the royals here did to Cylla—forcing her into marriage, childbirth, wardship, and an early death alike. Never mind that the entire polis thinks that Skyllea and its unwarded, wild-hued bloodmages are mad.

The Skyllean prince, Alldan, doesn't have a bloodline, and neither does he seem to be in Thanopolis against his will. He's flanked by a small, official delegation of other bright-haired individuals—the most subtle hair color among them a purple black—and he wears a polite, welcoming smile. It seems like this, his engagement, is precisely why he's come. Perhaps the two peoples are trying to mend their rift and fight the blight together, despite what happened to Cylla and my father.

What will the Skylleans think, then, when they see my father? That's probably why he wasn't allowed to come to the ball, I realize. Who knows what version of events the royal family has told the Skyllean delegation? And now, if everyone is striving for peace, maybe our chances of crossing the blight to Skyllea and being welcomed there have just grown a lot slimmer.

King Tyros stares down at the newly betrothed couple as if they're rats in a bucket. And despite how beautiful they look together with their silver and gold attire, raven's wings and stag horns, it doesn't seem the rift between Thanopolis and Skyllea will be closing anytime soon, if Lydea has any say. She gazes at Alldan with cool disinterest, her black-winged head refusing to bow even as he takes up her sigil-lined hands and kisses them. He doesn't seem terribly eager to touch her himself, despite the smile painted on his face. His vivid violet eyes seem to shine as if from behind a mask.

Ah, the joy of arranged marriages, I think. My heart aches a sur-

124

prising amount for Lydea, but for the hundredth time, I thank the goddess—maiden, mother, *and* crone—that this evening's entertainments have nothing to do with me. Even if my hope of escape has dimmed.

"And finally," the king says, facing the crowd. "It is my greatest pleasure to announce the betrothal of my son, Crown Prince Kineas of the line of Athanatos"—he holds his arm out to the loathsome squid at his side—"to the daughter of Silvean Ballacra of Skyllea . . . Rovan Ballacra."

Oh, I think, as the seconds trip by like several missed stairs. *Shit*.

12

I hardly notice the king's nod to the Skyllean delegation after his announcement. I barely hear him say, "Our apologies Silvean couldn't be here tonight, but he sends his regards." I don't see Kineas's reaction. All my thoughts, my entire world, stutter to a halt. The pronouncement isn't horrible so much as it's unreal. I simply can't believe it.

I don't meet Kineas's or the king's eyes, or those of anyone around me on the crowded lower tier of the ballroom. I stare at the floor in front of my feet, at the red rose petals like spilled blood against the blue-veined pale marble.

Before I know what I'm doing, I'm turning, stumbling away from the dais, but hands catch my arms before I make it five steps. I don't even know whose. They tug me, laughingly, as if I'm merely a shy, blushing bride, right up to the foot of the dais. The strings of rubies trailing from my dress glitter and tinkle, the red flashes too bright, the delicate sounds oddly loud.

I taste copper. I've bitten my tongue. Maybe I can dip my finger into my mouth, wet it with blood, and hurl everyone—the king, Kineas, whomever stands in my way—out through the towering, twining windows, before this becomes real.

"Rovan," the dead man says over my shoulder, as I'm pulled to the front of the dais.

I've entirely forgotten him. I want to keep forgetting him, but the warning in his tone gives me pause, despite myself.

King Tyros smiles down at me, his eyes bright in a way that

makes me want to recoil. "Honor your mother, now," he murmurs softly. "You wouldn't want to disappoint her."

Another threat against my mother. Ensuring I'll cooperate. Just like the dead man, using the invisible leash he has around my neck to keep me at heel. I haven't fully experienced his power over me yet, but I know he can drop me if I try to run. Hurt me.

I can understand, now, how my father felt at the banquet. Not to mention how he felt when he was hauled off to the palace and betrothed against his will all those years ago. Alone and powerless, just as I am now. My heart breaks for him as it never has before.

I should never have blamed him. None of this is his fault. He's doing his best, trying to stand against forces that want to smash him into the ground. He's still putting one foot in front of the other. So what if his head bows occasionally?

I shudder to think what *this* will do to him. Even more than the Skyllean presence, this must be why he's been kept from the ball. I'm glad for it.

I stare back at the king, unable to do much else. If I once thought of his face as hard as settled marble, now I can see through the cracks to what lies beneath, and it's terrifying. He's *enjoying* this.

Japha was surprised at their uncle's change in behavior since he was crowned. Was that other face a mask, waiting to be torn free as soon as he was king and could act how he pleased?

Japha is at my side, whispering urgently in my ear—*I didn't know, I promise I didn't know*—and Lydea says something else to me, squeezing my hand, but her voice sounds like it's coming from underwater. I hear what the king proclaims next, though, his iron gaze still locked on mine:

"And now to celebrate, the newly betrothed couples will dance. Japha and Helena, Alldan and Lydea, Kineas and Rovan, please take to the center of the room. Others may join in at a respectful distance."

And then Kineas stands before me. The prince has extended his hand to me. What's more, he looks to have been holding it there for at least a few seconds, long enough for impatient fury to ripple across his face. He smiles to hide it.

"Are you simple, or is your common upbringing rearing its ugly head?" he mutters under his breath. "*Take my hand and assume your position, idiot.*"

Numbly, I rest my palm in his. And then I'm dancing with Kineas. Crown prince.

My *betrothed.*

I vaguely think I might vomit down the front of his midnight blue himation. Its golden embroidery matches the gold laurel wreath glittering in his pewter hair. He looks every inch a royal, and I despise every inch of him.

I come back to myself in a sudden, horrible crash, like a wave smashing me against a rock. I'm here, in this ballroom. This is happening. My hand is in Kineas's, his other touches my hip, and I'm following his lead. I still remember how Lydea felt in his stead.

So different. So *good.* And now this.

I can't stand it.

"I had no idea my father would do this," Kineas says through the bared teeth of his fake smile. "Though I suppose with Helena turning out to be a failure of good breeding, your bloodline makes you a logical replacement, if the rest of you is entirely unworthy. Imagine my disappointment."

"Oh, I can," I breathe. *Just breathe. Don't speak.*

His smile drops, fury replacing it again. "I'm sure you're *delighted.* You're an ignorant peasant, and now you will be queen." He smirks. "If you live long enough."

"Your mother certainly didn't," I say, before I can help myself.

The look he turns on me before he stares out over my head in polite disregard is one of pure, blackest hatred.

We dance in silence for a few more seconds, but those seconds may as well be years. I try to ignore him, focusing over his shoulder, but all I can think is: *This is my life now.* It's all I can do to not tear away from him. To tear out of my very *skin.*

"I can't . . . I can't stand to look at him," I nearly gasp, when I can't bear it any longer.

Since I'm trying to stare beyond him, Kineas misreads my meaning. "Your guardian?" he asks, at the same time the dead man says, suddenly standing at my side, "The crown prince?"

Of course Kineas can't hear the shade. I give a short nod, which Kineas assumes is for him, though I meet the dead man's black eyes as I do. "I don't know what I'll do if I have to look at him for much longer."

I mean that for my guardian, as well, but Kineas says, "That must be a bother."

The dead man's eyes widen ever so slightly. "You're in a highly public place, and you need to maintain appearances. Whatever you do, stay calm."

"Telling me that *doesn't help,*" I say through gritted teeth. My hand tightens on Kineas's enough to make him glare at me.

"I don't care if it helps," he says. "I don't care about you at all, as long as you stop crushing my hand like a barbarian."

I don't respond, but the look in my eyes, which Kineas doesn't deign to notice, must be enough for the dead man. He vanishes and reappears right over Kineas's shoulder.

"Focus on me. I'm right here, and you hate me more than you hate him, yes? Concentrate on that." His tone is still calm, but rushed, like the surface of a deep, fast-flowing river. There's a lot of weight, *warning,* in those words.

"I'll try," I say, and the answer works for both of them.

"Try harder," Kineas snarls, without even meeting my eyes. He's more attentive to everyone watching us, keeping his face smooth for the crowd.

"What does it matter if I slip up?" I whisper.

"You'll embarrass yourself," he says, at the same moment the dead man says, "Think of your mother."

Thinking of my mother makes me want to scream. "This isn't working."

"*Obviously*," Kineas mutters. "You're still strangling my hand."

"You're not focusing on me," my guardian says.

"Because all I see is him," I grind out.

"Stop looking at him," both the crown prince and the dead man say in unison. It could be funny, under other circumstances. "Look at *me*," the shade emphasizes, while Kineas adds, "I should be novel enough for you."

Perhaps it's because Kineas's words are the most infuriating that my eyes lock onto his—clear, silvery, and entirely cold. I want to do more than scream. I want to *burn*.

Kineas appears mildly alarmed by my expression, but the dead man's head cocks to one side. His eyes can certainly be cold, too, but there's calculation in them.

It's then I realize the shade looks more alive than the crown prince. The dead man is, well, *dead*, and Kineas very much breathing—too much. But my guardian has more feeling in him, despite all expectations. He looks especially alive now.

"I'm going to try something," he says, and then he sidesteps . . . *into* Kineas, taking up the crown prince's exact position, except a hair's breadth closer to me. He covers over Kineas entirely, dark curls and eyes masking the pewter and silver I hate. My guardian's pale left hand looks as if I'm holding it, and his right hovers just over my waist. His face is only inches from mine.

And then I'm dancing with the shade and not the crown prince, moving through the crowd with a black-clad, unearthly figure as if he were flesh and blood.

The dead man's lips twitch at my sudden amazement, a slight slyness touching his flawless face. "Is this better?"

At least I want to kill him slightly less than Kineas. I can almost, *almost* feel him through the pressure of Kineas's hands on my body, and it's a surprising relief. I study the details of him. He looks like a king again: a silver circlet on his brow, a long robe of black velvet and silver embroidery belted at the waist with his usual, starkly elegant swords, and a ruff of black fur around his strong, graceful neck.

"This is better," I say, and the shade's expression shifts into something with fewer edges.

I don't get to wonder at that for long, because the crown prince answers, his voice coming disconcertingly from right behind the dead man's face, "I would imagine so. You haven't experienced much like this." *Much like me*, he means.

"Keep talking," I say hurriedly.

Kineas sighs. "I'm not here for your amusement. That's *your* role to play for *me*." A suggestive leer comes into his tone that I blessedly can't see. But it's still enough to make my blood boil.

"It's nice to be able to talk face-to-face," the dead man starts somewhat hesitantly, as if he doesn't know where to begin, "without you throwing things at me."

"I'm only cooperating because your face is preferable, at the moment," I say. "That could change quickly."

"I don't care about your preferences in the slightest," the crown prince says. "And if you insist on misbehaving, I'll be happy to train those feral tendencies out of you."

"Wow, lucky me." I stare hard at the dead man. "Who could have guessed someone in my position would end up here?"

"A true oracle couldn't have predicted it," Kineas mutters behind the shade's somber expression.

"I hadn't known it would come to this," the dead man says, "you and the crown prince, betrothed. I would have warned you, which was perhaps why I wasn't told." He seems disquieted by the thought. "But it doesn't have to be the worst of fates."

"Oh?" My voice comes out high and brittle.

Fortunately, Kineas ignores me. And the shade realizes it's wise to change the subject, though he pantomimes spinning me in a circle before he does.

"I haven't danced in a very long time," he says quietly, "though it's nice to know I still can. I can't feel your body, of course, but it's easy enough to anticipate how you'll move." His dark eyes dart over me. "I've spent lifetimes studying exactly that in order to counter an attack."

To counter an attack against his ward or to defend someone *from* his ward, I wonder?

Perhaps the dead man realizes he's moved us back into dangerous territory, because he adds, "I don't mind doing this. I'll keep doing it, if need be. To make it easier."

"Will you do this even when we're in bed?"

"I'll do whatever I want." Kineas's voice is like a splash of cold water on my face. I can't help shuddering.

"I can't imagine my face would be more welcome to you in that situation," the dead man says, and then pauses. "But I'll do anything to keep you from burning down the palace. Anything *you* want."

His vow is in direct contrast to Kineas's.

"Why?" I ask.

"Because I'm the crown prince, and *you'll* do whatever I desire," Kineas declares.

The dead man briefly closes his eyes, not long enough to lose the dance but long enough to look as if he regrets Kineas's pronouncement. "Because," he says, "we both need something that the other has."

I blink. "What?"

"You heard me," Kineas grates, squeezing me so hard I flinch.

A muscle in the dead man's jaw clenches. "Dear goddess, won't he shut up? *I'm* about to kill him."

I can't help it; I giggle, and that's the last straw for Kineas. Fortunately the song is near its end, because he breaks away from me, appearances be damned. His body splits from the shade's abruptly, making me stagger. My hand passes straight through the dead man's chest. He blinks down at it, as if surprised to find himself a ghost, as well.

I stare at my guardian, marveling at the impossibility of him. Our eyes meet and hold for what feels like a very long second. There's something between us that wasn't there before. I just have no idea what it is.

"Th-thank you" is all I have time to stammer, before . . .

"*Rovan?*"

My father's voice. The dead man's eyes fly wide, his alarm mirroring my own. As he spins toward the voice, he vanishes.

My father is standing right across from me, no longer hidden by my guardian. His hair is an untidy mess of blue and gray, his himation crooked. He looks to have come in a rush, and has probably seen the tail end of my dance with Kineas.

And he's drawing conclusions as to what it meant.

"No," he said, shaking his head. "No."

He shouldn't be here, I know he shouldn't, but I can only stare at him, tears forming in my eyes. I should tell him to leave, but I want to fall on him and weep. I want to scream.

"I think it's too late," I manage, choking on a despairing laugh. "We just had our betrothal dance, after all, witnessed by both Thanopolis's and Skyllea's finest."

133

"Skyllea?" My father blinks golden eyes in shock, and then his gaze shoots to the dais, to the delegation of colorful-haired people gathered there. "What are they doing here?"

"I don't think they're here to help," I say as gently as possible. "Lydea was just engaged to one of their princes."

"*What?*"

He takes a step, as if he's about to march on the dais. Before I can try to stop him—or before the dead man can, once again alongside us—the king sidles in front of him, having stepped off the dais to head my father off. He places a strong hand on his shoulder.

"Now, Silvean, you were supposed to be resting," Tyros says, as if speaking to a child. "You're in no fit state to meet guests. You wouldn't want to give them the wrong impression, would you?"

"*Fuck* impressions," my father spits, shrugging off the king's grip. "What are they doing here? And what is this about Rovan's betrothal to Kineas?"

"They're here to celebrate new alliances," Tyros says smoothly, "as should you, if you won't return to your apartments. Rovan has been graced with the highest honor. Her mother would be proud."

Yet another veiled threat.

The king leans forward to whisper in my father's ear. I don't hear what he says, but whatever it is, the effect is immediate. My father jerks back, his golden eyes bulging, nostrils flaring. I see the dead man's eyes widen at the same time. There's no other warning.

The many windows in the great ballroom shatter all at once. Their white wooden frames twist like tree branches lashing in a gale. Their panes explode inward in a glittering cloud. Bigger shards rain down from the ceiling. People scream, sheltering their heads and ducking for cover as glass and spatters of real blood join the red rose petals on the pale floor.

But my father hasn't flinched. A sword of fire appears in his hand. He shoves me behind him, stronger than I could have guessed, and swings the blade at the king's neck.

The dead man hasn't flinched, either. He's there, stepping between the king and my father, catching the fiery sword on crossed half-moon blades. He moves like air. Like shadow. Like dancing. Then one of the ghostly blades vanishes, and his empty hand shoots out to seize my father's neck. And it's over, just like that. Because this is far more than a pinch. The shade not only touches him, but *holds* him in place. And it's not just me who can see the both of them. So can everyone else, based on their surprised, frightened reactions. Everyone leaps away, crying out.

My guardian *is* here now. And it's not good; it's terrible.

The sword of flame vanishes from my father's hand. The window frames stop twisting. The quiet is suddenly deafening. I can hear people's isolated sobs along with my own panicked gasping.

I've wanted my father to act, but never something like *this*.

The dead man seems to agree. "I thought you knew better," he tells his ward, sounding disappointed.

My father can barely respond. "Couldn't . . . help it. And if there was even a chance . . ." His golden eyes speak of pain and murder as they wander over the shade's shoulder to find the king— but then they roll back in his head, and his knees buckle. The dead man lets him fall to the ground in a tinkle of glass.

I can only stare in horror at my father's unmoving form, lying on a bed of rose petals and gleaming shards. Kineas belatedly draws his sword, the steel ringing awkwardly loud.

King Tyros turns slowly to face the Skylleans, grouped in a protective huddle on the dais. "We hope that Skyllea had nothing to do with this assassination attempt, or else we may need to revisit our negotiations for peace."

A woman with purple hair and what looks like a pair of white doves nesting on her head straightens and steps forward. "You have our word that we played no part in this. We wished to visit with Silvean Ballacra as we've had no contact with him for two decades, but we'd yet to arrange it. We'll take this opportunity to formally disavow him. His fate is yours to decide."

"Good," the king says, and then nods at my father. "Get this man out of my sight." Armed guards rush forward. "The next time I see any trace of him, I want it to be on *her* skin." He stabs his chin at me.

"My apologies once again, Rovan," the dead man says. His anger would be preferable to this . . . sympathy?

Before I can tell him not to call me that—*never* to call me that—or to throw whatever I can at him or to flee from him, he reaches out and brushes my cheek with a fingertip. Shockingly, I feel his skin against mine, like his pinch, but lingering, cool, and light.

And then I can't remember anything else from that evening. But I *can* remember after.

13

I dream I'm burning alive, and it's a dream I can't seem to wake from.

When I finally do, cracking tear-crusted eyelids, my throat is hoarse like I've been screaming. I remember fire pouring over me, coating my skin like burning oil. Or was it somehow blood? Wherever it is I'm lying now—my surroundings are too dark to see—I feel tight and tender, as if sunburned. Maybe I *have* actually burned, and someone has healed me . . .

Then I remember the ball. The windowed walls writhing. Glass falling like rain. My father collapsing to the ground. The king's sneer. The dead man touching my cheek.

I fling myself out of bed and crash violently into something—a chair—and find my way to a crack of light. It's peeping through window curtains, and I throw them wide. Light spills over me.

My arms are traced in unfamiliar red sigils, from my palms to my shoulders. So are my feet and legs. I tear off my shift. They line my belly and breasts and even my ass, when I twist to look, so likely my back as well. There's a mirror—I'm in my room in the palace, I now realize. I stumble over to my rose desk and the mirror entwined in thorns above it . . . and freeze. My entire body is covered, the sigils climbing like a high red collar all the way to my jawline. Not even my *face* is entirely free. One red sigil streaks my cheek below my left eye—a half circle like a bowl, with three lines of varying lengths dropping from it like red tears.

I don't know what else to do. I scream.

"It's all right."

Spinning around, I find the dead man standing near the window. He's less solid than usual, washed out by a beam of sunlight.

"It's not all right!" I screech at him. "*Look at me!*"

"I . . . see you," he says, nearly sounding awkward, and I secrete his discomfort away like a dagger up my sleeve. "You have a bloodline now, a very long one. It's normal to feel disoriented by the changes."

"To hell with disorientation. To hell with these changes. And to hell with *you*. I didn't want this!" I pause, chest heaving. "Where is my father?"

I know before he speaks, from the too-still expression on his face.

"I'm sorry, Rovan, he's——"

I scream again, and the sound splits open a pathway in my mind. This path jumps sigil to sigil, like stepping stones across a raging river. As I follow them, sketching them out with my fingers, the chair behind me breaks apart, splintering into daggerlike shards that rise up and fly like arrows at the dead man.

All they do is pass right through him, bouncing and clattering off the marble wall behind him.

He holds up a hand. "I don't want to put you to sleep again, so please don't make me. You're very powerful now. You have access to magic you couldn't dream of before. Calm down——"

"To hell with *calming down!*" I sense it, along the stepping-stone path in my mind: the fire all around me, burning in candles, lanterns, chandeliers. And I can seize every bit of it, hurl it at him, at the wall behind him, at the *entire* palace, watch it all burn . . . I raise my hand to trace the path with my fingers, to bring it all into being.

I feel a gentle ghost of a touch at the nape of my neck. The dead man's sigh—*behind* me now—is the last thing I hear.

When I next awake, everything is fuzzy. A candle flickers in the gloom nearby. I'm in my bed with its treelike posts and leafy living canopy. Blankets are cool against my skin and lightly scented with a soothing mix of herbs. I'm wearing a new night shift, and the chair has been replaced. The dead man is sitting in it.

The sight makes my head drop back onto the pillows. Maybe it's the futility of trying to escape him. Once again he knocked me unconscious with a brush of his finger. I suppose I should be grateful he didn't hurt me.

"It doesn't have to be like this," he says quietly. "But it will be, over and over again, until you can control yourself."

I squeeze my eyes closed. A tear leaks out. Because he's right. As many pathways as I now have, branching in my mind like a tree—a *thousand* trees in a forest—he still holds this strange power over me. *Why? How?* No matter the cause, it's a leash.

My father possessed this strength, but he was as trapped as I am. And now he's dead, and it's my fault. Not because I received the bloodline. Crisea was right—I should have kept my head down. I'll never regret saving Bethea, but I was foolish enough to get drunk and climb on top of the gazebo with her in the first place. And then I pushed my father to a breaking point by resenting him for the life he had no choice but to live these past twelve years. I as good as accused him of being one of the enemy, and forced him to prove he wasn't. I don't know what the king said to finally shove him over the edge, but it doesn't matter. My father stood up to him because of me. And now my father is gone, and I'm in his place, in his prison, with his bloodline, and with his guardian.

But that doesn't mean I can't win free of the dead man. My father never figured out how, but he told me to follow in his footsteps. Maybe there's a way out of this. If there is, I'll find it.

This, I silently vow.

"If you *can* manage to control yourself, you can get up and move about as normal," the dead man says. "You can do whatever you want, and I won't stop you. As long as you don't try to harm anyone else, or destroy anything significant, let's say."

"So burning down the palace is out of the question?" I murmur behind closed lids. He'll expect me to put up a show of resisting, at least at first.

"Most definitely. Splinter as many chairs as you like, as long as no one is nearby."

These chairs probably took some craftsperson days to make. The fact that the dead man doesn't seem to care about them makes me care all the more. I would be like a spoiled child throwing a tantrum.

"I'll just stay here," I say, without opening my eyes. I need these people—the dead man, the royals—to forget about me, to leave me alone for as long as possible. I need to figure out what footsteps my father meant, find my mother, and flee this place—flee Kineas. Where I'll go after that, I have no idea. Especially not if Skyllea is no longer an option. But I'll figure that out later.

I prefer the blight to Kineas, frankly.

"About that," the dead man says, almost reluctantly. "There are those eager to see you up and around as the crown prince's newly betrothed and now one of the most powerful bloodlines in the polis. You need to heal from this process, so you have some time to rest, but you can't hide for long."

I *do* open my eyes at that, and I feel my face split into a horrible grin. "Of course, my social engagements, where I'll be made to dance for the amusement of others. My father's death must not be enough to excuse me. Whatever shall I do to make amends?" My voice has taken on a shrill, broken note. "How long?" I ask. "Until the wedding."

He hesitates. "One month. That's part of the rush."

One month until I'm bound to yet another monster. Except this one will be worse than the one sitting next to me. More tears leak from the corners of my eyes. "Just leave me alone."

"I can do that, but only if you promise not to act out."

"What am I, a child?"

"Sometimes you behave like one."

For a moment, rage blinds me, but then it occurs to me that he might be testing me. I take a long breath out through my nose, my jaw locked. I grate out the words, "I promise."

"Thank you," the shade says. There's a heavy silence, and I wonder if he's going to speak again. I want him to *go*. But then I hear him say, "I meant what I said earlier, at the ball. We each have something the other wants. If—"

"*Get*," I enunciate slowly, "*out*."

The dead man vanishes without another word. Maybe he's telling the truth, but in the moment I can't care. He as good as led my father to the executioner's block. Even if he can help me, I spit on his help. I'll find my own way.

The way to be free of him.

I can't let him realize what I'm up to, of course, and so I'll need to do a better job of pretending to cooperate. And soon, I'll try discovering some answers for myself, starting *where* my father told me to follow in his footsteps.

For now, I roll over in bed and weep until exhaustion takes me.

At some point, lying in bed, I feel arms come around me. I almost think I'm dreaming the sensation, but all my dreams have been nightmares. This is too nice. For a moment in the darkness, I think it's my mother, comforting me like she used to, but the skin is too firm and as smooth as silk, where my mother's had been yielding and rough. And then I smell the perfume, and I recognize the voice near my ear.

141

"You don't have to say anything. Anything at all," Lydea whispers. "But I know what you're feeling. And I'm here for you."

I don't respond, and I soon fall back asleep in the sweet circle of those red-streaked arms, stained in her mother's blood. When I next awake, the princess is gone.

But she was real. As real as she has ever been, and I won't forget it.

———

No one else visits me. Not Penelope, not Japha, and not—I shudder even to think—my *betrothed*. I sleep fitfully, but never for long. I'm tired, bone deep, but as soon as I close my eyes, I see my father fall to the ground, and I feel blood and fire wash over my skin, leaving behind the burn of these sigils.

The bloodline itself doesn't hurt after a while. It swirls in my head like a braided river, beckoning me to follow its sinuous lines, to make a path of its sigils, to weave their glowing strands into a tapestry magnificent or terrible.

But not all hurts affect the flesh. Some reach the spirit.

My father is gone, nearly as soon as I got him back. It's almost worse this way—not only a fresh pain, but a reopening of every deep cut his absence inflicted upon me as a child, which I've tried so hard to bandage over the years.

But the thought of my mother always keeps me from falling. I try to stay strong for her, to see her safe at home and supported. There's still hope for my mother, and even for myself, much more distant. It's that hope that reaches out and lifts me up.

I'm not allowed to see my mother, no matter how many times I ask, and so I refuse to leave my bed until I feel ready. It doesn't hurt that I truly need the time to heal and regain my strength.

No more than a week after I've received my bloodline, no more than a week during which I cry all the tears I have inside me and heal all the wounds I *can* heal, I finally get up.

142

I have three weeks. Three weeks to either enjoy the last of my life as I know it, or three weeks to find an alternative to my fate.

And there's an alternative I haven't yet considered. I don't want to, but it's there, another path branching. Except this one is much darker.

The apartment has been emptied of all but my meager belongings and the furniture. Drifting around, I feel a little like a ghost here without my father or the others. It seems my aunt, now without her daughter *or* her husband, has moved out, leaving the whole place to me alone. I have a hunch where she's gone, but I have more important things to investigate and I don't really care.

I can't celebrate my solitude, besides. I won't be left alone here for long. Either I'll be forced to marry Kineas and join him in his quarters, or I'll escape from Thanopolis . . . or I'll be dead.

14

I assume I'll meet resistance trying to go to my father's office, either from the dead man or any number of people who might be overly curious about the whereabouts of the late Silvean Ballacra's daughter and Crown Prince Kineas's new betrothed. But everyone seems content to let my guardian keep track of me. It's the one benefit to being warded, I suppose, and the dead man doesn't seem to have any objection as I steal out of my palace apartments in the early morning and venture down the long, blossom-entwined marble corridors. It's peaceful at this hour, a breath of morning dew and the perfume of flowers in the air. It perturbs me that I'm already growing used to the ridiculous wealth surrounding me.

At my destination I finally meet some resistance, but only in the form of the vine-carved wooden door. It doesn't seem to be locked, at least not with any physical mechanism. My father opened it with sigils.

I have *thousands* of sigils as my disposal now, thanks to my bloodline, but I don't know how to use them properly. My father never got the chance to teach me like he promised, and now he never will. I hate the sight of them. Their true meanings come to me in flashes of inspiration or murderous rage—a glowing path of them opening in my mind, guiding me to wondrous or horrible possibilities. And yet, something as mundane as opening a door seems beyond my reach at the moment. Or at least nothing comes to mind, no magical way forward, as I consider the door.

Maybe if I simply try to *move* the door . . .

At the thought, the jamb explodes inward in a shower of splinters, whipping the door on its hinges to crash violently against the inner wall.

I glance around in shock. "Oops."

The dead man shoots me an exasperated look as he appears next to me. The only other people nearby are across the gardens that sprawl before my father's office. I quickly duck into the ruined doorway to avoid their notice.

I leave the dead man outside. He doesn't try to follow me, only looks mildly amused as I try to close the door in his face; it hangs crookedly now and doesn't latch. And yet *this* I can do. I simply move all the wood back into place . . . except with more delicacy this time. When I'm finished, it looks as if I never touched it.

After I'm standing inside, safely alone—though never *truly* alone with the dead man lurking who knows where—I don't know where to begin. I light a lamp near the door with a wave of my fingers, tracing the less familiar sigil in the air. Other lamps follow its lead, one by one, around the office. *Ignite* is a sigil I've only just learned from Japha. My father never trusted me with it as a child— perhaps with good reason.

I step carefully over piles of books and papers on the floor that my father already managed to displace since I organized the space for him before he died.

I have to blink the sting from my eyes as I imagine him leaning against his desk, tired but smiling at me. He was *just* here, in this spot, and now it seems so impossible and wrong that he isn't. That he's simply *gone*.

I *cannot* get lost in crying again. To distract myself, I move to study the piece of paper tacked to the wall, the one he seemed to indicate was important last time I was here with him. I stare at the sigil: a strange crisscross formed of thick, red lines, as if it's been drawn in blood by the tip of a finger. I still have no clue what it means. Maybe one of the many books scattered around could tell me, if only I could read better.

You might just have to follow in my footsteps.

Follow your eye.

My father knew I couldn't read well, sigils or otherwise. Maybe he left me more of a *map* to follow.

And maybe he drew that map on my skin, with his blood. He contributed new sigils to the bloodline as he gave me his life—his magical footsteps, in a sense.

I just have to use my eyes to find the path. He left me a starting point on the scrap of paper tacked to the wall. I look at the first place on my skin to occur to me, raising my right hand. And in the center of my palm, as if my father knew I would look there first, is the exact sigil on the wall. The only problem: It's surrounded by other sigils, just like every other sigil on my body aside from the lone one on my cheek. If this is a map, a pathway, I have no idea where to go from here. But I can't help the burst of hope that tears through me, and I grin like an idiot.

Then I realize I *am* an idiot, and drop both my hand and my grin. The dead man can't read my mind as far as I can tell, but he *is* incredibly adept at reading my body language. For reasons I don't want to consider, the thought brings warmth to my cheeks.

He doesn't reappear to ask what I'm up to. Maybe he's uninterested in my rifling, or he has no understanding of sigils as a shade, only an ability to sense oncoming blood magic of the potentially destructive sort. But that doesn't mean he's not watching. I pick up a book and pretend to leaf through it while my thoughts spin. At least the pages have pictures.

Follow your eye.

Perhaps I'm right about the map being on my body. And yet I can't guess the path from my hand, so maybe he meant to help me out with clues in the room. I lean against the wall in front of the tacked-up paper, facing the office from behind his desk. It's not too hard to bend my head toward the book while surreptitiously shooting glances up through my lashes.

There, indented in the back of his wooden desk chair, I find it. My father must have used his magic to put a sigil so lightly and perfectly there, so the dead man wouldn't notice or grow suspicious. This one has more sinuous lines like waves. I'm *fairly* certain I've seen it above the sigil in the center of my palm, but I don't yet want to check to make sure. If the pattern holds, I imagine I might find another one from the perspective of the chair. Shifting as if uncomfortable, I sidle over to the desk to sit down and scoot over a sheaf of papers before setting the open book in front of me.

Underneath the stack of papers is another sigil, sunken into the wood of the desk, this one like an angular hourglass. To get a view from the desktop, I'll have to look up. I wait a few moments, flip through a few more pages of the book, and then sigh as if I'm frustrated, stretching my arms overhead and tilting my face toward the ceiling.

This sigil has been pressed into the carved wooden clouds. It's directly over the one on the desk, so there isn't anywhere else I can look from there. I drop my hands into my lap and pick at my nails as if bored, studying my palm.

Those same four sigils in the room weave a diagonal line from the center of my palm onto the inside of my pointer finger, where a few more sigils continue until ending at my last knuckle, like they do on all my fingers.

Perhaps here is my path. Before I can try to trace it, either in the air or only in my mind, the dead man appears, making me jump and sit up straight in the chair like a child caught breaking the rules.

"Sorry to intrude, but I must," he says, before I can try to come up with an excuse for what I'm doing in here.

My guardian doesn't seem to want one. He merely waits, dark, silent, and strange.

"Were you going to say something, or just skulk around like a ghost?"

"Are you all right?" His voice is curiously soft.

And that makes me furious. "Don't act like you care."

"I do care," he says, as if somewhat surprised himself. As I hold his gaze, something in his guard seems to drop. To leave a tentative opening.

I remember the odd ways he's helped me, even as he's held me back. The moments of wonder when I truly seem to see him. *This* is one of those moments. I should use it. "*Why* do you care?"

"Because it's my duty." He hesitates. "And despite your rough demeanor, you're kind to those *you* care about, and right now you have no one else looking out for you but me. Maybe Japha, but they can't do much. Also . . ." He purses his lips. "You hate this place as much as I do, so it makes me more inclined to empathy."

The words almost sound like an accident.

I gape at him over the desk. "You hate this place?"

He folds his arms and looks away. "I didn't say that."

"You did, too. What the hell, Ivrilos?"

He blinks down at me. "You called me by name."

"Because maybe for once you sounded like a person and not like a corpse," I say quickly, trying to mask my embarrassment. "But an *absurd* person," I add. "How can you hate it here when you do all you do to uphold it? After what you *just* did to my father?"

"I have to."

"What's making you? I mean, I have *you* keeping me in line. What's keeping you here?"

Who do you *answer to?* I almost add, though I don't want to press my luck.

He doesn't respond, but his expression cracks open even more,

148

revealing something raw and weary. Hope flares in me. Perhaps I'm not wrong to try to reach out to him—truly, and not just as a ruse. To treat him as more than a dead man. Maybe I can convince him to break his shadowy hold over me, no scheming required.

"You could just . . . let me go?" I suggest softly. "*Please*, Ivrilos?"

His face doesn't so much harden as go deathly still—the openness shuttered—and I know I've made a mistake.

"I can't," he says firmly. "I told you, I need you."

"Why?" I nearly cry. "For what?"

"I can't say."

Of course that's his reply. "Because you know I won't like it when you tell me?" I guess.

His silence is answer enough. I collapse back in the chair.

The shade suddenly appears right next to me, crouching on my side of the desk, his eyes level with mine. His dark gaze swallows me.

"I'll continue to help you however I can," he says, his voice low. "Especially with *him*." He glances off to the side, eyes narrowing, as if he can see Kineas through the many walls of the palace.

It nearly makes me smile, despite myself. "But you won't let me kill him?"

He sighs. "No, I won't."

Fine. "Then I hope you like standing over top of Kineas, because you'll be doing a lot more of it if you don't want me to try killing him. It's not the *absolute* worst arrangement in the world," I add, leaning my head back. "At least you have nice eyes."

Ivrilos's smile—brief, barely there, but wholly genuine—is rather nice, too.

Then he frowns. "Unfortunately, now that you're up and about, you're expected at your lesson. That was what I came here to tell you."

I sit up in a rush. "Dear goddess, more lessons in *what*?"

"Sigils."

I nearly burst out laughing—I actually need to know more about sigils at this exact moment.

"Do please make a more subtle entrance than this." He casts a wry glance at the door I blasted open.

It surprises me to realize he can be funny . . . for a dead man. That doesn't mean I want him out of my life any less.

"And please don't try to kill your tutor," he adds. "I'm asking nicely."

"Who's my tutor?"

But the shade has vanished, leaving me to discover that on my own.

Bastard.

15

You must always strive to improve, push your boundaries, and hopefully reach beyond the knowledge of your bloodline so that you may add to it when you pass it on. Being able to read and write sigils is the *bare* minimum." With this, Captain Marklos looks at me.

I stand in a sunny courtyard lined in marble colonnades and troughs of water, a lush garden at the far end and a patio with a massive table coated in sand for practicing sigil-writing, and all at once I determine that magic lessons are the worst of the lot. It's not the subject so much as the instructor. Still, I need these lessons.

But it's no wonder Ivrilos warned me against killing my tutor. I don't hate the captain merely because he didn't like my father, or even because he treats me with a bloviating condescension that makes me want to stab him in the eye. It's because he was the one to expose me as a bloodmage. He hit me, cut me, set my blood alight like pitch in the Hall of the Wards, and he felt self-righteous about it.

He's self-righteous about everything, turns out.

Marklos is the rare bloodline within the palace who isn't female, due to the fact that he's a commoner. And yet, because of the captain's skill—according to him—he teaches all the new royal bloodmages, which now include me as Kineas's betrothed, along with Japha, Lydea, and two younger girls, cousins who have yet to inherit their bloodlines but who need a solid base in sigil work before then. A base that I'm sorely lacking, Marklos is happy to point out. Already this first lesson, he's gleefully reminded me several times of what I already know: Despite my incredibly long bloodline, I don't understand how to use the half of it—*most* of it, more like—and what I've managed to tap into has been through instinct alone.

I smile at him. "I'd say the bare minimum is being able to tell your ass from your face and to teach a class without constantly passing wind. Because that's all I hear from you."

Lydea chokes on laughter, half-heartedly concealing it with a slender hand. Japha raises an eyebrow, but keeps their expression otherwise neutral. I haven't really seen them since the night of the ball. They never came to visit me, unlike Lydea, and their last words to me, *I didn't know*, still echo in my ears. Maybe they think I blame them. I'm not entirely sure I *don't*, even though I know that's foolish.

I'm the most to blame.

The two young cousins, girls with sandy blond hair, stare at me aghast after my insult.

To be fair, Marklos *has* taught me a few things. I've learned the sigils most commonly used for opening magically sealed doors, and gleaned that a few of the sigils in the strange string my father left me have something to do with channeling life energy and shielding. Others the captain didn't recognize, and warned me that writing out mysterious sigils whose meaning I don't yet know could result in my early death and the loss of a nigh-legendary bloodline.

Despite seeming to care more about my bloodline than my life, he's shown he isn't a complete idiot. Though he does make an easy target.

Marklos scowls at me. "If you think all I'm telling you is wind, how about we practice dueling. Japha, come spar with me. Lydea and Rovan, you two are together. You girls," he says to the cousins, as if he hasn't bothered to learn their names, "pair up. Remember:

No using fire to attack. And sigils as external weapons only! Nothing internal. If one of you causes so much as a headache or a muscle cramp, you'll regret it."

Using sigils to harm a body's *insides* is something I've never considered, although I do remember seeing my father rip open someone's neck. Healers exist, so why not the opposite? It follows, even if the thought makes me shudder. I could just as easily have torn Bethea's blood *out* of her instead of gently lifting it.

Before Japha steps forward to join Marklos, they whisper in my ear, "I'm going to knock him on his ass. Or is it his face?"

It feels like a hand extended to me. I stifle a giggle, which earns me a relieved smile from Japha. Then their expression grows serious. "Rovan, I'm sorry. I accompanied you to the ball, and knowing how I felt after losing my sister and my mother . . . if I'd had someone to blame, I might have done it. And I didn't know if I could face that, with you. Also, I'm shit at comforting people when they're truly sad. Pouting and hungover like you were before, no problem." They shake their head gently. "This was something else."

My throat squeezes tight. Japha understands me so well. I appreciate their acknowledgment, and there really is nothing to forgive. I manage a shaky nod before Lydea slides between us, capturing my attention like a cat snagging a bird out of the air. Today, the princess wears a red peplos that matches her bloodline and offsets her black hair. She's a glorious, deadly thing. Something in my belly clenches in anticipation. Or nervousness.

The perfect distraction.

"He paired me with you because I'm positively evil at dueling and merciless in sparring sessions." Lydea folds her sigil-lined arms and smiles. "He probably thinks I view you as a threat and I'll happily put you in your place. Ah, Marklos and his ilk, always trying to stuff others into their own meager understanding."

There's no trace of sympathy for me in *her* voice. Though, after she came to hold me in the darkness while I cried, there doesn't need to be. Lydea is so strong. But it's a brittle strength, and I realize I *never* want to see her crack. She doesn't have to show me what's behind all that armor that she's so carefully built, living in this place—because I think I already know. I would never want to strip her, leave her naked.

Well, at least not figuratively.

I can't help grinning, despite the darkness still ready to swallow me, despite the bloodline staining my skin, despite Kineas—no, I can't think about him yet—despite *everything*. Lydea and Japha make me oddly *happy*, in the face of all odds. "So you're not going to knock me on my ass?"

"I didn't say *that*." Lydea assumes a position a few paces away, raising her hands, fingers slightly spread. "Besides, you need to be ready for what's coming. My brother doesn't play nice, either." Her voice drops. "As I'm sure you've heard. You're more than a match for him, Rovan, but . . . one can't help worrying." Before I can get too distracted by *this* revelation—*she's* worried about *me?*—she asks, "Are you ready?"

I doubt it. I've never dueled before, in practice or in earnest. Especially not with a princess who wants to kiss me or stab me—I'm not entirely sure which is the stronger impulse.

Marklos shouts, "Begin!" and Lydea pulls every wooden practice sword off a weapon's rack under the colonnade and hurls them at me.

I barely have time to slam them aside with a wave of flame, the pathway of sigils in my mind telling me how. Fire is the first thing to come to me, maybe because the weapons are wood, or maybe because I have the urge to burn things lately. The countermove works, and they clatter to the ground in a charred and smoking heap.

"No fire!" Marklos shouts.

I spin on him, where he's in the middle of his own duel with Japha. "I wasn't attacking, you b——"

But then I can't talk, because I'm underwater. Or at least my *head* is. From the shoulders down, I only feel the warm air of the courtyard, but my eyes can barely make out anything through the shimmering curtain of bubbles that rises from my gaping mouth. I can't breathe. I claw at my face, as if to tear off a mask, but I merely get my hand wet. The water stays put.

I manage to curse myself through my rising urgency. *Sigils, use sigils, not your hand, you idiot!*

My bloodline provides an answer once again, but as soon as I swipe at my face, parting the water and dragging in a ragged breath, the water closes over my head again. When I scatter it into mist, more water, flowing from its ample source in the troughs, covers back over my face . . . but not before I glimpse the princess's wicked grin.

I have to stop Lydea, not the water. *Stop Lydea.* Another pathway opens in my mind, and I follow it in a panic. Before I know what I've done, I'm thrown off my feet. I land hard on rough ground, bruising my tailbone and scraping my palms. But whatever I did must have been enough, because the water enclosing my head bursts apart, soaking my shoulders and chest. When I sit up, coughing and mopping wet hair from my eyes, I see that the patio tiles have erupted. Thick roots from the trees in the garden are lashing through the cracks like tentacles, seizing Lydea's arms and twining around her fingers. The princess manages a few more sigils, however, and a massive root whips around my neck, dragging me flat on my back and choking off my air.

But I don't need air to pull the same trick on Lydea. Soon we're both on the ground, being strangled to death. The only sounds are from the two of us thrashing, and breath trying to wheeze through my constricted throat. The others must have quit their sparring to watch.

"All right, that's enough!" shouts Marklos.

I suck in a rasping breath as the root releases me. I remain on my back, battered, soaked, and covered in grit, staring dazedly up at the gleaming, veil-covered sky through the stars in my vision. I actively appreciate the air in my lungs.

Lydea appears above, leaning over me, smiling. She isn't too much the worse for wear, only a few streaks of dirt and early bruising visible on her neck and wrists.

"If I'd known you wanted to tie me up, I would have approached you differently," she says with a smirk, offering me a hand.

Wincing, I lift myself onto my elbows first. "Now that I know what *you're* into," I croak, "I'm a little reluctant to tangle with you again." I rub my throat, where I no doubt have blossoming bruises of my own.

The princess laughs. "I'm not so cruel as all that. I can prove it to you if you'll let me." The look in her eyes dredges up heat in my wet cheeks—along with carefully buried hope in my chest. Maybe the princess *can* help me. But trust is so much harder than doubt. She waggles her hand again, and this time I take it, struggling to my feet.

Japha steps daintily across the overturned tiles of the courtyard to join us. "Not one for subtlety, are you, Rovan, dear?"

"I'm impressed," Lydea says. "I might have years of practice on you, but you were still a match for me."

"I suppose you could call that a draw," Marklos growls from where he stands between the two cousins, as if he's been shielding them, "though Rovan's technique is sorely lacking. All brute force and absolutely no finesse. She'd be a danger to others on a battlefield."

"You're no fun, Captain," says Lydea dismissively. "Who cares how she fights, if she puts on a good show?"

"*Who cares? Who cares* about their comrades?" Marklos shakes his head in disgust and begins sketching sigils to start clearing the mess. "Her father didn't, but I'm hoping Rovan can be taught differently."

Taught, like a dog. Trained to sit, stay. How to eat, how to talk. Made to be their pet bloodline and marry Kineas.

The thought reminds me that I have to focus, not indulge in distractions. I can't get caught up in their plans for me, or even with Lydea. And maybe I can glean information about more than just sigils today.

"Have you heard from your sister?" I ask the princess, as we both begin straightening our clothes and attempting to brush the dirt from our skin.

"No, but that's rather the point," she says, smiling sharply. The mask is convincing. "To cut off all communication with the living so as to better commune with the dead."

"Poor Delphia," Japha murmurs.

Indeed. Delphia, the youngest and kindest one. The one who looks most like her mother with her cloud of white hair and bright silver eyes. Is this newest injustice an echo of the one against Cylla?

"I don't see why such extremes are necessary," I say. "We bloodmages have no problem communing with the dead."

"Yes," Lydea says. "But to form a connection with *all* the dead, you have to be . . . well, dead, or very much like it."

"I wonder what the nature of our guardian bond is," I muse, as if merely curious.

Surprisingly, it isn't Lydea but the younger of the cousins, Namae, who speaks up, having drifted closer. "I think it has to do with royal blood," she says as haughtily as only a twelve-year-old royal brat might.

Japha rolls their eyes, but I force myself to ask patiently, "What do you mean?"

"*My* guardian says he was a royal living in the palace like me—that he *is* still royal, in the underworld, so of course that's why he chose someone like me. Aias died young. He likes me." She sounds very proud of this fact.

"You need some lessons in logic, because that says nothing about the connection," Lydea says. "There are commoners who are wards, like our *esteemed* tutor—"

"And like me," I put in, sounding waspish, but my mind is preoccupied. The girl's guardian is royal. Ivrilos certainly *looks* royal, with that circlet he's so fond of wearing, and he intimated that he's surrounded by well-bred people—though few of them women—in something like a palace in the underworld, and they likely serve someone like a king. Are *all* guardians the shades of dead royalty?

Lydea carries on, "And everyone, even commoners, can be elevated to heroic immortality in the afterlife, so no doubt there are common guardians as well."

I scoff, hoping I'm not overdoing it. "The afterlife is probably just as unfair as life, meaning only dead royals are awarded the highest honors. That's even how it goes in the stories: The kings and princes who wage the bloodiest wars or slay the biggest mythical beasts or steal away the prettiest maidens get to be immortalized as heroes." Quick and nonchalant, I add, "What about you, Lydea? Do you think your guardian is a royal?"

"Graecus?" She shrugs. "He's very stuffy, so he may have been. Who knows? I try to avoid conversation with him as much as possible."

"I'm nearly positive Damios was," Japha says, "though he won't tell me precisely."

"Graecus." Lydea glances off to the side, at the person the rest of us can't see. "Were you a royal, like Namae's guardian here?" She waits, and then turns back to the living. "He says he doesn't remember." Her mask is back in place. She's trying to look bored by the topic, but something in her eyes tells me she doesn't believe her guardian and finds it odd he would lie. She sighs theatrically. "Always so dull, the dead."

At least Lydea and Namae have let slip their guardian's names. I already know Japha's. I don't want to ask any more questions about royal lines so no one marks my interest, but I can't help asking the captain, "Marklos, what is the name of your guardian?"

"Why?" He's at the other end of the courtyard, still tucking roots back into the earth with sigils. "We're going to have to get a shadow priest in here for the stone," he grumbles half to himself.

"It's not for my own interest. My guardian wants to know."

Ivrilos suddenly appears at my shoulder. "Rovan, I know perfectly well who Klytios is."

I ignore him, saying to the captain, "But I don't want to do him any favors and I despise talking to you, so never mind." I turn back to the others, leaving Marklos sputtering. "I don't know about the rest of you, but I need to get out of these wet clothes."

Rather, I *need* to get into the royal gallery.

As I cross the destroyed patio, duck under the colonnade, and head down the hall leading back to my quarters, leaving everyone else blinking at my abrupt departure, Ivrilos keeps pace with me. "You *tricked* me. What are you doing?"

"Nothing," I say without looking at him.

He's scrutinizing me. "You're up to some mischief. I can see it in your eyes."

"No, I'm not. I'm upset. Tormenting other people, including you, makes my own torment less tedious."

"That's not like you."

"You don't know me very well at all, do you?"

"I—" Before my guardian can finish, another voice cuts him off.

"Rovan!" It's Lydea, hurrying between the marble columns

159

after me, Japha on her heels. "Japha and I were hoping you might join us for a glass of wine in my apartments. You know, unwind after our class."

I have places to be and secrets to discover . . . but I've never been one to say no to a full cup. Besides, this little gathering might be about more than just wine.

And perhaps I'm finding it harder and harder to say no to Lydea.

16

Sometime later that evening, I lie on a couch in the princess's parlor. The ceiling overhead is midnight black marble inset with silver stars and a glorious full moon at the center that actually glows. The couch underneath me is more of a bed, wide enough to stretch out in either direction, upholstered in silver and white silk patterned like billowing clouds and strewn with black and blue pillows. Wine cups are now scattered across the low surrounding tables carved in red wood to look like poppy blossoms. Japha's legs are tangled in mine—we've been trying something called "leg wrestling" that I lost at miserably and that ended in a fit of laughing—and my head rests on Lydea's stomach.

She feels *so* good. She's lazily running her fingers through my blue-tinted hair, while Japha rearranges the rings on their fingers and holds their hands up to admire them against the dark, starry ceiling.

A few weeks ago, I could never have pictured myself lounging in a place like this, entwined with people like this. And for once, it isn't horrifying to find myself here in the palace with *royals*.

Because they're not just that. They're . . . my friends.

And maybe more, in Lydea's case, though my stomach ties itself in nervous knots to think about the possibilities—and not all of them pleasant, if the princess isn't trustworthy.

"What about you, Rovan?" Lydea asks. She's been expounding on why she prefers women after we all soundly lamented our respective betrothals, as well as complained about Marklos, the king, our guardians, and pretty much anyone else on two legs who isn't us or someone we currently find attractive.

We've all carefully avoided mention of my father.

It hasn't all been idle chatter. They've warned me repeatedly about Kineas, even if none of us knows exactly how I'm going to avoid him. And, despite receiving reminders in no uncertain terms that access is restricted—that not even Lydea and Japha have been allowed inside—I've managed to find out exactly where in the palace the royal gallery is located, with the excuse that I want to see who among them is attractive or not. The silliness of my reasoning has hopefully allayed suspicion from anyone listening. But now I've had rather a lot of wine and the direction of my conversation has grown less focused.

"I go wherever beauty takes me," I say with a grand sweep of my arm, "whether that's to the lips of a man or woman." I grin and jostle Japha with a leg. "Or neither."

I try not to think about one particular man I find beautiful. A dead man. The beautiful *woman* running her fingers through my hair is once again enough to distract me.

"At least you're not entirely hopeless. Ugh, men." Lydea shudders underneath me. "Most of them are too hairy and not nearly pretty enough to even tolerate kissing, let alone . . . *ugh*," she repeats. "Alldan is a green-haired . . . *man*."

"He looked quite handsome," I admit. "If a bit unusual." My father looked "unusual," too, so I don't actually find Alldan's appearance all that strange. But I don't want to talk about my father.

"That's not the problem, I suppose. My mother had white hair as iridescent as an opal and silver eyes, as does Delphia . . ." Lydea trails off, no doubt trying not to think of her mother *or* her sister.

"Did you know, those features originally came from magic?" Japha asks in a light tone. "Rumor has it, Skylleans began altering themselves centuries ago, just for fun. The colors come naturally now." They gesture at my hair. "I guess they just stuck, over the generations. It makes sense. They've wielded blood magic and bloodlines longer than anyone."

At my surprised expression, they say, "Yes, I know that bloodlines weren't the first king Athanatos's grand innovation. My father's people kept their own histories." Japha's look grows distant as they stare up at the black ceiling. "This city was once a glorified cult of death worshippers. Here, they all say the first king—the first to conquer nigh everyone in the region and bring them all under the rule of Thanopolis—was the first to introduce blood magic into the fabric of his society. But really, it was his wife, a Skyllean. She brought with her knowledge of bloodlines and sigils, things that had once been seen as heretical witchcraft in the polis. Suspicious, is it not, that no one celebrates her as the 'first queen'? There are historical sources, now lost along with the once-great libraries of my father's once-great kingdom, that say the reason isn't just because no one trusted her. It's because she didn't share her knowledge willingly."

Everything that King Tyros did to Cylla, then, is an echo of what the first king did to *his* wife. I don't want to mention that in case the topic is too painful for Lydea . . . or if she doesn't know the full truth of her mother's past. Still, this all begs the question: *Why* has Skyllea come to make peace through Alldan and Lydea's betrothal? One would think they could never trust Athanatos's royal line after being twice betrayed.

Japha carries on in a casual tone, as if this isn't a risky topic all around. "The first king, like his people, despised blood magic, despised Skyllea, but not from fear. It was jealousy of their power. And you know what they say about keeping your friends close but your enemies closer . . ."

Something itches in my mind. Maybe Skyllea has the same idea now. I almost don't dare hope that they can still shelter me, maybe

163

even *help* me. And I certainly can't share the thought out loud, even if my friends wouldn't blame me for it.

Besides, the Skyllean delegation didn't help my father at the ball. They disavowed him. Left him to Thanopolis's vultures.

"We're still doing that to this day"—Lydea sighs as if this is a dull and dreary conversation—"bringing the most powerful bloodlines into the family like priceless works of art to add to the royal collection. My mother. Rovan's father." She says it quietly, but she doesn't shy away from it. For some reason, I appreciate that—the acknowledgment without dwelling. She taps me on the nose. "The *lucky* commoner here and there."

"Some of us royals aren't thrilled, either," Japha grumbles. "We get the long bloodlines, but the short end of the stick. The short *life*."

"And it's a burden usually borne by royal women," Lydea adds. "Fancy that."

"But that's because the women of Athanatos's line have the greater aptitude for blood magic, didn't you know?"

I don't need Japha's sardonic tone—or the evidence presented by Japha themself—to doubt this. It seems that royal women have been intentionally saddled with their bloodlines like horses and made to bear guardians.

As if reading my mind, Lydea laughs humorlessly, gently jostling my head. "Women get all the short sticks, so why not?"

I want to ask more, but our little trio has doubtlessly reached the limits of what's safe to discuss. After all, it isn't just the three of us in the room. Graecus and Damios might be listening in, not just Ivrilos. I don't want their dead ears perking up any more than they already might be.

Japha seems to sense my nervousness. "Now, are you *sure* Alldan's stick is short?"

Lydea hurls a pillow at them. "You're welcome to find out, if you want." She pauses, blinking. "*Would* you want? I mean hypothetically. I haven't ever asked your preferences, dear cousin."

Japha spreads their arms wide. "I'm with Rovan. Select the prettiest to kiss, whatever is between their legs, but also *be* the prettiest. I'm the best of both worlds . . . nay, my *own* world . . . something in between and also nowhere else. Perfectly unique." They frame their face with waggling, bejeweled fingers.

I laugh. "It's difficult to argue with that logic. Unfortunately, while we're together on our preferences in others, I'm with Lydea when it comes to herself. I feel pretty thoroughly a woman."

Japha shrugs. "Not everyone can be as perfect as I." They glance coyly at me through dark lashes. "You are gorgeous, though, so anytime you get sick of my sweet cousin Lydea . . ."

The princess nudges me with a thrust of her hip, giving me that wicked grin that I'm beginning to love. "You're not beholden to me, dear. I would neither expect it nor desire it, not with how many rules we already must follow. I would only appreciate it if you considered *sharing* your affections."

Something about that sounds almost exactly right to me, but then I squint at Japha, whose finer details may be a little blurred by the wine. "You're not serious."

Japha raises an eyebrow. "And cross Cousin Kineas?" They purse their lips, staring back up at the ceiling. "It would almost be worth it just for that, but no. In all honesty, I . . . I've never been inspired to do much more than kiss anyone, perhaps leg wrestle at the most. No matter how beautiful they are. I've never sought it out. Ever. I *can*, I just don't care to." Despite their initial hesitation, they sound matter-of-fact, not embarrassed. Japha is never embarrassed, and I admire that about them. "All the more reason I wasn't looking forward to this betrothal, even with someone as lovely as Helena. I know I should count myself lucky to have her, considering

165

my options. She's kind, someone I could care for, and I don't want to hurt her. Some hurts can't be avoided, for either of us, but I can try my best . . . which probably means not kissing *you*, my lovely," Japha adds with a wink for me.

"Wish I could say my betrothed was someone I could care for," Lydea mutters—accepting Japha, just like that. I admire that about her, also: her ability to take people like me and Japha exactly as we are. "I think Alldan dislikes me more than I him," she muses, "even if he does a better job at hiding it."

Here is where I'm supposed to complain about Kineas, but I don't want to. Not that I don't trust Lydea and Japha to commiserate. Kineas simply makes me sick to think about.

"What Alldan *doesn't* hide," Lydea continues, "is his abject horror at the thought of my sister in the necropolis. I can relate. But the two of them spent some time together before she was banished there, since *I* wouldn't socialize with him. I think he's infatuated. Under normal circumstances, I would encourage him. Poor fool. Now there's only me."

She doesn't sound very sympathetic.

"If Helena ever takes another lover because I can't offer her what she needs," Japha says suddenly, "I would welcome it. I don't blame my aunt Penelope, you know," they add, glancing at us sideways, "for charming my father in my mother's stead. They were all forced into roles they didn't want, and they were rebelling—something I can definitely get behind. But even if they *hadn't* been forced to be with anyone, and they wanted to be with more than one person . . . I wouldn't blame them, either. We each have different gifts to offer, so why *not* share? Be a *little* beholden, but to more than one?"

"Now, Japha!" Lydea says, sounding both delighted and calculating. "Indeed, why *should* I treat my dalliances as lesser than my betrothal when they matter to me more?"

I surprise myself by speaking. "I think I've always wondered something similar, but I couldn't find the words or imagine anyone understanding. So I kept everything . . . light . . . with everyone. Temporary. Well, also because I was planning on leaving the city. But now I'm stuck." *For now*, I think, and then I smile at Japha. "Just so we're clear, I can still share with you, too, only without the kissing and bed play. Those things don't make a friendship more important."

Japha smiles back at me. "I know. But I'm happy to hear you say it."

I want to savor this sudden feeling. Somehow I feel rich—truly rich despite the wealth that has already been showered upon me. An *inner* wealth. An *inner* warmth, like molten gold in my chest.

I hold Japha's eyes, trying to stay in this moment with my new friends, to let myself *feel* and to not brush everything aside with a joke . . . but I can hold out only for so long. "Frankly, I'm relieved you're not interested in me like that. It's better for me, too." I stretch like a cat, untangling my legs from theirs and draping my arms over Lydea, arching my back and yawning. "Having the both of you that way would simply be exhausting."

My yawn turns to a yelp when Lydea gooses my breast. When I roll to look at her in shock, she gives me another evil grin.

"I should already be enough to exhaust you," she says.

Japha sighs, sitting up and dusting off their shoulder in mock disgust. "Should I leave you two alone?"

I can't take my eyes off Lydea, who's staring at me with a heavy, liquid gaze I want so desperately to sink into.

Let yourself, I think. *Be here. Feel this. This might be all you get of happiness.*

So I dive in. I reach for Lydea without another thought, and soon my lips and tongue are too occupied to answer Japha. I'm lost in the silky softness of the princess, my hands tangled in her hair. Her own fingers scrabble to unwind my strophion, while she kisses me back with a ferocity that steals my breath.

Luckily, Japha has answered their own question and left the room by the time my shoulder clasps come undone and my breasts spill out of my peplos into Lydea's waiting palms. I sink down onto her, her hands digging into me. I put my own hands to much better use, unraveling her strophion.

I hated the sight of my own breasts covered in sigils, but Lydea's are beautiful. Perfect, not marred. I can't help kissing them, and she groans.

I should be nervous. I am, a little. I've done this a few times, but never with a princess. But it's her gasp that lets me know: She doesn't care that she's a princess and I'm not. She only cares that the two of us are here, right now. And we want each other.

We *do* trust each other, despite all odds. At least enough for whispered secrets, clandestine kisses . . . and the freedom to share such things with other people.

"Rovan," she murmurs, an ache in her voice that undoes me. Her armor hasn't cracked, but she's peeling some of it away voluntarily. I want to melt into those gaps. Soon, I'm clawing her peplos higher up her thighs. Finding the waiting, wonderful warmth between them. She gasps.

I lose myself in the moment for a long time.

It's sometime later, in the middle of blissful oblivion, that Lydea surfaces to whisper in my ear in the lowest possible voice: "Both Japha and I are in. Don't worry about cost. We can get a ship, or find some other way, but you have to take us with you. And first we have to get free of *them*. We hoped you might have some ideas."

I have no doubt whom she means—and I dearly hope my guardian isn't paying attention.

17

After leaving Lydea's quarters later that night—much later, the palace long asleep—I take a different path than usual back to my rooms, weaving drunkenly down torch-lit, empty marble corridors. At least, I want my guardian to think I'm drunk. I quietly sing a bawdy ditty to help with that, and perhaps to scare him away. Two birds with one off-key stone.

And then I slip into seemingly contented silence and find what I'm looking for: halfway down a long hallway of swirling blue and purple mosaics of grapes, illuminated only with scattered pools of flickering light, a pair of bleary-looking guards stand before an impressive, heavy set of double doors—exactly where Japha said they'd be during our conversation on Lydea's couch. Beyond the guarded doorway, the hallway turns a corner that's covered in enough vines and flowers to be the entrance to a forest glen. Wherever it goes, maybe to some private garden reserved only for the king, I don't need to know.

I duck out of sight behind a column, pretending to stifle giggles. "They can't see me," I whisper, seemingly to the air around me. "They'll know I'm drunk!"

"I think that's already obvious," my guardian says, appearing next to me, having finally lost patience with whatever silliness he imagines I'm up to. "Your rooms are *this* way." He points in the opposite direction.

"Ivrilos." His name is like magic—saying it gets his full attention. I keep a grin on my face, and he looks charmed in return. I hope it'll last. "I'm going to have a little fun, and nobody is going to get hurt. Trust me. *Please*."

His marble-smooth forehead immediately creases. "What—?"

I follow the path of sigils in my mind, my fingers moving, and the vines at the end of the hall come alive like writhing tentacles. The guards at the double doors exclaim in surprise, but their cries are quickly gagged. I can't see them, but I don't need to. Armor and swords barely clatter, muffled, as both guards are yanked off their feet and dragged as quietly as possible down the hallway, out of sight around the corner, by suddenly monstrous plant life.

I probably could have knocked them out by restricting the blood to their brain or something, but I don't trust myself enough to not accidentally kill them. They just need to be *occupied*.

"Rovan," Ivrilos says, alarmed. "What are you doing? Stop this, now!"

He's clearly *not* going to trust me long enough for me to get where I need to go. I'm amazed he's let me make it this far, frankly. I grope frantically for something to use against him. It's still too early to try the special set of sigils my father left me in his office.

But then I have it—Ivrilos's awkwardness, his prudish sense of propriety.

I let my eyes grow heavy lidded, my lips parting, and I make my voice as sultry as possible. "This . . . feeling . . . was too powerful to resist. I just had to be alone with you."

The words come up like cheap, too-sweet wine, but they seem to have the desired effect. Ivrilos's eyes widen in alarm.

"Why would you need to be . . . ?"

He trails off as my hands drift up past my collarbones. My strophion is already loose around my waist from when Lydea unwound it, so all I have to do is unfasten the gold pins at my shoulders and the whole top of my gown will fall away, just as it did for the princess. My fingers brush the clasps.

Ivrilos not only averts his eyes; he spins violently away as if the sight of me might catch him on fire.

Before he has any clue what I'm doing, I'm off, sprinting down the hall toward the double doors. I keep expecting to feel the cool touch of his hand, to grow dizzy, to fall before I make it. But I only hear Ivrilos's breathless and rather foul curse behind me, followed by his frantic muttering, and then my feet reach the low marble steps in front of the now-unguarded doors. I throw every sigil for opening at them that I know, and they fly open.

In seconds, I'm inside and the doors are closed behind me, seemingly undisturbed. I release the vines down the hall, and with them, the guards. With any luck, they'll have no idea I've dashed in here and will spend their time trying to find their trickster outside. Everything is suddenly quiet, aside from my rapid breathing.

I've *done* it. I'm in the royal gallery.

Which is almost pitch black. I lift my hand, and a small flame appears above my open palm—*plenty* of light to illuminate Ivrilos's absolutely livid face, looming right in front of me.

I nearly jump out of my skin. At least I manage to swallow a shriek.

"You insufferable, foolish creature," he hisses, leaning closer with every word.

I make my tone light. "First you curse, and now you're name-calling? I thought you were too high and mighty for that."

"This isn't a game!" he spits, his voice low but ferocious. "This place is *completely* forbidden, trespassing is punishable by death, and the entry wasn't guarded only by two mortals!" He tosses a hand at the doors. "Do you know how many invisible wards I had to dismantle before you stumbled into them like trip wires? I'm talking about *death* magic, put in place by shadow priests and other shades." He takes a deep breath, even though he doesn't really breathe, as far as I know. "But none so powerful as me, thank the goddess. And

171

now I have to put their protections *back* into place, exactly as they were, before anyone notices they're gone."

Already turning to the doors, he begins muttering again. I don't recognize any of the words; they sound *old*. I remember that while the written sigils for blood magic came from Skyllea, the spoken words of death magic originated here. Perhaps this is the parent language of the one we speak.

My voice comes out a little choked, and not only because I'm whispering—Ivrilos is scary when he's angry. "Why *did* you take the barriers down, instead of just tripping *me* before I reached them?"

He spins on me, apparently finished with his magic. "Because then the wrong people would have known you were here. I can't carry you, after all. Now let's go. I know another exit."

I square my shoulders, regaining some of my composure, and I don't budge. "But why do you care if someone catches me, *Ivrilos?*" I make a point to remind him we're on a first name basis now, for better or worse.

"No one can think I dropped my guard that much, *Rovan*."

My name on his tongue, in that throaty growl, thrills me for some unfathomable reason, lighting along me like fire touched to a line of pitch. Maybe it's because he *has* dropped his guard for me.

He must catch my reaction, because his eyes snag on mine above my flame's light and hold there. His tirade dies on his lips.

Something seems suspended between us then, heavy and charged. His gaze hits me like a punch to the stomach. It's hungry. Alight. An answering challenge to mine. My heart beats almost painfully in my chest.

I didn't expect this, not while he was busy yelling at me, not when he *doesn't* have a heartbeat.

I'm unready for the force of whatever sparks and flares between me and my guardian. My knees feel weak, like in the silly stories. Ivrilos seems taken by surprise, as well, and nearly looks as unsteady as me.

Finally, he tears his eyes away, breaking the strange spell. I can breathe again.

"I can't believe you tried to make me think . . ." He seems about to say more, and then shakes his head. "Only *you* would be so vulgar as to expose yourself as a distraction."

I nearly burst out laughing. "I wasn't actually going to. Besides, you've already seen *the girls*." I shimmy my shoulders. "It's not like they can bite you."

He glares back at me. "You tricked me. *Again*."

I arch a brow. "So you *wanted* me to drop my dress?"

"That's not the trick I meant," he says through gritted teeth, his expression strained. "You ran when I turned my back for decency's sake, when I was at least attempting to trust you. And before you can ask if that makes me angry, yes, it *does*."

I swallow whatever I was about to say. Not that I feel bad. Not exactly.

Ivrilos runs a pale hand back through his dark hair, nearly unseating his silver circlet. "I want to trust you, Rovan. At the very least, I don't want to hurt you. But if it doesn't at least *look* like I'm keeping you under control, it reflects poorly on me as your guardian. *I* won't be trusted, and I can't have that. I need to avoid scrutiny—the both of us do—as much as possible. Which ploys like this are making rather difficult."

I smile sweetly. "Then you should continue helping me and let me in on *your* ploys, and everything will be much easier."

His hands fall in fists at his sides. "No, I *should* have dropped you to the ground before you made it even close to this room. *Before* you attacked the guards. You've shown me exactly how far I can trust you—which is not far at all." His voice stays low, but he starts pacing before the doors, angry again, more animated than

I've ever seen him. He's mad at *himself* now, I realize. That doesn't happen often, by the looks of it. "I should have known. And *everyone* knows you're new to being warded, still resistant, and that you like your wine. If servants had found you passed out in a hallway, it wouldn't have created much of a stir."

"Disapproval of my 'vulgarity' and now my drinking—what a surprise! Aren't you virtuous?" My sneer twists into an evil grin. "But your virtue has been your downfall. You shouldn't have turned your back on me. And now you can't knock me unconscious in here. Like you said, you can't carry me, so you *have* to keep helping me."

He freezes, suddenly wary. "What *are* you doing here, by the way?"

I shrug, nonchalant. "I just want a look around."

"I wasn't sure you even knew what this room was—Wait!" he says as I turn away, flame in hand. "You can't be in here."

"We've covered that already," I say over my shoulder. "Don't shout, now. Better keep up."

He follows at a brisk pace. "I'm serious, Rovan. Nothing good will come of this." When I ignore him, he says, "I could . . . hurt you. Until you agree to leave. Make it too painful to go forward."

I know he won't, not after his meager pinch at the banquet, and not after that look we just shared. So I raise my flame and peer into the shadows. Statues loom all around me, and the musty smell of disuse hangs heavy in the air. The royal gallery appears as if it *never* has visitors. A thought occurs to me, and I whip around to see my footsteps marring the thick dust over the black and white mosaic maze on the floor behind me. My guardian, of course, doesn't leave a trace.

"Shit," I breathe. "They'll know someone was here."

"I can fix that, cover your tracks, but we need to *go*," Ivrilos insists, planting himself between me and the way forward.

He really doesn't want me seeing whatever is in here—which probably means I'm on the right track.

Apprehension stirs uncomfortably in my belly, but I step right through him and raise my flame higher, willing the sigil to burn brighter. Pale marble faces float up from the gloom like drowned bodies surfacing in dark water.

Most wear the faces of men.

"Look here!" I barely manage to keep my voice down as I hurry to the base of a statue. "It says 'Damios'—the name of Japha's guardian."

"I thought you couldn't read." Ivrilos sounds stunned, close behind me.

I would be more offended if I weren't so proud of myself. I turn to give him a grin. "I can read a *little*, thank you very much, and I'm good at capturing the shape of things. While I can't string complicated sentences together, I've been practicing certain letters and their matching sounds in my head ever since my first horrid lesson here. *Names*, in particular."

"This one is probably a coincidence," Ivrilos says, his voice weaker than usual. "Damios is a common name."

"Is it him or isn't it? You've seen him. And, remember, it's *vulgar* to lie."

Jaw clenching, my guardian doesn't say anything. I carry on, rushing down the line of statues, diving deeper into the shadows of the royal gallery.

"Klytios! Captain Windbag's guardian." A dozen marble plinths later, I gasp. "Aias." I hurry on, nearing the end of the line, the dates on the statues going farther and farther back in time, nearing what had to be the era of the first king. "Graecus. They're all here."

And then I freeze.

"Rovan." My guardian's voice is strangled.

"Ivrilos," I say. Except this time I'm not addressing him. I'm reading a name. *This* Ivrilos stands before me cut from marble, not shadow. He's just as beautiful, if sadder in his expression than

175

the Ivrilos I know. He holds a sword in one hand, a circlet in the other, and gazes at something far away. The sight makes my chest constrict. Even though I've been braced to find him here—but still hoping, somehow, I wouldn't—I'm not prepared for *this*. "These dates . . ." I face my guardian, the true Ivrilos.

His face is as pale and still as marble in the darkness, but the rest of him is cloaked in black. "I know."

"It says you lived four hundred years ago."

"I did," he says.

"That would mean you . . . and the first king . . ." I press the heels of my palms into my eyes. "Please read what it says. I can't—I can't manage that many words."

"I don't need to read it," Ivrilos says, his voice gentle. "It says that I was King Athanatos's bastard son, recognized by order of my older brother, who succeeded him, only after my father and I . . . passed."

I keep my eyes covered so I don't have to look at his face—either of his faces. They seem to mirror the dual visions of him in my mind: the guardian I detest and the Ivrilos I'm beginning to . . . *like*? Can that be?

"So it's true," I say. "You guardians . . . you're *all* royals, aren't you, of Athanatos's line? You've been trying to hide it so the polis won't rise against your living family." I drop my hands. "It's brilliant, really. We're your royal weapons in life and your royal meals in death." When he opens his mouth, I snap, "And *don't* lie to me about that. I know it's not just about controlling us. You *take* something from us, too, to sustain you."

He doesn't argue.

How many living wards, I wonder with a sick sort of awe, are being used like this? Our numbers are ever increasing because of the first king's law, requiring those with magic to establish bloodlines and take guardians. Which was intended not only to grow and catalog the city's magical army, but to accommodate the growing number of royal *dead* sustained by them. How many of Athanatos's line have died in the meantime, in the four hundred years since he ruled?

It also begs the question: Who, even among royals, makes it to immortality? I gaze out at the spread of statues all around, standing in the darkness like a small army.

An army of men.

"That's why there aren't many women in your underworld palace," I say. "Somehow, they don't last long after what you do to them. What you do to *us.*" I laugh. "You sacrifice the women in your family to bear the most powerful bloodlines—and you don't even give them statues in the royal gallery for their trouble! You just use them and throw them away. Not to mention every commoner, man or woman, whom you foist guardians upon, as if they're pack mules carrying you to immortality. Who cares about *them?*" I finally meet his dark eyes. "And *you.* You're one of the worst of them all."

"Rovan—"

"Don't call me that!" I shout. Ivrilos gestures for me to lower my voice, but it echoes throughout the gallery. I can't help it—the truth is too much to contain quietly. "You said you haven't been dead as long as some. You mean as long as only one or two of your *ancient* family members? Your father, *Athanatos?*" I wave about. "This is all of his making, and you've supported him *from the beginning.* For *four hundred years.*" Heat boils within me. "And now you've killed my father, just like you're going to kill me."

I should want to burn something—everything—but all I really want is to be rid, once and for all, of my so-called guardian. Those strange, charged moments between us are like the odd falling stars I've managed to spot through the veil: entrancing but fleeting, flashes of brightness here and then gone within a much vaster, lurking darkness. I can't let myself get blinded by them. Ivrilos is evil. *Wrong.* I need to remember that.

In my mind, I feel the shape of the special sigils my father left me in his office, unfamiliar but glowing—a new path to trace, calling to me like never before. Maybe now is the time, now that I know Ivrilos will never, *ever* be on my side.

Without a second thought, I follow the sigils, drawing them out like an artist with a brush or chisel. And what becomes of them is . . .

Nothing. They don't do anything. The shape of them falls away before it even comes into being. I feel something collapsing inside me. My father left me *nothing*? How can that be?

Ivrilos's eyes narrow, as if he can feel what I tried to do. But all he says is, "I hear something."

"What?" I say, anger overcoming my despair. "Don't try to avoid—"

"*Shh.*" He raises a finger to his lips, his other hand going to one of the swords at his hip, shoulders tense. I can't help it—instinct makes me freeze along with him.

And then I hear it, too. A key turning in a door, the thunk of a bolt. The sound of boots on marble, at the other end of the gallery, where Ivrilos and I came through the double doors. My breath catches.

"Who's in here?" a voice calls. "I bloody heard you."

"See," another voice says. "I told you it wasn't just that royal bitch toying with us. Someone got in here. Maybe *her*. Look at the tracks."

Royal? I wonder if they suspect Lydea—she would certainly be one to play magical tricks on anyone who annoys her. But the guards will find out in no time who's actually in here. Ivrilos said there's another exit. Even if they know *someone* has broken inside, maybe we can still sneak away and escape . . .

But then my guardian closes his eyes. His jaw hardens, and every muscle in his body goes perfectly still. Just like that, I know something bad is about to happen.

"Wait," I say in the tiniest whisper. "We can leave."

Ivrilos shakes his head without opening his eyes. "They know we're here. And *no one* can know we're here." He smiles faintly, as if in apology, and meets my eyes. "I told you."

He doesn't seem to move. One second he's in front of me, plenty of space in between us. The next, he's nearly pressed up against me, looking down at me with a shadowed gaze. His fingertips graze my cheek—feather light, almost sweet, as they undoubtedly steal everything from me.

And then he vanishes.

I half expect to collapse right then—that's what usually happens after he touches me. But I don't.

"Ivrilos, wait!" I don't care if I shout now. I know where he's going. I pick up my skirts with one hand, wield my small flame in the other, and run, heedless of the statues I nearly careen into.

I tear around the last line of them to find the soldiers both staring at me in surprise.

"It's *you*?" one of them growls. "You're not— "

Ivrilos appears behind him, dark and looming, a sinister shadow. Based on the startled cry of his companion, his hand flying to a dagger at his hip, it's not only me who can see my guardian. The first man has just enough time to turn, halfway drawing his sword, before Ivrilos's hand closes on his wrist. *Solidly.*

Horror flares inside me . . . and then dies as my knees buckle. All feeling drains out of my body at once, like a split barrel of wine. I hit the floor, hard. I expected this after he touched me, beginning whatever dark transaction that steals his ward's strength, but it's still an all-consuming shock that leaves me gasping like a landed fish, barely able to breathe.

All I can do is lie there on the marble, cold, empty, and numb, and watch what's unfolding.

Ivrilos moves like liquid darkness. He helps the guard finish drawing his sword, his shade's hand still clamped over the mortal man's, and in one fluid sweep he thrusts the weapon into the other guard's armpit, skewering him crosswise through the chest and expertly avoiding any armor. Before the wounded man can fall, my guardian appears behind *him*, taking the hand that clenches the readied dagger. Together, they both bury it under the chin of the other guard.

Both men fall to the ground. Dead.

Ivrilos vanishes again.

For a moment, it's just me lying there, as still and silent as the guards with their staring eyes. It's almost peaceful. Much like the blood seeping out around their bodies, the room grows slowly darker at the edges . . . darker . . .

And then I can see Ivrilos. It's as if I'm hovering over his shoulder. But he's no longer in the royal gallery.

He's in another world.

He's lit by a strange gray light filtering through the . . . snow? ash? . . . that billows about. All around, deep gray dunes crest like a stormy sea locked in time. The colors of the earth and sky are reversed here, and the dark snow is *floating*, not falling. Ashen earth drifts upward in lazy spirals, bits and pieces of the entire desolate landscape gathering in heavy, lingering clouds that blot out the shadowy gray sky. It's as if the power that makes objects drop to earth no longer works, as if this entire new world is upside down.

A fortress sprawls in the distance, as big as a small city. If our strange surroundings are dark, this structure is a splatter of black ink on the horizon. Many towers rise from behind its high, smooth walls, but one dominates the rest, ending in a point. It looks like an obsidian sword piercing the sky. For lack of a better word, the walled city seems *wrong*. More of a blight than the one consuming the land of the living.

The two guards I just watched die are standing with their backs to Ivrilos, perfectly whole, baffled by the sweeping gray dunes all around us and the terrible, dark stain of the fortress on the landscape and not noticing the creature stalking slowly and silently up behind them. They should have been watching for *him*. My guardian. Their murderer.

Ivrilos steps up to one, and then the other, inclining his head as if in greeting. I can't quite see what it is he does—it almost looks like he kisses their cheeks. Before I can even think to cry out to warn them, they're both disintegrating like so much ash. But instead of floating up and away like everything else, their remains are drawn into my guardian, like smoke he's inhaling. And then it's only him standing there, looking darker than ever, with me somehow peering down on him from above.

I still can't feel much of anything, even though I distantly know I should be screaming.

Ivrilos tips his face back. For a moment, he looks sated, almost blissful, a slight smile playing at the corners of his perfect lips as he gazes at the charcoal sky. Everything around us keeps twisting up and away like swarms of insects as far as the eye can see. And after a moment, I begin to rise with it all . . .

My guardian's dark eyes snap to mine, wherever I am. "Not you," he commands.

And then I'm back in my body, my spine arching against the marble floor of the royal gallery as a great gasp tears through me. Ivrilos crouches above, his beautiful face no longer filled with that strange peace but stricken.

"You're dying," he says. "I used too much of you."

I can't quite talk. My face is numb. I'm cold all over, so cold. The edges of the room are already fading again.

"You can't die," he insists.

I smile somewhat drunkenly up at him. My tongue is heavy, clumsy. "Just try to stop me."

181

Ivrilos lets loose a string of curses. "I *had* to use you, Rovan, but . . ." He turns away, as if searching for help, but then looks back down at me, wild-eyed. "I can't—"

"I know," I breathe, the words rasping in my throat. "You can't carry me. Or catch me." My eyelids begin to flutter shut. It feels so peaceful, like drifting off to sleep. My voice hitches. "I'm falling."

My eyes close. Maybe I'll wake up again in that strange place, I think dreamily. Maybe . . .

Darkness swallows me.

18

Deep within the darkness that blankets me, muffling all else, I feel the oddest thing: pressure on my mouth. *Lips* pressing against mine. At first they seem to draw more than a kiss from me, as if trying to pull me out of my body faster than I'm leaving it. But then, suddenly, they give something back.

Sensation floods me. It's wine refilling my broken barrel. And yet it's sharp, colorless, and cold, so different from what spilled out of me. This is more like ice water than wine. I'm already freezing, but *this* seeps into spaces within me that I didn't even know I had.

It's also like a crisp breath of air in my lungs after nearly drowning. Somewhere, I feel my first inhalation—through my nose, because my mouth is, well, *occupied*.

During all of this, an image floats out of the darkness, consuming my vision: a stark white temple, in front of which looms a man wearing a black hood and wielding an ax. The man shoves something like my head—but not *my* head—down onto a block of stone, already red and warm with gore. A voice—not my voice, but seeming to come from me—masculine and terrified and *familiar*, cries out and pleads to be let go.

It's Ivrilos's voice. This time, I'm more than just looking over his shoulder. I'm looking out of *him*. Is this a memory?

The ax comes down, and we next open our eyes on that strange, dark, dissolving world I just saw. But now there's another man, far more frightening than the executioner, with hair like Ivrilos's and a flat stare that burns with a sickly blue fire. He stands before a structure that looks like the sprawling fortress, except it's nowhere near so big as what I saw before. While it's still completely black, it's unfinished, ending in jagged points that pierce the half light, but only at the height of a few men standing atop one another. Those points seem to drip upward, running like melted candle wax, the drops falling up into the sky like reverse rain. There's no door, so I peer inside to the throne, also black, and angular and liquid at once. It, at least, is finished.

Ivrilos and I are on the steps leading up to the structure. The man stands at the top with two other women. Both are crying, even harder now that they see Ivrilos.

"There you are. Welcome," the terrifying man says, addressing my guardian. "Glad to see you come when I call." He wears a crown of gold laurels, just as kings in the living world do.

"Father." Ivrilos's voice again, seeming to come from the both of us. Begging.

So the man is Athanatos. And I know for sure, now, who rules the underworld. I'm not entirely surprised. It makes a sick kind of sense that the first king is *still* king, down below.

The two women with Athanatos, one older, one younger, are mother and daughter, I somehow understand.

"I could use you," the first king continues. "These two, however . . . they'll make a prime example of what will happen to you if you disobey me."

He seizes the women, both wild-eyed with terror, and presses their faces against the wall of the tower.

They scream. Ivrilos shouts, lunging forward up the steps.

Nothing keeps their skin from darkening, collapsing, until their whole bodies vanish into the structure as if submerged in liquid. It's as if they've *melted* into it, becoming part of it. Only smooth wall remains where they once were. But the jagged top of the tower rises, stabbing farther into the cold, heartless sky, sharp points dripping up and away like daggers drenched in blood.

I try to shout now. Instead, I open my eyes. My own, this time. The dark world—the memory of it—is gone.

And I merely stare, uncomprehending at first. Because peering right back at me with a strange expression on his face, less than a finger's breadth away, is Ivrilos. His cool lips are still pressed to mine.

He's *kissing* me.

My eyes fly wide. Without thinking, I sit up and shove him away. It takes me a second to realize I actually *push* him, my flesh-and-blood palm connecting with his chest. I can feel the solidity of him, the slight give of his tunic and the firm muscle beneath. I stare at my hand in shock, but it looks the same as always.

Now I'm more awake than ever, even as I glance around in confusion. Everything appears hard and sharp, all shining edges. Shadows sink darker and highlights flare brighter, despite the deep gloom of the royal gallery, my sigil-summoned flame long gone. And I feel . . . strange. I'm ice cold. My skin is prickling.

But at least I'm alive. I hope.

"What—?" I say, and I can't resist reaching toward Ivrilos again. He gives me a strange, almost longing look, and this time my hand passes right through his face, like normal. Well, if I normally tried to touch his face. "I don't understand."

Then I remember what happened. What he did. The bodies of the guards, blood congealing around them, are still here to help jog my memory.

I scrabble away from my guardian and the corpses, my limbs responding quicker, stronger than I could have anticipated. "You killed them. I saw."

I also saw something else, possibly *Ivrilos* dying in his own memory, but I can't think about that right now. That happened four hundred years ago, and *this* is happening now. My guardian still crouches, seeming dazed, glancing around like he's just now realizing where he is.

"I'm glad I put the room's protections back when I did," he says distantly. "It'll look like only the guards entered here, fought, and then killed each other, especially when I smooth over your footprints. We need to get out of here immediately, before anyone else sees you."

"Or else you'll kill them, too?"

He turns on me, eyes like daggers, no trace of longing for me anymore. "You should hope that I can, and that they don't shout for help. There's no way I could save you if the wrong people found out that I'd helped you like this. I couldn't save *either* of us."

My stomach drops. "Helped me like *what*? What did you do to me?" I touch my chest, my mouth. "I feel odd. Cold. And everything looks . . . the same, but different."

"Rovan, we need to go."

I let my hand fall, trying not to think about the cool press of his lips on mine. "Why should I care what you need?"

"Think of yourself . . . and your mother. If they find you here like this, it would mean death. For you, for me, *and* for her."

"You're already dead."

"I can die again. Forever."

"Why should I trust you?"

Ivrilos holds my eyes in that unwavering way that makes me want to lean into him. "Because I want to stop all of this. For the past four hundred years, I've spent every breath on stopping this."

I almost can't believe what I'm hearing. He makes me *want* to believe, despite everything. But all I can say, nonsensically, is, "You don't breathe."

186

The corner of his mouth quirks. "All I am is breath."

I remember my father defining *pneuma*, the essence that composes the spirit, as another word for breath.

"Fine. But you've spent the lives of others, too, or their *pneuma* or whatever. I've felt you take it from me." Maybe I've even *seen* him do it, to the two dead guards in that strange, upsidedown place.

"You're right." He isn't apologetic. "About everything. And I'll explain it all if you leave with me now." He bows his head, the thin silver circlet glinting in his dark hair. "I promise."

I stare at him, every line of him as sharp as a blade in the darkness. He's a knife's edge in human form, and for some silly reason I want to touch him again. The word escapes my lips almost involuntarily. "Okay."

His whole body relaxes like a sigh, but then he's on his feet, gesturing for me. I hop upright with surprising ease. A few of his muttered words send a breeze gusting along the floor, swirling over my footprints and blending them back in with the rest of the dust. The guards he leaves exactly as they lie. He hurries over to a blank stretch of wall, me in tow, along with a cool draft that chases me, covering my tracks.

"I thought you knew another way out—*oh*," I say, as the stone parts like curtains after a few more words from him. I walk through in stunned awe, staring at the almost liquid quality of what was perfectly solid only a moment ago. Before I know it, we're standing in a palace hallway, the wall once again smooth behind me, the royal gallery sealed off.

And yet, while I can see gleaming marble and columns of blooming flowers in the torchlight, I can't see *myself*.

Before I can exclaim, Ivrilos assures me, "I've masked you and the sound of your footsteps. It would be best if you don't speak until we are back in your apartments. There I will explain every-thing."

He sets off down the hall, beckoning for me.

Invisible, feeling like a ghost, and not entirely knowing what the hell just happened, I follow.

19

I can't get warm. As soon as I close myself in my apartments—happily able to see myself again—I start shivering violently. My skin feels like a corpse's, nearly white underneath the crimson lines of my sigils.

I drag a dark green blanket around my shoulders, woven with golden leaves that *actually* drift down the length of it to pile at the bottom edge. I use the sigil to ignite a fire in my massive stone hearth carved like a lion's roaring mouth. The thing is hideous, and for a moment I consider asking Ivrilos to change the shape of it—he can do that, after all, with death magic—but my knees practically give out before I can. I sit down on the floor right in front of the fireplace, not even bothering with a chair.

"Are you sure I'm not dead?" I ask.

Ivrilos crouches next to me, dark eyes looking softer, warmer, in the flickering light, though his expression is as marble smooth as ever. "I can't imagine your teeth would be chattering if you were."

"Okay," I say, gathering the blanket tighter. "Here's your chance to explain what the hell just happened. What you did to me. Why I'm *not* dead."

For a moment, he just stares into the fire, the orange glow playing over his ridiculous cheekbones. "I have to explain a few other things first."

"Perfect," I say, rocking back and forth, trying to get warm, "because as I recall, you promised to tell me *everything*."

He grimaces. "I did, didn't I?"

Sighing, he drops all the way into a kneeling position next to me. We're an incongruous sight—a disheveled young woman and a man who looks like the embodiment of death, huddled in front of the fire—but I've seen stranger things this evening.

"Think of your body like a small raft," he begins. "A leaky raft. It *wants* to sink, and sinking is death." He cups one hand, palm up, and gestures beneath it with the other. "The current is the force that spins the living world. It's exhausting, and it will eventually, inevitably drag you down. Your pneuma, your spiritual essence, otherwise known as your shade after you die, rides within the raft of your body, and your . . . living spark, your vitality, whatever you want to call it . . . is the bucket with which you madly bail to keep from sinking. Some people have bigger buckets, some smaller. Some"—he shoots a barely there smile my way, and it makes my heart kick—"can take their bucket, make it into whatever shape they want, and play with the forces of the living world. Blood-mages, like you."

His lips take a downward turn—*why* am I looking at his lips so much? "I don't belong here in the living world, frankly, as a shade—a being of pure pneuma with no body or vitality of my own with which to keep me afloat. Bound to you like I am, I'm using you. Especially when I make myself more . . . *present* . . . here. It's as if I'm hanging off the side of your raft, dragging against the current. In actuality, I'm drawing on *your* living pneuma, making you weaker as you bail. If I were to draw on you too much, I would swamp you immediately—kill you, like I almost did back in the gallery. To do what I did to those guards, I needed a lot of you. Too much. But even as an extra passenger taking care not to wear out my welcome, I'll still wear *you* out all the sooner."

"Finally, the truth," I declare, with a great exasperated breath. "Not that I hadn't guessed already. But *that's* why bloodmages age quicker here in Thanopolis. It's not the weight of our bloodlines, which, as you said, actually make us stronger." My lip curls. "You're like leeches who've found the fattest vein. My father knew this."

"He did," Ivrilos says shortly.

"But you didn't swamp me, back there," I continue, eyeing him sideways. "You did something strange. You *kept* me from sinking."

You kissed me, I don't add.

Ivrilos's eyes close and his jaw clenches, as if he regrets what he did. "Yes, I did. I . . . I gave you *my* pneuma in return."

"But you're dead!" I goggle at him for a moment. "You mean I have essence of *dead man* in me?"

He nods solemnly.

I bark a short, humorless laugh. "I guess that explains why I'm cold. And why the darkness looks . . . less dark." I shudder. "A dead man's breath in my lungs. Blech. Yuck." For some reason, the thought of a dead man's *lips* on mine doesn't make me squeamish, but I don't tell him that.

"Are you quite finished?" Ivrilos asks, but the words don't have bite. "I didn't actually know all the ways it would affect you because I've never done it before. It's entirely forbidden, the strictest law we have. I suppose now instead of weighing you down, it's more like I'm holding you up, *feeding* you as you bail."

As he says it, his eyes dart away from me. I wonder if, were he alive, there would be more than just firelight coloring his pale cheeks.

"So it's usually you feeding on me, but now it's the opposite?"

"Yes. We became a closed loop, at least temporarily—which is why you could touch me for a brief moment. We were of the same essence. Mine was almost entirely filling you, since yours had nearly moved on. But your pneuma came back to your body, once I revived you by giving you a . . . a breath for one drowning. This weakened me, of course, but I had the strength to spare."

"How?"

He gives me a look I can only describe as mildly chagrined. "As you've pointed out, I'm *old*. A shade can fade—they're sometimes called fades, in fact, those who are evanescing. Or, if one doesn't fade, one can . . . grow. Strengthen. Deepen their capacity to take in pneuma. Just like your capacity for wine is gained by drinking, we can draw more and more on the essence of the living over time, though only from those we are bound to. Live pneuma is more powerful than our own, and far more invigorating with blood to animate it. Which is why guardians, especially older ones like me, are much stronger than normal shades, linked to the living as we are, for as long as we've been."

"But still, you nearly killed me to . . . *take care of* . . . those guards. And yet somehow you were able to revive me and then death-magic everything"—I draw my hand out of the blanket to make a sweeping motion—"without finishing me off?"

His voice goes quieter. "We can also draw on the essence of other shades in the afterlife, without needing to be bound to them."

"But if they're already dead, and they don't have a way to replenish themselves, then that means . . . you kill them? Again?"

Ivrilos meets my eyes. "I told you, there is a second, more permanent death."

"You're avoiding my question."

"Yes, Rovan," he enunciates, holding my gaze. "I killed the shades of those guards in the underworld. I consumed them, giving them their second death far quicker than they would have found it by fading. I couldn't allow them to linger and tell any tales. Their pneuma also gave me the strength to *death-magic everything*, as you call it, and to keep you from dying."

"Why?"

He looks away again. "I need you."

"Why?" I repeat, throwing the blanket off and jabbing a finger at him. "Answer me. You said it yourself: You hate this place. I see why now. I *saw*, when you . . . fed me." I suppose that's less awkward to say than *kissed me*, but not by much, based on how neither of us can meet each other's eyes all of a sudden. Instead, I recall the terrifying man I saw *through* Ivrilos's eyes, and what he did to those two women. "I mean, I think I saw *him*, Athanatos, in a memory of yours. Your father arranged your death, didn't he? To bring you to him in the underworld? He did that, and . . ." But I don't want to bring up the rest, not with how shocked Ivrilos looks, his dark eyebrows climbing. "And yet you're still following his rules."

"You saw that?" He sounds horrified.

I'm not going to let him get sidetracked, not even by visions of his own death. "What do you want, Ivrilos?"

He swallows, staring off into the flames for a long moment. I cultivate patience I didn't know I had, waiting for him to speak.

His voice begins low, monotone. "I have a brother. Kadreus. Not by my mother, but by my father. As I mentioned, I was a bastard. My mother had only a daughter after me, and neither of them had long second lives, thanks to my father. And yet my brother, his son and heir, never ended up in the underworld. My father could have drained Kadreus after death, but . . . I don't think so."

"Why not?"

Ivrilos shrugs, another incongruous sight. It's like he's thawing, turning more human, less shade, the longer he sits in front of this fire. "My father loved him far more than me, and even *I'm* still around. So I guess you could say I'm looking for my brother. This is the only place he could be—perhaps trapped between life and death somehow. I need to find him, but there are places here I cannot go on my own. Only one, really." He takes a deep breath. "The king's quarters, which every king from Athanatos to Tyros has occupied, is surrounded by magic I cannot penetrate. To get inside, I need to get close to the king, closer than I have ever been able to get before."

I blink. "To Tyros?"

"Any king over the years would have sufficed, but yes, it's Tyros now."

I scoff. "You've been waiting four hundred years just to get near the king? You're in the palace now! You can't just, I don't know, walk up to him?"

Ivrilos makes a complicated gesture. "You don't understand. The magic shielding the king is incredibly powerful—it's both blood *and* death magic, woven together."

I gape. "I thought blood and death magic couldn't mix. Not without killing the wielder."

"Perhaps a bloodmage and a shadow priest worked in tandem? How it was done, I don't know, but it makes the barrier around the royal gallery look like a straw fence. It surrounds whoever is the current king, whenever he is where you or I can see him, and it is especially strong around his private quarters where no one is allowed, encircling it. I think my brother is there, perhaps having been bound to each successive king during the ritual they undergo when assuming the crown, somewhat like I am bound to you. The problem is, I need to be *let* in to discover the truth. If I tried to break in by force, I would either fail or the king would be alerted I was coming and have me stopped."

"So all you want to do is get in there and look for your brother? What happens then?"

Ivrilos falls silent.

"You have to give me something." I don't resort to threats. Instead, I say, "Please."

He tips his head back to look at the ceiling. His profile is downright statuesque. I try to think of something else while I wait.

The Goddess of Patience, I am.

The words draw out of him slowly, unbelievably, like one of those absurd cloths that street performers pretend to unspool from their mouths. "If my brother is here, I want to do everything in my power to take his essence for my own and end him, quickly, before either he or my father can stop me. And then I'll be strong enough to go to the underworld and destroy my father and everything he has built."

My mouth falls open. A laugh burbles out of me before I can choke it down. "And I thought you missed your brother. Maybe even wanted to rescue him."

Ivrilos's lips twist into a grimace of pure contempt. I've never seen anything like it on his perfect face. "My royal family, my brother and my father especially, are evil, Rovan. You have no idea to what extent."

"I have . . . some," I croak. "What I feel for Kineas and Tyros aside, I saw what Athanatos did. And he didn't just kill *you*." I take a deep breath. "There was a woman and a girl."

"You saw everything?" Ivrilos's expression is deadly when he faces me, but I know the sentiment is directed elsewhere. "Then you know the full horror: My family not only devours the essence of bloodlines from the living world, they hunt down the shades who end up in the underworld. *All* of them. And not just to glut themselves. Since there's only pneuma down there, it's the only material available to consume *or* to build with."

I remember the two women, their faces pressed to the wall. I still don't quite understand what happened, though I'm beginning to get a sense. "Build?" I whisper, feeling sick.

"They use *people*, Rovan, to pave the very streets. Pneuma is used like mortar to construct towers, to paint walls. And like everything in the underworld, these structures need constant replenishing, repaving, repainting—an endless parade of shades sacrificed at the feet of my family. I've seen these atrocities happen *so many* times after the first, when my father killed my mother and sister right in front of me." He smiles faintly, sadly. "Though none have been so bad as that. Their memory hasn't faded, over time. Just as I haven't. It lives on in me, growing stronger and darker. Like me." He adds, like an afterthought, "I witnessed their first deaths, too, in the living world. They were beheaded right before I was. I had to watch."

I can only stare. *That's* what Ivrilos has been waiting four hundred years to do: take revenge. To bring down his father and his underworld kingdom. To help the living who've had their essence stolen from them for hundreds of years. Who've then had their *second* lives stolen. *That* seems worth waiting for, to me.

Perhaps even worth the sacrifices he's made along the way.

"Okay," I say, throat dry. "So if I'm hearing right, you basically want to burn down the palace as much as I do." I take a deep breath, and then slap the tops of my thighs. "I'm in. What do we do?"

Ivrilos rolls off his knees and sits back on the floor, scrubbing a hand over his face. "You do nothing."

"What do you mean?"

He drops his hand to glare at me. "You should forget all that has happened tonight, all that I've told you, and everything should go back to normal."

I can't believe what I'm hearing. "Back to you *leeching* off me and swamping my boat while you carry out your own plans without me? Let's *not*."

"There's no other way."

"Yes, there is. You just tried it, tonight, when you *kissed* me." Finally, I can say it. My rage gives me the gall. "I thought a kiss on the back of the hand was supposed to 'suffice,' by the way."

Ivrilos's gaze skips away again. He's *embarrassed*. "I didn't think. I just did it. And I can never do it again."

Somewhere in the complicated tangle of my emotions, I feel a strange twinge—one thread, pulled too tight.

"You don't understand," my guardian continues. "Not only is giving you my essence beyond taboo, it's . . . not good for you."

196

"I've always heard that blood and death magic can't mix. That they would kill you. But I'm alive."

"I've given you a breath in your lungs that you can yet expel." He shakes his head. "No more."

"What would happen if you *did* give me more? Would I die?"

"Possibly. Most definitely, given enough. But that's not the only problem, or else the rules wouldn't be so strict. After all, we kill the living all the time." His smile is grim, but then it falls away. "I think some form of madness might take you before death would. And with how powerful you are, the consequences could be . . . horrific." I must look unconvinced, because he adds, "Just imagine, Rovan: If your father thought death magic was already too close to you, too close to the city with the guardians and shadow priests that walk its streets, then what would he think about death magic being *inside* you, right next to your bloodline?"

I felt it filling me, and I can still sense the coldness. It inhabits the shadowy space between the glowing lines of my blood magic—a space I can now feel the shape of.

A breath, filling my lungs. A shadow's kiss.

"But I feel fine!" I say, throwing out my arms, the blanket dropping farther away. Ivrilos's gaze seems to flicker over the skin bared by my loose gown, or maybe I'm imagining it. "At least I'm not mad, and this is certainly better than being dead or so exhausted and hopeless and defeated that I *wish* I were dead."

"As I said: for now. This is a poison, maybe a slow poison in small doses, but fatal nonetheless."

"So that's it, then," I say. "Just like that. You won't help me be free of you, and you won't help me be free of Kineas."

And you'll never kiss me again, I think. When I realize *that's* something I'm mad about, I curse myself for an idiot.

It's Ivrilos's turn to throw out his hands. "Your position is too valuable. I've come too far, pretended to be the perfect guardian for too long. I'm too close to risk anything now, until the perfect moment."

"How is my position valuable?" I demand.

"You're betrothed to the crown prince."

I gape at him. "So let me get this straight. You could have helped my father escape, but because he wasn't *perfectly positioned* and you had to maintain your mask, you let him waste away while you grew fat on his essence, extending your existence a few more steps toward forever?"

"I told you—"

"It doesn't matter if it's for a good cause, Ivrilos!" I cry, wadding up the blanket and hurling it right through him. He blinks. "It's shitty! That makes you a shitty person!"

His expression stills. "I never said I wasn't one."

"And what if they never let me close to the king, into his inner sanctum?" I continue, ignoring him. "Even if you're the perfect guardian, what if I remind everyone too much of my father and they keep me away?"

"Kineas will become king. You'll be close by necessity."

"Cylla didn't live long enough to become queen. Wards never last that long." By design, perhaps, so no bloodmage or guardian ever could come close to this inner sanctum?

"Your children will be his heirs, and I'll be assigned as a guardian to the one who inherits your bloodline. In four hundred years, I've never been this close. Never trusted enough. Until now."

I'm nearly spitting with rage. "So you'll use me and *them*, my nonexistent future children, to get to the king? *That's* what you want from me? You'll just ride your wards like a caravan, one generation to the next, until they take you where you want? I'm not a fucking horse and cart, Ivril! And I'm *never* going to have children with that monster, so you can get that thought out of your insubstantial skull right now."

198

"Ivril," he repeats. "Why would you call me that?"

"I don't know!" I explode. "Convenience? I'm busy yelling, and it's short?"

"I just haven't heard that in a long time. It was an old family nickname." He shakes his head, as if ridding himself of some memory. I can't bring myself to care.

He continues, "As much as I admire your determination, you might not have a choice in any of this. As you well know, Cylla didn't. She never wanted to be crown princess, let alone pass the burden of her bloodline on to her daughter Lydea like an heirloom in the family collection. But she did. She was made to."

"By her guardian." I meet his eyes. "I'll kill whomever I need to before I let that happen. I'll kill *myself*."

He stares back. "You know I can stop you. That's my job."

"Do you want to stop me?"

"From killing yourself, yes. At all costs. As you so delicately pointed out, your bloodline is my key. But for the rest of it . . . it depends."

"Right, if I were *perfectly positioned*." I pause. "So how do I do that?"

He raises an eyebrow at me. "Are you suggesting, somehow, in some way, you might be willing to work with me?"

"Maybe." I feel just as surprised as he sounds. "If you'll work with *me*. It's not like I have many other options."

Actually, I have other paths—sigil-lined paths, if only I can figure them out—but I can't let Ivrilos know that. I have to wear my own mask, pretend to be the perfect ward, just as he's pretending to be the perfect guardian. We'll be doing the same thing, really. Falling in line, waiting for the right moment to break rank. And if Ivrilos can help me in the meantime, so much the better.

It's not that I'm fine with bloodlines being used as the main course for a host of royal dead, or with the rest of the world becoming their paving stones in the afterlife. But I'm not going to simply let myself be a victim, a stepping stone for *Ivrilos*. And I can't risk my mother meeting the same fate. Because once I'm gone, having served my purpose, there will be no one to guarantee her safety.

Ivrilos can find some other way of accomplishing his ends. If his purpose is grand, mine is simple. I have to protect my mother and get out of here, with Japha and Lydea and whoever else wants to come with me. As soon as we're all safe, *then* I can bend my mind to figuring out how to free the bloodlines. Preferably when I'm as far away from Thanopolis as possible.

Not that I can do any of that without freeing myself from my guardian first.

I bury my face in my hands, half to hide any duplicitous thoughts that might betray me, and half because I can feel despair clinging to me, grasping, trying to pull me down. There are some things I *can't* pretend. And maybe that's where Ivrilos can help me.

"I just can't—" I choke for a moment. "I can't . . . with Kineas. I need some way to avoid him."

"I don't know that there is one," my guardian says slowly. "I doubt the king would break off the engagement—your bloodline is too valuable. And attempting to make that happen will only make him trust you less. Make your position less ideal."

"So, what, I'll just pretend to smile and you'll just pretend to kiss me in order to hide that it's actually Kineas? I'm afraid that won't work, especially not now that I've had the real thing from you."

His mouth opens. Then closes. Finally, he manages, slightly hoarse, "It might not come to that. You have three weeks until you wed."

"And then what? You'll charge in and interrupt the ceremony and maybe stab the crown prince while you're at it?"

Ivrilos breathes a laugh that's the opposite of mirthful. "I can't do anything like that until I've found my brother. But maybe, with your help, we can manage that task before the wedding."

Even *he* barely sounds hopeful. And why would he? It's taken him four hundred years to reach this point. It could take him another fifty, for all he knows.

I don't have fifty years. I have three weeks until my wedding, and the rest of my life at stake.

"You really want me to do it," I say incredulously. "Go throw myself at Kineas for the sake of your plan. I can't believe you."

"I'm just asking you to *wait*," he nearly begs, holding up his hands. "I will protect you from him however I can without raising suspicions. You can feign sickness to avoid engagements, and I'll vouch for you. I can use my magic to make you look less appealing, I . . ." He falters as I glower.

"*That's* your idea of helping me? To turn me into a sickly shadow of myself so he doesn't *want* me? He already doesn't!"

"Then you can carry on like usual, and we take it as it comes. You've been able to manage him so far. Admirably, in fact—"

"How could you ask this of me?" I force him to hold my gaze, to *really* look me in the eye as he says it.

To his credit, he doesn't turn away. "I have to. I wish that I didn't, more powerfully than I've wished for anything—anything *except* the end of my father's reign." He sounds nearly helpless.

And yet he *isn't* helpless. He wants me to think nothing has changed, but everything has. Now I know: He could help me if he wanted to, truly free me, but he's choosing not to.

Sure, the lives and afterlives of countless other people hang in the balance, but still, there it is—the truth, and it cuts like a knife. I'm not sure why. What else did I expect from him? Even so, a fierce heat stings my eyes.

"Rovan . . ."

I stand abruptly and stalk away from my guardian, snuffing the fire in its gaudy lion's mouth, leaving him in darkness.

At the door, I only turn enough to say over my shoulder, "I wish you luck." And then I shut him out.

20

Over the course of the next week, everything carries on *almost* as usual. Other than a royal luncheon where Kineas refuses to speak to me or meet my eyes, I'm not forced to see him. Lydea and I continue to exchange secret glances and discreet touches in the hallways, and much more in private. I spend as much time as possible with both her and Japha. I even manage to decipher some of Japha's notes and shakily scrawl a few of my own. We all long for freedom and adventure, and have the financial means to pursue whatever dreams we can think of—a strange new reality for me. But none of that changes the fact that we're all still engaged to other people, bound to our guardians, and trapped in the palace.

As usual.

My guardian won't help me, and I can't be rid of him. Discovering that all guardians are royal hasn't brought me any closer to figuring out how they're bound to their wards, despite the cost of that discovery—my near death and the lives of two guards lost in a "drunken brawl." I can barely think about the latter. And I haven't managed to decipher the puzzle of those special sigils my father left me in his office. I even double-check his office to see if I missed something, perhaps another sigil, when I find a spare moment between social engagements and lessons. Nothing works—neither looking for more pieces to the puzzle nor further experimentation with the sigils in private. They don't seem to *do* anything.

Even though Ivrilos hesitantly tries to talk to me about what happened in the royal gallery, I ignore him. He wants me to forget about it, after all—for everything to go back to the way it's been. As far as he's concerned, I'm obliging him.

But *some* things have changed. And for me, there's no going back.

I have to struggle not to gape whenever I pass a ward while walking down the spiraling hallways of the palace a full week later, heading to one of my lessons. Ever since that strange night, I can peer into shadows like never before. *All* shadows, including those that lurk near every bloodmage. In that once-murky darkness, I now glimpse faces, flashes of hands against dark armor, the gleam of weapons.

Guardians. I can see them now, after what Ivrilos did to me. After what he gave me. A week later, it hasn't faded.

I don't entirely mind. It's something different, powerful . . . and I like that. Even if it's dark and dangerous.

"Rovan, my *dear*."

The words make me flinch.

I turn to see Crown Prince Kineas, my wretched betrothed, striding down the hallway, attendants fanning behind him like a fluttery flock of birds. I'm pretty sure a few of them actually *have* birds perched on their shoulders. One has a milky white snake with yellow stripes wrapped around their neck. There isn't time to try to slip away and escape attention, though I find myself wishing I could open doors in solid stone like Ivrilos.

"Where might you be wandering off to?" Kineas asks, the pompous ass. Before I can answer, he tosses his perfectly coiffed waves of pewter hair and adds, "It can't be that interesting. Come." His attendants all gather behind him as he approaches, preening.

The dance lesson I'm heading to *isn't* that interesting, but it'll be better than spending time with him. Etiquette lessons would be preferable. Maybe even torture. But I can't think of a way to refuse him that won't end poorly for me.

Or, worst of all, in a threat against my mother.

I still try to step aside, nearly burying myself in a cascade of flowers along the wall. Their perfume engulfs me, and a bee drones near my ear.

"Are you sure we should be seen spending much time together before the wedding?" I ask. "Wouldn't that be unseemly?"

I have no idea if it would be. Royals seem to do whatever they want with whomever they want—I try not to think of Lydea and bring a blush to my face—but they *also* have endless rules of etiquette. Maybe this is one of them. I hope.

"On the contrary. According to some, we have seen far too little of each other. Besides, you should want nothing more than to spend time with me." There's warning in Kineas's cold, silvery eyes. *Of course.* This is the language he speaks best: insinuations and threats.

Before I can recoil he seizes my wrist down low where no one else can see, hard enough to hurt. He dips his head toward my ear, where no one else can hear. The bright, romantic flowers curling all around us and the happily humming bee seem to mock me. "That wasn't a request. Try not to embarrass yourself this time."

Embarrass *him*, he means.

I smile winningly at him for appearances' sake and murmur, "Take your hand off me before I burn it off."

"Come now, we know your guardian would never allow that." His voice remains low, almost sultry. For all anyone can tell, we might be flirting with each other.

My guardian might not allow me to use blood magic. But another path springs into my mind. I suddenly know how to use my *body*.

With a twist of my wrist, I break Kineas's grip. I have his own wrist pinched at a brutal angle before he can blink. He staggers to escape me, and then catches himself in an attempt to hide it, lurching awkwardly and in a very unprincelike manner. He massages the joint before he thinks better of that, too. His hands drop, and he glares daggers at me. I'm surprised he doesn't actually draw a blade on me.

But I know precisely how to dodge him. I'm already bouncing on my toes, anticipatory.

Where on earth has this knowledge come from?

I'm suddenly aware of Ivrilos standing at my side, a dark shadow framed in a profusion of blossoms. Normally I would appreciate the contrast—*why* does he always have to look so starkly beautiful?—but I spare him only a glance or two. He's busy staring in amazement. He never expected me to be able to do what I did, either, and yet there's a glint of recognition in his eyes. He's so focused on me that the bee flies right through his forehead without him seeming to notice.

And then I realize: I learned it from *him*. Or rather, I drank down some of his martial knowledge with the shadowy power and memories he gave me in his forbidden kiss.

"Perfect." Kineas masks his fury with a laugh that sounds razor sharp. "I was just headed to my sparring session. I wanted you to watch, but now perhaps I can practice on you. You seem to have some training yourself. Only blades allowed, of course. None of that blood magic of yours."

Shit, I think, as his attendants titter—some of them nervously, some in approval. I don't know *how* much knowledge I've absorbed from Ivrilos. I doubt it extends to full-bore dueling. But that won't stop Kineas.

He wants to hurt me. I can see it in his eyes. *This* is the man who will be my husband, and there's no one here to gainsay him.

Ivrilos finally blinks as if coming back to himself. "Convince him this is a bad idea."

"Be my guest," I mutter.

"You know he can't hear me," my guardian bites out.

"After you," Kineas says with a murderous smile, once again assuming my words are for him.

He assumes everything is for him.

He gestures the way forward, down the hall. I have no choice but to accompany him.

"Shit," my guardian breathes.

"And I thought you were supposed to be my protector," I say, picking my words carefully so Kineas won't know they're not for him.

"Rovan—" Ivrilos begins, almost desperately.

"We're not married yet," the crown prince interrupts without realizing. "What's a little blood between friends? Although"—he leans for my ear again as we walk—"I hear there's supposed to be blood on the wedding night, too."

I laugh, but I still keep my voice down. "You think you'll be my first? Besides, you must not have much experience yourself if you think all women bleed the first time."

I hope that will fluster him, but he only smiles unsettlingly. "In my experience, it's not difficult to make them bleed. Granted, with you, I might have to get creative." His voice drops. "You wouldn't be the first woman I've cut."

I remember Japha telling me about the accusations of abuse from some of his lovers, and worse, the rumors of missing lowborn girls . . . all swiftly silenced.

"For the love of the goddess," Ivrilos practically hisses in my other ear, "would you *stop* provoking him?"

I could, but then I might lose whatever pride I have left. I wish I could extend my arms, or even just a sigil-weighted thought, and pitch both men into the walls on opposites sides of me. And then maybe strangle them with flowers. But I can't hurt Ivrilos, and he would never let me hurt the crown prince.

"Rovan, you can pretend you don't feel well," Ivrilos says. "I can *make* you feel unwell . . ."

"Don't even try it," I growl through gritted teeth. "Or else I'll tell the truth about you."

"And why would anyone care to listen?" Kineas asks lightly, carrying on *our* conversation. He adds, just as light, "I can't wait to hear you change your tune. Someday, I'll even make you beg for it. It will be music to my ears. Not this insufferable squawking."

I don't give him the satisfaction of a reaction, even though I want to shudder. My skin is crawling from being so near him.

Twin or not, how could Lydea *ever* think she was anything like him?

The crown prince and his gaggle of attendants walk the rest of the way in anticipatory silence to a sunny, wide dirt courtyard, columns open on one gracefully curving side of the palace to the city sprawled below. Between the columns, light streams in from stacked arches that rise three stories overhead to a pale, curving ceiling punctured by oculi and draped in flowers. Weapon racks line the other walls.

Kineas dismisses several men already waiting there to spar with him and spreads his arms wide to encompass our arena. "Choose your weapons, my dearest."

"Your Highness," says an older attendant, standing deferentially apart. "Shouldn't you both be limited to wooden practice weapons, or—"

"Of course not," Kineas snaps. "My bride-to-be surely knows how to handle herself. You dare insult her, and you're insulting me. We fight until first blood."

Clever, I think. *Sick, but clever.*

I march right over to where the real weapons hang and draw a pair of half-moon blades off the rack. They give me a good feeling—a sense of comfortable familiarity, despite my never having held anything like them before.

I *have*, however, seen them both strapped to the waist and gripped in the hands of my guardian.

Said guardian appears in front of me, speaking rapidly. "Ideally you'd use something with better reach, but I don't think you have the arm strength for a two-handed sword. My advice?"

I meet his eyes.

"Lose as quickly as possible."

My expression must be response enough, because he says, "I didn't imagine you would listen. So I'll try to give you tips, but Kineas has trained as a warrior nearly since birth."

He sounds less than hopeful. I turn away from him and walk toward the center of the arena, grateful I'm wearing a shorter chiton for my dancing lesson, so as not to tangle up my legs. I face Kineas, who draws the sword on his hip.

"Let's see how experienced you truly are," he murmurs, a smile on his face for anyone who's watching. "I'm betting you'll bleed after all."

I charge first. Kineas is probably hoping I will—hoping to goad me into making an immediate mistake. And then he'll poke and prod and make a fool of me, if he isn't planning on *truly* hurting me. But I have something other than fury fueling my limbs. I can feel it alongside my bloodline, swimming in the dark spaces between it. Maybe Kineas has trained as a warrior since birth, but *Ivrilos* has, too, since both the beginning of his life *and* his death—four hundred years ago. And he's given me a breath I have yet to expel.

I'm happy to expel it now.

My barrage hits the crown prince like a storm, and he ends up retreating almost before the spectators can let out a collective gasp.

"Feint left!" Ivrilos barks.

I don't know what the hell that means. I only have the dark instinct curled like smoke inside to guide me. And Kineas is indeed skilled. He only allows himself a single look of wide-eyed shock before he's back on the offensive. Twisting, he swings at me viciously, seeking an opening. The force of his strike, deflected by my half-moon blades, vibrates up my arms hard enough to rattle my teeth. Suddenly, it's all I can do to keep up with *him*.

"You've fought, now let him win!" Ivrilos says, practically at my ear. If I could spare the hand, I would bat him away like a fly. "He can't wonder at how well you can fight. No one can discover . . ."

He chokes off, but I know what he was going to say: Discovery is too risky. And yet, I'm supposed to let Kineas cut me to hide the truth?

As another rush of blows makes my elbows creak, I know what else Ivrilos would say. It's what he argued that night: A little pain, a little misery, is worth it, for the sake of his plan. At least to him.

And yet he's hovering so close, reluctant to let Kineas hurt me. My guardian doesn't want to be the one to allow it. He wants *me* to allow it, so he doesn't feel responsible.

Fuck that.

I pummel Kineas back once again, gaining more ground and making someone in the crowd actually squeal. But I can already feel the weight of my blades. Already I'm flagging.

Kineas must sense this, because he swings so hard I have to catch his sword on both blades, crossed above me—exactly how Ivrilos caught a sword of fire when my father attacked King Tyros. It was effective for Ivrilos, but the distraction of the memory costs me. The crown prince's blade grinds down along both of mine, driving close to my shoulder, bared by my sleeveless chiton. His edge strains to reach my flesh. If it does, it probably won't stop at first blood. It might even bite into bone, such is the force behind the blow.

I let out a ragged gasp that's nearly a sob, my grip slipping even more. Kineas's grin is a feral snarl.

This is it. He'll win. And, oh, will I bleed.

But then, pale hands close over each of mine. I can't feel them *or* the phantom arms overlaying my own, even though they look as solid as I am, wrapping around my shoulders from behind. I sense the ghost of a cheek next to my ear. My eyes dart back and find Ivrilos's as he glances at me through his fall of dark hair. Then he looks ahead to Kineas, his gaze determined and . . . furious. And he *pushes*.

I can feel his hard chest lining my spine, his thigh planted alongside mine, the strength in his fingers nearly crushing my delicate bones against the hilts. I thrust my blades forward at the same time, and together Ivrilos and I send the crown prince staggering back so abruptly he trips and falls on his ass in the dirt.

I spin to stare at my guardian in shock. He's backed away slightly, though he's still nearly stitched to my side. Not that anyone else can see. He didn't appear long enough, or perhaps with enough of himself, for the spectators to notice. I only felt him at a few key points of contact—places on my body that are still tingling, both with the force of him and something else. Some heightened awareness.

I expect to topple over, to fall harder than Kineas. However little my guardian materialized, he used a lot of strength. Which means *my* strength, in the end.

But it's Ivrilos who looks winded, leaning forward, black-gauntleted arm braced on his thigh, hair curtaining his face.

He hasn't stolen from me at all, I realize. Affecting the physical world takes a lot from the dead, and it all came from him.

He straightens and practically hisses when he finds my gaze on him. "Eyes forward, blades up. End this now. You could conceivably have hidden martial talent and get lucky, but you can't prove to be thoroughly stronger and more adept than him."

And then Kineas is on me again, swinging in a flurry of blows.

But he's angry, his cheeks flushed. I've embarrassed him. And that makes him sloppy.

I know where to strike: a low thrust to the left, which Kineas is able to block, barely. What he can't do is parry my higher strike on the right, which is once again propelled by Ivrilos's palm against the back of my hand—just a whisper of it, there and gone—lending me speed.

The red gash appears practically like magic across Kineas's bicep.

The crowd is silent as the blood wells up and then drips down the crown prince's arm. He stares at it in disbelief. I almost laugh as I let my half-moon blades fall to the dirt, never mind that *I* feel like dropping to the ground with them.

"I guess it's you who bleeds," I manage to say.

Kineas's face twists in fury. He raises his sword. I'm too stunned, too exhausted, to try to block him with sigils, let alone fast enough to pick up my blades.

Another blade flashes in front of my face to meet Kineas's— keeping it from cleaving my head from my shoulders. I turn, half hoping, half dreading that I'll see Ivrilos standing there, dark in the sunlight, revealing himself for all to see as my true guardian. Enemy of the crown.

But no. It's *Alldan*. He tosses Kineas's blade wide in a shining arc of ringing steel.

"I heard tell of your skills, my lord, and came to see for myself. And yet this is beneath even the lowliest of fighters." His voice has an odd, lilting accent, but otherwise betrays nothing. "The lady put down her weapons."

Kineas is panting. I don't doubt the crown prince could—and would—bully anyone in his own court. But the uncertainty in his sharp gaze tells me that he doesn't know how to approach a prince of Skyllea. It isn't just because of his title. The man is a striking sight

212

to behold: deep green hair crowned in gold antlers, copper-flecked skin, and a russet tunic so patterned in bronze-edged leaves that it appears to be made of them, layer upon layer, all of him glittering in the bright courtyard. Even his sword is a wavy piece of rose-gold steel as odd and elegant as the rest of him. If he reminded me of a summer forest at the betrothal ball, today he looks like an autumn wood incarnate.

Kineas seems to shake himself, his empty hand spasming into a fist at his side. "It was all in jest. My beloved and I were just sparring."

"Of course. Your beloved." Alldan's smile dies well before it reaches his violet eyes. "And she won. So weapons aren't necessary anymore?"

"Of course," Kineas echoes, dragging his gaze away from Alldan. He skips over me as if he's already forgotten me.

But I know he'll remember this. Everyone probably will. It doesn't matter that *I* didn't challenge Kineas to a duel, that he brought this on himself. The next time he tries to hurt me—and there will undoubtedly be a next time—it will be much worse for me.

So much for falling in line and making myself the perfect bride-to-be. If I could see Ivrilos's expression right now, I doubt he would be pleased. But he's vanished. I have a hunch that he's too drained to easily appear in the living world, even if only to me.

Kineas walks away, lurching across the courtyard somewhat stiffly, I'm pleased to note, hand clutched to his arm to stop the blood. His nervous flock of attendants scurry out of his way as he departs between the columns. But then they follow at a safe distance, which leaves me blessedly alone for the moment.

Except for Alldan, prince of Skyllea and Lydea's betrothed, who is still standing next to me.

21

The Skyllean prince turns to me in the sunlight of the sparring yard, brow arched, golden crown flashing against his hair like a flicker of deer antlers in a dark forest. "Is this one of the stages of courtship in Thanopolis? Should I challenge Lydea to a duel?"

"Not unless you hate her," I say before I can think better of it. "Or unless you have a death wish."

Alldan's lips quirk. "So then . . . Prince Kineas hates you?"

I try to equivocate to make up for my slip. "No more than Lydea hates you, I'm sure."

His mouth flattens into a grim line. "And why would she have cause to do that?"

There's a slight challenge in his words, and I'm not sure why. Does he know, somehow, that Lydea and I are involved? Does he think I'm turning her against him in some other way? Or does he mean something else entirely?

"I didn't say she did." So as not to be entirely ungrateful, I nod at his strange sword. "Thank you for that. Kineas can get carried away, with his games."

"I'm pleased to help. I've been wishing to speak with you. Pardon my forwardness, but you're difficult to get alone." If I didn't know any better, the comment would sound flirtatious. In a flicker of bronze embroidery and rose-gold steel, Alldan sheathes his sword and gestures down at my own blades in the dirt. "That was a remarkable fight. I didn't know the royal women of Thanopolis trained as warriors, aside from the Princess Penelope and her daughter."

"Well, I'm not royal," I say, not bothering to put my weapons away as I trudge toward a marble bench between the shady columns of the courtyard. "And I'm only partly of Thanopolis."

Alldan follows me, hands folded crisply behind his back. "Yes, your father was Skyllean." A pause. "At one time."

Is he rubbing in the fact they disavowed him? Or is the Skyllean trying to unearth my father's loyalties and my own?

Before I do anything else, I need to sit down. I sink gratefully onto the cool marble. "My father was always a Skyllean," I say as Alldan takes a seat next to me on the bench, looking the very picture of a poised prince. "He made no secret of it here."

"Ah." His tone is perfectly poised, as well. "Then it's a shame we never had the chance to meet."

"Disavowing him was a funny way to show that."

A grimace flickers across Alldan's face. "That was political theater, you understand. Our alliance with Thanopolis was at a critical juncture. It's strange—years ago, your father reported something very disturbing happening to him and the other Skyllean bloodmage who journeyed here with him, Cylla. We were quite literally preparing to go to war with Thanopolis over it, but first Cylla and then later your father recanted those reports in documents officially sealed by the royal family here. Apparently, Cylla eloped out of love, and Silvean defected to Thanopolis, preferring life here. We would have liked to have spoken more to them about why they made the choices they did, but we never had the chance. It's a shame: Cylla's desire to pass on her bloodline so early and your father's unfortunate attack on the king so recently. We've since been told he was sick. Unstable. So perhaps he wouldn't have been able to tell us what we wanted to know, anyway."

I know the truth, of course. But I don't need to risk trying to tell Alldan. I can see, as plain as the violet of his eyes, that he knows what really happened.

215

"We've realized how little we understand of life over here," he continues. "Perhaps there's wisdom to be found. So we're here to create more formal ties, along with a more open channel between our two peoples."

They're here to keep their enemies close, as I've suspected. As I've *hoped*.

"My father always wanted to go back home," I say, willing Alldan to get the message. I swallow a sudden lump in my throat. "And it's been my greatest dream to go to Skyllea someday."

"Perhaps you can." He says it politely, maybe not understanding what the dream means to me. Or maybe he's trying to tell me something else . . .

Lately, I've preferred danger to despair. I want to trust him, but I have no reason to believe he can help me even if he wants to. My laugh is a broken thing, echoing among the columns. "Oh, I doubt it."

"Why is that?"

I don't feel like saying more aloud than would be wise. Besides, he must know already, if he knows the truth about Cylla and my father. So I snort. "If you can't see what's in front of your face, I can't help you."

He points at *my* face so abruptly I flinch and lean back, nearly falling off the bench. "That's an interesting sigil," he says.

The upright bowl with the three dripping lines, directly under my left eye.

"You know sigils?"

"My people created them."

I fight my blush with a scowl, shifting back into place. "I know, but since you don't have a bloodline . . ."

Alldan shrugs. "We still study them, especially those of us who have the time to do so."

The nobility, he probably means. Some things don't change, city to city.

"So . . . do you know what it is?" I ask, gesturing toward my cheek. I don't *quite* want to admit I don't know myself.

"I think so," he says, resting his hands on his knees. "Though I've never seen this particular one before. Your father must have created it, and yet it looks similar to another sigil that is relatively new in our lexicon. I believe that one was used, among others, to create the veil that protects Skyllea from the blight." He glances out through the columns to the iridescent ripple of the veil in the sky over Thanopolis. "Something like it was probably used to create the veil here, as well, though they've jealously guarded that knowledge. It's a sigil for blocking."

He holds my eyes for a pregnant pause.

Blocking. That sounds like the special set of sigils my father hid in his office, a map for me to trace along my hand, which I've identified as having to do with shielding. But the sigils haven't resulted in anything when I've tried to use them. They've been *missing* something. This sigil on my cheek is in a more prominent place than any other, so maybe it's somehow connected to the others. My father's words suddenly come back to me:

Follow your eye.

Goddess. My breath comes faster. He didn't just want me to follow the visible clues he left behind. He also meant for those clues, those sigils running along my hand and up my finger, to literally point to my *eye*.

I know I now have the final piece to my father's puzzle. The final sigil in the secret pathway he wanted me to follow.

My mind is spinning. If my father intended these sigils to shield only against the seeping poison of the blight as I journeyed to Skyllea—to safety, to freedom—then they won't be of much use if I'm unable to escape Thanopolis in the first place. And the force keeping me here is . . .

My guardian. The one whom I've suspected the sigils were

217

meant for all along. But Alldan seems to be telling me they could block out the blight, as well. Perhaps they're a shield against both, somehow?

I need to make sure. And for once, Ivrilos isn't around to eavesdrop. I can somehow feel he's farther away than usual. Perhaps it's my greater sense of his death magic or his underworldly essence. Not that I'm perfectly safe, but this is as close as I'm going to get until I can win entirely free of him. I still need to be careful.

Besides, Alldan is likely assuming my guardian is listening. He'll want to be just as careful.

"There are a few here who believe that the blight didn't just happen, like a drought or a cold spell," I begin hesitantly, picking at my fingernails in my lap before I still my hands—Alldan's are perfectly at rest. "I count myself among them. Maybe it comes from somewhere specific, and is made of something . . ."

"Darker?" Alldan suggests, almost casually. "It is not blood magic that our veils protect against, after all."

He has to mean death magic. That must be what the sigils are meant to block out. Aside from the greater, frightening implication that the blight is caused by death magic, perhaps knowingly from within Thanopolis, as my father suspected, that means the same sigils used to protect against it can work on my guardian.

I want to test my theory this very moment, but Ivrilos isn't here, and besides, if he learns I can shut him out, he might report me, shaky truce or not—and whatever confusing feelings lie between us or not. I can only try it when I'm ready to move; otherwise, the palace will come down on my head. Without Ivrilos to stop me, I'll be more than formidable, but I can't fight off all the wards in the city at once. As soon as I put my escape plan into motion, I'll need to be quick.

218

What that plan might look like, I'm not sure. Not without Lydea and Japha weighing in.

Not without my mother.

"So the king understands the true nature of the blight, and is willing to join forces with you?" I ask. I shouldn't care. I need to help myself before I can consider anything else. But Ivrilos said his family is evil, and for the king to know about the blight, to know that the death magic he so trumpets is the cause, to know that it originates from Thanopolis . . .

"Oh, I think he has known for a very long time," Alldan says, seemingly without judgment. But the words are like a sheath disguising a honed sword.

"And you're eager to make peace?" I press.

"We are eager to find allies."

Allies that don't necessarily include King Tyros. Maybe Skyllea will help me after all. Maybe Alldan will. I suddenly look at him in a whole new light, this strange prince sitting calm and collected next to me, while I'm anything but.

And yet Alldan has only given me a clue—an important clue—to what my father already knew. So why didn't my father use these sigils to block out Ivrilos, flee across the blight years ago, and bring the truth to Skyllea? Maybe he grew too weak before he discovered them. Or maybe it's something else.

"Shielding against the blight," I start. "Do you know how it works? I mean, you said it's a jealously guarded secret *here*, but maybe . . ." I make a muddle of it, but I hope he understands what I'm asking. Talking with Alldan is like pretending to dance with Ivrilos—we're making all the proper motions, but we're really up to something else entirely.

Alldan's expression darkens. "There's a reason it took us much longer to create a veil of our own. There are certain practices here that we find . . . distasteful . . . in Skyllea." By *distasteful* he means *abhorrent*, and by *certain practices* he means *death magic*—I know enough from my father to translate. "It led Thanopolis's mages more readily to the solution of the veil. You see, you must have a *piece* of what you wish to shield against. I believe bloodmages here worked with these . . . shadow priests . . . of yours to safely contain some of the blight. If one wished to create a similar veil, they would need similar . . . assistance."

Both excitement and sorrow stab at me. *That's* why my father never used the sigils. He would never have touched death magic. It's supposedly too dangerous for bloodmages, and he hated it, besides. And he never trusted any shadow priests or Ivrilos enough to ask for help.

But Ivrilos has given me something. A piece of himself. I don't even need to find a shadow priest to assist me.

Suddenly I can't sit still, no matter how exhausted I am. I stand from the bench and pace between columns. Underneath the arches overlooking the polis, I come to a marble balustrade and lean over it. I'm chewing my lip, trying to spot my home as Alldan joins me, resting his elbows on the warm stone. The sunlight practically makes him glow.

I can't see my home from here, and I wonder if I'll ever see it again.

Alldan may have already told me all he wants to share, but curiosity gets the better of me. "How did Skyllea create their veil without shadow priests?" I ask, watching the iridescent shimmer in the sky that's our own veil.

He shrugs, his eyes shuttering. "If one wants a piece of the blight, it's happy to oblige."

He obviously doesn't want to elaborate. He also hasn't said their approach is safe. The blight infects *people*, as well, so did bloodmages in Skyllea knowingly expose—and perhaps sacrifice—

220

themselves to erect a barrier against it? I shiver. It makes the weight of what Skyllea is attempting to do here in Thanopolis all the heavier.

I try not to think about the other person who wants to fix all of this. An amusing thought occurs to me before I can stop it: If Alldan could ever get over thinking of Ivrilos as an abomination, he might actually *like* him.

And yet, what does Alldan want from *me*? Why is he helping me? I'm sure he's seeking allies, but there must be more to it than that. He's a royal, after all, Skyllean or not.

I turn to face him, pushing back from the balustrade. "Are you enjoying your time in Thanopolis? I'm not much more familiar with the palace than you are, but if there's something I can help you with . . . ?"

"Thank you," Alldan says seriously. "I appreciate it. Anything you can share with me about the culture of Thanopolis would be wonderful, or about the royal family that you think might be useful—in wooing Lydea, that is."

Of course. Spying. I'm as *perfectly positioned* for that as I am for what Ivrilos wants.

I close my eyes, letting the sun warm my lids. Am I selfish for wanting to run the other way? Instead of figuring out how people can help me, should I be trying to help them? Should I be offering myself up as a sacrifice to Ivrilos's grand plan, or volunteering to spy for Skyllea?

"Ideally," Alldan continues, "I would like for Lydea to come live with me in Skyllea someday soon, to complete our cultural exchange. Do you think she would be willing to do that?"

I blink. Leave Thanopolis, yes. Accompany Alldan to Skyllea to no doubt be used as a political bargaining chip? I'm not so sure.

"Perhaps?" I say. "But she's one of the most . . . beloved . . . people in the polis, so King Tyros might not want to let her go."

She's *valuable*, I mean, if only for her bloodline and keeping Graecus sustained in the afterlife. Not to mention that *I* might not want to let her go.

"Ah, see, I've gotten the opposite impression. I feel like daughters are neglected here. Look at what happened to Delphia—a child practically of Skyllea, sentenced to the necropolis. It's a shame." He sounds truly bitter about that, and I wonder if indeed there's something between him and the young princess, as Lydea said. He hesitates, a slight breeze ruffling his forest green hair. "But you might be right. If something were to happen to the crown prince, Lydea would become precious indeed."

If something were to happen . . . It hits me then, what he's saying.

If Kineas's thread were plucked from the royal tapestry, Lydea wouldn't inherit the crown because of the rules laid down by the first king of Thanopolis proscribing female rulers. But she *would* become queen regent, and her son would be in line for the throne. Alldan's son. And if Lydea were safe in Skyllea, a shift in power could more easily occur. Once the king was removed as well, whether through war or assassination, she and Alldan could bring true change to Thanopolis. Free bloodmages from their guardians, and perhaps reveal the source of the blight. Destroy it.

Skyllea doesn't only want to keep their enemies close; they want to infiltrate and overthrow them.

But that would require Kineas's—never mind the king's—*permanent* absence.

"We wouldn't want that, now, would we?" I ask carefully.

"Skyllea cannot come under any suspicion if we are to maintain our alliance and encourage Lydea's visit. But of course we cannot be held responsible for accidents . . . or the actions of others."

I feel dizzy for a few heartbeats, and my hand returns to the marble balustrade to steady me. They want to assassinate the king and his heir. But does Alldan want *my* help? I'm close to Kineas by necessity, and I've as good as admitted that we hate each other. But if I help kill Kineas and anyone finds out, I would be handing myself and my mother a death sentence.

I almost laugh in despair. Alldan and Ivrilos do indeed want the same thing, in the end: a change in leadership. But Ivrilos is more focused on the underworld than on Thanopolis, and Alldan wishes Kineas dead, whereas Ivrilos forbade it. Killing the crown prince is far more appealing than marrying him and bearing his children. But either way, I might not survive their quests to destroy the royal family.

I want to survive. I want my mother to survive. I don't want to be someone's sacrifice.

"It would be horrible . . . ," I begin slowly, turning back to the view. "Horrible if any accident were to reflect poorly on *me*, as well. I couldn't dishonor my mother like that."

"Of course," Alldan says immediately. "And there would be far less risk of that if you and your mother were to accompany Lydea on her visit to Skyllea. If you can help me convince her to come, that is. You said seeing Skyllea was a dream of yours, correct? Perhaps you can share that enthusiasm with her."

It certainly is my dream, and my mother and I would be safe there from the rippling damage Kineas's and the king's deaths would cause.

"What about Japha?" I blurt. "They might want to see Skyllea, as well. I would hate for them to be left behind."

Alldan nods. "They are more than welcome to visit, and so is Delphia if she can gain leave from the necropolis. In fact, we would highly encourage it as part of our diplomatic mission." Something in his tone suggests it matters far more to him than that.

Maybe only because Delphia could be used in Lydea's absence as a potential path of succession to the throne. Japha, too, or even Crisea. But if they're all absent from Thanopolis, none of Old King Neleus's grandchildren would pose a threat to Skyllea's plan for Lydea's son to wear the crown.

Maybe Alldan doesn't want my help killing anyone. He probably has people aplenty for that. Maybe he wants my help with something else. His line about *wooing Lydea* might be closer to the truth than I thought.

But if all this comes at the cost of Lydea's freedom, then I'm beyond hesitant.

Besides . . . "The king may not allow me to abandon Kineas, even if I insist it's temporary," I say.

"Ah, but you like breaking the rules." And then, I swear to the goddess, he actually *winks*. It looks about as awkward on him as it would on Ivrilos. "Don't worry; I won't reveal your secret."

He could mean my penchant for disobeying, but I think we both know he means that he'd hide me if I managed to escape to Skyllea. It would probably be easier for the Skyllean delegation if they had me to help Japha and Delphia escape, anyway. They could then focus on extracting Lydea, through open channels or otherwise—if she agrees to go with them. And Alldan thinks I might be able to convince her to do so.

But this would put us all in Skyllea's debt—and in their clutches. And even if it's *my* dream to go to Skyllea, I highly doubt it's Lydea's or Japha's. I'm not sure about anything other than the knowledge that runs as deep as my bones: I can't marry Kineas. Which means I can't stay here.

But I also can't trade Lydea's freedom for mine.

I look out over the polis again. I have to find my mother. And in the meantime, I can teach Lydea and Japha the sigils to shield themselves from their own guardians, though I'm not sure what they'll use as a source of death magic. Maybe someone in the necropolis—even poor Delphia or Crisea—can help them. Even if I could block all their guardians by myself, there's no telling if I'll be able to sustain that for as long as we'd need to escape. Ideally, they could do it themselves, and we need to find a more permanent way to break the bond. Once we've figured that out, and I've reunited with my mother, we can all flee, fight whom we must, and cross the blight. King Tyros will send people after us, no doubt, especially if the veil alerts him to our passage like my father warned it would. But if we can move quickly enough, especially if we have horses, we can stay ahead.

If we have help.

Lydea's paying a more official visit to Skyllea still might be our best option, but it has to be her choice.

I meet Alldan's violet eyes squarely. "What if I can't help you . . . woo Lydea?"

He shrugs, though I can see the weight on his bronze-edged shoulders. "We feel it's our moral imperative, so to speak. You would still be welcome in Skyllea if Lydea refuses to come, but we might have to resort to less diplomatic measures to effect change. Broader strokes, on a larger scale."

He means that without Lydea as a less bloody path to the throne, Skyllea might have to go to war to stop Thanopolis. Many more people than only Kineas and King Tyros would die.

It wouldn't be my decision to start a war. It's ridiculous for Alldan to even place that burden on me, when Skyllea hasn't done *anything* for me or Lydea.

But he's also offering us all asylum in the near future. And that's not nothing, if he's telling the truth.

He must see the doubt in my face, because he says, "I mean it when I say you are still welcome no matter what. You only have to find me or one of my envoys, and we will get you there."

I don't know how he thinks he could get me out of the city so easily, but I think, *Okay, then*. My dream of Skyllea is still within reach. Winning free of Kineas is still possible. I don't know what to do about Lydea, but I haven't felt hope like this in a long time.

It feels like a promise of fire.

22

I get in touch with Lydea and Japha as soon as possible, passing them notes. My guardian's absence makes this less tricky than usual. I still have Graecus and Damios to worry about, but the fact that I can see where they are now makes them easier to avoid.

I can't help being concerned about Ivrilos, too, but in a different way. He helped me in my duel with Kineas, after all, and I appreciate it more than I care to admit. I haven't seen him in a couple of days. That's not entirely uncommon, but the timing and circumstances are odd.

The thought of him suffering somehow, unable to tell me, makes my chest feel tight and fluttery in a strangely panicky sort of way. And yet, while I might be my guardian's responsibility, he's not mine. I shouldn't care about him beyond trying to get rid of him.

Or at least that's what I keep telling myself. My silent reminder that *he doesn't care about me* doesn't ring quite as true, though.

After I wrestle with nigh-too-much reading and writing for my fledgling abilities, Lydea, Japha, and I agree to meet at the palace's private entrance to the necropolis. When we arrive, we're all wearing somber ceremonial death shrouds. It's the traditional garb for visiting the necropolis, *and* the draping cowls and sleeves cover our heads and bloodlines, lending us some measure of anonymity. Even the torches burn low in this stretch of hallway, and the floor is a dark swirl of black and gray mosaics.

The solemnity doesn't stop Lydea from winking at me. "Hey, beautiful."

I can't help smiling back. "Hey."

I shouldn't smile, because it feels dishonest somehow. Like I'm hiding something.

I've told them I have a way to escape but that we need more information from the necropolis, which suited Lydea just fine. We hope not only to learn more about our guardian bonds from Delphia and Crisea, but to let them in on our plans. Lydea intends to take Delphia with us when we flee the city, and I wholeheartedly encouraged the idea. She also says there's a place in the necropolis where we all might be able to talk without our guardians being able to overhear. Her mother, Cylla, took her there once or twice.

I *haven't* yet admitted that leaving with Alldan is perhaps our best bet. Even though it seems to be the easiest way to help the warded bloodmages, halt the spread of the blight, and avert a war between Skyllea and Thanopolis, I'm afraid to.

Because it might not be what's best for Lydea. For *us*.

Japha waves a hand in front of our faces. "Hello, I'm right here, and I'm also beautiful."

I laugh and throw my arms around their neck. "Of course you are. You were also being less obvious and more appropriate, for once."

Japha returns my hug warmly. "I can't help being unremarkable, wearing this." They shift their shoulders uncomfortably under their cowl. "I wouldn't be caught dead in this."

"My dearest, I don't think you'll have a choice when the time comes," Lydea says. "It's a *death* shroud."

"Even so. Fashion is always a choice. That will be my final request: 'Don't dress my corpse in a shapeless sack.'"

Lydea laughs and points us to a doorway between columns that are uncharacteristically naked of vines or flowers. I realize now that there are skulls inset over the head of the door, and the surrounding columns have segments between their knobby ends, like finger bones.

"This is the private entrance to the necropolis for members of the royal family. We don't have to deal with the common masses this way." She smirks at me to let me know she's teasing. "Shall we?"

Ostensibly we're visiting so I can pay respects to my father in the afterlife, and Lydea and Japha to their mothers and grandfather. Attempting to speak to the dead is a common-enough ritual in Thanopolis, even if it's more often practiced by the wealthy. It's expensive unless you're royal; then it's free. Somehow that makes sense to everyone. Of course, I've never done it.

"Let's," Japha says. "Despite our dreary outfits, I've actually been looking forward to this." There's a bright gleam in their eyes.

They march straight over to the darkened doorway and open it without further ado. Lydea and I both follow after a few cautious glances down the hall. I give her a subtle nod to let her know that my guardian isn't paying much attention. She and Japha return the nod, not realizing that I can see both their guardians. Graecus and Damios take note of where we're headed, but they aren't following very closely. I only catch flickers of them in the gloom. The thought of a visit to the necropolis must not be terribly exciting for dead men.

Ivrilos himself either truly doesn't care what I'm up to, which I doubt . . . or he can't spare the energy.

The way beyond the door slopes downward, continuing in twining mosaics that look more like flowing shadows than cut pieces of stone. Torches, surrounded by alcoves filled with skulls, barely light the way. This underground passage will connect us to the necropolis, built partially into the cliffside of the plateau upon which Thanopolis sprawls. The rest of the edifice looms on top like a vulture on its perch. The massive main building has no ornament, only weather-beaten pillars like bundles of bone. I've never wanted to go near it, and my mother, probably because of my father, never encouraged it. Aside from this underground palace entrance, only the poorest part of the polis abuts the orderly mausoleums outside the necropolis. Because who wants to live near the dead, other than shadow priests?

"They have a consistent sense of style here, I'll give them that," Japha murmurs, before carrying on down the hall.

"Were you able to get word to Delphia that we're visiting?" I ask Lydea, as low and as close to her as I can manage after we close the door.

She nods. "She's not supposed to meet us during this part of her training," she says out of the corner of her mouth. "Seeing family can make adjusting to life like the dead . . . difficult . . . so she'll have to sneak away." Her lovely lips cant downward. "I'm nervous for her."

"Don't worry," I say, squeezing her hand discreetly under my baggy sleeve. "We'll find her."

I let my fingers slip away from hers quickly, and not just to avoid being seen. Lydea gives me a glance, but she's too preoccupied by our mission to do more than that.

We wander on down the dim passageway until abruptly it's no longer narrow. It spits us out under a deep column-lined aisle, which in turn opens onto a cavernous central chamber. Columns and arches disappear into the shadows overhead. A statue of only one aspect of the tripartite goddess, the crone, stands stooped at the far end, a staff in one hand and a raised lantern in the other. Eerie blue fire burns there, throwing a sickly glow around the room. In the light, Japha's lips look blue—suffocated, drowned—and Lydea's skin as pale as a corpse's, her mouth bloodied. I pull my cowl tighter around me, as if I can keep the light from touching me.

"Hello, benighted ones." The hissing voice from the shadows next to us nearly makes me leap out of my death shroud. A person shambles forward in an outfit matching ours, except where a cowl would cover their head, twisting bands of ropelike iron bind them. The mask leaves only their mouth exposed, lips darkened to an unhealthy black at the corners, teeth jagged and rotten. As far as I can tell, it even covers their eyes. As much as I hate the sight of it, it's almost unfortunate it doesn't hide everything.

"Benighted?" Japha says with ill-disguised distaste.

"Shadowed by death. Bound to darkness." A skeletal hand flickers out from a sleeve, not taut with age but something worse, and reaches for Japha's face. Japha takes a hasty step back. "How I envy you. No matter how close to death I come, even touching the *shadows*"—they say another word after that, an old word, like what I heard Ivrilos speak, and something like black smoke coils around their thin fingers—"I will never be as close as you." The iron-strapped head tips nearer to all of us, and I can hear a raspy inhale. "I can smell it on you."

Whatever death smells like to the shadow priest, I hope it's not as bad as the stench they're giving off. *Glorified cult of death worshippers*, Japha once called Thanopolis, and that's never felt more apt.

I want to recoil like Japha, maybe run, but Lydea only smiles calmly. She might be the bravest person I know.

"Yes, lucky us," she says without a hint of the sarcasm I know she feels. "Excuse me, shadow priest, but we wish to try to commune with our royal family. Pay them our respects. There is a place where other shades cannot accidentally interfere with our summons?"

"Yes, there is a place for that." The shadow priest cocks their horrible, half-faceless head. "But your connection with your guardians may become disrupted. You see, the room has deep, dark magic in its stones. Its *bones*. By blocking out the many voices of the dead, it serves as a channel to those you call." The priest hesitates. "And just know that not all shades come when summoned."

Probably because most of them can't *come*, I think. *Because they've been used as mortar in the underworld. Or worse.*

"Of course," Lydea says placidly, "but it is our devotion to the dead—and the crone that shepherds them—that makes us try."

The priest hisses something that might be satisfaction. "The crone smiles upon you, as does her king." They gesture behind them, trailing a ghostly sleeve from their bony arm. I squint until my eyes adjust. There, at the end of the massive central chamber, behind the statue of the goddess, I finally see it: a darker, taller statue, deeper set against the far wall. It must be the first king, Athanatos, looming in the shadows behind the goddess.

I shiver.

The priest's head snaps in my direction. "Do you find death uncomfortable, you, whom darkness has kissed the most?"

My face blossoms with heat. Now I appreciate the sickly lighting making me look pale, because it's not just the shadow priest who's staring at me through the impossible iron bands of their mask. At least Lydea and Japha only appear confused.

"No, death and I are . . . um . . . pretty well acquainted," I stammer. "My apologies. I'm just cold." The opposite of cold, more like. My armpits prickle with sudden sweat.

The priest licks their lips with a blackened tongue, and I can barely suppress another shudder. "You should welcome the cold, because cold is the embrace of—"

"Of darkness, death, whatever, we get it," Japha says, looping their arms through Lydea's and mine. "If you'll excuse us, we have respects to pay and places to be. Um, where is the room we want?"

"There is only one place we will all be, in the end . . . but go in peace," the priest says with a terrifying smile. "Behind you, third door on your right, and at the end of the hall."

"Thank you!" Japha sings, practically dragging us away between the columns.

I lean toward Japha and mutter, "Do you even remember the directions?"

They keep their eyes forward. "No, but if I had to smell that priest's rancid breath one more time I was going to prove how alive I am by vomiting on their death shroud."

"I remember the way," Lydea says grimly. Determined. She paces ahead a few steps, and we follow. "Here, this door."

The entire frame is lined with skulls. All but the skull at the apex are lacking jawbones.

"It gets the message across, I suppose," Japha says, eyeing it as Lydea opens the way for us. "The dead are silent in here, unless it's the specific shade you're calling."

In other words, *no guardians allowed.*

The hallway stretches forward, darker than ever. And it's *completely* stacked in jawless skulls. They even curve around to cover the arched ceiling. The priest wasn't joking when they said the room's magic is in its stones *and* bones.

"Delphia said she knew where to meet us," Lydea murmurs after closing the door behind us. She hurries down the hallway. "Dear goddess, we have to get her out of here."

I hope that whatever magic keeps out unwelcome shades is already working and that it for sure applies to guardians. Because what she's just said could definitely raise suspicions.

As if my thought summoned him, I hear a voice behind me:

"Rovan? What are you doing?"

My heart leaps into my throat. Halfway down the hallway of skulls, I spin around to find Ivrilos standing behind me. He's squinting, a pale hand on his dark crown of hair, looking for all the world like he's just woken up with a hangover.

"Where have you been?" I demand.

"As close to resting as my kind can get," he mutters, as if talking hurts. "What is this?" He gestures down the hall with his other hand, still clutching his head. "I felt the strain in our bond. It . . . woke . . . me, if you want to call it that."

"Rovan?" Japha says over my shoulder. They're looking at me with a concerned expression, as is Lydea. Of course, neither of them can see or hear my guardian.

"One second," I say to them hurriedly. "I'm sure he'll go away like the other guardians." I turn back to give Ivrilos a significant look.

"How do you know *they're* not here still?" Lydea asks.

Because I don't see them. But she doesn't know I *can*. Damn her, she's sharp.

"So you show up now, of all times?" I hiss at Ivrilos as he seems to get his bearings. "I'm about to go . . . uh, pray. Commune. Whatever."

"No, you're not," he says, dropping his hand and glaring at me with more frustration than he usually betrays. The familiarity strikes me as sweet, somehow.

But I'm not going to let that ruin everything.

"Yes, I am. I'm going to try to talk to my father."

Ivrilos's face falls flatter than flat. It nearly *sinks*.

I didn't have much hope, but I can't help my breathless whisper. "Is my father down there? Have you seen him?"

He gives a single shake of his head, more like a twitch.

My throat tightens, and I feel a terrible pressure behind my eyes. He knows better than anyone what can be done to shades in the underworld. But I can't think about that right now—either about my father lost in that horrible place or, worse, becoming part of that nightmarish city, just like Ivrilos's mother and sister.

Gone, forever.

"Just be careful," Ivrilos says, shocking me out of my dark reverie, "whatever you're doing. I can't do much when you're in that room." He nods toward the end of the hall. "To help you, that is. Graecus and Damios couldn't even make it this far."

I'm baffled that he would first think of helping me instead of

234

hindering me. He must know I'm up to something that I don't want him to overhear.

I try to cover my surprise. "How can *you* be here, then?"

"Rovan, we need to hurry," Lydea says, but Ivrilos's words keep me from turning away from him.

"You and I have a . . . deeper . . . connection, right now," he says, wincing slightly, "that even the magic here has a difficult time silencing."

You, whom darkness has kissed the most, I can't help but remember the shadow priest saying.

"I gave a lot back to you when I . . . you know," he adds, shifting awkwardly. Awkwardly for him, at least, which still looks like a dance somehow, even amid all the skulls. Wreathed in flowers, wreathed in bones, Ivrilos stands apart from it all. "More than I should have. There are pathways open between us now that shouldn't be. That's why I didn't have much to give you during your sparring match." The apology in his tone is a small knife, stabbing me. "I think I'm *still* giving, without realizing it."

And he's not taking, like he normally would.

"It's okay," I force myself to say. Force myself to ignore that *he* might not be okay. Force myself to twist the knife. "If it's too much for you we can try to figure something out later, but I'm fine." I hope I am. "I need to go. Keep resting. We'll just be a moment."

I turn away from him quickly, because I can't stand to see his expression anymore. It's a little tired, a little pained, a little lost. It's like he's trying to reach out to me, and I'm smacking his hand away.

Lydea and Japha have twin "you'd better explain" looks on their faces, but they continue down the hall without another word. They obviously don't want to speak in front of Ivrilos, and they don't know if he's gone. I don't know, either, because I refuse to look back as I follow them.

I refocus on our purpose here. Finding Delphia, learning from

235

her, and eventually getting her—and the rest of us—out of this city. None of that has anything to do with Ivrilos.

We walk the rest of the way in heavy silence, the jawless skulls around us somehow adding to the weight of it.

"It should be just in here," Lydea murmurs, reaching the black door at the end of the hall.

Delphia should be just in here.

And she is, as we open the door onto a strange, dim room. The glasslike walls are all dressed in black. The only furnishing, if you can call it that, marring the equally smooth, dark floor is a raised stone slab. Luckily there's not a body on it. Only a lone sconce burns on one wall, casting barely enough light to see by. This room is much like the one I found myself in—or at least my spirit in—when I was first bound to Ivrilos. Delphia's cloud of white hair is like a torch in the darkness, even half-tucked in the cowl of her death shroud. Her silver eyes are wide.

Because she isn't alone. Two girls stand with her—one at either shoulder, as if she's pinned between them—on the other side of the stone slab. It's as if they want a barrier between us and them. I recognize the first girl immediately. Even in her death shroud she looks more like a warrior, shoulders squared, face set. Crisea. The second takes me far longer to place, because of the dark circles under her eyes, her pallid skin no longer sun-kissed, her lank hair like wheat that's dying instead of thriving, and the iron collar crawling in spirals up her throat as if already reaching to cover her face.

Bethea.

And she doesn't look happy to see me.

23

Lydea, Japha, and I freeze in the doorway to the strange, dark room. We've been expecting—hoping—that Delphia would be here, while planning to ease Crisea into talking to us if she would tolerate it. But we never expected to find both of them. And definitely not Bethea.

Japha and Lydea don't even know her, I realize. Of course. How could they? My two lives are colliding in this windowless room with no escape.

"What's going on here?" Lydea snaps, closing the door quickly behind us.

Delphia tries to move around the stone slab toward us, but Crisea places a firm hand on her shoulder.

"Shouldn't we be asking you that?" Bethea demands. She keeps the stone slab firmly between us. "This is our temple."

"And a *lovely* one it is," Japha says, tossing a hand at the glassy black walls. They pause. "Who the hell are you?"

Bethea shakes her head. Her neck is chafed under the iron collar, and her throat sounds scratchy. "Again, I'm not the one who owes the answers. You trespass here under a false purpose. You're leading our acolyte astray. Who do you think you are?"

"I'm your princess, you wretch," Lydea declares, sounding every bit as royal as she is, "and that's my sister you have there. My cousin, too," she adds, "if she still recognizes me."

Crisea's set expression deepens into a scowl, but she doesn't say anything. And she still doesn't let Delphia approach us.

Bethea shrugs. Even her shoulders look bonier than I remember. "In death, we're all made of the crone's breath."

Lydea bares teeth that look sharp between her red lips. "Are you telling me you want to die?"

"Are you threatening me, an acolyte studying death magic in the grandest temple of death?" Bethea scoffs. "You're lucky I haven't turned you in already."

"Now, now," Japha says hastily. They slide to stand in front of the stone slab as if it's a negotiation table. "There's no need to threaten anyone. We're only here to speak with the shades of our illustrious family, and we invited Delphia as *part* of that family. We didn't mean to break any rules. Right, Delphia, dearest?"

Delphia looks between us desperately. "I—" Her voice breaks. "She caught me with one of your notes."

"I only said we wanted to meet you here," Lydea supplies quickly. "There's nothing wrong with that."

"*Where no one can overhear*," Crisea recites in a hard voice. "I wonder, were you going to invite me to this secret meeting? I didn't get a note."

"Because you make it *so* easy to talk to you, now, don't you, dear cousin?" Japha asks breezily. "Or should I say *sister*? I suppose there's no need to hide it now that you're locked away in here."

Lydea rolls her eyes. "Of course we were going to contact you eventually, you dolt. We just didn't know how you'd react, so we were playing it safe. You're proving our caution was wise."

Bethea steps forward as if reasserting her authority, and yet she looks too sickly to command much. She grips the opposite edge of the stone slab more to steady herself than anything. "You're all forgetting there *is* something wrong with this, beyond misusing this room. Acolytes aren't allowed to meet with outsiders, let alone family, until they've been raised to the rank of shadow priests. You're breaking the rules by even sending notes to Delphia, never mind speaking with her."

"Then we're breaking the rules by speaking with you, too," Lydea says cannily. "So why are *you* here instead of some withered priest to reprimand us?"

"Maybe I want to talk," Bethea admits, both her gaze and voice dropping. She picks at the stone with a ragged fingernail and then looks up at me. "And you, Rovan? You have nothing to say to me?"

She's right: I've been standing here, mostly frozen, my mouth open like a simpleton's, unable to take my eyes off her.

"Or have you forgotten me?" she continues, before I can speak. "You didn't try to pass me any notes or pay me any secret visits. It must have been hard to remember me, living in the palace, in luxury, while I was sent here to die in dust and darkness."

Japha arches a questioning eyebrow. "I'm guessing you two know each other?"

Lydea looks back and forth between Bethea and me, understanding dawning in her eyes. "Is this about us breaking the rules or your feelings getting hurt?"

"I didn't know that they'd sent you here!" I insist to Bethea, willing Lydea to stay quiet.

"And you didn't bother to check," Bethea says, her hand tightening on the stone, her knuckles whitening. Her fingernails look bluish. "You didn't even try to find me. You didn't care. You're just like the rest of the royals, throwing us commoners away like we're trash when you're done using us."

"I am *not* a royal."

"Your new friends are," she says. Her glare takes in Lydea and Japha. "Your *betrothed* is. Yes, I've heard about him, even in here."

"You think I wanted this?" I burst out, throwing up my arms. My baggy sleeves fall away to reveal the red sigils streaking my skin. "You think I want the crown prince *or* this bloodline?"

"Oh, I'm sorry. What has your powerful blood magic done to hurt you?" Her voice is flat, but her sarcasm sharp. "Has it given you a new life in the palace? Status and wealth? Must be terrible."

"It got me caught, bound to a dead man, and engaged to a monster! It *killed* my father when he gave me his bloodline, and my mother—"

"Death magic killed my mother, too!" Bethea nearly shrieks, and I briefly hope the walls block the ears of the living as well as the dead. "They sent her here with me, and she died almost immediately."

For a moment, I'm too stunned to speak. I didn't know Bethea's mother well, but she told fortunes and communed with the dead in a manner not exactly sanctioned by the necropolis. She charged people a lot less than shadow priests do, for one, and she didn't have any formal training. My mother knew her better, and had often given her spare loaves of bread or fabric.

Gone.

"And I'm dying almost as fast!" Bethea continues, reaching up to grip her lank hair. "The whispers are louder in my head every day, telling me what to say to call the darkness. Sometimes I can't shut them out. Sometimes I can't resist drifting closer to them." She chokes on a half laugh, half sob. "You should have just let me fall from the gazebo that day. You saved my life, but then you threw it away. I was left all alone, with only death for company. I *needed* you," she nearly spits, slapping the stone slab. "I *loved* you."

I can't hear anything over the thudding of my heart. I don't know how I feel about Bethea—how I *ever* felt—other than temporarily happy to be with her. What I do know is that a pit of shame is opening up inside me. "But I couldn't—I don't—" I stammer. "You're not even allowed to . . . you know."

"I didn't need you like *that*," she snaps, jerking her hand back. "It's not only passion that holds off death. It's any light in the darkness. The warmth of a friend is just as powerful."

I know this from Japha already. It's something I could have given Bethea without question or hesitation. And yet I didn't. She's right. The thought shames me even more.

Bethea takes a deep breath. "If not for Crisea, I—"

"*Crisea?*" I can't help but exclaim.

Crisea takes a strong step forward and seizes Bethea's hand. "Yes. We're friends. Maybe we'd be more, if we were allowed. What of it, bitch?"

"Nothing," I say, stunned. "I just didn't think you could *make* friends, is all."

She sneers. "I didn't think you could, either. Not true friends, I mean, who you weren't just using to get ahead. You even used your father's life for gain."

For a moment, my vision narrows to Crisea's face and what I'm going to do to it—with sigils, fists, *anything*. Then I feel a hand take mine and squeeze tight, anchoring me.

"Rovan's not using me," Lydea says. "She's my friend. And more. Because we *are* allowed. Or rather, we don't care enough about the rules to bother with them."

Bethea stares at our entwined hands, and then at me. "So that's why you didn't *bother* to remember me. Why think about a commoner when you have a princess—"

Crisea scoffs. "I'm a princess, too. Trust me, it's not all it's made out to be."

A smile, as brief as it is, breaks the pall over Bethea's face, and for a second she looks as I remember her: bright, happy, beautiful.

"Bethea, I'm sorry," I say. "I was so caught up in my own misfortune that . . . you're right. I was completely selfish. I *am* still selfish."

More than I want to admit, especially as I'm holding Lydea's hand and yet hiding what I've discussed with Alldan about her.

Bethea doesn't say anything, only stares back at me. Her smile chased away some of the shadows on her face, but she still looks hollow.

Crisea cuts in again. "Don't worry. Rovan will forget Lydea, too, as soon as she's done with her."

Lydea's eyes flicker to me. There's not doubt in them, exactly, just the slightest hint of a question.

I should speak up, reassure her, but I'm frozen. It's like Crisea has found the beating heart of all my guilt, taken it in her hand, and squeezed.

It's Japha's turn to burst. They throw up their arms. "Dear goddess, can we do what we came here to do? This romantic drama is killing me piecemeal! No offense, death acolytes. But can we get on with it?"

"Yes," Crisea says. "What do you want to say to us? *All* of us? Because I'm not leaving, in case you were going to ask." She lets go of Bethea's hand to fold her arms, the picture of stubbornness.

Japha throws a cautionary look at me and Lydea. "Maybe we shouldn't . . ."

But if we can't talk now, when will we ever be able to? Lydea must be thinking the same thing.

"If you try to betray us, I'll say you're lying," she pronounces. "And that you were breaking the rules, to boot. Rovan, Japha, and Delphia will support my claims. Who will they believe? At the end of the day, we have more power than you."

"Well, then," Bethea says wearily. "What do you want with Delphia?"

"We want to leave, and we want her to come with us. You, too, Crisea, if you want."

For a moment, Delphia brightens so much I think she might lift off her feet. She truly doesn't belong here, if anyone does, surrounded by so much heavy darkness. But then her silver eyes dim. "Father will never let us go," she says quietly. "He put me here himself."

I can see how much that knowledge hurts hers, and I hate King Tyros all over again.

Lydea's voice is almost gentle. "It won't exactly be with his permission, little dove."

"How do you propose to manage that?" Crisea demands. I wonder how long it would take the necropolis to snuff that fire of hers, and the thought doesn't give me any pleasure. "You have guardians, remember? I can't believe they even let you come in here where they can't follow."

"Why should their guardians care?" Bethea asks, distantly, bleakly. Even an extra week in the necropolis has faded her so much in comparison to Crisea. "What can they even do in here?"

"We can *scheme*," Japha says.

"It doesn't matter," Bethea says. "You're bound to your shades forever. When you leave this room, you still will be. Nothing can change that."

"That's *one* thing I wanted to ask," I say hesitantly, stepping up to the stone slab. "How long is forever? Is there a way to be rid of them, even if it means using death magic?"

Bethea shakes her head. "Death is the only way. Your *second* death, or your guardian's. You'll still be bound to your guardian even in the afterlife. The bond is deeper than the flesh—it's of the spirit. Pneuma. And only with the dissolution of pneuma will the bond break."

It makes a horrible kind of sense. Blood magic dies with the flesh, death magic with the spirit.

That's it, then. There's only my father's special set of sigils. I can only block what I can't sever. It will have to be enough. Because for some reason I don't want to think about, I can't imagine giving Ivrilos his second and final death. If even such a thing could be done, I don't think I could do it. I wouldn't want *anyone* to do it.

"Okay, say we have a way to avoid them anyway, however we manage it." I take a deep breath. "We're going to leave Thanopolis. Will you come with us? *All* of you?" I ask, looking straight at Bethea. Lydea, Japha, and I never talked about her coming, because they didn't know she existed. But I'm not about to leave her here.

Delphia barely lets me finish speaking before she squeaks, hopping on her toes, "Yes!" She looks ready to leap over the stone slab and head for the door.

I can already see the answer in Bethea's eyes, but surprisingly, it's Crisea who answers. "I can't leave. This is my duty. If Delphia wants to shirk hers, it's not my business. That's between her and the goddess. I serve the crone now. For my mother." She looks away from me, sheepish, almost. "And I won't turn you in . . . for your father. He"—she chokes slightly—"he wouldn't have wanted me to."

Tears build in my eyes. Once again, she's found my heart and stabbed it. But as much as I want to hate her for being closer to my father than I ever was, I can't.

Bethea says softly, "And I'm with Crisea. I'm not leaving. It's my duty, too."

"But how can you stay in this horrible place?" I demand, gesturing at the stone slab and all it stands for. "This isn't your home. It's everything you're not. It's *killing* you."

"This is what I am now, for better or worse," Bethea says. "This *is* my home now. I'm sworn to the crone, and I'm loyal. I

244

haven't always had one foot out the door, like you." She glances at Crisea. "Crisea is keeping me alive, pulling me back from the dark, and I'm helping her. And for her sake, I won't turn you in, either."

Making it clear it's not for *my* sake. I never thought I would be dependent on Crisea's goodwill.

Delphia lets out a quiet cry and comes dashing around the stone slab. She throws herself at Lydea first, then Japha, and even me, surprisingly. When she pulls back, she doesn't go far from us, as if not wanting to let us go.

Japha pats the back of Delphia's head and smooths her cloud of white hair. "Now, can we get to the scheming part?"

"Yes, what exactly *is* our plan?" Lydea asks, facing me. "I've said we should buy passage on a ship—or hell, buy the whole ship—but you told me to wait."

Nervousness stirs in my belly.

"That must be the smartest thing Rovan has ever said. Because you have guardians?" Crisea sounds almost grimly satisfied. "Remember them?"

I still want to strangle her, but instead I say, "About that." I pull two pieces of paper from beneath my death shroud and pass them to both Lydea and Japha. "You'll know what these are," I murmur as they unfold the papers to find my string of shakily written sigils. "My father left them for me. You just need a piece of what you want to block out, and then it will be like the veil between us and the blight."

"And it will work on . . . all blights?" Japha asks, amazed. "Including the shadowy, brooding type?"

"That's the idea, but you have to have a *piece* of that shadow."

Delphia's silvery gaze darts back and forth between us. "I think I can help with that. I've learned enough to . . . gather it." She grimaces. "And after I do that for you, I'm never touching it again."

"Delphia, Rovan, this is fabulous," Lydea nearly gasps. "With this we can leave as soon as we want. We can go *wherever* we want—"

I don't want to say it, but I force myself. "I have some thoughts on that, too."

"Yes?" The eagerness in Lydea's eyes nearly makes me wince. Because I know it's about to vanish.

"Perhaps we should consider Skyllea," I say quickly, as if to get it over with. Never mind that the worst is yet to come.

"Skyllea?" Lydea's brow furrows. "Why would I want to go there? Alldan is a Skyllean prince. It's not as if I could easily avoid him."

"I was actually talking *to* Alldan about this plan."

She blinks. "You were talking to Alldan? About our *escape?*"

"Yes," I admit. "He wants allies. Skyllea thinks the source of the blight is here. They've been studying it, and found out death magic is causing it. From within Thanopolis, Lydea. And they think they can do something about it."

"Great," she says abruptly. "But I don't see how this concerns us *leaving* Thanopolis. If Alldan wants to stay here and study the blight, he's welcome to."

"This *does* concern us," I insist. "It concerns everyone. The blight is still expanding. It's going to devour the whole world! Skyllea has done their best to develop shields against it like the veil. These are shields against *death magic*, like this one my father discovered." I gesture at the papers still clutched in their hands. "But they're not enough. This all has to do with Thanopolis's dealings with the dead, everything that's wrong here—the blight, guardians, condemning people to the necropolis." I wave at Bethea and Crisea. "And Skyllea wants to *fix* all of it. They want to stop the blight, free bloodmages from their guardians, and keep more people from dying. If we can help them, we should at least consider it, don't you think?"

Lydea is silent. Her expression is unreadable.

"This is all very noble, Rovan, dear," Japha says. "But how can we help?"

I swallow. "Alldan thinks if they plan things just right"—*kill Kineas and the king*, I don't add—"they can use your position, Lydea, to really change things."

"My position," she says flatly. "With Alldan, you mean."

I flinch. "Yes. If you go to Skyllea . . ." I hesitate. I'm not sure how I'm going to explain everything without mentioning the murder of certain family members of hers—family members of almost everyone in this room—but she doesn't give me the chance.

"Wait, wait," she says, closing her eyes and lifting an elegant hand. "This plan involves me *marrying* Alldan, still?" She opens her eyes to stare at me, red lips parting in shock. "And you're fine with this? You *want* me to marry him?"

"No, of course not! I wish there was a better option. But they can help us escape, offer us sanctuary, and we can help—"

"*We?*" Lydea cuts in. "You mean *me?* You and Japha will both escape *your* marriages," she says, glancing between the two of us, her gaze sharp, "but I still have to go through with mine even after I've gone to the trouble of abandoning everything I know to run off with you?"

"Hey, this isn't *my* plan," Japha says, raising their hands.

She ignores them, holding my gaze. Hers is shadowed. Sad. "That's not what I meant when I said, 'Take me with you.'"

The look in her eyes is killing me.

"I'm sorry. I just thought . . ." I don't know what I thought. The plan sounded much better in my head than it does now, and it didn't even sound fabulous then. It's still a way for Lydea, Japha, and me to escape; for me to help Ivrilos and Thanopolis, Alldan and Skyllea; and to reach the land I've so long dreamed of seeing all at the same time.

And it's utterly selfish. I know that.

"I just figured it might be a way for everyone to win?" I finish feebly.

Lydea's gaze hardens. "Everyone except me. I can't believe you would deny me the same freedom that you seek for yourself. I can't believe your grand plan involves only *my* sacrifice and not yours. I don't see *you* volunteering to stay behind with Kineas—using yourself to achieve some noble end. Only me."

The worst part is, she's right. Ivrilos tried to convince me to do exactly what she's suggesting, but I refused. I came up with *this* plan instead. Because I couldn't stand Thanopolis's prince, and I thought maybe Lydea could tolerate Skyllea's.

"I would never ask you to stay with my brother," she adds. "I would do anything in my power to get you away from him."

"Kineas is *cruel*, Lydea!" I exclaim. "Alldan isn't—"

"You're going to sing his praises?" she demands, folding her arms. "My, you move quickly! He's a complete stranger to me and yet you know him so well?" She shakes her head in disgust. "Why don't *you* marry him, then, and leave me out of this?"

"I'm not royal," I say, exasperated. "Skyllea has no path forward through me."

"You mean no path to the throne," Lydea says coldly. "And I suppose my *womb* is that path?"

"Only if you agree to it!" I say.

She stares at me. "Was I just a diversion for you? Did I ever mean anything more than that?"

"See, I told you," Crisea says. "Rovan will use you and forget you, just like she did Bethea."

This time, Lydea seems to listen to her. She takes a step back from me. Then another, toward the door.

"Lydea, wait!"

She ignores me as she speaks to the dark room around her. "Maybe I'll just take *myself* out of here, along with Delphia and Japha."

"Hey, now, that's not my plan, either!" Japha says, backing away from both of us. Delphia looks helplessly caught in the middle.

And just like that, our little group is drifting away. Literally and figuratively. It feels like my heart is breaking apart with them.

"I still want you to come with me," I say desperately to Lydea. "We don't have to go to Skyllea! Forget I said anything about it."

"Maybe I don't want to go with you anymore," she says. "Maybe I don't want to go anywhere with anyone who would even *suggest* such a thing. For me to let myself be used as just a part of another man's scheme." She smiles cuttingly. "Or should I say *woman's* scheme?"

"Lydea, that's not fair!" I cry. "I never meant to use you!"

She shrugs slender shoulders, as graceful as ever. It doesn't matter that I can barely see them under her death shroud. I see them in my sleep. And that might be the last I'll see of her. She retreats all the way to the door.

"Maybe," she says. "And maybe I don't care about your intentions, if it all ends in the same place." She reaches for the door latch. "Delphia, await word from me. Japha, decide who you want to go with." And then she slips out of the room, just like that. Leaving me behind.

I can only stare at the door as it closes behind her. Japha doesn't say anything, their eyes downcast. Delphia sniffles.

"You deserved that," Crisea says, her hands on her hips.

I spin on her, fists clenched at my sides. She's lucky she's still on the other side of the stone slab. "Shut. *Up.*"

Bethea shakes her head in wonder. "You really don't care about anyone other than yourself. I tried to tell myself I was being too hard on you, but you've proven it again and again. First with me, and now a *princess*. I actually feel bad for her." She gives a feeble, disbelieving laugh. "All you think about is helping yourself. You've barely even *mentioned* your mother."

"I'm doing this for my mother!" I cry. "I'm trying to get her out of here. To get *all* of us out of here, and not leave the world to rot!"

Bethea blinks at me. "What do you mean? She's not . . ." She trails off.

"Wait." I squint at her as if trying to see her better. "What do *you* mean?" My breath hitches. "Do you know something about my mother?"

Her expression freezes into place. She doesn't respond. Crisea glances at her, looking afraid for once. Delphia covers her mouth with her hands. Only Japha looks confused.

"What about my mother?" I ask. I can't get enough air in my lungs. "She's being held somewhere . . ."

"No, she isn't," Bethea says quietly. "When you mentioned your mother earlier, I thought . . . You really don't know?"

"Know what?" Already I feel something horrible building inside me. Some hidden knowledge. And when it bursts free, I might break.

"Rovan, I . . . I saw her here."

"Where is she?" I gasp.

"She isn't—" Bethea chokes, tears in her eyes. "She's gone."

"Where did she *go*?" I shriek. "I need to find her!" I'm suddenly moving toward Bethea, reaching.

"Rovan—" Japha tries to grab my arm, but I throw off their grip. Still, it's enough to stop me in place. My hands are in my hair. The pressure builds and builds.

This can't be happening.

"You won't find her," Bethea says, her voice light as a whisper.

"She went where most people do after they come to the necropolis. I helped prepare her . . . her body."

No, no, no, no, is all I can think.

"I'm sorry to be the one to tell you this." She meets my wide-eyed stare as a tear tracks down her cheek. "Rovan, your mother is dead."

And then I break.

24

I shatter inside, and yet somehow everything stays the same. I continue to breathe, and my heart to beat. Bethea and Crisea remain on the other side of the stone slab in the strange black room. Japha and Delphia keep close to me, but Japha watches me carefully and then reaches out to tug their cousin behind them, as if shielding her from whatever I'm about to do. Lydea is still gone. The same weak torchlight flickers over us all, and yet the glossy walls seem to be closing in on me. Crushing me to dust.

"How?" I say. My voice sounds hollow. Far away. Like it isn't mine. "How did she die?"

Bethea shrugs helplessly. "I don't know. Your mother and I were both brought into the necropolis together, after your trial. I was isolated with acolytes, and she was taken away. The next thing I knew she was laid out on a stone table a lot like this, and I had to wash her—her body. Her skin was very pale, like she had no blood—"

"Stop." I can't hear any more. I even cover my ears.

That's why the royals wouldn't let me see my mother. They haven't been keeping her somewhere safe to ensure my cooperation. They killed her for whatever reason, practical or evil, and they've been lying to me this whole time. Using my gullibility to their advantage.

But no more.

I'm moving through the doorway and out of the room before I know it. The black walls and the people vanish, replaced by the skull-lined passageway. Gaping eye sockets flash by me. Japha follows, trying to keep up with me, saying something. I can't hear them. I don't see anything around me, really. My focus has narrowed to a single, needle-sharp point: the door at the end of the passageway.

Move, move, move. It's the sigil I've used most of my life. The one I can form with barely a thought. I'm like the embodiment of that sigil. If I don't move, I don't know what will happen.

But then something stops me in my tracks. *Someone.* He appears as soon as I exit the skull-lined hallway.

"Rovan? What's wrong?"

He's so beautiful that for a moment I want to cry. But those tears belong to another person. "Ivrilos," I say. "Did you know that my mother's dead?"

His expression—pure devastation—is answer enough. And yet he doesn't look even close to how bad I feel. "I knew as soon as your father did. That's what King Tyros whispered to him at your betrothal ball. Rovan, I'm so sorry. Silvean didn't want—"

"It's fine," I interrupt, even though it's not. "It's fine."

And then I take all of that shadow inside me, that *piece* of Ivrilos, and drag it to the surface. I feel him in my very skin.

But I don't use that to block him out. Not yet. First, I want to bring him closer. And now I can do that.

I *seize* Ivrilos by the back of the neck. I actually touch him, pull him into me, using his own substance to do it. What he gave me of himself. We crash into each other, nearly losing our balance. He's taken completely by surprise. I fight against my *own* surprise at how wonderful he feels under my fingertips, curls of his dark hair tangled in my hand. My other palm rests on his chest, above where his heart would beat. I want to keep touching him.

His eyes are wide, his body tense, but he can't do anything before my lips are on his. I kiss him hard. Deep. He responds, and the feel of his tongue moving against mine sends a distant thrill through my body, like lightning far across the night sky. His hands rove over my flesh as if he's never felt anything like it before. He probably hasn't touched someone like this in a very, very long time. And then I feel an answering call inside him, and it's more than just his kiss, his hands. It's his very essence. What makes him *him*. He's right: We're connected in ways we shouldn't be, in ways he can't control. He can't help but open himself up to me—exposing that deep well of shadowy darkness inside him.

And then I *take*.

I take so much. Much more than a breath. His hands tighten on my shoulders, and he sucks in a ragged gasp as if trying to get it back.

"Rovan," he grates against my lips. "What—how—?"

How could I do this to him, after everything he's done to help me? But he hasn't only helped me. He's also hurt me. And this is what he gets. I need something he has, so I'm using him to get it. I'm finally just as selfish as everyone has accused me of being.

And I can live with that, if only because I might not be alive much longer. If *this* doesn't kill me, then what I'm about to do probably will.

"I truly am sorry," I breathe. I don't mean for the words to be double edged, but I realize it's an echo of what he said to me when he bound me to him.

Ivrilos's knees buckle. It's as if he's been gutted. He tries to use me for support, but his grip fails and I let him go. He crumples to the ground.

"Don't be too mad at me," I say, my voice numb. "I'm actually helping you. Maybe."

I leave him there, staring, convulsing on the floor of the necropolis. I keep moving. I don't look back.

Move, move, move.

254

I feel so cold, so *full*, brimming with his icy essence. Powerful. I still can't help stumbling. Memories blind me. I see the ax falling. I see his mother and sister screaming. I see terrible Athanatos in front of that horrible, dark city. And then . . . I see my father smiling, tears in his eyes, as the strange earth in that upside-down place drifts up and away around him.

So Ivrilos *did* see my father in the underworld. He lied to me, like everyone else . . . But no, I can't look closer at that memory, or else I'll lose my focus.

My father is gone. My mother is gone. I can't do anything to get them back.

But I can sure as hell make someone pay for it.

I move quicker, as if trying to outrun the sight of my father. I lurch through the main chamber of the temple and into the underground passage leading back to the palace. The movements of my body are all wrong. I'm trying to walk like Rovan, the nineteen-year-old girl, *and* like Ivrilos, the twenty-three-year-old swordsman who's had an additional four hundred years of experience as a shade. It doesn't help that my skin is numb from the cold, my limbs deadened. I nearly fall over at several points. When I catch myself against a wall, I'm forced to look at my hand, splayed out on the marble in the torchlight.

My fingernails are blue like Bethea's, but worse. The skin around them is black. Not just like I'm freezing, but like I'm diseased. Rotting. *Dying.*

Stealing from Ivrilos may not have been the best idea.

I have to shove down a spike of horror. Drawing too deeply on death magic *is* bad for a bloodmage, I think with grim humor. *That*, at least, wasn't a lie.

As long as I don't die too soon. I just need my legs to work in the meantime. And the worst of my imbalance is coming from the link between Ivrilos and me that I can now feel, like a chain made of shadow. He's still trying to control the pneuma I've taken from him. He still thinks it's his.

But it's *mine*.

Now I use my father's parting gift to erect a barrier around me, keeping what I have of Ivrilos inside and cutting off the rest. I only have to sketch the sigils in the air. My bloodline does the rest, calling forth the sigils now that I know where to look for them. I draw them out along with a tiny pinch of what I've stolen from my guardian.

Something settles over me, as light as silk. It warms my limbs and muffles Ivrilos's influence through our bond, nearly silencing his presence. I still know how to use a sword—oh, how I know— and I still remember things I don't want to remember, but Ivrilos's movements and memories are no longer trying to bring me to my knees. And now he won't be able to stop me.

Lydea is nowhere to be seen. A small, distant part of me is glad that she's not around to see this. Japha is still here, though. They're shouting from behind me, heedless of who might hear. But we're alone in the underground passage back to the palace. They manage to snag my arm and drag me around to face them in the middle of a pool of torchlight, next to a skull-filled alcove.

So much death around me, and now it's *inside* me.

"Rovan!" Japha cries. Their expression is more horrified than I've ever seen, the shadows on their face darker and sharper than my usual eyes would be able to detect. Now I have another kind of sight. Deeper. Keener. "What the hell is happening to you? Look at you! Goddess, you're . . ."

I pull away, forcing their grip down to my bare wrist. "I don't care. I have to go."

Japha recoils at what must be the coldness of my skin, and wipes their hand briskly on their death shroud, as if whatever is plaguing me might rub off. "Go *where*? You're falling apart! We need to get help!"

"You can't help me. Only I can do this."

"Do *what*?"

Alldan wants the crown prince and the king dead. Ivrilos wants to breach the king's inner sanctum. I wanted to help them both without sacrificing anything of myself. I even considered offering up the woman I love in my place.

Not anymore, I think. And then, *Love?*

I do love Lydea, don't I? I think I might love Ivrilos, too, but luckily I don't have to worry about that right now.

Or maybe ever.

"Just keep yourself safe and get out of the city," I say to Japha—forgetful, for once, that someone else might be listening.

"Abomination," a voice says over Japha's shoulder. "Did Ivrilos do this to you? If so, he will answer for his crimes."

I meet Damios's eyes as he appears in the underground passage. Now I can see Japha's guardian as clearly as I can see my own.

"No," I say. "I did it."

Japha blinks at me, looking back and forth between me and their guardian, realizing we're speaking to each other.

"Well, then," Damios says, drawing his sword. "Prepare to die."

Japha spins on him. "What the fu—"

Damios places his other hand on Japha's shoulder, and his ward drops like a bag of rocks. Their head cracks on the stone floor. The sound is loud and sharp, echoing deep inside me.

Damios did that. He's stealing Japha's life energy to stop me. And for that, I'm going to kill him. *Again.*

Because I love Japha, too. And I can't stand to watch them hurt. Not that I haven't hurt those I love, myself. Sometimes I feel like I love too much and not enough.

Fire appears in my hands with barely a sigil-lined thought, two blades of flame in the shape of bright half moons, and they burn an unhealthy blue. The fire of life tainted by death, perhaps.

Damios lunges to meet me, moving like liquid shadow. But I move like that, too, despite my numb, sickened flesh. Blue flames spark off shadowy steel. And as we clash, I remember I found Damios's statue among the somewhat recently deceased in Athanatos's line. Which means the strength and experience I gained from Ivrilos is far greater.

Never mind my bloodline—my father's life experience. *His* long family line.

I hope both threads of life and death, of blood and breath, are enough to hold me together for as long as I need. As I swing my blades, whirling around Damios and carefully stepping over Japha at the same time, I notice some of my fingernails have fallen off. The distraction nearly costs me my head, but I duck just in time. A clump of my hair, its blue tint gone dull, almost gray, drifts to the floor. It's more than his blade should have dislodged.

Japha was right. I'm literally falling apart. Ivrilos's essence is sucking the life out of me, like a blight inside me. I took too much of him. But there's nothing for it now. And it's Ivrilos's instinct that tells me exactly how to end this.

Damios seems to understand I have the upper hand in swordplay—he's staying away from me, backing down the hall. He must see I don't have long, and he's trying to tire me out. But blades aren't my only weapon. With a few sigils, I create a raging fire on the floor underneath the dead man's feet, just as I once saw my father do to a different shade. But Damios jumps clear of it.

I hurl one of my half-moon blades, end over end, right at him. He freezes, staring down in shock at where it lodges in his chest. His own sword falls to the ground. Where there should be a clatter of metal against stone, the weapon simply vanishes, because it's only made of pneuma, like him.

I'm about to bring the fire underneath him again, burn him away like so much smoke. But then an arm comes around Damios's neck from behind. Ivrilos's head appears alongside his.

"Goodbye," Ivrilos says. "For good."

He kisses him on the cheek, as if in farewell. Damios does indeed turn to smoke, a final look of horror blurring with his face. Instead of disappearing or dispersing, that darkness *flows* into Ivrilos, vanishing into his mouth like an inhalation.

Not only is my guardian on his feet, he seems a lot stronger now—as dark, beautiful, and deadly as ever. I expect him to be angry, but he only stares at me across the hall. Japha is still sprawled on the stones between us. I feel a distant relief when their body stirs and they give a feeble cough.

Japha is *free*, I realize, no longer bound by their guardian. But I don't have time to celebrate on their behalf.

"Rovan," Ivrilos says quietly. "Stop this. *Please.* You don't have to do this."

Even though I'm resolved in my plan, I still don't want him to see me like this. I'm not sure how I look, but it can't be good. I lift my cowl back over my head, but even that loosens more of my hair. "Don't try to stop me. You can't. It's too late anyway," I say, picking away the strands and dropping them with a strangled laugh.

"Maybe," he says, the very picture of calm. "But you can still give back what's killing you. You don't need to steal it from me, because I'll help you. Together, we'll do this. I'll stand with you." He holds a pale hand out to me.

His offer is more than tempting. Even when I had only a limited amount of his essence inside me, I still knew how to fight like him. With this much, I'm not sure what I've gained other than too many memories and too much death magic.

I stare at his hand, and he lifts it higher. "Come on," he says, oh so reasonable. "I promise I'm only here to help."

Carefully, fully aware that my barrier is still intact, I raise my own hand. He lunges for me.

I repel him, even seem to hurt him. He yanks his hand back, hissing, like I'm a fire that has burned him.

"You're going to stand with me, huh?" I snarl, backing away from him. "You're such a liar. You were trying to knock me out."

"I promised I was here to help," Ivrilos says, shaking his hand. "I don't know how you've shielded against me, but I'm *still* trying to help. That wasn't a lie."

"Your definition of help is very different from mine." I keep backing away. "You also said you didn't see my father. Down *there*."

Ivrilos follows slowly, like he doesn't want to scare me into fleeing. "I said he wasn't in the underworld, which was true by the time you asked."

"I forgot you like to mislead and pretend it's not lying out of some stupid sense of honor. But try to get out of *this* one," I spit. "What you just now did to Damios . . . You did that to my father, didn't you?"

Ivrilos freezes. Closes his eyes. "It would have been worse for him, down there, if I hadn't."

"Maybe." I don't stop moving. "That still makes you my enemy."

Ivrilos opens his eyes. The look in them is agonized. He doesn't try to deny it, but then he says, "I might be your enemy. But you're not mine. Rovan, I . . . I *care* about you. I might even—"

"Shut up!" I shout. It's hard enough to think I might love him, but to imagine he might feel the same . . . I can't, not when I'm on this path.

As if in response, Ivrilos's memory of my father surges back into my mind, stronger than ever. But this time, he's still alive, standing over me, my body once again laid out on something too much like a funeral slab. Marklos—that *bastard*—is the one to slit his wrists. My father's blood pours out, but it doesn't fall. My father uses it to sketch sigils—so many sigils—in the air above me. Ivrilos must be standing at my head, watching it all happen. No, he's keeping me under, trying to deaden my pain, even if I feel it in my dreams. I shift and moan in my sleep. Eventually, my father's blood looks like a complex web ready to settle over me.

And then, my father, sounding dazed, drunk, his eyes nearly rolling, says, "Goodbye," to no one in particular. And then to Ivrilos, he says, "Take care of her."

"See you soon," Ivrilos says. And then my father collapses, just as the bloody net drops down on me.

Before long, they're both standing in that dark world. It's much like the glimpse Ivrilos gave me of my father before, but now there's more. I realize my father no longer has his bloodline.

"Don't tell Rovan about her mother," he says. "I don't want her to do what I did, throw herself madly at her own death. If the thought of protecting her mother can keep her safe—as safe as she can be in that den of snakes—then I want her to hold on to it."

"As you wish. I, too, think that's for the best," Ivrilos says.

My father seizes Ivrilos's shoulders—he can now, like he never could in life. "I'm begging you, as a father, as the one who has given my life to you, and soon my second life, if you can help her, if she can help you . . . please, consider it."

Ivrilos clasps his shoulder in turn with a firm hand. "I will."

The fire goes out of my father, but not without a final spark. "If you don't," he says with a weak bark of laughter, "then I hope she ends you. For good."

"She's welcome to, once I've done what I need to do."

My father sighs. "There's nothing else for it. You've told me what happens to wandering shades down here, and I'd rather you do it. I'm ready." But then he asks, his voice heartbreakingly small, "Do you know what comes after this?"

Ivrilos shakes his head. "I have only died once."

"That was a long time ago, I imagine."

"And yet someday—maybe soon—even I will follow you." My

guardian hesitates. "I hope. Until we meet again. Honor to you, my brother."

"Farewell," my father says with a crooked smile and tears in his eyes. "Bastard."

"That I am." Ivrilos leans forward and kisses him on the cheek.

The memory clears, leaving the Ivrilos of *now* still standing before me. "I'm sorry I kept it from you, but I was trying to keep you from doing *this*."

I shake my head. I know my father wouldn't have wanted me to do this. But now I understand: *He* couldn't help doing the same, after he heard about my mother. And neither can I. "You only want me safe for the sake of your revenge," I insist.

Ivrilos throws a hand behind him, toward where he . . . *ate* . . . the other guardian. Tendons stand out in his powerful arms. "I ruined my chances at revenge when I finished off Damios." He's trying to stay calm, but it's a struggle. "Killing some common guards is one thing, but one of the ancient royal line?"

I shrug. "You can blame me. Hell, you can *report* me, if you give me a minute. And if I fail in my task, you can carry on your plan with the next bloodline you're bound to. Maybe they'll even give you a promotion."

I sound indifferent, but part of me is dying inside.

"I don't want a *fucking* promotion," he snaps. I don't think I've heard him use that particular curse before. He reaches up, gripping handfuls of his hair, nearly unseating his circlet. He looks more disheveled than I've ever seen him. In more pain. "I don't know what I want. I'm not sure I want to save this kingdom if you're not in it."

"Don't," I say, raising a hand to silence him. But then I drop it because I don't want to see my mottled skin, missing fingernails. It's appropriate that I'm wearing a death shroud. "Revenge has driven you for four hundred years. I don't believe you've forgotten

262

it as quickly as that." I take another step back down the dark passage. "And right now, it's time for *my* revenge. But maybe you can get yours soon, too. I might even be helping you." I turn. "Follow me, if you want."

"Rovan!"

I ignore him, moving as fast as my limbs will allow me down the rest of the underground passage toward the palace. I refresh the shield between me and Ivrilos, resketching the sigils as I move, for good measure. I know he's following, but I don't look back.

I'm on a warpath.

25

The gold-threaded marble and flower-wreathed columns of the palace pass by in a flurry of jagged edges because of my strange, enhanced vision. In every line, I see a blade. In every bit of red, dripping blood. And in every shadow, spirits that scream in agony as they're devoured.

All I see is violence. Death.

I think I might be losing my mind. And it's only getting worse. Another memory rises unbidden, and I can't tell if it's Ivrilos's or my own. We're both sitting before my gaudy lion's mouth of a hearth, cast in flickering firelight, and he's saying, *I think some form of madness might take you before death would. And with how powerful you are, the consequences could be . . . horrific.*

Well, here we are, I think hysterically. I try not to let it slow me down.

Hidden by my shroud and deep cowl, I make it all the way through the palace to Kineas's door without anyone raising the alarm. Ivrilos obviously hasn't reported me to the underworld authorities, nor have Bethea or Crisea to any shadow priest. Damios's second, final death has gone unnoticed. The guards at Kineas's door, however, try to stop me.

"Excuse me, miss, but the crown prince has asked not to be—"

I follow the path of sigils in my mind, and I raise my rotting hand. My fingers map it out.

Both guards collapse on the ground, staring at the blossom-covered ceiling. The only evidence of the violence done to them is their blood-red eyes, flooded by the force I exerted on their skulls with my indelicate sigils. It's good that I've never tried to knock anyone out before now.

If I hadn't previously crossed some invisible line, I know I just did. These sorts of sigils had never come easily to me, because I never wanted them before. I do now.

Behind me, Ivrilos lets out a string of curses and vanishes. I know where he's gone—to devour their shades in the underworld.

He's also eliminating witnesses. Which means he still has hope that this can turn out any other way than how it will. I already know: I'm going to survive neither this nor my second life as a shade. There will be no immortality for me.

So I leave the bodies where they lie.

I'm equally discreet with my entrance. Kineas's elaborately carved, gilt-lined double doors are made of wood, and I blast them open with a wave of my hand. Perhaps I could move stone now, too, with a word—I hear an eerie whisper in my mind, trying to tell me how. If blood magic can shape life through written symbols, death magic must shape what is lifeless through spoken words. Two sides of the same coin, really: the breath of the dead, sigils written in the substance of life. But I don't want to use it. If I start channeling death magic, I'm worried my body might just disintegrate.

Blood and death magic really do seem to want to destroy each other.

Kineas's apartments make mine look positively common. Gold is in abundance everywhere, not only veining the deep blue marble of the outer room's pillars, but lining every piece of furniture with elaborate filigree. Gold practically rains from the ceiling with chandeliers molded like draping branches, their leaves wrought in silver and blossoms cut from pearly glass. Even the wall sconces are gold cast in the shape of naked women lifting their bright flames high above their heads, exposing their ample bosoms.

Of course Kineas would be that tacky. It's a small consolation I'll never have to join him in these apartments.

I hear a muttered curse past another gilded set of doors. His despicable voice rises: "I *said* I was not to be disturbed!"

I kick in those doors with sigils. They slam against the inner walls, sending one of several large mirrors shattering on the mosaic-tiled floor. I try to avoid my reflection in the others, though I glimpse grayish, flaking skin beneath that once-hated red sigil on my cheek and black mottling around my mouth. Revulsion crawls up my spine. Luckily the light is dim in here, the thick curtains tightly drawn and only scattered candelabras lit—for a purpose I soon see.

Kineas flies upright from under elaborately embroidered covers, his hair tousled. He's in a massive bed at least twice as big as mine, the four corner posts carved to look like naked women upholding a canopy of midnight blue silk embroidered with gold and silver stars that actually sparkle and drift. His bed also has about that many flesh-and-blood women in it. There's a gasp and a yelp from where they're half-buried under the covers. Even a giggle.

They probably think I'm here to catch them in the act. I don't care about them at all.

"Get out," I growl.

Several pairs of kohl-lined eyes widen in the shadows of the deep bed. One girl makes a move to slide out of the covers, but she freezes when Kineas snaps his fingers at her and shakes his head, like she's a dog.

"Rovan, *darling*," he drawls, tossing his pewter hair out of his eyes. He leans back languidly against a luxurious stack of pillows. "Why don't *you* get out? I never granted you permission to enter. You might be eager for the marriage bed, but need I remind you we aren't wedded yet?" He blinks. "Where are my guards?"

"I killed them," I say, and then look at the girls. "I only want you to leave so I don't have to kill you, too."

266

One of the girls screams, and then they're all out of bed, stumbling and running for the doors in various states of undress. Kineas snarls at me, hurling the covers aside. He tugs a himation hastily around himself, but not before I see more of him than I ever wanted to. It makes me doubly grateful I'll never have to again. He also grabs a long, wicked dagger from off his bedside table. A ruby the size of an eye winks from the pommel.

I hope it's there to use against unforeseen threats like me, and not against the women who have the misfortune to regret being in his bed. But I've heard the stories, and I have my doubts.

"There's no chance you killed my guards. Your guardian would have stopped you." He marches toward me, but his steps falter as he gets a closer look at me in the dimness. "What in the goddess's name is the *matter* with you? You're hideous!"

I shake my head slowly, vaguely hoping more hair doesn't fall out. "No, I'm dying, and I'm taking you to the underworld with me." I get no small satisfaction in watching the blood drain from his face. "But first, let's take a walk."

Kineas raises the dagger in shaking hands, the blade and ruby glinting in the candlelight. "I'm not going *anywhere* with you, you disgusting witch. Look at you!"

Of course he wouldn't want to come with me because of how I *look*, not because I threatened to kill him. I should be angry, but instead I start laughing. I can't help it. It's just so *funny*.

"You're insane!" he shouts.

I swallow my laughter with difficulty. "I might be."

"Guards!" Kineas yells. "Help!"

"I told you, they're not coming." Another giggle escapes me. "Can we go now?"

Kineas lets out a wild cry and charges at me with the dagger upraised.

Merely sketching sigils, I break every one of his fingers. The snaps are loud, like chicken bones popping when you twist the leg from the thigh. I'm actually impressed with my accuracy, though I wouldn't want to try anything requiring more delicacy than that. Healing must be terribly difficult.

I'm not here to heal.

Kineas howls and drops the dagger. He tries to catch it, fumbling it in useless fingers and slicing his palm open, before it hits the floor, the ruby clacking loudly. Bent with pain, he stares down at his reddening, rapidly swelling hands, one now dripping blood. He releases a strangled groan.

"You *bitch*," he half sobs. "You're going to pay for this."

I'm staring at his hands, too—rather, the red oozing from the one. I can't *stop* staring. It's like something has seized control of my body, and I just need to get closer . . .

I reach for Kineas's hand, but he jerks it away—understandably, though I can't have that. With a wave, I slam him against the wall, breaking another mirror, and seize his wrists, feeling the warm wetness ooze over my fingers. I marvel, because where his blood touches me, the dark rot recedes from my skin.

That isn't why I do it. I do it because I can't help it. I feel a need, a hunger so strong, that nothing, not even my own screaming thoughts, can stop me. I press his palm to my lips.

Blood pulses into my mouth, warm, thick, and coppery rich. I drink.

Kineas screams. But I choke off his throat with sigils until the noise is a mere rasp. I keep gulping. It tastes so good; it's like his blood is filling a yawning void inside me.

Satiating the darkness.

"Rovan." Ivrilos's voice is soft. "What are you doing?"

I spin to look at him almost guiltily, Kineas's hand still pressed to my mouth. I have the misfortune of catching myself in yet another mirror as I do—how many mirrors can one person *have?*—and I

268

see how I must look to Ivrilos, who stands in the shadows behind us. I actually look *better*, as far as the death rot, but my eyes are feral and red tinged, and my cheeks have a high, feverish flush. Otherwise I'm starkly pale underneath my sigils. Worst of all, I have blood running down my chin and neck.

Ivrilos swallows as he takes me in. I can't decide if he looks sick or . . . something else. Hungry?

"You should stop," he says. "You don't want to kill him. Not yet."

Right. Taken with this strange craving, I've nearly forgotten why I'm here.

I pull Kineas's hand away with a wet slurp and wipe my mouth, unable to meet Ivrilos's eyes or my own in the mirror. It's easier to look at Kineas, who's still making strangled noises, his face drawn with pain and terror.

I clear my throat. "I don't know why I did that."

"I have some idea," Ivrilos says quietly. "I've heard stories of . . . of what death magic can inspire in a bloodmage. Of the hunger it creates. You can't easily sustain yourself with the pneuma of others like a shade would, because you're still in this world, of this flesh, but you *can* drink the substance that powers your blood magic. Do you feel better?"

I nod, running my tongue over my teeth. Trying to savor it.

"Good," he says, "but it won't last. If you reopened the way between us, unblocked our bond, I could still help you. I could help you focus. I could take back some of what's making you hunger, or I could try to feed you in a way that's not—"

I shake my head. "No! I don't trust you!"

"Who else do you *have*, Rovan? You can't approach anyone else like this! You're . . ." He trails off despairingly.

A monster, I think. "I don't need to see anyone else. Just the king. I thought you wanted to get a glimpse into his inner sanctum?"

269

My guardian cocks his head, going as still as a cat spotting a mouse. "That's where you're going?"

When I gesture at Kineas, I'm pleased to see my hand no longer looks like it belongs to a festering corpse. It just looks *freshly* dead under the smears of drying blood and the sigils of my bloodline, but even my fingernails have grown back. "With him. I'll get as close as I can, and then after that . . . I figure the king might listen to me if I threaten the life of his heir."

Ivrilos arches an eyebrow. "And you think Kineas will cooperate?"

"Let's ask him." I release my invisible hold on Kineas.

As soon as I do, the crown prince takes the opportunity to vomit all over the floor. I'm struck by the absurd urge to apologize, but I ignore it. It would be useless to say, *I'm sorry for drinking your blood, but not for breaking your fingers. And just so you're aware, your life is completely expendable!*

"Kineas, *darling*," I say instead. He flinches away from me. I probably still have blood on my mouth.

"Goddess, you're a sick freak! Who were you talking to?" He coughs, flailing a bit with his damaged hands. "Are you deranged, or is that your guardian? If it's him, I command that he stop you this instant!"

"He can't stop me, because I've shut him out. And this is all my doing," I add, just in case Ivrilos wants to take up his revenge plan another time, if all else fails. "Are you ready to accompany me to visit your father?"

Kineas is shaking. He holds both forearms crossed at his chest. "Why should I do that? If you wish to make an attempt on the king's life, it's my duty—"

"You'll come with me quietly, as if we're on a lovers' stroll, because if you don't . . ." I use sigils to seize the part of him that will hurt the most. Down *there*. Kineas jumps and lets out an undig-

nified squeal. "I'll break other . . . *things*. Squash them to pulp."
Sweat instantly breaks out on Kineas's forehead. "After that I'll rip
out your tongue. And I'll *still* drag you to the king."

I'm unable to smother a grin. Drying blood cracks on my face.
I must look demented. For good measure, I pick the dagger up off
the floor.

Ivrilos shakes his head. "Rovan, this cannot end well for anyone. I beg you, please. I can't—"

But I'm already using a spare length of peach cloth from the
ground—a piece of one of the girls' outfits, I imagine—to scrub
the blood off my hands and face. I have more on the sleeve of my
death shroud, but I fold it to where it doesn't show. My outfit isn't
ideal for visiting the king, but I have to work with what I've got.

"Kineas," I snap. "Tuck your arms into your himation to hide
your hands—yes, like that. Now practice smiling. If we run into
anyone along the way, tell them everything is fine."

"No one is going to believe that," the crown prince hisses as he
adjusts his arms under the draping cloth. His grimace is the opposite of a smile. "My father is going to *kill* me," he groans.

I shrug. "What's worse—that, or me crushing your balls and
ripping out your tongue?"

The smile he gives me is sickly, but it's a smile.

I gesture with the dagger toward the door before I flip it
around in my hand, ruby pommel flashing, and tuck the blade up
my sleeve. "Lead the way, then."

Ivrilos tries to stop me one last time, a tortured look on his
perfect face. "Don't do this."

I ignore him.

Kineas walks ahead of me, stepping far more gingerly than his
usual confident stride, arms crossed carefully against his stomach
under the folds of his himation. Ivrilos stalks behind me, resigna-
tion sharpening him, one of his half-moon blades drawn. I keep up

271

my shield against Ivrilos and a subtle pressure on the crown prince to remind him to behave.

Even so, we don't make it very far.

There are about a dozen guards already outside, weapons drawn, as we step through the broken-in doors and out into the palace hallway. It makes sense: I left a mess at the entrance to Kineas's apartments, not to mention the corpses of his guards, and the fleeing girls no doubt raised the alarm.

"Oh, thank the goddess," I say breathily, "and thank *you* for getting here so quickly! Someone attacked while the prince and I were chatting. We were waiting for reinforcements before we came out."

The guards all stay back, at the ready. The one in charge says, "We have a report that *you* attacked."

"That's absurd! I'm the crown prince's *betrothed* and a loyal subject." I pluck at my death shroud. "I was just paying respects to Old King Neleus in the necropolis. Besides, my guardian would never allow that. Our attacker must be spreading these lies. Right, dearest?" I ask Kineas, increasing the pressure on him.

He nods quickly, his face coated in a sheen of sweat. It looks like he has to stifle a gag. "Yes! Yes, that's correct."

Subtlety is definitely not my thing. Marklos was right about that. If I see him again, I'll be sure to thank him, especially for what he did to my father.

The lead guard squints at the crown prince. "Are you all right, Your Highness?"

Maybe it's good that Kineas's appearance is drawing all the attention. It distracts from *mine*. But he still needs to play the part.

"I'm fine," Kineas says, giving his sickly smile. I want to elbow him.

"It was just a bit of a shock," I say. "We're going to go report to the king now."

"There's no need for that," says a commanding voice that traces a cold trickle down my spine. "I'm right here."

I hear footsteps approaching from down the hall. And then the group of guards parts down the middle, bowing their heads, to make way for the king.

26

Down a marble hall infested with gold and choked with flowers, King Tyros comes striding purposefully. A gold-embroidered, deep blue tunic drops heavily around his legs, and a gold laurel crown glints in his salt-and-pepper hair. He has even more guards in tow, led by General Tumarq and the Princess Penelope in bronze breastplates and leather pteryges. Lady Acantha, whom I haven't seen since my trial in the Hall of the Wards, and Captain Marklos head up a few bloodmages, all of them in black and red uniforms and silver helms. I thank the goddess Lydea isn't among them.

I can see the guardians perfectly clearly. All in black, they look less like their wards' shadows and more like looming captors, ready to bring them to heel—or even kill them—at a moment's notice. A pox on flesh. And maybe it's my strange eyesight, but the king is a dark stain at the center of them all, despite his bright embroidery, almost like a guardian himself. The worm in the apple.

All of this death mixed with life, I think somewhat deliriously—in the end, all you get is rot, whether it's in this city, in the outer blight-covered world, or even in my own body.

My game is up already—I know as soon as I see the look of panic that crosses Kineas's face when he sees his father. He's more afraid of the king than he is of me. The loathsome squid won't do what I say. Not even for the sake of his tenderest parts.

But maybe his father will.

I slide behind the crown prince, grab a fistful of his pewter hair, and bring the sharp edge of the dagger that was hidden in my sleeve to his throat. He tries to struggle, but the movement makes him nearly crumple in pain. Not only that, his neck gets nicked by the blade for his trouble. I try to ignore the trickle of blood.

"Trust me, I don't want to be this close to *you*, either," I mutter in Kineas's ear, and then I raise my voice. "One move and your heir will no longer be able to make heirs. And then I'll slit his throat just for fun."

The blade is redundant, since I could splatter Kineas's guts on the floor with little more than a thought. But it's a good visual clue for the guards who might need to see the threat plainly to be dissuaded from any heroics. The ruby winks at them for good measure. And yet I'm regretting it because of the blood.

I can *smell* it, and it's like the scent of everything my body has ever thirsted or hungered for, all at once. It makes my love of wine seem like child's play. Through an act of sheer will, I don't drag his throat down to my mouth to lick it.

Tyros halts in his tracks, throwing out a hand for everyone with him to stop. They do, with varying expressions of alarm. Tumarq is calculating. Acantha stares at me aghast. Marklos downright seethes. The king's face remains stony.

"What is the meaning of this?" he says, eerily calm.

This man killed my mother. Or at least ordered her death *and* my father's. The urge to throw Kineas aside like so much trash and fly at the king with sigils and dagger alike is almost as strong as my thirst.

Because while killing Kineas might be one of Alldan's goals, I don't really care about him. The king, however . . . he's mine. Alldan wants him dead, anyway. Ivrilos might want to stall to see where his brother is hiding, and I'll help with that if I can. But if all I can do is end Tyros, that's good enough for me.

"I need to talk to you," I force myself to say instead, nearly as calm as him. "Just you. And him out of necessity." I nod toward Kineas without moving the dagger. "Otherwise he's not worth the air he breathes."

It's my only chance to get the king alone. And I need to get him alone. I'm not going to be able to get close enough to kill him if he's surrounded.

Tyros cocks his head at me, and for a brief second—very brief—he reminds me of Ivrilos with his predatory focus. The gold laurels in his hair flash. "Why? And why would I agree to that?"

"Because I have a few things to say to you alone, and because you want your heir to live?" I pull Kineas's head back harder, and he gasps as if on cue. "Or maybe you don't care. Let me tell you now: I don't care if *I* survive this, and so I'll do whatever I must to get your attention."

The king's blunt eyes don't leave mine. And then he smiles, which nearly makes me shiver. "Trust me, you have it. But where is Ivrilos in all of this? Why hasn't he stopped you?"

Ivrilos is standing by my side, but of course Tyros can't see him.

"He can't," I say. "I've blocked him."

"You figured it out. Clever girl," the king says. And then he blinks slowly. Once. Twice. "All right."

Tumarq and Marklos both look at the king in surprise, but it's Penelope, in full fighting attire, hand on her sword pommel as if ready to cleave me in half, who says, "You can't honestly consider humoring her?"

Tyros doesn't even look her way. "I'll consider what I wish."

"But, Your Majesty—*brother*," Penelope insists, "she's wearing a death shroud. She may have been to the necropolis. What of Delphia—your *daughter*—or . . ." She doesn't say the name, though Crisea is obviously her primary concern. Ever the warrior mother. "Aren't you worried this girl is taking revenge on our family for the perceived wrongs against hers?"

The king shrugs a single shoulder, barely. It's like a boulder shifting. "Check the necropolis," he says to Penelope, without taking his eyes off me. "See if anything is amiss. Report back and don't dawdle."

She doesn't look appreciative of his dismissive tone, but hers is unmistakably grateful. "Yes, Your Majesty." She peels off, heading back down the hallway, a few of the guards accompanying her at her signal. I don't miss the flash of relief on Tumarq's face, even as worry flickers through me.

Bethea, Delphia, *Japha*—I hope they'll all be fine. That's all I can do. At least Crisea should be safe, because she's royal *and* not plotting to escape. As safe as she can be in the necropolis. But the king seems to mark how little he cares about them when he adds, "Marklos, go find Lydea. Guard her with your life."

I guess I'll have to kill Marklos later, if I survive.

The captain bows his head, flashing the sigils that climb up the side of his neck, and departs immediately, with only a glare for me. He doesn't take anyone with him. He probably doesn't need to. His bloodline is long and powerful enough to guard . . .

Lydea. I hope she can still get herself out of the city. In making my move, I've drawn attention to *her*, too, not just myself, and now she has Marklos to deal with. Whatever the outcome, by attacking Kineas so soon I've betrayed her importance to Thanopolis. It's not just Skyllea that understands it now.

I'm still selfishly hurting her, even as I'm trying to give myself up. The thought makes me sick. I try to swallow the feeling.

"Care to step inside with us?" I ask, as if this is a casual encounter in the streets and not a standoff in the royal palace—with the king, no less. I begin backing toward Kineas's destroyed apartment doors, dragging the crown prince with me.

Tyros follows slowly, step by careful step, his tunic's gold embroidery glinting, his eyes unblinking. It's unnerving. When

277

Tumarq and Acantha make a move to follow, he waves them off. "Stay," he says.

Now I know where Kineas gets his tendency to treat people like dogs.

I slip back into the outer room of the crown prince's chambers, dodging debris. Ivrilos is somewhere behind me, but I face forward, holding Kineas and watching the king. Tyros traces my steps without looking down, like we're dancing. Once we're fully inside, I use some quick sigils to drag the doors closed and brighten the lamps.

"Well." The king smiles, holds out his hands, palm up, as if in offer. "What can I do for you?"

"You can tell me why you killed my mother."

He doesn't even bother denying it. "She had no use other than reining you in, and I believed we could do that well enough without her."

"How's that going for you?" I spit, holding the knife tighter against Kineas's throat. His indrawn breath is harsh. Frightened.

"Yes, I admittedly overestimated Ivrilos's abilities as your guardian," Tyros says, unconcerned, folding his arms, "as well as underestimated your father's influence. I didn't end him quickly *enough*, apparently, before he could put ideas into your head."

I don't glance at Ivrilos. "My father was *cooperating* with you! First for Cylla's sake, and then for my mother's and mine. And you betrayed him. You only wanted his bloodline."

"Cylla." The king's lips twist around her name. He seems to ignore everything else I said. "She deserved worse than she got."

"Father," Kineas chokes, trying to look Tyros in the eye despite my fist in his hair. "You don't mean that."

Even in the midst of everything else, *this* is the first thing the crown prince mentions? His mother is definitely a sore spot—I remember that from our betrothal ball.

"You *abducted* her," I add to the king, vaguely horrified to be siding with Kineas. "You *forced* her to marry you. She was the mother to your children."

"Yes, just as you were to be the mother to *his*," Tyros says with a dismissive nod at his son, gold laurels glinting. "Warmth of regard isn't necessary, as you can see."

"There's something wrong with you," the crown prince gasps against the dagger's edge, surprising me yet again. "You felt sorry for Mother. You were always giving her gifts, trying to make her comfortable here. You *loved* her, even if she didn't love us." I hear the mixture of both yearning and disgust in his voice—how he both admired and pitied his father, how he both adored and despised his mother. Perhaps because Cylla both loved and hated Kineas, especially after he grew up to be more of his father's child than hers. "You never denied it before. You're *different*."

I don't know how Kineas can presume to judge his father for anything, but I don't interrupt. I remember Japha, and even Lydea now that I think about it, hinting that Tyros has been acting strange since his coronation. I squint at him over the crown prince's shoulder.

Ivrilos comes up to stand next to me, studying the king just as avidly. Tyros only stares off into the distance behind his son.

"Perhaps you see more of yourself in me than you ever have before. Pity it's not enough." The king seems to shake himself, as if knocking a piece of mosaic tile back into place—completing the picture of a ruler with everything under control. He turns back to me, disregarding Kineas entirely. "Love or cruelty doesn't enter into it. I did what I did because that's what I was *told* to do. Like Kineas would have if he'd had the chance to do his duty. But neither he nor Ivrilos appear to be up to the task of managing you. Perhaps Skyllean bloodmages are too much of a challenge. Perhaps we should rid the world of them entirely." He sighs. "We're certainly finished with *you*. Kineas needs someone more biddable. I thought your bloodline would be too great a shame to lose, but it's not worth the trouble."

I shake my head, marveling at him. "Why do you hate blood-mages so?"

"I don't hate you. You're tools," he says bluntly. "Meant to be used and discarded when no longer useful."

And almost all these so-called tools in the palace are women. They're doomed to short lives and even shorter afterlives, while royal men go on to become immortal guardians.

"Why do you hate women, then?" I ask.

"I don't, as long as they do as they are told." His eye twitches, giving away the lie. "As must we all."

"You're the king," I say incredulously. "Who do *you* answer to?"

"Certainly not you," he says, some sharpness entering his tone. "Now, where does all of this pointless talk leave us? What do you want from me that I could possibly wish to give?" He raises his eyebrows, shifting that marble face. Exposing the cracks again. "What do you want—your freedom? An apology? I'm afraid I can't bring your mother and father back to life, but is there *something* I can do to make amends?"

The falsely honeyed tone of his voice, his disdainful sarcasm, his sheer arrogance, is enough to make my hand tighten on the dagger and my vision leap into strange, unearthly focus. He's right about one thing: This conversation is pointless. He's not going to give me the answers I crave, and he can't bring back what I've lost. But he can do *something* for me. It's the real reason we're all here.

"Yes," I hiss. "You can *die*."

With the hand hidden in Kineas's hair, I hurl sigils too quickly for the king to dodge. A column of fire as thick as my leg shoots from my sketching fingertips and blasts toward Tyros's face. I've unleashed the heat of a forge. It will burn everything in its path—shadow, flesh, even stone.

But the flames don't touch him. The burning column *parts* around him like water, dissipating in the air behind him. His arm is raised as if it were a blade that cut my fire in half. In the dying glare I see his hand fall still.

His fingers were *moving*. Sketching sigils. Maybe someone like Kineas won't have noticed, but I have. So has Ivrilos, next to me. His eyes are wide. Before I blink, the invisible hold I have on the crown prince is ripped away by more sigils, rendered as ineffective as my fire.

The king is a bloodmage.

I don't have much time to consider it, because he charges for me, where I stand with the blade at Kineas's throat. I don't know why he doesn't use sigils now—maybe to hide his power. But I *do* know that he can't affect metal with his magic. A blade should be able to pierce him like anything else. He's not wearing any armor, just his thickly embroidered tunic.

And I have a hidden power, too.

I whip the dagger away from Kineas's neck. With the same motion I used against Damios and borrowed from Ivrilos, I hurl it at the king. The ruby flickers as it flies end over end.

The blade slams right into Tyros's heart, burying itself up to the hilt. He jerks back midcharge, teetering to a halt. And like Damios, he looks down in surprise at the jeweled pommel protruding from his chest.

But he doesn't fall. He *frowns* at it. "This is inconvenient," he says.

My mouth drops open. Kineas is too shocked to even pull away, let alone attack me. We both just stare as the king reaches up to take the hilt and slowly draw the dagger from his chest, as if he's in no particular rush.

No blood comes pouring down the gold embroidery of his tunic. There's none even on the blade. Tyros doesn't seem relieved by this, or disturbed. He merely looks from the dagger in his hand up to us.

"Father?" Kineas says. He doesn't say it like he's asking if he's all right. He says it like he's asking if it's *him*.

"No," Ivrilos says. And when he speaks, the king looks *right at him*.

"No," the king agrees. "Hello, brother. It's been a while. But I've seen *you* around, of course."

"Kadreus," Ivrilos breathes. "Rovan, *run*."

The king smiles, and the hair on my arms stands on end. "She's not going anywhere," he says, and then turns to me. "While this business with Kineas is unfortunate, you actually did me a favor by drawing me away. If you'd betrayed what I am in front of so many witnesses, it would have been much more bothersome. Why *else* do you think I agreed to come with you alone?"

"Because you care about the life of your heir?" I suggest, shifting closer to Kineas. Maybe there's a chance I can seize him again, try to use him as a shield. He's still unmoving, useless, staring at the man who's not his father. It would be easy to overpower him.

But then the king says, "No more than the lives of my many other heirs. There are always more, to keep me alive. To keep our legacy alive."

And then he lunges. I'm not ready for it, and neither is Ivrilos.

And neither is Kineas. Because the king goes for *him*. The knife flashes toward his throat. Kineas jerks. Gurgles. Unlike the king, Kineas can bleed. Blood cascades everywhere over his chest from the gaping wound in his neck. It's like a red smile.

I can't help turning for Kineas. Not because I want to save him, but because of the blood. My guard utterly drops, no thought in my head other than the overpowering urge to drink. I lunge . . . right into the king's dagger.

Ivrilos is ready this time, but he only manages to throw his hand between the king and me, to make that one part of him solid. The dagger still slides right through the back of his hand, like a knife through bread.

And pierces my heart.

It pins Ivrilos's palm to my breast for a moment, which at another time might have been funny. Not now. My guardian shouts, agony in his voice, especially as contact with my shield burns him. But his cry cuts off as he vanishes.

There is a terrible pressure in my chest. It's cold. So sharp. I can't breathe. I can't speak. When I reach for the dagger, my hand closes inadvertently around the king's, which still clutches the handle. I want to coil around that spot, but I can't bear to move. It's like a muscle cramp has seized my entire body.

The king grips the back of my neck, pulling me into his chest and making pain explode through me. I scream. But he holds me tight, steadying me, shushing me. And then he whispers in my ear, "I could have used sigils or something else, but this is just so much more *personal*, yes? It's personal between us, Rovan. Especially since you've forced me to kill my heir far ahead of schedule. He couldn't know what I am."

What are you? I want to ask, but I still can't speak. I want to lie down.

I know who he's *not*, at least—not Tyros.

He keeps me upright, embracing me. Perhaps I should focus on the dagger in my heart, but I glimpse something strange on his arm as he touches me. It's like a shadow lifting from him, revealing a bloodline marking his skin. He was hiding it. Along with everything else about him.

I still have my shield against death magic. It would be the only way to hide a bloodline—my father could never hide his with blood magic alone. Which means the king wields *both* blood and death magic. And he can't die.

Obviously, if he's somehow Ivrilos's brother, Kadreus.

I look up into his eyes. They're bright red now, but other than that, he's much like Ivrilos. About my guardian's age, maybe a little older. Slightly lighter hair, cropped closer to his head. But it's his eyes and the expression on his face that are different. He's so cold and . . . utterly mad. I was looking through the cracks in his previous mask to something hidden underneath. I just didn't realize how far down and dark they went.

And yet, the shadow behind him is even worse. I see it even as the gilt-lined room dims at the edges. Something like a guardian, looming over us both, mostly too dark to make out but with burning, sickly blue eyes I recognize now and I'll never forget. I've only seen them in Ivrilos's memory before now, but there's no mistaking whom they belong to.

Athanatos.

The king gently brushes my hair aside and leans toward my neck, lips parting.

"I can't wait to taste you," he says. "Your mother was delicious."

But then there's a shout, and the already-bedraggled doors to Kineas's apartment shudder. Maybe the guards out there, or Tumarq or Acantha, heard me scream.

The king's eyes flicker in that direction. "Damn the timing, but we must all keep up appearances, hmm?" He grips my shoulders and pulls back, only stooping to kiss the side of my mouth where a trickle of blood has escaped. He licks it from his lips. "Congratulations, you've succeeded in your mission. You've just slit my *son's* throat and stabbed yourself in the heart. Tragic, really."

And then he rips the dagger out of my chest. The pressure escapes in a rush—and everything keeps rushing, all of it, gushing out of me in a hot burst. I wish I could pull it back. Instead, my knees buckle. I sink into the flood—the river of life carrying me away.

I collapse onto the ground, but I feel like I'm floating.

His voice drifts above me. "Farewell, Rovan. I doubt we'll see each other again. If you run into Ivrilos before your final end, which will be swift, tell him *someone* wants to see him."

I want to see him, I think. I want to see Lydea. Japha. I still want to kill the king. There's so much left to do. But it's too late for all of it.

Mother, I think. *Father*.

My heart kicks once.

And stops.

27

IVRILOS

Ivrilos falls hard into the underworld. Sometimes the sensation is like drifting off to sleep and then waking up suddenly—or at least how he remembers sleeping and waking, since he doesn't exactly do that anymore. And sometimes it's like being thrown into a cold, dark lake and launched out of it again, saturated by the chill and dark. This time it's the latter.

He immediately crouches into a fighting stance among the drifting gray dunes, drawing both of his half-moon blades. He's tired, weak. Damios's pneuma was enough to bring him back from whatever brink Rovan sent him to, but it wasn't enough to fully restore him. And then he made his hand tangible and shoved it in front of a dagger.

Idiot! You know better. It was a useless gesture, one that hurt instead of helped.

I couldn't save her. The thought is far more excruciating than the dagger was.

He needs to find her. He doesn't let himself dwell on what it will mean when he does.

. . . But of course it'll mean that she's dead.

Don't think about it. Everyone dies eventually.

But it means something to him that *she'll* be dead. He's not entirely sure what, but it might amount to more than what anything else has meant to him in his long, dreary existence.

Worse, he doesn't know if he's strong enough to keep her safe down here.

She still may be better off here than up *there*. With his brother, whatever he has become. Not fully alive. Not fully dead. Caught somewhere in between, like a venomous spider at the center of its own vast web.

"Where am I? Who the hell are you?"

Ivrilos spins to find none other than Crown Prince Kineas standing next to him. If a death occurs near Ivrilos in the living world, and he crosses over to the underworld at the same time, he's likely to turn up next to that new shade. Now here they both are. Kineas looks confused and alarmed, but otherwise every bit as whole and arrogant as he ever looked in life.

"Finally," Ivrilos says with a sigh, approaching slowly through the dark sand and bowing. "I've been looking forward to this for a while."

The crown prince arches an eyebrow. "I wish I could say the same, but I've never had the pleasure."

"*I* have, though 'pleasure' is not the word I would use." Ivrilos pauses. Smiles. "Rovan sends her regards."

He doesn't even give Kineas a chance to scream before he lunges. The crown prince tries to struggle, but he's no match for Ivrilos, who quickly traps his hands and draws him in.

Drinking Kineas's essence is every bit as satisfying as Ivrilos thought it would be. And as it comes from a life taken in its prime, it's strong.

Delicious.

When the crown prince is gone for good, Ivrilos rolls his shoulders and cracks his neck, readying his weapons.

Much better. But like any fresh kill, it will likely attract other predators.

Ivrilos casts around, his eyes tracing the horizon. He can't see far, with the dark dunes cresting around him like a wave-tossed sea. An unfelt wind whips sand into the air like spume. The sand never falls, just drifts up into the sky in darkening funnel clouds. The world dissolving.

As always.

Ivrilos feels unseen bits of him try to drift up and away, but he holds them firmly to himself. A little dissipation is always natural, but he can't spare anything.

The link between him and Rovan means she should arrive close to him. The bond always keeps him near to his ward in the living world, and the same is true down here. But he doesn't see her.

Could she . . . *not* be dead? He saw the blade enter her heart. He *felt* it, and not just through his own hand, but through their shared essence. She doesn't have long to live, if she isn't already here somewhere.

"Look, it's the illustrious Ivrilos."

That's not the voice he wants to hear.

They don't even try sneaking up on him; they know he would sense them. They approach, five shades all from opposite directions, pinning him between them. Creating a web of their own.

But, little do they know, Ivrilos is the spider.

"The king sent us," the first shade says. "You have the choice to come along quietly. But just to warn you, he's not pleased. And he especially won't be pleased when he learns you took the lad for yourself. He was of the family. It's for the king to decide whether or not he was worthy to stay."

"Standards are slipping, clearly," Ivrilos says. He struggles to remember the shade's name, a minor lord who died twenty or so years ago, not yet elevated to a guardian. Which means he's hungry. The rest are even younger shades.

The king is testing Ivrilos—the king *here*. His father.

There are two kings, one above, one below, though there may as well only be one with how tethered the two of them are. His brother's barriers never before faltered enough for Ivrilos to catch a glimpse of his father lurking in the background. But for a moment, he sensed Athanatos in the living world. And he's probably been there all along, standing behind Kadreus.

Ivrilos doesn't have time to consider the implications of that. The shades are closing in.

His feet shift in the sand as he tries to keep an eye on them all at once. If he fails to go with them, to explain his actions to his father in a way that will excuse him—and he doesn't think he can—then these shades are meant to take the measure of his strength and wear him down. Only then will his father come to finish him, to make good on his four-hundred-year-old threat. It might not be immediate. And even if Ivrilos wins the fight against these shades, he's likely to lose as much essence as he gains. And his father can keep sending shades to harass him across the dunes until, like a man dying of thirst in the desert, Ivrilos begs for mercy.

His father will give him mercy in the only way he knows how.

And yet. If Ivrilos uses this test to his advantage . . . If he loses *nothing* . . . His hands tighten on the hilts of his half-moon blades. He thinks of Rovan.

The other shades take note of his resolve. And, as one, they charge.

They come at him in predictable ways. After all, he's seen just about everything.

When Ivrilos meets them, he's smiling again.

———

He doesn't know how many hours or even days later, how many shades have hunted him and become the hunted, when he sees the dark silhouette on the horizon. He's been steadily making his way in the direction of those black towers, and now his goal is in sight.

He's given up on finding Rovan. There's a chance she never died, but since he can't use their bond to go to her, he doubts it. His access to the living world has been cut off as if she were dead. She must have slipped through his fingers and either passed directly to her second death, or else their bond was so weakened by her shield that she appeared somewhere else. Maybe she fell victim to another shade before he could find her. Packs of the young and weak roam the dunes for exactly that purpose.

He can't think about that, or he won't be able to put one foot in front of the other.

His father never came for him. Maybe because of those shades he sent in advance; Ivrilos defeated and drank every last drop of their essence. They stopped coming a while ago, because Athanatos realized they were only fodder.

Maybe his father is scared. Hunted, instead of the hunter.

Ivrilos still doesn't believe he's strong enough, not without the essence of someone as powerful as his brother, but there's nothing left for him now. Early on, he did his best to reach Bethea or Delphia or whoever could hear him and answer whether Rovan might still be alive, but he never heard anything back.

It's over.

His feet eat up the sand beneath him. They're powered by the energy of the dozens of other men he's consumed. He's stronger than he's ever been.

This is it. He's going to defeat his father or die trying. His final death.

As he starts down the last, massive crest of sand that will carry him like a wave to the front gate of Athanatos's dark kingdom, he suddenly feels a tug in the opposite direction. Like an invisible string running behind him that's grown taut. He tries to take another step, and the tug becomes a sharp *jerk*.

And then he's ripped off his feet. Gone in a blink, as if he were never there.

The dark towers remain. Waiting. Hungry.

28

A great breath tears through me. Based on the ripping sound, I feel like it should hurt, but I don't feel any pain. I open my eyes and immediately have to shield them. The scene around me is so bright, colorful, and soft after the sharp-edged, blood-soaked violence of what came before. And especially after the darkness that swallowed me for so long. I have a feeling it almost consumed me entirely. Wherever I am, whatever is happening, I simply bask in the knowledge that it *didn't*.

"Rovan?"

His voice sends a bolt of shock through me, followed by delirious, giddy relief. "Ivrilos?"

I squint into the blinding light, and a shadow coalesces nearby. My fingertips brush against a silk coverlet, and the scent of roses is overpowering. It covers a distant odor of rot. Birds chirp outside some window nearby. My body feels cool, heavy, and comfortable. I'm on a bed, I realize, and my guardian is standing over me.

My shadow. I've missed him, after being in that darkness for so long without him. I should dread the sight of him, but looking at him is easier on my eyes than anything else is. Maybe my body understands what my mind doesn't yet: He's not my enemy. Not anymore.

His beautiful features come gradually into focus. Dark gaze and gently curling hair. Pale skin, black tunic—shorter and simpler than usual, and there are neither bracers on his arms nor swords at his hips. He almost looks exposed, vulnerable. And yet, in the folds of his tunic, underneath the fall of his hair, and beneath his brow, his shadows seem deeper and darker than before. *Sharper.*

He also looks baffled. Then amazed. Then *overjoyed.* It's like watching a sunrise play out on his face. I've never seen anything like it with him before. He stares at me like I'm the most wonderful thing he's ever seen.

"Should I still be shielding against you?" I croak.

He shakes his head, smiling a beautiful, gentle smile. "You'll never need to again. I promise. You're safe . . . for now."

"Where am I?" I ask, looking around. The room is filled with roses. They grow up the sunny marble walls in intricate curlicues and in every color. I can't see anything but the veil-shimmering sky through an arching window of glass cut in the pattern of a leafing tree. My voice is rough, dry. It's like I've been sick, and just woken from a fever dream.

"I'm not exactly sure," he says. "I . . . I haven't been with you this entire time. And since I joined you, I've been shut in here, too. We're in Thanopolis somewhere, from what I can tell, but not in the palace or the necropolis."

"What entire time?" I ask.

"I'm also not sure. I spoke to Delphia briefly—"

"Delphia is here?" I interrupt.

"Yes, but she can't maintain contact with me for long. She hasn't yet mastered the trick of speaking with the dead—and she won't, now that she's free of the necropolis. But she said it's been a couple of days since . . ." He trails off.

"What happened?" I can only remember pieces in fits and starts. The flash of a dagger. The gleam of a ruby. The liquid shine of spilled blood.

My stomach suddenly wakes up, as well. I'm hungry. *Ravenous.*

"Rovan," Ivrilos says. The sound of my name on his lips is music to my ears. "There's something you must know."

"What?" I feel like I'm missing something important. Maybe something terrible. "Is Japha okay? Lydea?"

"Japha is fine. They're here as well. Lydea, I don't know. She's still in the palace." The first bit of news is great, the second not so much. "But this isn't about either of them. It's about you."

I stare at him, as a strange sensation starts to creep over me.

"While you're safe, you . . . you're not yourself," he says, stumbling, looking down at his hands, which are suddenly knotted. "At least not in the way you're accustomed to."

And then I realize what I'm missing. After that first, instinctual breath, I haven't breathed much at all.

I don't need to, unless I require air to speak.

I tear my gaze away from him, hauling myself onto my elbows. I seize the neckline of my shift—clean, white—and drag it down. I'm in a bed with silk sheets, but it might as well be a stone funeral slab. Because I immediately see the wound in my breast that goes straight to my heart. It looks fresh, but there's no clotting or scabbing. No blood at all.

The smell of rot was coming from *me*, I realize, though it's almost gone. The roses were masking *my* scent.

"What the fuck?" I say, staring down at my chest. There's no rise and fall of breath, only that deep rift separating me from the living.

"You're different," Ivrilos says. "But we can get through this. I'm right here, by your side."

I draw my knees toward me on the bed. "Get through this? I'm *dead*!"

Something swells from deep within me. It's not my breath. More like the urge to vomit. But nothing happens. There's only the inescapable truth, with no relief.

"Rovan, just breathe," Ivrilos says, and then he winces. "I mean . . . *damn it*."

But there's nothing I can do. I can't breathe. I can't even cry out. I just freeze as horror sweeps through me like a tide. My mind is a silent scream. But it passes, at least just enough for me to blink again. Or maybe I grow a little numb to my horror as it inhabits me.

I flex my toes experimentally. Wiggle my fingers.

Several times in life, I've felt like my body was simply monstrous. When I first bled on what disappointingly became a monthly basis, it was as if my body had decided to betray me, wounding me from the inside out. And when I woke up with the bloodline covering me head to toe, it was as if I'd been *turned* inside out, exposing my family lineage and my veins to the world. I've heard that pregnancy and childbirth are raw and primitive in their violence, one's body nigh splitting itself in twain with plenty of blood and gore to go around, but I don't know firsthand, and now I'll never know, because I'm dead.

I'm *dead*. My body moves—responsively, sensitively—but it doesn't breathe unless I tell it to, out of comfort or the need to speak. I'm not a shade, and yet I have a stab wound in my chest that goes to my still and silent heart.

Except . . . before my eyes, the wound begins to fill in, eventually sealing over. The pink fades from my skin in mere moments, leaving only the smooth, too-pale expanse of the inner curve of my breast underneath my bloodline. It's as if a healer is working on me with blood magic. But it's only my body. It simply heals on its own. Because it's powered by magic and not life.

I am a horror now. A monster.

Distantly, I hear how strained my voice is. "Ivrilos, this is bad. Wrong. *I'm* wrong."

He tries to smile. "You know I'm the last person to judge you for being dead, right?"

"What am I?" I nearly shriek. "What is this?"

"Shh," Ivrilos says. And he puts a hand on my shoulder.

He puts a hand on my shoulder.

He deals with the shock of it incredibly well. Surprise only flits over his face, there and gone. And then he leans into me. It's a weighted, wonderful feeling. So different from the still, horrible presence of my own body. He pushes me back onto the bed, sitting next to me in the same motion. He pauses for just a moment, makes a decision, and tosses his legs onto the edge of the bed. He slides down next to me, facing me on his side.

For a moment I can't think of anything except his body, lining the entirety of mine. We're in bed together. Sunlight plays softly over us, gilding our limbs. Making us look alive.

I've been in bed with a few people. But never Ivrilos. It's hard to focus on anything else, even though he's trying to show me something. His arm propped beneath him, he keeps a hand on my shoulder, his fingers playing casually along the bare skin over my collarbone as if this is the most natural thing in the world. As if we've always done this. The other hand, he raises above me, palm up.

"Remember how I said your body was like a raft, and I was weighing it down, because of our bond?"

"Yes," I whisper, even though I'm struggling to remember anything at all.

"Now it's like we've completely rebuilt it to hold the two of us. I'm not dragging you down anymore. You're alive . . . but not. Only now, the problem is that we're too much." His hand, glowing warm with sunlight, dips toward my chest. I want it to keep dropping, despite what it symbolizes. "We're imbalanced, like the blight. The river—the living world—doesn't really want us anymore. It's trying to shove us out. We're running aground rather than sinking."

"So . . . I need a stronger life force to paddle. To stay in the current." My eyes widen. "Someone *else's* life force."

296

Blood. That was why the thought of it made me ravenous. *Still* does.

"It's a temporary solution to the problem, and one only an undead bloodmage—a revenant, I believe you're called—can fully utilize." His voice is so gentle. As if trying to soften the name, something with so many edges and so much violence.

"Utilize? You mean *digest*," I say, disgust rolling through me. "Magically speaking?"

I feel him nod.

I turn into him, bury my face in his shoulder. Goddess, he feels so good. He even *smells* good. Cool and clean, if ever-so-slightly musty. Like the stone of a cave. It's almost enough to take my mind off what he's saying:

I'm a *revenant*. I drink *blood*.

My body is separate from the living world now, a dead end, tethered only by blood. I can feel it in the stillness of my limbs and belly: I'll never get sick again. I'll need no food. I'll never need a chamber pot again. I'll never have children.

It's a small consolation that I won't have my monthly bleeding anymore. Not that this is a fair trade.

Ivrilos reaches up to smooth my hair. "At least this way, your body can contain my essence safely. You're more than my anchor here now—you've become my vessel. I imagine that's why we can touch. You can't rot anymore, because you're not alive. You're . . . preserved?"

Again, his tone is so gentle. I like him touching me. I like not rotting. But everything else makes my gorge rise.

"Ugh," I say, burrowing deeper into his neck, wishing I could block out everything but the feel of him. "So what is the permanent solution?" My voice is muffled.

His words are all too clear, unfortunately. "There isn't one. You maintain a steady diet of blood until . . . well, you're already dead, so until your body either starves or gets damaged enough that it can't sustain us, and then your shade and mine finally pass to the underworld. My own feeding might help with your hunger, though I'm not entirely sure. I fed . . . a lot recently, down there, and I think that's what gave you the strength to wake up and heal."

I go still. He wraps an arm around me. I can't believe we're lying in bed together, but I can believe other things even less. It's all so awful, what he's saying. The hunger I'm feeling. The silence of my heart.

"I'm afraid I consumed Kineas," he adds after a long pause. "I hope you don't mind."

That's enough to jar me out of my frozen reverie. I can't help my bark of laughter. It's *sick*, but Kineas's demise is the least of my concerns.

"I can't believe I'm dead," I say. Maybe if I say it enough I'll get used to it.

What will *Lydea* think? Maybe that's the one bright side to losing her trust. If I already disgust her, being dead won't make much of a difference.

"You still have flesh and a life force," Ivrilos says hopefully. "You're just . . ."

"Living dead. Right." It brings back all the stories of ghouls and other creatures of the night I heard as a child. "That makes me want to vomit."

"Don't do that," Ivrilos says, leaning forward to kiss my temple. Into my hair, he adds, "You need to *drink*."

I jerk my head upright to stare at him, his face only inches from mine. "You *want* me to?"

He holds my gaze levelly, a flat lake of an expression. "If you do," he says calmly, his dark eyes beginning to trace my face, "I believe you'll become one of the most powerful forces in Thanopolis, Skyllea, or the entire blight-ridden land. I believe the king—

kings—have tried very hard to keep someone like you from coming into existence. Someone like *themselves*."

"I'm . . . he's . . . you mean . . ." It all comes flooding back. How the king swatted aside my sigils like they were flies. How my shield against death magic briefly lifted his long-held disguise. How he pulled a dagger out of his heart without bleeding or flinching, and then stabbed it into my own.

How he's Ivrilos's *brother*, Kadreus, still alive after four hundred years. Well, not exactly alive. But he's *here*. Affecting the world of the living as if he were alive—*too* alive. Far too powerful. Imbalanced.

And now I'm the same.

"The king, my brother, is a revenant," Ivrilos says, "by some combination of the magic in his blood and his bond with my father's shade. My father, king in the underworld, is his guardian. He has been, this entire time. They must have discovered what could happen from mixing blood and death magic ages ago, and so they forbade it. The insanity, the rot, when a living bloodmage is exposed to too much death magic is bad enough. But for them, the worst possibility must have been the creation of other revenants—someone to rival their power."

"That's why only royal women receive bloodlines and can never inherit the throne," I murmur, my mind starting to piece it together. "Not *only* because the . . . kings . . . hate women. It's so a male heir could never risk becoming a revenent—first as a bloodmage with a guardian—and then challenge their rule. It's so your brother could steal their faces and only *pretend* to give up the throne, generation after generation."

"Even so."

I pull back enough to glance up at him. "Why pretend, though? Why doesn't Kadreus just show his true face to the people? With your father, he has all the power . . . in this world *and* the next."

Ivrilos shrugs one shoulder, his fingers tracing my collarbone again. "Do you think people would follow him? Bloodmages are frightening enough. Binding them to shades allows the polis to accept blood magic in their midst. A revenant is far more frightening. If people found out, it could cause mass panic. Revolt."

I look away, toward the ceiling. Like the walls, it too is covered in roses: a mask for cold stone, the smell of rot. "And now I'm just as monstrous as they are."

"Two of the same force can balance each other, if they're on opposing sides. *You* can restore balance." We're lying so close together on the bed, I can't help but notice the gleam of excitement in his eyes.

It stirs an answering response in my belly. One tinged with hunger, yes, but also eagerness. I want to *hunt*. I try to ignore it.

"You're not upset with me?" I murmur. "I ruined your plans."

He sighs, tucking a strand of hair behind my ear. His fingertips brush over my cheek. "It's honestly a relief. I'm not alone for the first time in centuries. Someone knows my secrets. I have a partner in treason, even if she upended all my carefully laid plans." He pauses. "That is, if she'll have me. I'd rather start over with the planning, if it's with you. Do you want to bring down a kingdom with me, Rovan?"

It's his goal. It's my goal. It's revenge, and yet it's a solution to right so many wrongs.

It's also quite possibly the sexiest thing anyone has ever suggested to me. I'd be breathless even if I weren't dead. I nod into his hand.

"I hope this is okay," he whispers, fingers running down my jaw. "Touching you, I mean. Tell me if it's not."

"It's okay," I whisper back. It's more than okay. My eyes grow heavy lidded as his fingers skim over my lips.

His long, dark lashes shadow his gaze as he studies my mouth.

"It's just that I haven't touched anyone except to hurt or to hunt in a very long time. This is——" He pauses. Has to swallow. "To touch someone just because, or even better, out of desire . . . Rovan, I . . ." Now it's his turn to be lost for words.

"Keep going."

His fingers find my chin, turning my head gently as he continues his careful inspection. His voice is low. "I didn't think I would see you again, and I wasn't sure how I could bear it. I couldn't, actually. I was going to throw myself at my father, just like you threw yourself at my brother. So I can't be upset with you."

I don't interrupt, mostly because I want him to keep touching me.

His eyes flash back up to mine. He shakes his head as his fingers trail down the other side of my jaw. "I'm sorry. I know what I've done to you. I know the situation is awful. I'm so sorry about your mother, your father. I understand if you hate me. And if you hate what you've become."

I can't think about my mother at all right now—my thoughts recoil when I even try—and I think about my own . . . *situation* . . . far less when he's touching me. His hand drops, but I catch it. Before long, his thumb runs over my knuckles, caressing my fingers. He can't seem to help it. I crave the feeling as much as he seems to.

Maybe I should feel guilty, enjoying this after everything he's done, but right now I can't find it in me. It's not that I don't care about his actions, but dying maybe put it all in perspective.

"I have no right to expect anything," he continues. "And I *don't* expect anything." He marvels at our interlocked hands for a moment, and then he looks up with a crooked smile. "But even in the midst of all of this, I can't help but think how beautiful you are. To appreciate more than anything that I have another chance to tell you that I love you."

My eyes sting. I'm not sure if I can cry anymore.

"I love you, too," I whisper. "Despite everything. Even if I shouldn't."

He buries his hand in my hair and leans in to kiss me.

Before he can, I say, "But I have to tell you that I also love Lydea. I've been a complete ass, and I don't know if she loves me anymore—or if she ever did—but that doesn't change how I feel."

His grin appears a mere finger's breadth from my lips. He draws the tip of his nose to mine and rubs it back and forth a couple of times. "You don't think I already know that? And after all that I've seen, I don't believe love is a finite resource. How could I begrudge something that should be celebrated? As long as she doesn't mind me, that is."

I know she won't—rather, if she cares about me at all anymore, in her anger and disappointment. Like every other painful thing trying to get my attention, I can't dwell on that right now.

If it's Ivrilos's intention to distract me, it's working.

"Goddess, you're beautiful," he whispers.

I stare at him in the same awe with which he's looking at me. "Now I want to kiss you until I can't breathe." I grimace. "I mean—"

He leans the rest of the way forward, his fingers tightening in my hair and sending a thrill through me. "I know what you mean," he whispers against my lips. "Don't think I've forgotten how."

And then, *oh*, he's kissing me. And he's using every bit of that focus he usually devotes to stalking and fighting. Maybe it's better that I don't need to breathe. The other times our lips have touched felt almost incidental in comparison. A means to an end. This, now, is the end.

Or so I think, until he extracts his hand from my hair. While he kisses me with slow deliberation, his fingertips slide luxuriously down my neck, my arm, my side, until his palm comes to rest on my thigh, which I've unconsciously lifted to meet him. He tightens his grip, pulling me into him. My legs part just the right amount. I gasp as I make contact with him and a burst of heat radiates out from my hips, tingling all the way up my scalp.

It occurs to me that my shift is short and it wouldn't take much for us to fit more completely together.

"Ivrilos," I murmur between kisses. "I want you." And then, "Um, can we? Does everything still work?"

He groans into my mouth, shifting his weight. "I haven't exactly been practicing, but there's only one way to find out."

His strong arms close around me, and he drags me on top of him. After that, it doesn't take much wriggling until I have him where I want him. Part of me can't believe I'm doing this, and the other can't wait. There's a pause: that breath—or lack thereof—before the plunge. And then I sink down onto him just as he surges to meet me.

The look of wonder that crosses his face is beautiful. Almost like it's his first time.

I guess it *has* been a while.

We both gasp. And we keep gasping, as if we're trying not to drown in each other. But as his hips keep lifting to meet mine, wave after wave of him, an ocean of sensation, I'm happy to drown. At the same time, that warm, delicious feeling begins to rise inside me. I guess some things do still work.

But then Ivrilos cries out. Too soon.

"I—I'm sorry," he stammers when he can form words again. "It's . . . uh . . . been a long time. That was fast." He looks blissfully disheveled, discomfited.

I grin. "It doesn't have to be over yet."

He goes completely still beneath me. His gaze is fixed. Hungry. Giving me the confidence I need.

I lean forward, both to kiss him and to adjust my hips. But then there's a shout, and the door to whatever room we're in flies open, making us both freeze. Japha comes charging in, their hands raised to sketch sigils.

Those hands fly immediately to their eyes. "Oh my goddess, what did I even just see? Who is *that*? Aren't you supposed to be dead, Rovan? What the *hell*?"

I'm mortified, but at least they didn't see much. I'm only sitting on top of Ivrilos, although our clothing is hiked a little high on our thighs. I roll off him and onto the bed, dragging my white shift down. Ivrilos launches to his feet, tugging his own black tunic lower.

And yet, I'm not ashamed. Hell, if I have to be dead, I'm happy I can still make love. I'm only sorry I was slower to arrive than Ivrilos.

Not that I know where to begin explaining to Japha. They look as radiant as the sun-drenched room, in a berry-colored peplos woven with peach-colored birds, a gilt-lined sword belt at their waist. They have a dagger strapped to it, its gold sheath studded in jewels to match their crown of multicolored rose blossoms. They're a sight for sore eyes, but they obviously don't feel the same, since they keep their own eyes covered.

I start with, "You can see him?"

"Yes, almost too much of him! Is it safe to look?" Japha asks, peering out between their fingers before getting an answer. "Oh, phew." They blink. "Where did the strange man go?"

I look over at Ivrilos. He looks back at me, shrugs, and then to my great surprise, he bursts out laughing.

"Very helpful," I say, but I can't help grinning. Ivrilos doubles over, shaking, and nearly tips into a rosebush. I've never seen him laugh this hard. Or much at all.

"*What is going on?*" Japha cries.

"Ivrilos is having a fit, and I'm trying not to melt in embarrassment."

"That was *Ivrilos*? Why could I see him? I'm so confused."

"You must be able to when we're touching."

"So you *have* come back to life, somehow?" Japha asks.

My grin falls away. "Not entirely."

"Okay." Japha gives me a solemn nod. And then they shrug. "I don't understand how that's possible, but we'll figure it out."

"You're not horrified?"

"*Please.* I'm not going to abandon you just because you're dead. At least now you don't smell anymore, thank the goddess. You actually look frighteningly magnificent."

That wrings a smile from me—until I burst into tears. It's all been so much: realizing what I am now, making love to Ivrilos, and now *Japha's* love and acceptance.

It's almost enough to give me hope for when I next see Lydea.

Japha comes to me without hesitation, wrapping their arms around me. "Shh, dearest, it's okay." They pat my hair but then pause. "I don't mean to alarm you, but you have blood running down your face and I'd prefer not to get any on me."

"*What?*" I wrench away from them, wiping at my cheek. My hand comes away red. "Now *that* is disgusting. Ivrilos, what is this?" I demand, holding out my palm. "I cry *blood?*"

He grimaces. "It's part of being a revenant who thrives on the substance, maybe?"

"*Goddess.*"

"What did he say?" Japha asks, staring somewhere in the direction of Ivrilos.

"I'll tell you later," I mutter. I hope Japha won't want to rethink staying by my side when they learn I drink blood. "Do you know where we are? Is there any word from Lydea?"

Japha is about to answer when the door bursts open once again. We all spin.

It's Alldan in the doorway, with a pair of incredibly

strange-looking people standing behind him, a man and a woman. Their washed-out hair is something like gray, even though they don't look that old. Their cheekbones stand out like a skull's. They have towering crowns woven from dead twigs, what look like mice bones dangling in the branches. Sweeping robes made of myriad fabrics in diaphanous grays hang from their emaciated bodies. Oddest of all, their lips are stained black and their eyes are red. Bloodlines cover the too-pale skin of both.

I can also smell the death magic on them. And yet, I can still hear the faint beating of their hearts, as well. They're alive.

"Good. You're awake, Rovan," Alldan says. But there's no warmth or even the respect I once knew in his voice. His violet gaze is hard, and his tone is almost disgusted. "And now we will decide if you will live—such that *this* is living," he amends, his lip curling, "—or if you need to be destroyed."

29

J apha and Ivrilos both step between me and Alldan. The strange bloodmages accompanying the Skyllean prince track the movement with their red eyes. They can see Ivrilos, then, even if I'm not touching him. The sunlit, rose-covered room suddenly has the air of a potential battleground.

Ivrilos, surprisingly, gives the man and woman a nod of acknowledgment. They nod back. The woman even smiles, but her teeth are a little too grayish for comfort.

"You never mentioned anything about destroying Rovan," Japha says dangerously.

"There was no cause to alarm anybody before we knew if she would wake up or not." Alldan raises a hand, forestalling any objection. "Don't forget, we helped you. We've sheltered you, Delphia, *and* Rovan."

"How?" I manage. Everything is changing so quickly. "Where are we?"

"We're in the quarters of the Skyllean delegation in the city, where we've been staying when not in the palace. Your body was smuggled here from the necropolis, where it was taken for your death rites," Alldan says with a disapproving twist to his mouth. His distaste for Thanopolis's rituals is plainer than ever. I suppose he's not worried about diplomacy anymore.

"I was hiding in the necropolis," Japha elaborates, "after you freed me from my guardian. Delphia, Crisea, and your, uh, *friend*, Bethea, helped me. It wasn't pleasant, but I didn't know where else to go. Back to the palace wasn't an option. I didn't want to be given another shadow to suck the life out of me. No offense," they add in the general direction of Ivrilos.

"None taken," Ivrilos says, even though Japha can't hear him.

"Meanwhile, *your* guardian"—Alldan's mouth gives the same twist as he turns to me—"found Princess Delphia and told her you might not be truly dead. She couldn't speak with him clearly, but it was enough for Japha to sneak out of the necropolis and find me here."

"Because Rovan said you might be willing to help us escape." Japha's tone is biting as they glare at Alldan. They cross their arms, fingers drumming over their elbows, as if still ready to sketch sigils.

"I am helping." Alldan looks back at me. "We got your body and Delphia out under cover of darkness, and have offered both her and Japha asylum in Skyllea."

But not me. Not anymore.

"We haven't yet accepted," Japha says.

I shoot them a grateful glance. They've proven time and again to be the best of friends.

I still have questions. "Let me guess, you also had help. From them?" I nod at the strange bloodmages. "If it was so easy to skip in and out of the necropolis, their acolytes would be escaping all the time."

Alldan frowns. "Yes."

"They're the ones who helped create the veil around Skyllea, aren't they? Bloodmages infected with death magic? And that's how they could sneak undetected through *this* veil. You've had blood-mages here with you all this time." He nods reluctantly, and I say, "And yet you're so disdainful of the magic they wield."

"I'm not fond of it, no," Alldan says coldly, "especially when it's allowed to fester and spread unchecked until the *entire world* is at risk. But we keep it strictly under control in Skyllea." He pauses.

"Which is why creatures like you are problematic. You upset the natural order."

I scoff. "Oh, so green hair and purple eyes are *so* natural? Just because you've been altering yourselves with magic for longer doesn't make you the arbiters of magical purity."

"You're not *alive*," Alldan insists.

"I'm not the first to become like this," I burst out. "And you're toying with the same power." I toss my hand at the infected blood-mages. "Aren't you worried about them becoming exactly like me? If they die—"

"If we die, we return, yes," the woman says, her voice as thin and dry as paper. "But it is without thought or emotion. Only hunger."

"We are not bound to a shade that will keep us focused in death, like you," the man adds, his red eyes flickering to Ivrilos. "We have only the blight inside us, which is mindless. We struggle against losing ourselves to it in life, and we succumb in death. And so we are swiftly destroyed when our time comes."

Thinking of an undead bloodmage with no mind of their own, only a bottomless need for blood, makes me shudder.

"In Skyllea, we have dealt with such creatures more than you have," Alldan adds, "as we battled to keep out the blight. Whole communities were consumed until we belatedly created a barrier— but not before some of those very people, no longer human, went on to consume other communities. We call them bloodfiends."

Maybe that's why I heard stories of ghouls and fiends as a child, and so many warnings against mixing blood and death magic. And yet we've forgotten what the blight *is*, what it can do to people. We're so safe behind our veil here, sheltered from the ruins of those destroyed towns and cities. From the truth. And that's exactly how the king wants us. Blindfolded.

Especially since he's the cause of the blight.

"But I'm not a . . . bloodfiend," I say, trying out the word uncomfortably.

Alldan regards me, unblinking. "No. But maybe you're something worse. Intelligence does not equate to virtue. Or *humanity*."

"So why go to all that trouble of getting my body out of the necropolis if you're just going to kill me again? How *will* you, anyway?"

"A wooden stake through the heart," the creepy man hisses, "or one of bone. What was once alive interrupts undeath. The stake cannot be removed, and then the body must be burned."

"Great," I say. At least now I know why a steel dagger had no effect on the king's heart.

Ivrilos takes my hand. Japha can't help starting away from us, and Alldan's eyes immediately go to Ivrilos.

"Prince Alldan," Ivrilos says politely. "My name is Ivrilos, son of Athanatos, as much as I rue my lineage. You and I are not enemies. But if you threaten Rovan again or try to make good on such a threat, we most assuredly will be." His tone is as calm as ever, but it's that dangerous calm that once made my skin prickle. "And trust me when I say you don't want to be our enemy." His dark eyes flash to mine, and then back to Alldan. "You'll find we make much better friends."

My grip tightens on his.

"Like I said," Alldan says, looking a little disconcerted, "we didn't wish to be hasty. Before any steps were taken, we wanted to see what Rovan would become."

I gesture down at myself, though I keep hold of Ivrilos. "A monster? Well, here I am. What do you want with me?"

"Have you seen yourself yet, girl?" the woman asks. She whispers a few words, waving a bony, colorless hand—blood and death magic intertwined—and the air shimmers between us. Suddenly it's like I'm looking into a reflective pool.

In it, I can't see Ivrilos even though I'm holding his hand, but I can definitely see myself. I'm standing in a simple white shift. My skin is abnormally pale, so my bloodline's scarlet sigils stand out all the more vividly—and I still have blood smeared on my hands and face. But that's not the weirdest thing. My eyes are bright red, like the two bloodmages'—or the king's, after his disguise dropped. My hair, unlike theirs, is lustrous, a midnight blue that shines like a tumble of water. My lips are fuller, and almost as red as my eyes.

I'm more beautiful than I ever was before. But mine is the beauty of a predator: eerie, sharp, lethal-looking.

"You might be a monster," Alldan says as my reflection ripples and fades away. "Even one that deserves to be destroyed. But it's not for me to decide. Come."

He gestures the way out the door. There are guards waiting outside. They've brought armor and steel, as well as blood and death magic to protect against me. I have little choice but to follow, unless I want to prove right here and now that I *am* a monster and fight my way through them.

"At least let me put on a damn robe," I say.

Alldan points to where a square of plain white material is folded on a small table under the window. I thought it was a towel.

Japha makes a face. "No way will she be caught *dead* in . . . Never mind, I have something better."

I leave the room wrapped in a luxurious plum shawl woven with butterflies. *Fitting*, I think.

I grow amazed as I walk barefoot through a series of rooms, perhaps part of a whole building, that Skyllea has claimed as their own. While the bones of it belong to Thanopolis's architects, everything else is Skyllean. They prefer greenery over flowers, unlike Thanopolis—sustained life instead of a brief pop of color and then

311

death. They have more greenery than the greenest places in the polis. The interior walls are a profusion of life, from tiny, lacelike fronds to glossy leaves as wide as my head. One wall has an entire tree growing against it, flattened out along the marble. There are also whole surfaces, even columns, with thin sheets of water running over them. The actual curtains, covering windows and various archways, are just as sheer and liquidy. I can't help but envy their rugs especially, the fibers seemingly spun with sunlight or moonlight in silvery blacks and rich warm browns. They cover the floors in a rippling, velvety glow that's plush beneath my toes.

But the most remarkable thing is the woodwork. Wood must be like clay to their artisans. Columns that aren't covered in water or greenery are braided with wood. The simplest table, desk, or screen is a work of flowing art, one practically blending into the next. It's almost like they're trying to cover up the stone.

It looks like I'm walking through a forest. A *magical* forest. A hummingbird even flits by me, and some peacocks saunter by the next room over. The Skylleans we pass look equally flamboyant, with iridescent hair and eyes and extravagant clothing. Alongside such a celebration of life, Thanopolis really does look and feel like a subdued, death-obsessed city.

We finally make our way into a spacious courtyard, the sky above covered by a glass canopy. Blue and green fragments make swirling patterns in imitation of the veil itself, sending down filtered sunlight that makes everything look like it's underwater. There's an inexplicable shimmer in the air, golden motes floating in shafts of light. I expect more vibrant extravagance in so large a space, so I'm surprised to find it empty, save for Delphia and a small knot of Skyllean guards wearing intricately layered armor that fits together like overlapping leaves. The princess wears a beautiful cerulean gown in Skyllean style, her cloud of white hair tinted blue-green by the glass canopy. She first sees Japha and Alldan and brightens. She positively *glows* at the sight of the latter.

"Prince Alldan! And Japha," she adds belatedly. "Will we speak with her again? She said we can when—oh! Rovan, you're alive! Ivrilos was right, I knew it!"

"Um," I say, but before I can clarify, the gold in the air glimmers to life, seeming to gather in a rippling sheet. Suddenly, inside a strange flickering outline, is another world. I don't really understand what I'm seeing, because this view should be impossible.

Towering gray trees rise in the background, with spiraling walkways twining around their trunks, wide enough for carriages. Buildings nestle in their massive branches. I can see lights in the tear-shaped windows, glowing like drops of dew from among wide swaths of curtaining, silver-green leaves. Bridges stretch between them, as intricate and numerous as the strands of a spider's web, glowing with an internal light. Right at the forefront is a deck of swirling pale wood, as if we're looking out over the view from a nearby tree.

It's a city in the trees. Swarming with people.

I'm looking through a *portal*.

There is pride in Alldan's gaze as he turns from the view to where Japha, Ivrilos, and I stand frozen in awe. "I'm pleased to present Skyllea and our capital city, Lyridan."

It's so beautiful I can't speak—the land I've so long dreamed of seeing. My *father's* homeland.

"How . . . ?" I begin, extending my hand toward the sparking gold frame.

"It won't hurt you, but you can't pass through," Alldan says. "It's how our delegation here stays in communication with Skyllea. It's something like a living echo, if you will, created through blood magic, of course. We've been developing the sigils for ages."

I'm hardly paying attention to him, because I've spotted

something else through the portal. On the ground in the distance, I see the ranks of an army beginning to assemble. A massive army. They're far away in Skyllea, but I know where they're headed.

"We sent some of our most magically powerful here before, in Cylla and Silvean," Alldan says, and then waves at himself. "And now our least powerful, with promises that Thanopolis will soon have access to our greatest assets: our bloodlines." He smiles. "Oh, we will deliver Skyllea to them, but not in the way they think."

"Don't give away all our secrets, my son," says a voice.

A woman steps into view on the other side of the magical window, followed by a coterie of attendants, and, stunningly, a pair of white tigers at her flanks. Her hair is spun gold, her skin a dark, metallic bronze underneath an endlessly long bloodline that even drops down both cheeks like red tears. Her eyes are entirely white to match her flowing gown. She's just as impressive as the city behind her, with a towering white wooden crown, rising and curling at the ends like an elaborate tree complete with dangling diamond and emerald leaves.

"And may I present my mother," Alldan continues, "Kytharae, Queen of Skyllea."

I'm not sure what I'm supposed to do, so I bow my head. Japha goes a little deeper—maybe they're more used to royalty than I am. Delphia curtsies.

Ivrilos, mostly unseen, stands unmoving, staring at the white tigers. His face is avidly alight. When he notices my attention, he blinks, looking almost embarrassed. "I haven't seen one of those since I was a boy, and it was a poor, starved creature. Brought to the arena to fight, back when they used to do such things. They haven't been hauled across the blight in ages." He smiles wistfully. "I wanted to free it."

He looks so much like that boy that my heart breaks. How far he is from his past, and yet he's still that child somewhere deep inside. And it makes me realize: Ivrilos may be protecting me, but for the first time, I want to protect *him*.

If the Skylleans don't execute me first.

"Greetings," the queen says, without nodding back. But she smiles radiantly at the princess. "Delphia has agreed to foster with us in Lyridan, in the absence of her mother, our beloved Cylla."

Japha blinks at her in surprise. Obviously, Delphia didn't mention it to them first. And yet she *is* of an age to make her own decisions. She's only slightly younger than me, even if at times her timidity and her innocence make her seem far younger. But I still can't help but think that since the Skylleans don't have Lydea within their grasp, they're already looking toward the next heir to the throne.

"We all miss our auntie Cylla," Japha says, "but I *am* curious how Delphia's father might feel about this."

"I'm not," the queen says bluntly. "He sent her to a place of death to be forgotten. To die young."

And then I realize: They don't know. No one knows who—*what*—the king truly is. Kadreus, the revenant. Ivrilos wasn't able to tell them, and no one other than the two of us witnessed what happened.

I'm not sure how to bring it up as Japha continues, lifting both hands, "I also think Skyllea is a better place for my cousin, mind you. It's just that certain kings in certain cities might view smuggling the princess out of the city as a royal kidnapping and an act of war." They glance off into the portal, at the troops assembling far below. "Though it looks like you're preparing for that eventuality."

War. It's a distant, terrible thought—that might soon be too close and real for comfort.

The queen disregards Japha, turning to me. "So this is she. Is she sane?"

Alldan opens his mouth, but I beat him to it. "As sane as anyone here."

315

"I knew your father," the queen says, her white eyes seeming to look everywhere and nowhere at once. "Silvean came from a family of famous scholars. I wonder, did you inherit his wit?"

"I'm not sure. But I did inherit this." I lift my arm, my plum sleeve sliding away to reveal my bloodline. "He left me clues that would bring me to Skyllea. To you. But now I'm wondering at the intelligence of *that*."

"He did not know what you would become. Had he, perhaps he would have directed you elsewhere."

"Well, now I'm here, which is still in Thanopolis last I checked. Alldan wouldn't tell me what you want with me. Hopefully you can. Your Majesty," I add belatedly.

She tilts her head at me. "Show me what you truly are."

I stare at her. Does she want me to do tricks?

Japha leans over and whispers out of the corner of their mouth, "You might want to show off your shadow puppet."

"He's not a *puppet*," I grumble, but I look at Ivrilos. He reaches for my hand with a half smile.

As soon as he takes it, several people gasp at the strange appearance of a dead man in their midst. More Skylleans from the delegation have gathered at the entrance to the courtyard behind me to watch the show.

Ivrilos nods at the queen, but she ignores him. "So it's true," she says. "You have a bond that transcends even your death."

Delphia's silver eyes fly to me in shock. "But I thought you weren't truly dead?"

I smile sadly at her, shrugging.

The queen, it seems, requires more. "What else can you do?"

"I can still wield blood magic, if that's what you're asking," I say, squeezing Ivrilos's hand tighter, "with my father's bloodline at my disposal. And I believe I can use death magic as well, though I haven't tried."

316

"Try."

I frown, feeling like one of the poor monkeys in the marketplace, forced to do a dance on command. I glance at Ivrilos, and he gives me a reassuring smile.

"Why not?" he asks. He doesn't seem concerned about the predicament we're in. His calm confidence seeps into me.

Maybe it's his essence, *his* knowing, that tells me how to do it. But my lips and my mouth move, trying to form the shape I have in mind, and using the space of my lungs. I *breathe* it.

"Skia," I whisper. *Shadow* in the older language of Thanopolis. Like a curl of smoke, darkness coils into the air before me, twining around my upraised hand. It feels cool and almost comforting against my skin. "This magic doesn't hurt me anymore," I murmur, half in wonder. And then I summon fire with barely a thought. Flame twists around the shadow. Darkness and light entwined. "It feels like it complements my blood magic instead of fighting it."

"Because you are living a half life," the queen says. "As good as dead."

"Maybe," I say, trying not to feel the sting in her words. "But I'm still here, aren't I? And death would mean the loss of my bloodline, and it's still here, too. Maybe this is the only way to truly use blood magic and death magic together. To inhabit the space between."

The queen practically sniffs. "I'd rather be alive."

"And go mad and rot?" I snap, and then nod at the two fading bloodmages, standing right next to me. "I hope they have fun with that. I'm trying to look on the bright side here."

"Still, what else can you offer?"

I drop my hand in disbelief, the shadow and flame vanishing. "Shall we turn this into a trial by combat?" I look around and smile, and I know it's feral. "Because I can also fight"—I toss my head at Ivrilos, whom they can all see standing with the relaxed confidence of one of those tigers—"like him."

"No," Ivrilos says. "Like never before. Like *I* never have before." He looks at me with pride. "You're much stronger than I was in life. *We're* much stronger."

I turn my smile on the queen. "There you have it."

"Even so," the queen says. "There's one thing you're forgetting." I blink at her.

"What do you need to sustain yourself?"

Oh yeah, that.

She nods at Alldan, and he signals to a couple of guards. They leave the courtyard for a few moments and return with a bedraggled man suspended between them. He's wearing a stained, nondescript gray chiton, its edges fraying. He's obviously a prisoner of some sort.

"What is this?" I ask nervously.

"I just want to show everyone what it is that you eat, before we decide what to do with you," the queen says.

I want to snarl at her. "I'm pretty sure *I* decide what to do with me, and don't they eat the same thing?" I gesture at the two blighted mages, whose red eyes track the man.

"We limit them to pigs' blood when we can help it, but our worst criminals we sentence to satiate the darkness. We . . . borrowed . . . this one from Thanopolis's prison. He was destined for the chopping block." She nods at the man, whom the guards force to his knees in front of me. He stares at me with wide, frightened eyes. He moans but can't seem to open his mouth. A bloodmage has probably locked it closed. Nobody likes to listen to screaming, after all. "This man is a murderer."

I'm a murderer: of the two men guarding Kineas's quarters and the other people I've gotten killed. My father. My mother. Bethea's mother. Kineas. The guards in front of the royal gallery. The list probably goes on.

And it's going to get longer if I can't avert an oncoming war.

"He's also a rapist," the queen adds, watching me carefully.

Well. I'm definitely not that. I try to picture Kineas as I look at him.

Maybe it's my hunger trying to convince me more than anything. I want to decry this as disgusting, and say I won't have anything to do with it. But my stomach gives a strange, slow twinge. Not like a growl, as if I were alive, but the feel of an awakening beast rolling over.

Oh no.

I can't stop staring at his neck. *Now* Japha looks a little sick. Delphia starts backing away, as if ready to flee the courtyard. Alldan surveys the situation with righteous distaste.

I want to slap him. All I did was *die*—trying to help him, no less—and this is what I get?

But next to me, Ivrilos merely shrugs. He obviously doesn't find this whole display as horrible as I do, not after everything he's done to survive life after death.

"You need to eat," he says.

Still, I refuse to perform like some monkey. I sneer at the queen. "If he's so tempting, why don't *you* eat him?"

She stares back at me through the portal. And then she signals to the two blighted mages. They close on the man like dogs on a bone.

Maybe the queen understands me all too well. Because shortly after the blighted mages have lunged forward, the queen signals again. The gray man and woman—looking slightly more pink cheeked now, their black lips smeared with red—pull back from the prisoner.

Leaving him bleeding from his neck and elbow, and kneeling before me.

It doesn't help that Ivrilos nudges me gently. The novelty of his casual contact sends a thrill through me, only inflaming my hunger further.

319

"Go on," he says.

And then *I* can't help it.

I dive for the man, feeling a strange pressure against my gums. My eyeteeth are suddenly longer. Sharper. I'm barely aware of biting the other side of his neck.

Because all my attention is focused on what comes after: the flood of blood into my mouth.

It's exquisite. It's the finest wine, the most mouthwatering food, all stirred into one. It's everything my body wants. *Almost.* Ivrilos and his touches have given me a clue as to the rest.

I am a creature of hunger.

I barely notice when I drop the man. But I can feel his blood thrumming through me as if it's mine. As if my heart is still powerfully beating. I feel like I can do anything.

Everyone is staring at me in horror. Except the blighted mages. They look jealous of my meal. And Ivrilos.

He's respectful. Appreciative. In a little bit of awe. And more than a little in love.

So different from the look the queen is giving me.

"See," she says sadly. "You can't control yourself."

I spin on her, everything razor sharp around me. I can hear a dozen different people breathing, a dozen hearts beating. All but my own, Ivrilos's, and the man's on the ground. "You wanted to humiliate me, prove I'm some kind of an animal so you might easily condemn me, but you've only made me stronger. *You* can't control me, either."

"That's what worries me most of all. An uncontrollable animal can turn against those who feed it."

I glare at her. "I *really* hope one of those tigers tears out your throat one day."

"Is that a threat?" she asks. The blighted mages and guards on this side of the portal tense, their hands ready for sigils or swords.

I shake my head. "I could be on your side. You could have me fighting with you. Or you can try to kill me, but your royal schemes? I will *royally* fuck them all up before I go." I lift my gaze to the glass canopy, wondering what it would take to bring it down. Not much. "And yes, before you ask, *that* is a threat."

More hands move for their weapons.

Japha's eyes flick around, their expression hard. "I'm with her. I didn't deal with a pile of bigoted shit in the palace just to put up with more of it here."

Goddess, I adore Japha. I try to hide how grateful I am. I stand tall and confident. My next words are loud and hard, so everyone can hear: "You worry that you can't control me? Why don't you worry about the fact that someone like me is *in* control of this entire polis?"

Silence answers me, aside from the odd creak of armor or shift of a boot.

The queen's eyes narrow. "What do you mean?"

"I mean the king is a revenant," I proclaim, "exactly like me, except he's been ruling Thanopolis for four hundred years. He's Ivrilos's brother, bound to their father, Athanatos, who is lord of the underworld. He kills—*drinks*—and assumes the identity of every crown prince who tries to succeed him. Tyros is gone."

In the murmuring chorus of heartbeats, quite a few quicken. Japha's and Delphia's eyes widen as the realization sets in. It doesn't take long for them to believe. Japha releases a shaky breath, while Delphia's face crumples. She doesn't have either of her parents left anymore.

"His name is Kadreus," Ivrilos volunteers, taking my hand again so all can hear him.

"And we're willing to challenge him so you don't have to," I continue. "But obviously not if you try to destroy me. *Or* if you intend to destroy the city."

321

"What she said," Japha adds.

I flash them a grin and turn back to the queen. "So are you with us or against us? Because *we're* going to take down an undead king and make the war you are about to start unnecessary."

The queen regards me a moment longer, her expression oddly calm. "And you think you can succeed?" she asks.

It's Ivrilos's turn to squeeze my hand. "Rovan is the best chance we've ever had."

I smile at him. "Only with you."

Unmoved, the queen asks, "Why would you do this? What's in it for you?"

"Revenge," I say bluntly. "The man killed my mother and ordered the death of my father. And this is my city. The king is my responsibility. If your army invades to take care of him instead of leaving him to me, so many more people will die."

"A trifle, next to what his blight has destroyed." She pauses. "I will grant a temporary stay on your execution and on the deployment of our army. *But*," she adds, "you must destroy this king *and* his blight."

I blink. "The blight can be destroyed?"

"Just as your guardian is drawing upon you, something—some*place*—is causing the living world to wither."

Ivrilos gives me a meaningful look.

"The dark city," I say.

"You've seen it?" the queen asks, raising a golden brow.

I suppress a shudder. "I wish I hadn't. Athanatos has used the pneuma of others—*all* others, aside from his family—to build it."

"We've suspected." Her lip curls in disgust. "Even so, it would fade, deteriorate, like all dead things do. So he bound it . . ."

"To the living world," I finish. "Like a guardian to a ward."

The queen nods. "There is a point of contact between the

worlds, the source of death and decay in the living realm, and it's there. In your city. In the palace."

"But I thought only death could break a bond like that."

"The living realm and the underworld are veritable tapestries of souls—the dark city literally built, piece by piece, as you say, from the dead. So this is not like the bond between a guardian and a ward, straightforward, one point connecting to another." She gestures at me and Ivrilos. "You're attached to him wholly, and he to you, so only a final death can separate you. The living world is too strong and vast to be bound fully, and the underworld too disparate. The grip is less sure, less complete. It's more of a bridge than a chain, with myriad strands that all tie to a precarious point—an anchor point."

"It must be in the king's quarters," I murmur.

"That would be my guess," Ivrilos says.

The queen shrugs. "Wherever it is, you must find it, and sever the connection. If you fail, both Thanopolis's sovereignty and your life, such that it is, are forfeit."

I bare my teeth more than grin at her. "I'm pretty sure if I fail, I'll be gone anyway."

The queen abruptly turns away from the portal. "Then you may live so long as you are helping us in our efforts to restore balance to the living world. But if you step too far out of line and upset the balance yourself . . . we will end you."

I shrug. "You can try."

Alldan glares at me.

The queen, for her part, ignores me. "Make yourself ready. We'll not grant you much time before we put our plans back into motion."

Nervousness, excitement, and fear all coil inside me, my too-quiet stomach like a basket of waiting snakes. "How long do I have?"

She glances back at me at the edge of the portal's frame. "Tonight."

Now I have a bellyful of *writhing* snakes.

"Wait, wait, wait," Japha says, holding up a hand. "You're giving her *tonight* to kill the king? What happens if she succeeds, and yet no one else understands why she had to kill him? They'll just see an inhuman assassin—sorry, Rovan—backed by a foreign influence. We need to get the word out to key people, to convince them what we're doing is right, so everything doesn't devolve into chaos even *if* Rovan succeeds."

"What do you suggest?" the queen asks.

"I would speak with my father, General Tumarq, on your behalf," Japha says. "He leads Thanopolis's army."

"What if you regret your new alliance with us and wish to betray our plans to the general?" Alldan asks.

Japha raises their hands. "I don't see how I could put you in a worse predicament. You're already under suspicion for aiding in Kineas's assassination, and"—they wave around at the courtyard—"you're all trapped here anyway—you, Delphia, your whole delegation. Unless you wish to flee the city before Rovan makes her move?"

The queen shakes her head. "That could draw too much attention. Besides, Alldan needs to remain there. Rovan must act now, and Alldan make ready. It's *you* I'm less sure of," she says to Japha.

"I can help, too," I say. "I'll get Japha into the palace, and I'll . . . I'll help seal our alliance another way. Before I kill the king, I need to get Lydea out of there. I'll bring her over to our side while Japha is doing whatever they're doing." I force myself to say it, even though the words taste rancid. "If Thanopolis's own princess, who will be queen regent and whose son will be heir to the throne, takes her place at your side—on *Skyllea's* side, don't you think that's worth the risk?"

324

"If you"—the queen holds my eyes with her strange white gaze—"bring Princess Lydea, Alldan's betrothed, out of the palace, you might tip the scales of balance ever more in your favor. Not to mention secure my trust. And you," she adds to Japha, "if you convince your father not to turn on my son, who *will* be Lydea's consort, you will win more than my trust. I will grant you whatever you wish."

She walks entirely out of the portal's frame, not even waiting for our response. Delphia shoots me an agonized look and says, "Please go get her."

I will. I'll do whatever I can to free Lydea from those who would use her.

Even if it means betraying Skyllea's trust.

30

The night air feels warm and alive against my skin as I slip through the shadows of the palace's outer courtyards. The perfume of garden flowers rises thick about me, and cold dew coats my feet through my sandals. My tunic is black, hooded in the Skyllean fashion, but not too long to tangle up my legs. My limbs are twined in black cloth to cover my too-pale skin. I have two half-moon blades strapped to my hips, courtesy of the Skyllean armory.

I feel so unbelievably free for the first time since my arrival at the palace that the smallest, most selfish part of me just wants to leave this all behind. Prowl through endless night—go where I want to go, see what I want to see, and be what I want to be, with Ivrilos at my side. Dodging the guard patrols, opening a door in the outer garden walls for Japha, using air and shadow to cloak us while my eyes picked out every detail in the darkness—it was all so easy. I could vanish into the night.

But I can't leave Lydea trapped in the palace. I can't leave Japha by themself, at the mercy of either Thanopolis or Skyllea. And I can't leave a revenant king ruling over the only city I've ever known.

Still, I can't help but wonder what storm I'm about to unleash on Thanopolis. It needs it like a cleansing rain, but I still feel like everything is moving so fast. And Lydea . . .

How will this storm hit her?

Blessedly, the night air is mostly calm as I begin my climb. Scaling the outer spiral of the palace is death defying, but I have no problem with that. And it's even easier for me when I whisper a few words that come to mind. Handholds sink into the stone when I reach for them, almost as if I'm scooping them out with my fingers.

I still almost fall when Ivrilos appears in the air next to me, startling me. One would think I would be used to that by now.

"That is really weird," I mutter, a breeze tossing my hair. "You look more like a ghost than ever when you just *float*."

"You should see yourself," he says with a grin, and then tucks my hair behind my ear, midair. I'm still not used to his touch, either; I find it more startling than all the impossible flying and climbing.

It doesn't take me long to find the outer wall of Lydea's quarters, many stories above the distant gardens below. I know the view and the shape of her windows well. I peer in through the glass but see only dim candlelight through a crack in the curtains.

I use sigils to widen the wood around the metal latches so they don't hold properly anymore. I figure it's the quietest way in. Thank the goddess the hinges are well oiled—the window swings silently open. I part the curtain with a fingertip, and see the sprawling, bedlike couch of her sitting room, silver and white as a cloud, empty save for the blue and black pillows strewn across it. I slip my legs over the sill.

Sigils grip my ankle in invisible fingers and drag me the rest of the way inside. I could break their hold—I see them so clearly now, and they're not as strong as me—but I don't.

My hip and elbow thwack loudly as they hit the floor in rapid succession. I feel pain, but it's different. Like it's a memory, or as if my flesh is nearly numb.

"Ow," I say, mostly out of habit, as more sigils pin my shoulders flat to the ground.

Lydea stands over me, staring, open mouthed. She looks every bit as beautiful as I remember her. Her black hair falls in a long braid over her shoulder, a few pieces sticking out in disarray, and her midnight blue robe is sheer enough to make my eyes trip

327

over her. Her red lips and bloodline look as vivid as if a painter just limned them on her pale skin. I don't have any clue how I look to her in my black tunic and bound limbs, with my hair wind tousled. But I know I probably look different from how she remembers me.

"Rovan," she chokes, a hand going to her mouth. "I thought . . ." She can't finish, because her eyes are flooding with tears. I've never seen her cry before.

"That I did something stupid?" I say with a nervous laugh. "Well, I did."

"How . . . I thought you were dead! That's what they told me." I take a breath to respond, but too quickly she follows up with, "Did you kill my brother?"

I hesitate. I didn't kill him, but I didn't exactly *not*.

When she flinches, I say, "No, I—"

She shakes her head, but before she can speak, Graecus, Lydea's guardian, appears over her shoulder. He sees me—and sees me *seeing* him, and his eyes widen. But then his gaze whips up to Ivrilos, who appears right in front of him.

"Graecus," Ivrilos says. "I'll give you one chance to—"

But the shade draws his sword and lets out a shout.

The outer doors to Lydea's chambers burst open, and Marklos comes striding through. "I know I felt something, and Klytios just said . . . What's this?" And then he sees me, and the words die on his lips.

I can't help it; I wave at him from the ground.

He throws his hand out, sketching, and Lydea's rug blows apart to twine around me like ropes. But I simply pick apart his sigils, like plucking at a thread in a tapestry and unraveling it all. The pieces of rug fall limply to the floor.

I whip my legs in the air and catapult to my feet, something I was never able to do while alive.

Lydea stares back and forth between us. Graecus and Marklos—and, invisible to her, Klytios and Ivrilos—ready themselves.

Three against three. *If* Lydea sides with us. *If* she doesn't hate me most of all.

"Graecus first," I say to Ivrilos. If only so Lydea's guardian can never hurt her again. So she'll be free after this, with any luck. I taught her the sigils to shield against him, but she doesn't have anyone here to help add that pinch of death to her blood magic.

I do it now, sketching out the shield for her.

"Choke on that," I say with a smirk for Graecus. And then, to Lydea, "Us against them?"

She only has a split second to make a decision, and thank the goddess she makes the right one. With the force of her sigils, a small table, shaped and stained like a red poppy blossom, lifts off the ground and smashes into Marklos, just as Graecus and Klytios charge Ivrilos.

The shades can't easily fight me until they materialize. I've made it impossible for Graecus to do so by shielding him from his source of energy, and Klytios knows that if he does so he's dooming Marklos, who is the only one capable of fighting me and Lydea otherwise.

But Marklos is definitely capable. He hasn't made a career of training royals for nothing.

He deflects the table with more sigils, sending it right into my face as the shades become a blur of clashing darkness around us. I split the table in half while Marklos redirects the shredded rug to twine around Lydea. At least he has a handicap: He can't truly hurt Lydea, whom he's sworn to protect. While he takes that small but critical amount of time to be careful with his sigils, I open up the stones under him, sinking his feet into the floor.

His eyes widen at my death magic. "You—" To his credit, he

doesn't give himself much time to wonder before he snuffs all the fire in the room, plunging us into darkness.

He doesn't know I can see in the dark. And yet that's nearly not enough to save me as he sends a splintered leg of the table flying into my chest.

Thank the goddess I see it coming and twist just enough that he misses my heart. As it is, I feel a horrible dull pressure in my shoulder. It could be worse, never mind that there's a giant spike of wood sticking out of me.

Lydea, having fought free of her bonds, waves the lights back on. Her ragged cry at the sight of my injury hurts me more than anything Marklos has done. She raises her hand with a scream. Another jagged piece of wood rips free from the couch—and flies right into Marklos's chest.

I don't hesitate. Gritting my teeth, I rip the wooden table leg out of my shoulder. I can already feel the wound closing up, but I need blood, fast. Marklos's is gushing down the front of his chiton. Dizzily, I stumble toward him, falling to my knees where he's sunk in the stone floor.

"I watched your father bleed to death," he burbles, blood at his lips. "By my own hand."

I already knew that, but it reminds me not to feel the slightest bit bad about what's coming.

"I'll be glad to do the same to you," he wheezes. Hilariously, he still thinks he has the upper hand.

"No," I say, feeling the pressure against my gums. "After you."

My fingers find the stake in his chest and jerk it out. Marklos gives a strangled cough as I press my mouth to his wound. Vaguely, somewhere, I hear Lydea gasp. Maybe gag.

I also hear a fading cry. Someone dying a final death, though I'm not sure who. I guess it's Graecus, Lydea's guardian.

Marklos gives an agonized scream that has nothing to do with me. His body arches, wrenching away from me. Then Klytios, fully materialized with Marklos's "help," is swinging a sword for my neck. I tuck and roll as he swings for me again. I move even faster now with Marklos's life force coursing through me, but Klytios is also keener after draining Marklos's pneuma. Nobody has said what will happen if I'm struck with a blade made out of shadow, or if my head is no longer attached to my shoulders.

I come to my feet, drawing my half-moon blades, to find Ivrilos by my side. He gives me a flashing glance, his eyes so dark they're like ink.

I'm eager to fight together with Ivrilos, to see what we can truly do—but then Marklos's guardian suddenly goes up in flames. His face twists into a hideous scream that's quickly lost in the blaze. It's so bright I flinch, throwing up my forearm to shield my eyes. When the inferno burns out, there's nothing where he stood but flakes of ash on the scorched stone.

Lydea stands behind a dissipating curtain of smoke, her arm still raised. She's breathing hard, chest heaving, and her dark eyes are wild.

The room is a wreck. The cloudlike couch that she, Japha, and I often frequented is a smoking ruin. The poppy-blossom tables are splintered, scattered around like petals. Marklos lies staring blankly at the ceiling, his chest its own kind of ruin, his legs still submerged in stone. Lydea's mouth works. I think she might scream again, or maybe vomit. I realize she's probably never killed anyone before.

"You are not your family," I say, before I can think of anything else. "This was all me. And even if you helped a little, you're *not* them."

That seems to snap her back to herself. Her gaze locks onto me. She asks, her voice nearly a whisper, "Are you okay?"

She can't see Ivrilos, standing next to me with his own blades drawn. She doesn't know anything—about the king, about Skyllea, about my . . . reawakening . . . or about my feelings for Ivrilos.

He steps away, giving us space. "I, um, I'll go make sure there's nothing left of Klytios down below." He vanishes.

"*Well?*" Lydea demands, some of the usual command coming back into her tone.

I glance down at my shoulder, where my wound is healed over completely, my pale skin and bloodline perfectly intact. "You might say I'm okay."

"Or I might not?" She still doesn't drop her hand. "What's happened to you?"

I grimace. "It's a long story."

"Then can you at least wipe your mouth first?"

"What? Oh." I realize what's covering it. It's a simple matter to use sigils to clear the blood away. "Of course. I know it must look—"

Before I can finish, her mouth is on mine, and she's kissing me. Her arms come tight around me, heedless of my blades. I drop them in an effort not to cut her, and they clatter loudly on the stone floor.

I raise my hands, trying to speak around her lips. "Lydea, wait—"

"Shut up and let me enjoy this before I inevitably want to kill you."

"Lydea," I say through her kisses. "There's a body on the floor."

"I don't care and neither does he."

"I'm a revenant. I'm not really alive, either."

"You feel alive," she says as her lips trail down my neck. Her hand gives my ass a squeeze as if verifying.

I nearly laugh, but what I say next dries up any humor completely. "The king is a revenant, too. He's not your father. He's Athanatos's son—Ivrilos's brother, Kadreus."

"Mmm" is all she says as her lips drop lower.

I grab her chin and force her to meet my eyes. "I'm serious. I need to kill him, or else Skyllea will attack Thanopolis with the full force of their army."

Her eyes darken at that. "Does that mean I can call off my engagement?"

A laugh bursts out of me. She smiles in response.

"Your eyes are amazing. So red," she says, and then she's kissing me again.

This time, I kiss her back. Ferociously. When she lets out a little yelp, I remember I have to be careful of my strength. I try to pull away from her, but she seizes me. Doesn't let go.

"I thought I lost you," she murmurs into my hair.

"I almost lost *you*. Lydea, I promise I'll never ask anything of you that I'm not willing to do, ever again. I'm so sorry I was selfish. After this, I'll help you go wherever you want, gain whatever you want, even if I have to fight my way through everyone who stands against you."

A faint smile quirks her red lips. "Are you my guardian now?"

"I'm whatever you want me to be."

We stare at each other for a long moment, and then her forehead creases. "Are you really dead?"

I grimace. Nod.

"But . . . how dead? You're still here. Still moving. I can feel you."

"I have no heartbeat. I don't really need to breathe, other than to speak. I heal quickly, I can use death magic as well as blood magic, and I, uh, drink blood."

"Huh," she says. I expect more questions about that, but then she asks, "And my father is gone?"

I nod again.

"Good riddance," she nearly spits. "But what happened? They all say you tried to assassinate the king and that you succeeded with Kineas."

"*He*, the undead king Kadreus, actually killed Kineas, because your brother discovered who—*what*—he was. The king is actually worse than your father, believe it or not. He's a revenant, like me, but insane after four hundred years of ruling this kingdom while his father, bound to him, rules in the underworld. Before I knew who Kadreus was, I was trying to use Kineas to get to him."

She shakes me. "*Why?* Why did you attack him like that?"

"I'm sorry about Kineas," I say, even though I'm not, really.

"I'm not," Lydea says. "He deserved everything he got, and more. The pig."

His death must not be what's upsetting her, then. "I know I drew more attention to you. I made it so you couldn't escape on your own, and—"

"I'm not mad about that, either!" she interrupts. "I'm mad because you got yourself *killed*. How could you put yourself at risk like that?"

She still cares about me. And she accepts what I am now, just like that, like she always has for those she holds dear.

I swallow. "My mother is dead." It's still hard to say the words out loud, too horrible for me to think about. The pain will overwhelm me, and I can't have that right now. "The king killed her. Back when I believed he was your father, I thought I could get revenge."

Her eyes close, and she drops her forehead against mine. "I'm so, so sorry."

"If it weren't for Ivrilos, I would be completely dead, not half-way there."

"Ivrilos?" Her eyes pop open. "I thought you hated each other."

"We . . . um . . . don't. He's actually been trying to help this entire time—to help the living for as long as he's been around. He's as little like his family as you are, or as Japha is." Which might explain why I love the lot of them. Or how we all found each other. "We might actually care a lot about each other."

Her eyes widen. "Like *that?*"

334

There's nothing else to do but say it, so I do, in a rush. "Yes. I fought it as long as I could but I can't anymore. Not now that we've joined forces and that I'm . . . like this. We can touch each other now. We've actually touched each other a lot. And yes, like *that*."

She stares at me for a long while. This is where, in one of those horribly dull tragedies as Bethea called them, someone would murder someone in a jealous rage or swallow hemlock in grief, and then someone's head would end up on the chopping block. Except Lydea . . . *giggles*.

"I didn't know shades could do that," she says, swallowing her laughter. I keep waiting for the explosion, for her to pull away, but then she asks, "How was it?"

"*Lydea*."

"Fine, you don't have to kiss and tell. But you still have to kiss me. I mean—" She falters, utterly unlike herself, her grin fading. "If you want to, anymore."

"Of course I want to! And, really, if you never want to see him, you don't have to. I mean, he can choose not to appear around you. But I just had to tell you what we did, before you and I go any further. It's less weird than it sounds now that I'm dead, too—"

Lydea taps my nose with her finger, interrupting me. "Rovan, shut up. I love you. And if he does, too, I'm fine with it."

I freeze. "You love me?"

"Obviously, you loon. Which means, if he hurts you . . ." She trails off, her eyes narrowing threateningly.

I snort. "I'm already dead."

"You know what I mean."

My smile drops. I've long known that many hurts run deeper than flesh. "I do. I love you, too." I hesitate. "Want to meet him?"

"Now?" She blinks. "Okay."

At first, I'm amazed. But, as Ivrilos said, love isn't finite, and

Lydea, Japha, and I already built a foundation for sharing. It just needs to expand a little to include Ivrilos.

I say his name, and he appears at my side instantly. I take his hand. He lets me, only raising his eyebrows slightly in surprise. Lydea steps back at his sudden appearance, but otherwise her expression is smooth. "This is Lydea. You've seen her before, but now you can have a true introduction. Lydea, meet Ivrilos."

Lydea's mouth quirks. "I would offer my hand in greeting, but . . ."

Ivrilos adjusts his grip in mine, layering his palm over the back of my hand. His skin is cool and firm, still surprising, and his fingers graze my knuckles in a minute caress. He lifts our hands together.

In a flash, I realize what he's doing. Using *me*, he takes Lydea's fingers and lifts them toward his lips. He brushes her knuckles with a kiss she can't feel. And for a moment, the three of us are holding hands, through mc—a bridge between life and death.

"It's a pleasure to meet you, truly," Ivrilos says.

Lydea looks charmed, despite herself. "I can see why she likes you. I'm not about to reconsider men, but—I can see."

Reluctantly, I drop everyone's hands. "If you think all of this is weird," I say, "wait until we climb out the window."

"What?" Lydea says flatly.

"We need to meet Japha, and we can't go through a palace full of guards and bloodmages and guardians to do it. With any luck, Japha has convinced their father that he needs to support us against the king. And if they haven't, maybe you can help sway Tumarq—if you want."

"Of course," she says, "but you still haven't clarified the most important detail." I wait, expecting questions about succession or Skyllea, until she says, "*I'm* climbing out the window?"

I smirk. "No, I am, and we're going to strap you to my back." I gesture over my shoulder. "Hop on."

31

Lydea and I skulk through the shadows alongside Ivrilos, who is currently invisible to everyone but me. After we avoid a pair of guards on patrol, I peer around a pillar across the wide expanse of courtyard between the palace, its outer wall, and the royal barracks.

This is where I've seen Tumarq and Penelope drilling troops. More importantly, Tumarq's and now Penelope's quarters are nearby, and bloodmages are unlikely to be wandering through this part of the royal grounds with their guardians, who might spot us.

To avoid the eyes of the living, I cloak us with even more shadow as we dash into an arcade-covered alley between the barracks and a storage outbuilding. Once there, our only company is a few broken sparring dummies and an empty weapon rack in need of refinishing.

"This is where Japha said they'd tell their father to meet us," I whisper, nodding at the outbuilding. Their plan was to send a palace servant with a sealed note for Tumarq with instructions. I hope it worked.

Ivrilos steps straight through the building's wall, and only a few moments later sticks his head back out. "They're inside. Several guards accompanied the general, but Japha rendered them unconscious."

So Tumarq didn't fully trust Japha's note telling him to come alone, even though it was written in the script of the general's blight-swallowed homeland. Which means he might not be convinced of *other* things, such as the fact that his king is an undead, maniacal tyrant, as well as the bringer of the blight—two things we were hoping would win Tumarq to our side.

Keeping us shrouded in shadow, I head for the door.

"You go first," I whisper to Lydea. "I'll keep myself hidden so he doesn't shout while you still have the door open."

Lydea nods and squares her shoulders. Instead of her diaphanous midnight robe, she's now wearing something more befitting a princess about to have a discussion with her top general: a wine-colored peplos embroidered with a maze of intricate black lines and tied with a silver strophion. She marches right inside. I follow closely behind, hidden by my magic like a true guardian shadow.

The storeroom smells of wood, leather, and dust, and wall sconces cast flickering light over shelves and weapon racks. A few guards lie on training mats of woven straw. Tumarq, despite the hour, is wearing a bronze breastplate and leather pteryges over his red chiton, his arms and legs armored in bracers and greaves. At our entrance, he looks like he might shout, but when Japha raises their hand for silence and the general sees only Lydea, his princess, he grudgingly subsides.

"Japha." Lydea rushes forward to give them a hug. "I'm so glad you're all right. I didn't know what happened to you after I left the necropolis. I never should have deserted you. I'm sorry."

Japha gives her a quick but sincere kiss on the cheek. They're wearing a deep indigo peplos twined in russet leather straps almost like an armored strophion, with more kohl on their eyes than usual—Japha's attempt at subtle. Their dark gaze flits around her, no doubt seeking me. "I'm okay, Cousin. I'm in fact *happily* unprotected, if you know what I mean. Have you come alone?"

Lydea grins. "Free of my guardian *and* my babysitter, Marklos."

"I won't ask what happened to the captain," Tumarq says gravely. "For now."

"That's for the best," Lydea says, giving him a nod. "Hello, Uncle."

He nods in return, his tone just as formal. "Niece. If you're here, I imagine you also support a coup?" He smiles grimly. "You would become queen regent, after all, until a son of yours came of age."

Her expression turns to ice. "And you think that's what I want?"

Tumarq gestures at Japha. "How else could you support such an outlandish claim as this? That the king is not only a bloodmage and a wielder of death magic in disguise, but a . . . *revenant* . . . as you so call him? Did this accusation originate in Skyllea? Did Alldan put it into your heads?"

Lydea opens her mouth angrily, but Japha grips her arm. "Father, you know the king hasn't been himself, not since he was crowned."

"And yet not to the extent that I could suspect him to be a *different person entirely*."

Japha raises their hands, as if they've been over this before. "He sent Crisea—your *daughter*—and Delphia, his own, to die in the necropolis, never mind that he always humored Aunt Penelope and Crisea's training as warriors, and Delphia was his favorite!"

Tumarq's face has grown stonier after the mention of Crisea. "Are you sure you're not upset because he's no longer humoring *you* and your inclinations . . . or lack thereof?"

Japha takes the question in stride, their voice calm. "Frankly, I drew the luckiest lot in getting betrothed to Helena. I knew I would have to get married sooner or later after I inherited the bloodline. But you're right, Uncle Tyros often indulged me, just as he did Penelope and Crisea. He respected those in his family who wanted to forge their own paths—as long as it was a path that didn't conflict too much with his own," Japha adds. "Don't get me wrong, the man had a heart of stone, but not like this."

"He never indulged me," Lydea grumbles, folding her arms.

Japha rolls their eyes. "Because you hated him. Tell me, Cousin, have you not noticed a difference?"

"I have indeed. Because now he hates me, too. I can feel it." Lydea frowns in thought. "And I once overheard Father in one of his darkest moods telling Kineas that he would never inflict a marriage like his own on us. That he would never force someone to marry a Skyllean like he was forced to marry my mother. That he pitied his sister Penelope for being bound to Silvean against her will." She shrugs. "And yet, what does he do as soon as he's crowned? He not only punishes Aunt Penelope for trying to rebel against her fate, but betroths Kineas to Silvean's daughter, a half Skyllean, and me to a full-blooded Skyllean prince. True, he never liked me, but not even I thought him capable of doing to me what he so hated having done to himself."

It's Tumarq's turn to frown, and I feel a flare of hope. "And now you argue this . . . revenant . . . has no issue doing it in your father's place."

I take this as my cue. I let the shadows around me dissipate and step forward as he takes me in, his mouth dropping open and his hand reaching for his sword.

"Just like Old King Neleus wanted—because he *is* the old king. Kadreus is the same king who's ruled Thanopolis for four hundred years, and he's always wanted Skyllea's power," I say. "He wants their bloodlines for the polis. He claimed Cylla's. He wanted my father's bloodline. And Lydea's betrothal to Alldan was a safe way to gain access to more of Skyllea's knowledge. But the king may be regretting his choices now." I rub my chest. "He made it clear he was getting sick of Skylleans when he stabbed me in the heart."

"You stabbed yourself in the heart." Tumarq shakes his head, eyes wide. "I saw your body. What witchery is this? No blood magic can resurrect the truly dead."

I raise my arms. "Because this isn't blood magic alone. It's also death magic. I'm a revenant, like the king. Here is your proof, at least, that creatures like us exist."

The general draws a few inches of steel. "You're not proof of anything. You're a traitor. You assassinated the crown prince—"

As he's been talking, Lydea and Japha have both sidled closer to me, their hands at the ready to protect me. A burst of warmth in my chest lends strength to my voice. "The *king* killed Kineas to protect his secret, and then he killed me. I'm not the liar. The king is."

"Why should I believe you?"

I extend a hand. "Because you don't have to take only my word for it." Ivrilos's palm slides into mine. The general gasps as he appears. "You once saw Ivrilos defend the king from my father. Now hear what he has to say."

I can't help but notice it's the four of us facing Tumarq in a line: Ivrilos, me, Lydea, and Japha. I'm so grateful for them. My odd, wonderful little family.

Ivrilos gives the general a short bow. "General Tumarq, I have long admired you as a man of strength and integrity. I like to think of myself as one, as well. So please believe me when I say the king you serve is my brother, Kadreus. He was my father Athanatos's legitimate heir; I'm a bastard. We both died over four hundred years ago—I was sent to the chopping block with my mother and sister, because my mother tried to hide me from him. But, unlike my brother, I found my way to the underworld, where I was pressed into my father's service. Kadreus remained here, bound to my father as Rovan is bound to me, ruling the living world, while Athanatos rules below."

Tumarq's eyes widen, and he shakes his head. "Even if what you say is somehow true, Athanatos is worshipped as a god in this city. If we rise up against him and his son, would that not be a greater treason than a simple coup against a mortal king?"

341

"My father is seen as a god because that's how he wants it," Ivrilos says. "I'm here to tell you that he's just a man, if a monster. He is trying to supplant the goddess. He has reshaped the underworld to reflect his tyranny, and he has used the essence not only of his people, but of the living world to do it. To sustain his dark city, he's caused the blight that swallowed the kingdom you were once heir to. To stop him—to stop the blight—we must first remove my brother and sever my father's connection to the living world. Otherwise, more kingdoms will be devoured like your own."

True fear—or fear of the truth—flashes in Tumarq's eyes.

"And if we don't remove him ourselves, Skyllea will," I say. "Because they're next to fall to the blight. They'll be forced into war with us instead of an alliance. They'd rather have us as allies, though. Think about how many lives we could save, fighting back the blight together *instead* of fighting Skyllea."

The general's lips press into a grim line. Still, he waves at my guardian. "How do I know this isn't some sort of trick? Some conjured magic to convince me to commit treason?"

"Because I promise you it's not?" Japha suggests.

"You don't know death magic. You can't know for sure."

Japha shakes their head, staring at their father. "Will I ever be enough for you?" they ask flatly. "Despite what you *perceive* I'm lacking?"

The general doesn't seem to know what to say. But he looks far more clueless than dismissive.

I sigh. "Do you think she's coming?" I ask Japha.

"Who?" Tumarq asks.

Japha shrugs. "If anyone can get her out of there, it's those creeps."

It was the one bit of help Skyllea offered us: The blighted bloodmages were to run a special errand for us. They were supposed to be here by now. Just as worry tightens like a fist in my belly, there's a knock on the door—one that comes in a distinctive pattern.

"That's—" the general starts.

Japha waves the door open with some sigils, and a dark shadow flows in. At first I can see nothing beyond that, but then Crisea steps out of the gloom, blinking in the flickering light of the storage building.

The circles under her eyes have grown darker, her brown skin chalkier, but her eyes are still sharp, and she still looks like she belongs in armor more than a death shroud. Lydea drags her the rest of the way inside.

Japha is about to close the door when Crisea squeaks, "Wait!" and hauls Bethea in after her.

We agreed that after the blighted mages brought Crisea out of the necropolis, they would remain hidden until needed so as not to frighten anyone. No one said anything about Bethea, but I'm glad she's no longer in there. Although I *am* surprised she left.

I'm less surprised when I see how her eyes follow Crisea, as if the other girl is her lifeline. Or her ward to protect. Even so, Bethea looks half-dead already. Her iron collar has climbed a few rounds higher up her pale throat. It's going to reach her face soon, at this rate. Her gaze snags on me, and she freezes, while Crisea only has eyes for Tumarq.

"Crisea," the general breathes, and all his stony stoicism melts as she throws herself into his arms. She herself nearly caves in. She's always put on a strong face, but not now.

"I'm sorry," she sobs. "I've failed in my duty. They told me if I didn't come, that you and Mother might die—that the whole polis was at risk!"

The general glares at us over her head.

"It's true," I say. "And *she's* going to die if she doesn't get out

343

of the necropolis. Look at her, General. The king did this to her. To your *daughter*."

"You think I don't know that?" Tumarq nearly spits. "But it is my duty—"

"To fight for the polis. For your king. But he's not the man you thought he was. He's a monster who will doom the polis and the entire world for his own gain. Crisea, look at me."

She turns, sudden fire behind her shining eyes. But then they widen as she takes in me and Ivrilos. Bethea hasn't stopped staring at me.

"Tell him who this is, and what I am."

"He's a shade," Crisea says. "I've seen him before, in glimpses. That's Ivrilos. And you, I thought you were dead, but—" She gasps.

"She *is* dead," Bethea whispers. Her hand covers her pale, chapped lips. "And you have death magic. Oh, Rovan."

I nearly flinch away from the pity in her voice. "The truth from someone you can trust," I say to Tumarq.

Lydea sniffs. "He should have trusted Japha, if not me."

"Forgive me, Princess, if I doubt your motives," the general bites out.

"What you know about my motives wouldn't fill a—"

"Shh, everyone." I raise my hand, cutting Lydea off. There's a muffled sound from outside. The blighted mages were too quiet to detect because of their magic, but this is the sound of someone *trying* to be quiet. "Someone's coming."

Ivrilos drops my hand, vanishing from anyone's view but mine. This time, before I can react, the door is kicked in . . .

. . . to reveal Penelope, bristling with armor and weapons. She stares at Tumarq—along with Crisea, Japha, Lydea, me, and Bethea—and her jaw drops. To her credit, she doesn't drop the sword in her hand.

344

She levels the blade at me. "Out. Get away from the general and my daughter. And Princess Lydea," she adds belatedly.

"Your priorities, as ever, are painfully clear," I snarl. Lydea shoots me a wry look.

"Penelope," Tumarq says slowly. "You might want to hear them out."

Hope flares in my chest.

"We can talk when she's in chains! This girl is a traitor! She murdered our nephew and is supposed to be dead. What is Crisea doing here?"

"You still might want to listen to what Rovan has to say, as well as Lydea and Japha."

"Then they're with her?" Penelope shakes her head. "I won't ask why you slipped out in the middle of the night without telling me, Tumarq, but I imagine it has something to do with *them*." She tosses her head at Japha. "Missing, presumed dead or to have played some role in the assassination of the crown prince."

"Mother, Japha would never have," Crisea says, and for a moment I appreciate her presence more than I thought possible.

Tumarq's jaw hardens as he faces off with Penelope. "Don't make Japha . . . or me . . . your enemy in this."

"I thought I was rescuing you from an assassination attempt!" she hisses. "I didn't know I would find you with a secret . . . *cabal*." She whistles sharply, and I hear the distant scrape and clank of armor out in the square.

"Soldiers," I say.

Turmarq curses. "Stand down, Penelope."

"Stand down?"

Crisea looks desperately back and forth between her parents. Japha is grim-faced, and Lydea furious. Bethea is like a shadow. Ivrilos *is* a shadow, already heading through the wall outside.

"That's an order," Tumarq says. "I outrank you."

"As a general," Penelope snaps. "I outrank you as a *princess*."

"Oh, so now you want to be a princess, when it suits you," Japha says.

"I outrank you all," Lydea bursts out. "For the goddess's sake, Aunt, the king isn't your brother. He's a monster who's lived for centuries, and he needs to be put down."

"*What?*"

Before anyone can explain, I hear it—the sound of hooves. More than a few sets. It doesn't take long for the rest of the group to hear them, too.

"You ordered in the cavalry?" Tumarq exclaims.

Penelope curses. "No. No one mounted." She rushes outside.

We all look at one another and follow, making a rather jumbled exit from the storeroom. I seize Lydea's arm and drag her back.

"Stay here," I say. "You're too important."

She grimaces. "To Thanopolis or Skyllea?"

"To me." That makes her freeze. "Please stay and hide." Saying that dredges up a distant memory of my father once telling me the same thing. I hadn't listened to him. Before I can dwell on that, I draw the shadows around me and conceal myself in darkness. Invisible, I head outside.

Out in the square, it's like a military drill has been ordered in the middle of the night. Dozens upon dozens of soldiers are gathering, torches flaring and steel flashing, apparently in preparation for whatever assassination attempt or treason Penelope thought she might find brewing.

And now come the bloodmages on horseback. It's not every bloodline in the Hall of the Wards, but as many as could be assembled at this late hour, led by Lady Acantha . . . and the king. The two of them are nestled in a phalanx of mounted bloodmages cloaked in black and red, silver helms glinting in the night. Acantha is swathed in crimson, the king in midnight, his true face hidden behind that mask of stony middle age, iron eyes, and salt-and-pepper hair crowned in golden laurels.

The horses come to a stop, facing the ranks of foot soldiers. Everyone looks confused—the bloodmages, the troops, and Penelope alike.

"What is the meaning of this?" the king asks calmly into the awkward, heavy silence. His eyes skip over me—but several times, as if they're fumbling for what they know is there. I swear I see a flash of red in them.

Penelope's gaze is alarmed as she glances back and forth between the assembled ranks and the mounted bloodmages, backed by the king. "Your Majesty, how . . . why . . . ?"

"You don't think I'm aware of what's going on in my own palace?" the king asks coldly. "I suspected you might try something, Penelope."

I watch a war play out in her expression. She neither wants to let herself be accused of treason nor to accuse Tumarq of it. "I'm not trying anything. I'm trying to *stop* it. Something was amiss, and I wanted to investigate before I disturbed you, Your Majesty."

"The company you keep is far more disturbing." His eyes flicker over me again, and then settle on Tumarq. "And perhaps oddest of all is finding my most trusted general here with you, alongside truants from the necropolis and potential traitors." He pauses. "Order your men to stand down."

"No," Turmarq says before Penelope can speak.

"Then you"—the king tosses an unconcerned, arrogant look at Acantha—"order your bloodmages to attack any who will not surrender. If they resist, take no prisoners."

He doesn't look back as he turns his horse away. He's not even going to watch his people kill one another by his command. And with him will go my chances for revenge, and for averting a war.

I move.

32

Surprisingly, it's Bethea who moves first. Before Acantha can open her mouth to give the order, Bethea casts off a length of the iron from around her neck and flings it, her spoken words of death magic whipping it through the air like a blade. For a split second I think it's going to cleave the bloodmage's head from her shoulders, but instead it binds around her throat, choking her off and knocking her from the saddle.

Bethea's face is set in grim satisfaction. Acantha was the one who sent her and her mother to the necropolis, after all.

The king pauses, barely sparing Acantha a glance where she wheezes and gags on the ground, and turns his horse to face Bethea. But Crisea has already stepped in front of her, shielding her.

"Cris," Penelope cries. "Don't!"

Maybe it's because that's the nickname my father once used for her. Maybe it's that she's protecting Bethea like I was already moving to do. But I step out in front of both of them and the lines of troops. The phalanx of bloodmages points at me like a crossbow, the king like the bolt about to fire. I doubt he'll lift a hand to do it, so as not to give his hidden powers away, but he'll use someone else's.

"*Wait*," I cry as I let the shadows around me dissipate. The king's eyes shoot to me, and I don't imagine it this time—they flash red. In that moment, his mask cracks, his lips move, and his hand rises.

This is my chance.

Metal darts wreathed in blue flame lance from his fingers—

blood and death magic that only I could block. Instead of trying, my own hand flickers and my breath exhales the words. A stone clacks at the king's feet as I brace for his unearthly projectiles to hit me.

Ivrilos appears before me, stepping back against my chest so he materializes fully. His blades, along with a huge gust of air that rises with his whisper, hammer aside the metal darts, and a gout of water douses the flame, leaving only steam in the air. Japha stands next to me, hand extended—the one that guided the water.

I didn't have to save myself, because they did it for me.

"That was death magic, from the king!" Bethea cries.

"And blood magic as well," says Japha, their voice carrying. "The king is a bloodmage."

"More than that," Ivrilos shouts. "He is my brother, dead these four hundred years. But whereas I am a shade, he is a monster. A revenant in disguise."

"And I can prove it," I add, and I sketch the final sigil, the one under my eye that my father left me. The stone I threw toward the king shimmers. And then the light expands—the shield I cast on it—billowing out like a blown glass bubble, encasing the king like a miniature veil. Inside, he flickers and ripples like a reflection in water. At times, you can see the king everyone knows as he struggles to maintain his mask against my magic, and other times—red eyes in a too-young, too-mad face; short dark hair with no gray; a leaner chest heaving in anger; muscular arms streaked with a bloodline. Kadreus.

A different person entirely.

The bloodmages, at least, would know what sort of sigils I used. It's much like the city's own veil against the blight. Some of them pull their horses away in surprise and horror.

"They speak the truth," Tumarq declares. *Finally.* "The king has fallen to this blighted impostor, who sits in his place on the throne.

Rally to me!" He raises his sword, and all the foot soldiers draw their own.

The king looks around at his bloodmages. "Kill them," he says.

Even though a few horses shy sideways, none of them move forward.

"*Kill them*," he repeats, growling. "I am still your king. And a truer one you've never had since Athanatos."

"It's literally been *only* you, since him," Japha says, their sardonic tone carrying across the courtyard. "But that doesn't mean you're true. You've kept the throne through an endless string of lies and regicide. You've ruled by deceiving your people. I'd say we're done with all of that."

"You did this." The king turns slowly to Japha, those flickering red eyes finding them across the gap between the two forces. "Tumarq would never betray me otherwise, not for the little blue-haired witch. You're a disgrace. You've never belonged in this family."

If the words are meant to be damning, they don't have their intended effect. Japha grins. "Or maybe *you* don't belong anymore."

The king's eyes don't leave theirs. "Indeed. Our blood is too diluted. This latest generation is a shame. I've had to tolerate you as a bloodline because your sister was inadequate and took her own life. Kineas was a fool, Lydea willful. And Crisea has always been her mother's greatest weakness."

Tumarq's hand tightens on his sword. "Never mention my children with your foul lips ever again."

The king ignores him and looks at Ivrilos, his brother. "Children are always a liability. He should have entirely rid himself of *you*, bastard."

"You too, then," Ivrilos says.

"No, because I made myself indispensable. His greatest strength."

Tumarq takes a step forward, moving closer to his children. *Both* of them. "Then Japha and Crisea are mine."

I hear Japha's breath catch. And then I hear a door slam open. Footsteps over the courtyard's cobblestones.

"And perhaps I will be my father's," says a voice that makes me flinch, "even if he doesn't have a say in it." Lydea comes striding out from the storage building. Her wine-colored peplos flows around her like a storm, her dark eyes practically sparking in the torchlight. I shake my head at her, willing her back inside. She's in too much danger out here. And yet she stands in a line with the rest of us, hands held ready by her strophion-twined hips.

The king smiles down at her from atop his horse. "Why would I not have a say in your significance, daughter dear?"

"Because you're not my father," Lydea says, and then waves a hand over the bloodmages. "No one will be charged with treason if you resist this man . . . if you stand with me. I am Thanopolis's future, so help me. Help your polis. Because my father is gone."

The king stares at her, death in his red eyes.

"Children are nothing without their fathers," he says. "Headless beasts without guidance. *You* are already nothing. But some of you are still too much." His gaze flickers. His hand moves even faster.

I realize what he's doing, but too late. I've been focused on protecting Lydea. Japha, Bethea. Even Ivrilos. I spin toward Tumarq just as the king reaches for him.

The father of Japha and Crisea. Head of the army.

I try to block whatever it is the king has thrown. It looks like liquid darkness, slithering like a snake through the air. I rip up the stones of the courtyard as a shield, but his magic just flows around it. *Fire*, I think frantically—I could burn it, turn the liquid to mist, but that much heat would scorch everyone around me.

The toxic darkness coils and strikes.

351

And hits *Japha*, square in the chest, who has thrown themself in front of Tumarq at the last second.

Japha stumbles. They look around, almost in confusion. And then I see the poison streaking up their neck, deeper and darker under their skin than their bloodline. They collapse to their knees.

"No!" I shriek.

Tumarq cries out at the same time. He catches Japha's shoulders as they topple sideways, cradling them in his arms. The darkness is bleeding into Japha's eyes, turning them fully black. Their limbs shake uncontrollably against the cobbles. Their chest convulses.

"Fight this," Tumarq commands, his strong hand cupping Japha's cheek. "You are my greatest strength. You always were. You were always enough. Now fight. I'm begging you."

Japha opens their mouth to respond, and blackness like tar bubbles out.

Tumarq's words grow more frantic. "I'm supposed to be *your* shield. It should have hit me." His voice breaks. "*Why*, Japha?"

I've moved without realizing it. I'm almost to them, fingers outstretched, mouth opening to stop this however I can. But no words come, no sigils, because I hear Japha's heart stutter . . . and stop.

Tumarq lets out a bellow of anguish. Lydea stands frozen, hands over her mouth, eyes flown wide in horror. Crisea and Bethea both dive for Japha, taking their hands and muttering frantically, but there's nothing either of them can do.

Japha just called themself the luckiest of us. And now they're dead.

"No," I say. "No." I can't believe what I'm seeing, what I'm feeling. Pain tears through me, starting in my chest and dropping, leaving me with no sense of the bottom as it turns me inside out. I fold forward, clutching my useless, empty stomach as a cry rips out of me.

Behind me, my back turned on him, the king says calmly, "Attack."

"*No*," Ivrilos breathes.

Because the king isn't speaking to the bloodmages anymore. He's speaking to their guardians. I spin just in time to see every bloodmage collapse in their saddles, some sliding to the ground, backs arching, eyes and mouths wide in anguish, as an army of darkness steps out of the shadows.

An army of the dead facing an army of the living.

Behind them, the king wheels his horse around and rides away from the field of battle, out of the courtyard and toward the palace.

The guardian shades flood forward. I flex my fingers and say the word, and the shield I used against the king expands, encasing a dozen or so bloodmages. They cough, stirring feebly, suddenly blocked from what was drawing the life from them. A few of their shades are likely vanishing from sight, no longer able to fight the living.

But not enough of them.

"Rovan," Ivrilos says. "Save your strength. We have to—"

"I know. We have to follow the king." I look around frantically. The general is still down on his knees next to Japha, along with Crisea and Bethea. Penelope stands above them, gripping Tumarq's shoulder hard. I can't tell if she's comforting him or urging him to get up. The lines of soldiers look terrified even as they raise their steel. Flesh meets shadow in a flickering clash of swords, and already there are screams among the living. Our group knots together, Ivrilos whirling around us, fighting off other shades, as I maintain my shield over the few bloodmages I can cover. "But how can we leave everyone like this?"

"Because we will help them," say the two blighted mages as they appear alongside me. One raises their hands, one whispers, and my shield suddenly lifts from me like a weight—and then expands. More of the fallen bloodmages stir back to life. "We will hold this, but you should open the gates."

Through the chaos, my eyes find a pair of thick wooden doors studded with iron. They're mounted in the outer wall of the palace, where the royal barrack could deploy itself into the city quickly if necessary. I'm not the only one who spots them.

Penelope is eyeing both the gates and the blighted mages with horror. "Open them to *Skylleans?*"

Lydea nods, her face settling into something like calm. "Open the gates."

"We will not have a foreign queen!" her aunt shouts.

"We won't. I will be queen," Lydea says, and somehow the bottom drops even further out of me. "And Alldan my consort. We will ally with Skyllea, not submit to them." She glances down at Japha's body and then quickly away again. She meets my eyes. Hers are shining and flat at the same time. Depthless lakes. "You've all sacrificed so much. I can, too."

"As you will it, my queen." Tumarq stands, tears streaking his face.

Penelope is at his side, drawing her sword with a ferocious expression. She meets my eyes briefly, nods once. "Open the gates!"

It's Lydea who does it—taking full responsibility, I suppose—throwing out her hands and sigils. The wooden doors fly open, and a small group of Skylleans come streaming in, their rose-hued steel shining. Alldan is in their lead, his stag-horn crown glinting in his forest dark hair. He lets out a strange, high battle cry and launches immediately into the mix of living and dead, hacking right into a shade that was about to skewer one of Thanopolis's soldiers from behind.

Both Tumarq and Penelope let out their own battle cries and charge forward to join him.

But still, I don't move. I'm frozen in the storm of motion

around me. I know I don't have time for this, but my eyes keep going back to Japha.

"We need to get to the throne room," Ivrilos says alongside me. "This was all a distraction—everything since you unveiled Kadreus and he knew he'd lost. He's stalling us. He's gone to protect the most precious thing in all of Thanopolis, because he suspects that's where we might be headed."

The source of the blight. The anchor point between Thanopolis and the dark city. The greatest source of their underworld power.

"Ivrilos," I say, spinning on him. As soon as he sees my face, he shakes his head, because he knows what I'm going to ask. "Find Japha. Do everything you can to make sure they're okay down there."

"I'm not leaving you right now."

"*I can't just leave them alone.*" My voice breaks. "Please."

Ivrilos swallows, nods, and then he's gone, just like that. Still, I can't move. I can't look away. Crisea and Bethea drag the body to the edge of the courtyard, Lydea following them with a fierce determination I've never seen in her face before.

She turns back only to say, "Go, Rovan. Do what you need to do. I'll"—she chokes—"I'll take care of Japha, make sure nothing else hurts them. I promise. Go!"

I know it's just a body, that Japha is no longer there, but her assurance is the only thing that allows me to tear myself away.

"Don't follow me," I say. "It's too dangerous."

The ferocious look on her pale face burns into my mind like a torch in the night. "You think you're the only one who wants to make that monster suffer?"

I can't fault her for what she's feeling, but where I'm headed is no place for her.

"You made me a promise," I say, "and you have to keep it. For me . . . and for Japha."

Maybe it's manipulative, but if it will keep her here . . . Pain streaks across her face as I turn away.

Thank you, Japha, I think, and then, tears choking me, *Japha, Japha*.

And then I'm running after the king who took my father, my mother, and now my best friend from me.

I'm going to take *everything* from him.

356

33

I raise a shimmering curtain of blood and death magic as fine as any cloth I've ever woven to cloak me from the eyes of the living and the dead—something probably like what the king has used all these years to disguise himself. I dodge forces of flesh and shadow, invisible, pausing only to send burning blue fire like spears through the hearts of as many shades as I can reach as I pass.

Still not enough.

I can almost hear Ivrilos hissing at me to save my strength, but I can't resist. I feel as if *I'm* on fire.

I quit attacking once I reach the edge of the courtyard, dropping my disguise and breaking into a sprint, bending all my focus on moving as fast as I can. The arcade blurs and the night air rushes around me, my feet slapping the marble tiles at an inhuman pace. The king was on a horse, but if he's going where I think he's going, he'll need to abandon it.

His path up the spiraling curve of the palace's main hallway is even easier to follow than I imagined. After leaving his mount, he didn't raise any guards. In fact, quite the opposite. He's left a trail of their bodies. And their blood. Their life force is splattered along the gold-threaded and blossom-choked marble.

It's deathly quiet.

I only bump into one living soul. He must have gone to relieve himself, and when he came back . . . He stares at the body of his companion guard, wide-eyed. The moment he sees me, he throws himself in my way, swinging his sword wildly.

I dodge the blade, locate his neck, and soon he joins his companion on the floor. I'm moving again before I even bother to wipe my hand across my red-stained mouth. I needed the blood, and, besides, I couldn't leave the danger of a panicked man with a sword for someone else to stumble into. It's a pity, but better I take care of him than let another shoulder that burden.

I'm already a monster, after all. At least in this moment, I'm fine with that. It takes a monster to hunt a monster. But it does make me wonder if there will be any coming back from this, beyond simply surviving.

I know where the king's quarters are, his hidden throne room, despite never having been inside. The trail of blood shows me the way. And when I finally see the column-lined, high black doors that reach almost to the ceiling, what has been invisible in the past is all too obvious: the magic wreathing the place, made of intricate sigil work and twisting shadow. It makes my own magical cloak look like child's play. No wonder Ivrilos has never been able to sneak in on his own. It's almost like a cage, and I can feel something dark and pulsing within. Maybe Kadreus. Maybe something worse.

Like the king, I can also weave both blood and death magic—and pick them apart. And yet I can see he's protected himself from the likes of Skyllea's blighted mages who can do the same. Even if they were to unravel the magic, the final thread of it would stop their hearts.

Good thing my heart is already still.

Despite my readiness, when I approach the entrance, I don't have to do anything. The magic falls away like a curtain. More alert than ever, I brace myself as one of the black doors cracks open for me.

Maybe the king knew such barriers would be useless against me. Still, I feel a stirring of unease. The voice I hear doesn't help:

"Do come in, Rovan."

It's not the king's voice as I've known it. He's let his illusion drop away, just like the protective magic on the room.

Part of me is screaming in warning. But a greater part of me is eager to end this. Furious for revenge. Hungry for blood.

I throw both doors entirely open. I see the king all the way through another set of double doors on the other side of an elaborate sitting room. Gold veins lace midnight marble. Gold-plated skeleton hands hold wall sconces. Elaborate mosaic scenes on the ceiling in more black and gold depict skeletons and shadows in flowing shrouds. Death and opulence. Perfect for a royal revenant.

Atop a dais, the king is sitting in a high-backed throne carved of the purest obsidian. The only thing interrupting the almost-liquid darkness of the stone is a skull set at the crest, wearing a golden laurel crown. One that perfectly matches the chair's occupant.

Somehow, I know it's Athanatos's skull. Just how I know it's the source of the blight—the anchor point to the underworld.

Red eyes meet and hold mine. Kadreus could almost be handsome, if it weren't for the cruel madness simmering right under the surface of his skin. He's pretty wrapping over a deep, festering wound. Maybe similar to how I'll look someday.

Don't think about that, I tell myself. *Not right now.*

There's still blood on his lips as he smiles at me slowly. "Always you think you're getting me exactly where you want me when, in reality, it's the other way around."

"Are you well acquainted with reality these days?" I ask.

"More than you, it appears. You seem to think you have a chance of beating me in my inner sanctum, alone. It's why I let you in. Shall we dance?"

He abruptly stands, his black himation flowing around him like shadow, his muscular arms lined in deep red sigils. He steps forward, and I have to resist stepping backward. A dance, indeed.

"I can't help but feel as though we've done this already," he says, slowly walking down the dais. "Except you didn't stay dead. I should have known. I couldn't see what you were becoming. But I can see you now. You *burn*. And you can't be left to exist."

"Then neither can you," I say. "Everyone knows what you are now."

He shrugs. "This is not an insurmountable obstacle. It will only require a little effort and time, and I have plenty of time. Once I destroy you, I'll send out every guardian still tethered to a blood-line and eliminate all who know my secret. I'm already doing a fair job of that right now."

"No," I say, squaring my shoulders and standing tall as he gets closer. Refusing to cower. "You're losing. The Skylleans brought reinforcements."

He waves a hand, golden rings flashing. "Only more to sweep up, then. This family, this *polis*, needed a cleansing, especially of Skylleans. Time to start fresh."

"Yes. Which is why Lydea will rule, and you will die. For good."

"Lydea," he snorts. "She isn't fit to preside over a dinner party, let alone a kingdom."

Now he's standing less that a body's length from me. Sigil-lined paths open up before me, and deathly whispers drift in my ears. My hands, my breath, are held ready.

"So what was that about my dying for good?" he asks. "Show me how that will work." Despite what he says, he's teasing, almost flirtatious, and it makes my skin crawl. "*I've* already practiced on Japha, so you need to play catch-up."

For a moment, my vision flashes red. I remember Kineas toying with me like this, trying to goad me into making the first move. I tell myself I'm not going to fall for his trick.

But then Kadreus reminds me he is not Kineas. Without warning, he swipes at my face with his hand, which has suddenly grown foot-long iron claws. I duck away, barely, from where they would have made ribbons of my cheek. At the same time his other hand, sketching sigils, sends a ball of fire into the space I step into. I barely deflect that, too, and singe my fingers doing it.

The blisters subside immediately into smooth, unblemished skin.

The king shakes his head and smiles at me as if I'm a willful child—an incongruous sight with his grotesque claws and red-stained lips. "You're fast and you're resilient, but you can't win this alone."

"She's not alone," Ivrilos says, appearing next to me. In the same motion, he seizes my wrist in one hand, drawing from me, and swings at Kadreus's head with the other, a half-moon blade in his grip.

Kadreus should have fallen like wheat to a scythe. Instead, he throws himself into a standing backflip to avoid the strike, lithe and graceful as a cat in midair. Which simply isn't fair.

I glance at Ivrilos long enough for him to jerk his head, a weighted look in his dark eyes.

He couldn't find Japha, or he couldn't save them. Maybe he had to watch as someone got to them first . . .

No, don't think about that. Don't think at all. Just move.

"Ah, indeed, she's not alone!" the king announces theatrically, as if he's the villain in a dramatic play. He grins. "And neither am I."

A dark shadow coalesces behind him, growing darker and darker while the figure's eyes glow a bright and icy blue until they burn with cold. If Kadreus is all fire and madness, Athanatos is pitiless darkness. He's empty, but it's an emptiness that is vast and terrifying and self-aware.

This is bad. Ivrilos has always said he would need to absorb his brother's strength before facing his father. But now his father is here.

"My son," Athanatos says in a voice like death. "I've been waiting for you."

"Likewise," Ivrilos says shortly. Neither one seems much for words. Maybe after this long, they've said all they needed to say.

But one thought keeps my joints from locking up in fear. Ivrilos isn't like his father, not one bit, and not after four hundred years of being in a similar state. Maybe I don't have to turn into a monster like Kadreus. Maybe I can kill the monster without becoming one myself.

My hands tighten on my half-moon blades just as Ivrilos's do on his. I wanted to see what we could do together, after all. We exchange a glance, and then we're both moving.

Kadreus and his shade of a father take a split second longer than we do. Perhaps they can afford to take their time. I barely see Ivrilos and Athanatos clash out of the corner of my eye. Not only are they dark shadows, trailing even more darkness, they move at an inhuman speed. Unearthly. Godlike.

Kadreus—I don't want to give him the satisfaction of thinking of him as *the king* anymore—doesn't even draw a weapon. He conjures a blade from the air: obsidian, just like his throne, and dripping with blood. It's dramatic, but it's an effective combination of blood and death magic, so I line my half-moon blades with blue fire. Just as dramatic.

I know they probably won't work on his heart for the final strike, but I have something special for that.

Kadreus bats my weapons aside as if they're twigs and almost casually sends a blow my way that nearly beheads me. I remind myself that he benefits from Athanatos's experience as much as I do Ivrilos's. My only hope is that maybe, in ruling Thanopolis and the underworld, both he and his father neglected to practice throughout the years, overly confident in their power.

But it soon feels like Kadreus has everything I have and more.

His sigils are as precise and efficient as his blade work. He trips me by bucking the stone under my feet and lands three more burns on me that heal over just as rapidly as before. I'm barely able to throw any sigils at him. Flame comes so naturally to me, but when I encase him in a massive sphere of it, he simply snuffs it and steps out from behind a curtain of smoke.

Death magic might come easier, but he keeps me so much on the defensive that all he has to do is purse his lips and blow away my attempts to open the floor under his feet or pin him down with metal spikes.

I'm surprised when he tries to poison me like he did Japha. I still don't let it reach me, utterly vaporizing the snaking black tendril.

"Pity you didn't do that for Japha," Kadreus says conversationally. "Since you're already dead, it can't actually hurt you. *Physically*, at least." His smile cuts like a razor.

I scream and launch myself at him, flaming blades twirling, but he batters me back. As I dodge, something nags at me. It comes from Ivrilos's knowledge, no doubt. Kadreus *isn't* as efficient, even leaving slight openings whenever I try to move a certain way and he's forced to stop me.

He's keeping my focus elsewhere. Keeping me from going deeper into the room, putting himself between me and the throne. Keeping me *away* from the skull. He doesn't even know for sure that I want to reach it, which tells me for certain that I do.

I throw a few more blows at him while I think. He's the better fighter. For now he's testing my limits, maybe even toying with me. But if he realizes I'm going for the anchor point, he'll end me as fast as possible. Whatever I throw at it, he'd probably put himself between me and it, even at risk to himself.

Unless . . . unless the risk is too great. Maybe it's time to tip my hand. Just not in the direction he expects. He needs to believe

I want to kill him even more than I already do. He needs to score a hit on me, which means I need to leave him an opening. And not a physical hit.

I start crying, even as I swing my blades. It's not difficult to start. I see red on my cheek out of the corner of my eye, a blood tear. Hard to miss.

"I forgot that's what happens when we cry," Kadreus says, locking my blades for a minute to stare. He sounds almost curious. "I haven't in so long. Nothing to cry over."

I toss his sword aside. "Because you're alone."

The bastard doesn't even bother to raise his guard again. "I'm never alone."

"And yet everyone hates you. Your people. Even *him*." I nod without looking at the clashing black shadows around us. "Your father. He loves no one, and you know it. You can see it in his eyes." Something flashes in *Kadreus's* eyes to show me I've scratched at some long-buried hurt. "Ivrilos's and my bond is stronger than yours and Athanatos's could ever be, because we love each other and we have people who love us."

I realize even as I goad him that it's true. I *do* have something Kadreus doesn't—a caring family. My father and my mother. Ivrilos. And Lydea and . . .

Japha.

Kadreus must see it in my face, because he says, "So how does it feel to lose someone who loved you? Do you feel stronger now, after watching the light fade from your friend's eyes?"

My cry of rage is real. I use a quick sigil to slice the dark cloth wrapped around my wrist and reveal the stake: half bone, half wood, twined in a spiral of steel to keep both sides together and the point sharp. It's a tool designed specifically for putting down creatures like us, courtesy of Skyllea.

Kadreus's red eyes only have a split second to take it in, to widen, before I throw, aiming right for his heart. I've never thrown something so hard, so fast, so accurately. I could have hit the eye of a needle, threaded it.

Kadreus dodges with a mere blurring flick of his shoulders, his eyebrow already raised in derision. It's too dangerous a weapon against a revenant, too solid a throw, to risk anything else.

Except I wasn't aiming for him. I only lined his heart up perfectly with his father's skull.

He hears the sharp crack as soon as I do. His father's outraged shout is even louder.

The shadows stop moving, revealing Ivrilos, hair disheveled, panting, gashes up on his arms and one on his thigh that ooze darkness instead of blood. He looks grateful for the respite. Athanatos appears untouched, except for his face twisting in contempt.

"Fool," he snarls at Kadreus.

It's there and gone on Kadreus's face—the same look I saw when I said his father didn't love him. The briefest flash of a little boy's pain in a man's rage.

When he turns to me, all I see is hatred.

"Kill her," Athanatos says. "I may be forced to leave this fight unfinished because of your mistake. Hurry if you don't want to face them both alone . . . although perhaps that would serve you right." He doesn't wait for a response. He simply launches himself at Ivrilos with renewed speed, and the two of them meet and melt back into a blur of shadows.

Kadreus wastes no time. He has a hand around my throat, metal claws digging into my skin, before I can blink. I jam one half-moon blade into his side, but he doesn't even flinch. I raise the other, and he catches my wrist, his own sword abandoned, and squeezes until my bones crack and snap, and my blade clatters on the ground. I scream, but he lifts me off the floor by my neck, choking me off.

I can't use any death magic without breath. For sigils, the fingers of my broken arm are useless. I hesitate too long in letting go of the weapon jammed in his side—long enough for him to sketch sigils of his own that break all those fingers. Pain lances through me, enough that my mind stumbles when I try to use the only sigil I know well enough to follow without sketching. When I finally *move* him, it's feeble. He only pivots, still dancing, and slams me up against a wall. My toes dangle a foot off the ground.

"Any more tricks up your sleeves?" he hisses. "Ah, yes." It doesn't take him long to find the second stake, bound beneath the wrappings on my other arm. His retrieval of it, jostling my fractures, would have made me scream again if I could.

He raises the stake eye level between us, twisting it back and forth to examine it.

I gurgle at him. My straining eyes follow the stake in his grip. I can feel my wrist and fingers quietly knitting back together. When the inevitable blow comes, I hope they're strong enough to catch it before it reaches my heart.

"I'm not done with you just yet," he says. "First, a toast."

He strikes like a snake, lips parting to reveal elongated eye-teeth. I don't have much of a glimpse before they're buried in my neck. I can't even gasp in shock or pain.

I hear Ivrilos shout, but he can't stop this.

It's like the old days, when I was still alive and my guardian would steal from me. Everything feels like it's draining out of me. My wrist and my fingers stop healing. The world wheels around me. Without my feet on the ground I soon lose track of what is up or down, and the lights begin to fade. I barely notice the hand at my throat or when Kadreus's teeth pull away; I feel so empty. Adrift.

"Just delicious." Kadreus's voice floats toward me from far away. All I see are his red lips swimming before me. There's a current I can feel against me, trying to carry me off.

Part of me just wants him to let go.

"It's not broken, you realize," he says, and I have a hard time understanding, at first. "The link to my father's domain. It's like severing only one rope of a bridge. It might not work correctly, be too precarious for proper use, but it's not *gone*. And it could always be repaired." Maybe he's trying to reassure himself, or perhaps his father. "Are you prepared to go to the underworld to finish the job, Rovan?"

Kadreus smiles into my face as he watches the news sink in. "I'm certainly planning on sending you there, for all the good it will do you. You've lost. I told you, you can't beat me alone."

Then there's another voice, and a face behind him that sharpens my focus and drags me against the current, closer toward the surface.

"She's *never* alone," Lydea says over his shoulder—just as she rips Kadreus's heart out through his back. The sigils she uses are magnificent, more powerful and yet more delicate than I've ever seen her use. It's a work of violent art.

Oddly, I can almost hear Japha's voice echoing her. But maybe that's because I'm dying. Again.

It doesn't stop me from smiling as Lydea tosses his heart aside like so much trash. Not even when Kadreus hurls *me* aside, and my head cracks on the stone floor like an egg.

34

If only Kadreus getting his heart torn out would kill him. But he remains standing, just with a gaping, impossible hole in his back.

I can still see him from my vantage on the floor, my body like a broken doll's, even though it looks as if I'm staring down a long dark tunnel. A tunnel that's underwater. I hear Ivrilos crying out again. His memory of his mother and sister dying rises in my mind, clearer than my own vision. He's trying to feed more of his essence into me, and his foremost memory must be coming with it. But it's not enough, not after I've lost so much blood. And he can't spare much of himself, not while fighting his father.

"Don't," I try to say, but it comes out as a rasp.

Kadreus thinks I'm talking to him—they always think that— and he turns to give me a grin, right before he seizes Lydea by the throat.

She wasn't ready for him. She obviously thought ripping out his heart would slow him down. But no. Only a stake of wood or bone *piercing* the heart can kill a revenant. The only stake like that left within reach is clenched in Kadreus's hand.

I can't sketch sigils to snatch it away from him, not with my unhealed fingers. As my brain sluggishly tries to think of something to do from within the empty ruin of my body, I can only watch his hand tighten around Lydea's throat as his sigils bind her limbs like invisible rope, even down to her fingertips.

"Where is your sense of honor, dear Lydea?" He *tsks* at her. "You came at my *back*? Your king, no less?"

"You can't speak of honor. And you are no king, not anymore," Lydea hisses. "I am your queen."

"We *definitely* can't have that," he says. I can't see his face directly, but his rage is barely concealed under the calm mask of his tone. "I guess my line ends with you. So be it."

Lydea, absurdly, grins. She looks fierce, bright, even as Kadreus is trying to snuff her fire. "You forgot Delphia. She's the one Alldan truly wants anyway. She's the continuance of your line, and an alliance with Skyllea your end. They're coming for you."

"I'd best make ready, then," he says. And then he snaps her neck.

It's the sound of my own heart breaking.

He tosses her body on the ground, shattered, like mine. The only difference is hers is unseeing. Her peplos is like spilled wine around her, and those dark, beautiful eyes stare sightlessly across the floor at me. Her limp hand, freed of its binds, almost looks like it's reaching for me. But the stretch of black marble between us may as well be an ocean.

Or the divide between worlds.

Kadreus turns to me, flipping the stake in his hand, but I don't even bother looking up. All I can see is her. If this is my end, I want her to be the last thing I see in the living realm.

. . . And yet, I can't help noticing the lumpy, wet shape on the floor right over her shoulder.

Kadreus's heart.

I don't have a stake, but I have something like it. *Two* things.

Move, move, move. The simple sigil I know better than any other. The one I can sketch without lifting a finger.

Kadreus is too focused on me and my imminent second death to see what comes flying toward me. My ruined hands meet his heart and slam it numbly to my lips, crushing it to my open mouth. My teeth sharpen, stretch . . . and stab as deep as they can into the slippery muscle.

Teeth. *Bone.* Close enough to stakes.

Blood squirts into my mouth as I bite and suck. I squeeze his heart like a sponge in newly healed hands, tearing into it with renewed vigor. It feels so good, more intoxicating and potent than any blood I've had before. I barely hear Kadreus gasp. Then he screams as he falls to his knees.

He keeps screaming. My teeth aren't long enough, I suppose, to pierce *all* the way to the other side. But I'm working my way through it like a juicy slab of meat.

My visions clears, my senses sharpen. Over the delicious meal pressed to my face and Kadreus's shrieks, I realize I don't see blurring shadows or hear any more fighting. And then I see Ivrilos stalk up behind his brother. He's limping, but that doesn't stop him from looking like the deadliest creature I've ever seen. He leans over Kadreus's shoulder, and his dark eyes meet mine.

He asks, "Mind if I share?"

I nod without stopping my own feast, blood running down my arms and soaking into my skin.

Ivrilos kisses his brother on the cheek. The screams stop. Kadreus's red eyes roll back into his head until I can only see white. Ivrilos must be catching his essence as it tries to escape to the underworld.

Once I reach the center of the heart, I know it's a useless, drained thing. I elongate my nails and tear the rest of the way into it, and then I burn it to ash.

By the time Ivrilos and I both straighten, Kadreus's corpse is turning to ash just like his heart. I'm entirely healed and fully satiated on such rich blood. Ivrilos is as dark as an inkblot, no more cuts on his arms or legs or exhaustion in his face.

We've done it.

My eyes find Lydea's sprawled body. *But at what cost?*

First Japha. Now Lydea. I can't fathom it.

And where is Athanatos?

"He left," Ivrilos says, as if hearing my question aloud. "He returned to his dark city. And yet it's unstable. I can feel it. Everything wants to fall apart, drift away after being leashed together for so long. But it's still holding. The *bridge* is still holding."

"I know," I say. "Kadreus told me. The only way to fully sever the connection between worlds is down there. The second anchor point."

Ivrilos nods. "And that's where my father is." He glances down at Lydea. "Rovan, I'm so sorry." His voice very nearly breaks. "Words are inadequate."

I only nod. Because, yes.

I don't cry or scream. I feel the urge to do those things like a distant pain. Even if I'm healed, my heart is still broken and dead. Or maybe I'm just numb, and this won't last. Maybe I'm going to truly fall apart.

Which means we need to move fast.

It's just then that the tall outer doors to the king's apartments slam open, and a whole crowd floods into the entry room: Alldan, Tumarq, Penelope, Crisea, and even Bethea. They're flanked by too many soldiers to count, quite a few of them spattered in blood.

Though not even *close* to as much blood as I'm covered in. It's dripping down my chin, my arms, and the front of my tunic.

To them, I look like the only one left standing. Ivrilos is invisible. Every weapon in their group bristles, especially once they see Lydea sprawled on the marble floor.

Crisea gasps, covers her mouth with a hand. "But I thought . . . no." She just shakes her head, and Bethea seizes her other hand in her own.

Alldan's violet eyes are locked on the body of his betrothed. "I can't imagine you did this."

"I can't imagine you would suggest such a thing and expect to live for much longer," I say calmly.

371

Weapons bristle even more, if that's possible.

Crisea says, choked with tears, "She didn't do this, you idiots."

"Hold." Tumarq raises a hand, and the weapons lower.

Before anyone can ask, I say, "The king killed her. And I killed the king."

"Then Delphia will be queen," Alldan says, and it takes everything I have in me not to kill *him* right then. He's so quick to move on to the princess he truly loves, apparently with no care for this one—*my* princess. Queen of my heart. Now gone.

"Is it done?" Alldan asks, after receiving only silence. He doesn't realize how close he came to dying. "Did you destroy the anchor point?"

"Yes, but there's still one on the other side. Down there."

"So you need to cross over to destroy it, too."

"Do I?" I say.

Ivrilos seizes my hand, startling my onlookers and causing a few weapons to jump back into the air. "No, she doesn't."

"But those aren't the terms of her agreement with Skyllea," Alldan insists. "She destroys the link to the underworld, and we allow her cursed existence to continue."

Tumarq and Penelope look uncertain, but then Crisea snarls, "*Fuck* Skyllea. That's something for Thanopolis to decide, and I doubt Delphia would approve."

I'm surprised and heartened that she came to my defense—as surprised and heartened as I can be, with everything that's happened and what has to happen.

"She's too dangerous to exist," Alldan says, and Tumarq and Penelope look half convinced.

I raise a hand. It's red. "It's okay. Thank you, Crisea. *No* thanks to you, Alldan. But I'm going down there anyway."

Ivrilos blinks at me. "No. Let me go alone."

I shake my head. "You need my help. Besides, you're all I have left." I take his other hand so we're facing each other. Suddenly, it's as if only the two of us are in the room. I don't care about anyone else, I realize. My family is gone. "I couldn't bear it if you didn't come back. If you die for good, I will, too, anyway."

"The only way to come with me is a stake to your heart," Ivrilos hisses, "and the only way to get back, even if we succeed, is if *they* remove it." He tosses his head at the crowd in the entry. "That is, if they don't decide to just burn your body immediately."

I shrug. "If these will be our last moments before our final death, I'm going to spend them with you."

"This is exactly where they want you, Rovan!"

No one really argues. Lydea and Japha would have fought for me—fought *me*, and then fought others if they had to, to get me back. But they're both gone now, and I'm not sure there's anyone else who would do the same.

I smile. "Dead if I do, dead if I don't." The stake rests on the ground next to Kadreus's pile of dust. I summon it to my hand with my favorite sigil.

I hold it out to Crisea. If there's anyone I would trust to want to ram a stake into my heart, it's her. Or maybe Bethea. "I imagine you'd like to do the honors?"

Crisea raises her chin and folds her arms in defiance as she stares me down, tears in her eyes. "You think I'd want to?" she asks. "You asshole."

I don't have time to apologize.

Bethea looks at me sadly. She seems like she's about to say something, but only shakes her head.

"I guess the pleasure's all mine," I say.

I lean forward and give Ivrilos a lingering kiss.

And then I jam the stake into my own heart.

35

The underworld appears the same as I remember it from Ivrilos's memories. Like before, the ground rises slowly, drifting like a reverse snowfall until it funnels up into the gloomy sky in twisting clouds. But I'm not thinking about the stark unearthliness of the landscape as I scan the dark dunes before me.

I'm looking for her.

"Rovan, you——" Ivrilos starts.

"Do you see her?" I interrupt. "Can you tell if you've caught someone's death current?"

"Rovan . . ."

"You said if you cross soon after someone dies, you'll end up——"

He takes my shoulders. "She's not here. And if she was, she won't be now. Look where we are." He turns me toward him, away from the dunes, and I see we're standing before the immense dark gates of the black city.

My throat seizes. I'd really hoped I could find her, at least make sure she was safe down here for as long as I could. See her one last time. It's finally starting to hit me that she's gone, and I don't know if I'll be able to withstand the blow.

Ivrilos takes both of my hands and presses his forehead against mine. "No words," he says again. Despite where we are, the danger we're in, he closes his eyes and just leans into me for a moment, the dark world dissolving around us. "I'm so sorry she's dead . . . and

I'm sorry you are, too. I've never wanted to see you here." And then he blinks. "You still have your bloodline. You should look at yourself."

I pull away enough to glance down at my arms. I'm wearing the same black tunic I wore just moments ago in the living world, but without any tears or burns or bloodstains. My bloodline stands out on my skin, brighter than ever, like fresh blood. It nearly shimmers, crackles, red lightning over my skin.

And it *definitely* has an effect on what's around me. Whereas Ivrilos looks the tiniest bit . . . *fuzzy* . . . as if the smallest pieces of him are trying to fly away, I churn up everything around me simply by standing still, like I'm the eye of a storm. It seems as though everything nearby wants to flee from me.

Ivrilos shakes his head. "You're like no shade I've ever seen before. It must be your bloodline. You're supposed to lose it when you die. But your connection to the living world isn't severed—you can still go back to your body if the stake is removed—so you've brought your bloodline with you. It's something from the living realm in a land of death."

"I guess this is why you're supposed to burn the body, or at least the heart," I say. "No coming back to life, and no bloodline down here."

The very air around me feels charged, disturbed. Ivrilos and I face the gates of the dark city together, hands clasped. The walls, from the ramparts to the sky-piercing towers, are rippling like black water. It's as if they're having a hard time containing what's inside. The city is like a thin layer of ice over turbulent depths, and it's melting—literally dripping up into the air.

And we have to walk across it.

"Can you still shield yourself?" Ivrilos asks.

I answer by throwing up a shield. I cast it wide enough to include Ivrilos.

"Just don't go too far from me," I say, "or it will work against you, too."

He nods. "Good. It should keep any shades from touching us. Or the city from swallowing us. I don't know how long this place will remain standing, especially when we sever the other anchor point to the living world. It's restless, unstable."

It's hard to imagine that the walls were once *people*.

"You don't think Athanatos found her and took her in there, do you?" I ask, nearly breathless with pain at the thought.

Ivrilos is grim. "I hope not. But we'll make him pay if he has."

We walk up to the gates, our feet kicking up dark sand that whips away from us. At Ivrilos's whispered urging, the massive doors part soundlessly.

The wide black street inside, dimly glinting under a stormy sky, is eerily quiet and empty, as are the towering gatehouses on either side. It's the same as we make our way into the strange structures of the city, the architecture like glass, somehow both flowing and sharp at once. And black, always black. Our footsteps sound loud, echoing against the buildings. I see the faces of shades—men, of course—darker than shadows, from only a few of the unglazed windows that stare down at us like eye sockets. I don't know if the multitude of the city's occupants died their second deaths during the battle above, or if they're staying away from us or from the tenuous stability of the walls. Wherever they are, either in the living world as guardians, out in the dark dunes taking their chances, or finally all the way dead, they don't seem to be here.

Ivrilos keeps his hand in mine as we make our way through the barren, terrifying city alone. I still can't shake feeling like we're walking to the chopping block. Our final deaths.

We reach a massive square that terminates at another set of doors so tall they look stretched, and I recognize where we are from the earliest memory Ivrilos shared with me. The towers of the keep weren't finished back then like they are now. But I remember seeing a throne through the doors.

They're shut tight against us now, but I can feel Athanatos in there, just like I could feel Kadreus in his quarters. I can also feel the other anchor point. It seems to vibrate—the source of the city's instability. And yet it's also the thing still holding it together. Like Ivrilos, I have a feeling that, once cut, it'll all come tumbling down—or up, rather.

Once we're standing in front of the doors, I have to crane my neck to see to the top. The black surface seems to ripple *away* from me.

"Should we knock?"

Ivrilos smiles briefly, and mutters a few words of death magic under his breath. The doors don't budge. "He's holding them against us."

Athanatos isn't making the same mistake Kadreus did and arrogantly throwing them open.

"Let me try."

I use the same words for opening that Ivrilos did, but also sigils, since at least some of them seem to work here. I also walk right into the door at the same time. My shield repels the magic holding it closed, and on top of that, the doors don't seem to want to get near me—or at least my bloodline. They practically leap away, slamming open.

The floor rises to greet us. It ripples like a wave to lift and carry us out, but it breaks against my shield.

Then we feel the wind. Even though it parts around my shield somewhat, it creates a drag against us. Putting one foot in front of the other is difficult. I think of Lydea, Japha, my father, and my mother, and I keep moving forward, Ivrilos at my side.

Athanatos is inside, surrounded by darkness—the rotten heart of this place. His blue eyes flare in surprise and anger. He stands next to his throne, which is exactly as I remember it: both spiking and liquidy, black as ink. It's practically humming.

Lydea isn't here. I'm both relieved and heartbroken all over again.

"If you insist upon entering," Athanatos says coldly, "I suppose I'll just have to kill you." He takes a step toward my shield and then hisses away from it. "What is this? How have you brought this here?"

"Magic," I say. "We're here for your throne."

"You will not approach," Athanatos says though gritted teeth. Under his anger there's a note of frustration, and it's music to my ears.

Ivrilos must hear it, too. "You first brought me here to watch as you destroyed everything dear to me," he says. "Now, no matter how powerful you are, you get to feel just as helpless. You don't get to fight, not even to lose. You just get to *watch*."

For a king who has been taking what he wants by force for hundreds of years, in life and in death, I can't imagine anything more humiliating.

I take that as my cue and head for the throne, the glassy black floor rippling under my feet like I'm walking on water.

"Are you too cowardly to end this properly?" Athanatos snarls, waving at Ivrilos. "Don't you want to try to best me, take my essence for your own?"

Ivrilos sticks close behind me. "I don't want you to be any more a part of me than you already are. They can have you." He nods at the walls, which are now quivering like jelly the closer we get to the throne. "They're probably hungry, after so long."

I realize, with some joy, that Athanatos can't flee. We're blocking the way out, and he has no bond of his own to follow to the living world, without Kadreus. There's only the three of us and the throne.

It *hates* me; I can feel it. If its connection to the living world is anything like a guardian's bond to their ward, then only the destruction of what's bound can break it. I pierced the skull with the stake, but the throne is made of pneuma, like a shade. How exactly does one break that? Its essence looks too concentrated, too dangerously unstable for Ivrilos to try to consume.

And then I remember that once-living substance can interrupt death, just like the skull or a revenant's heart. And I've brought something like that with me: my bloodline. It's the stake that I'm going to ram into the heart of the dark city—into Athanatos, his throne, and everything he has built with it.

I'm the stake.

Athanatos howls as I reach the throne. The hum grows to a whine of straining tension—a stringed instrument plucked to the point of breaking. The noise pierces my brain, makes my ears want to bleed, but it's nothing to the pain I've already felt.

I sit on the throne.

The screeching vibration abruptly stops. The throne falls still, though a shock wave blasts out from it, rippling through everything—the snapping tension of the link to the living world felt throughout the entire city. Then everything falls quiet.

Too quiet. Like a held breath.

I face Athanatos. His expression is scorched, empty. I merely cross my legs, as if getting more comfortable. "It's done."

As I say it, the walls begin to run. Down, not up, pooling on the floor like thick paint. It must have too much weight, the essence too condensed, to just float away.

"Rovan . . . ," Ivrilos says, eyeing it. "We should go."

Athanatos has been too busy staring hatred and murder at me to notice it puddling at his feet. By the time he glances down, it's too late. He tries to lift his leg, but it's stuck fast to the floor, and the blackness only rises, beginning to crawl up his leg like shapeless fingers.

Like hundreds, thousands of the nameless, starving dead. So ravenous and held here unnaturally for so long that they caused the blight, their hunger so toxic and mindless that it can make blood-fiends out of bloodmages and drain the entire living world dry.

I stand and head for the doors with Ivrilos.

"Wait!" Athanatos's blue eyes are now wild with fear as he flails, almost losing his balance. "You can't just turn your backs on me." His voice grows more desperate. "You can't leave me like this! It's a disgrace."

"Enjoy your mausoleum," Ivrilos says. "You built it, and in it you'll lie." He looks around, his dark eyes suddenly soft. Sad. "Fare-well, Mother. Aeona." His sister, I remember through our bond, though I never knew her name before. "Embrace this man like he embraced you, and then rest in peace." He touches his fingers to his lips.

I turn to the city, blinking away sudden tears as Athanatos's screams rise behind us.

Everything is melting around us. The entire city.

"We might want to run," Ivrilos says, and a whole building comes down, suddenly liquid and thrashing and containing what look like hundreds of submerged, amorphous limbs, reaching blindly toward anything and everything. The walls of Athanatos's keep begin to sag behind us.

Athanatos's screams abruptly cut off.

We run. The liquid darkness parts around us, though it strains against my shield like nothing I've felt before, not even Athana-tos's attacks. Such is the force, the sheer *mass* behind this unfath-omable amount of essence, now unleashed. We pass other shades, flailing in the black muck, crying out, and we ignore them. They helped build this. Now they're reaping what they sowed.

And what they sowed is reaping *them*.

It's when the street beneath us begins to soften, slurping at our feet like mud, slowing our progress despite my shield, that I really begin to worry.

"Almost . . . there," Ivrilos pants, his hand at my lower back, propelling me forward.

The city gates practically burp us out in a shower of slippery darkness, though thankfully it only sluices off my shield. We scramble our way up the side of the first wave of dunes, not stopping until we've reached a safe height. And then we turn to watch the city walls and towers collapse into churning, clawing, slithering waves.

Eventually, everything falls quiet. And Ivrilos and I are looking out over a black lake where a city once stood.

Even now the lake isn't entirely still. It ripples like there are gargantuan creatures swimming beneath the surface. Horrors. But they're just the shapeless remains of *people*, finally finding their rest. As we watch, the lake begins evaporating, just like the dunes are dissolving. The strange drips that once fell upward into the sky now lift off from the lake like reverse rain.

My knees give out, and I sit none too gracefully in the sand along the dune's side. Ivrilos drops down next to me. We stay that way for a long time, watching the weight of all those souls finally relax and drift, eventually rising to find some measure of peace.

Hours, or maybe days later, Ivrilos looks at me sitting next to him, and he smiles.

He's strangely bright, even all dressed in black. Maybe it's that the landscape is somehow darker. Maybe it's that he almost looks . . . *happy.*

I take his hand. "You look young, Ivril."

Ivril. His childhood nickname. A look so wistful crosses his face that I touch his cheek.

"Sorry," he says. "You . . . all of this . . . I don't know quite what I feel. I don't know if I want to sprint or lie down or . . ."

"You did it," I say. "Finally."

He sighs. "And yet I'm more aware than ever of everything I've lost."

It's hard not to be, sitting at the side of a lake at what looks like the end of the world. It's certainly the end of life. And *lives*. Maybe ours, and so many others.

My father. My mother. Lydea. Japha. I've also lost so much. My grief feels as deep and dark as that lake, with things swimming in it that I don't want to think about.

So I won't think about it, because this might be one of the last moments I have in any realm, the living or the dead.

"You haven't lost *everything*." I grin and nudge his shoulder. I even give him a suggestive wink. If anything, it might distract us both.

But he looks at me in a strange way. One that isn't awkward or startled, but open and . . . new. "No, I haven't."

I can't take the intensity of his look. *I* suddenly feel awkward. But as I try to turn, he catches my cheek and gently guides my face back toward his. His eyes pore over me, and his expression is one of wonder.

"You are so beautiful," he breathes. "Body, mind, and spirit. And sometimes I can't believe my blessed fortune that I've met you after so long. That I've found one bright, glorious thing toward the end of this long bleak existence that makes it worth continuing."

He presses his lips to mine, and I forget everything else. I might as well be drifting away with the rest of our surroundings.

"End?" I murmur, when I can breathe. "Who wants this to end?"

"It must," he says, leaning his temple against mine and exhaling, long and slow. "Probably sooner rather than later."

"Let's not rush toward that." Never mind that we haven't left ourselves many alternatives. "Let's enjoy the moment. Besides, I'm pretty sure we have unfinished business."

He opens his eyes. Holds mine. "All right."

And then he kisses me again, for a long, long time.

<hr />

It's sometime later, as we're lying back against the dune, arms wrapped around each other, staring at the dissolving sky, that I feel a strange hollowness in my chest.

I sit upright abruptly, dragging myself out of Ivrilos's embrace, hand at my breast.

"What is it?" he demands, startled, reaching toward his bare hip where armor and a sword suddenly reappear.

"I think I feel somethi—"

And then I'm gone.

36

When I open my eyes, it's onto a ceiling lined with skulls. Of all my waking views—from the veil on top of the gazebo with Bethea, to my body on a stone slab when I was bound to Ivrilos, to sunlight spearing my hungover eyes, to a canopy of roses masking the smell of my dead body—it's probably the least appealing.

Until I turn my head and I see who's standing nearby, looking down at me with anxious faces. And then it's the most beautiful view I've ever seen.

Lydea and Japha. Even Ivrilos appears next to them.

I fly off the hard surface I'm lying on—another stone slab, as it turns out—and I throw myself at Lydea. I crash into her so solidly I almost bring us both to the ground. That doesn't stop me from smothering her face in kisses. Neither do her red eyes, nor their tears of blood.

It doesn't hurt that she starts kissing me back just as fiercely, never mind my own red tears.

Someone clears their throat. And that someone is Japha. I don't care if I'll get blood on them; I spin away from Lydea to throw my arms around them.

. . . And I fall right through them.

"Yeah, that," says Japha. "I'm dead, if you recall."

I pull away, staring at them. Unlike any shade I've ever seen, they're wearing a bright orange peplos patterned in blooming white lilies. Japha never did like black. And they're no longer wearing their bloodline. Good thing—it would have clashed horribly.

"But y-you're here," I stammer. "How—?"

They jerk a thumb at Lydea. "I'm bound to her. I'm . . . her guardian? And she's . . . um . . . you're not really my ward, are you? My revenant?"

Lydea smiles at me, her eyes almost entirely red now, with the blood. "I guess I'm dead, too, just not as thoroughly. Like you, Rovan."

Except I *was* thoroughly dead, just a moment ago. I paw at my chest. There's no wound there. Lydea lifts the stake between two fingers as if it's disgusting, wood and bone bound in steel.

"How?" I gasp again. I'm having a hard time finding words.

"Well, we pulled the stake out—"

"No, I mean, how are you *here*?"

Lydea's lips twist. "I didn't exactly have time to tell you before I ended up with a broken neck, but Crisea and Bethea, with the help of one of those creepy Skyllean bloodmages, trapped Japha's shade before they could wander too far, and then bound them to me. I offered, and Japha didn't resist, so . . ."

Japha throws up their hands. "Why would I resist? Have you *seen* the underworld? Who wants to stay there?"

"Indeed," Lydea says. "That's why I left the battle to find you, Rovan. I fulfilled my promise to keep Japha safe. At that point we were still a normal ward and guardian, but then I tore that bastard Kadreus's heart out and made him angry, to say the least. As he was strangling me, Japha tried to help."

Japha cringes sheepishly. "I guess I helped too much, even if it didn't amount to much at all. Still, I gave her everything I had. And here we are. She died—mostly—and we both came back."

I stare at them, agape. Japha waves in greeting at Ivrilos. Ivrilos slowly lifts a hand in return, nearly as shocked as I am.

Lydea smiles at him—of course, she can see him now, too, as a revenant—but then drops her red eyes and stares down at her twining fingers. "I know this is weird, but we woke up here in the necropolis next to your staked body—"

She might be shy about her eyes, or about how she looks otherwise, but to me she's more gorgeous than ever.

"It's amazing," I interrupt, choking, my throat almost too tight to speak. I take in all of them slowly, standing awkwardly together. My *family*. "It's the most beautiful, wonderful thing anyone could come back to." I glance at the black walls, which remind me uncomfortably of the dark city. "Despite the decor."

"You think *we're* beautiful?" Lydea takes my shoulders and steers me over to a narrow window. "Look at this." I try to focus on what she's showing me instead of the feel of her hands on me. We're high up in the necropolis, peering out from its vulturelike perch on the edge of the plateau that holds Thanopolis. We have an unobstructed view of the blight.

Except . . . there's golden sunlight now on the icy peaks in the distant north, with no endless, wintery white billowing off them. Snow has even melted away from the craggy rocks and old ruins in some places. And toward the south, where barren desert once was, I see streaking rain clouds on the horizon, and already the faintest hues of green beginning to dapple the brown stretches of cracked dirt and sand. I can even *smell* the moisture on a warm breeze.

"The blight," I gasp. "It's fading."

"It is," Lydea says, squeezing my shoulder.

I lean into her touch, running my cheek over the back of her knuckles. But then I can't help glancing at Ivrilos in sudden concern. He only gives me a beautifully crooked grin.

"Yes, dears, the view is amazing, but let's get the hell out of here," Japha says, shuddering. "I hate this place. We were just waiting for you to wake up."

Feeling overwhelmed, I back away from the window, but I hesitate before going straight for the skull-lined door. "Can we? I thought they might decide to leave the stake in and burn my body for good measure. And now that there are two of us, the Skylleans might decide that's two too many."

"Pshaw!" Japha sweeps a hand as though brushing away the thought. "I took care of that. The queen owed me a favor. Remember, she promised me whatever I wanted if I brought my father to Skyllea's side. I *died* for that damned promise, so she'd better keep it. With Lydea's help I could appear to her, and I asked her to never kill, imprison, or otherwise subjugate anyone I care about—which includes you two, revenants or not. Also future Queen Delphia, and, as a happy coincidence, the rest of Thanopolis."

It seems much has happened since I staked myself; it's dizzying. "How is Delphia?"

"Only so blissful she might float away, with Alldan at her side," Lydea says with a soft smile. And then it flattens. "I've never seen *him* so happy, either. He certainly never looked at me like that."

"Nor you, him," Japha says, barking a laugh. "For now, both my father and Penelope are helping Delphia to rule. They've refused to allow any advisers from Skyllea—other than Alldan, of course—to join them in that task, but that doesn't keep the Skyllean queen from asking."

It's really not a bad arrangement. Delphia is truly sweet and kind and the least likely to want to rule, which is why she's perfect for it. Tumarq and Penelope are more than capable advisers. Even Alldan, clever and noble, won't be terrible at her side as her consort, even if he can be a self-righteous, pompous ass.

"As long as the queen doesn't make threats to get what she wants," I say.

"If she does . . ." Lydea makes a fist.

"She won't," Japha says.

"You're brilliant," I say, grinning at them. I still can't believe they're here, even after dying. That I'm awake. That I have everything I could ever need, despite what I've lost. My grin falters a bit. "How are Crisea . . . and Bethea?"

"Crisea and Bethea have officially left the necropolis, along with a lot of other acolytes. Only the old die-hard priests remain. Or should I say *die-easy?*" Japha smirks.

Ivrilos groans, which makes Lydea laugh in delight.

"Anyway, Bethea and Crisea are together," Japha continues. "Death magic, as you know too well, is poison for the living. They need to stop using it, get it out of their systems. It's hard, but Penelope is training with Crisea again, helping her, and Crisea and Bethea are helping each other."

"They're actually rather adorable together," Lydea says grudgingly.

I'm glad to hear it, truly. "So that just leaves you two," I say. "Are you . . . okay . . . aside from being dead? Being a revenant is an adjustment, as I also know too well."

Lydea shrugs. "I'll get used to the eyes . . . and everything else. It's worth it." Her lingering look warms my cheeks. *You're worth it*, she seems to say.

"And being a shade . . . ?" I grimace at Japha.

Their lips quirk. "I get to see my father and you all again. I'd say that's worth it. I can't marry Helena, obviously, but I'd rather not. I mean, I didn't *intend* to sacrifice myself. I was fighting for the freedom to be *me*, and in a strange way I got it. Thank the goddess I don't mind Lydea's company," they add, smiling at her. "She's my anchor. A new ground beneath my feet. I'm happy to be here, even if I'm bound to my dear cousin more than I ever thought I would be." Lydea gives Japha a worried frown, and they take her hand. "I don't mind, I promise. I know where I belong. And it's right here with you and Rovan."

I reach for Lydea's other hand, as well as Ivrilos's.

"You're bound to all of us," I say. I can't help smiling again, like a fool.

Japha eyes Ivrilos. "At least he really is something to look at. And if he's your family, he's mine." They take Ivrilos's free hand, startling him—and me. I shouldn't be surprised. Not only is Japha touching Lydea and Ivrilos touching me, but shades can interact with one another without any help. And Japha has always been affectionate.

We all form a circle. Our strange little family. Only two related by blood, two of us dead, and two of us *un*dead. And yet, despite our deaths, we've been reborn, more vibrant than ever before.

Like Japha said, I don't mind this new arrangement. Not anymore. Not alongside them.

"You were there for me," I say, squeezing their hands. "And I'll be here for you, forever."

"Until the end and after," Lydea says seriously.

I just say it outright. "I love you. All of you."

"I love you," they all say back, nearly in unison. Japha and Lydea laugh, and Ivrilos smiles. "Forever," he adds.

He's so beautiful it's heartbreaking. Except my heart can take it now. It feels unbounded instead of dead. Expansive and free.

And maybe even strong enough to face what I've lost. My father. My mother. The life that I once had. But I'm not quite ready yet. Because now is the time to celebrate what I've gained.

Blinking bloody tears from my eyes, I blurt, "Where to next?"

"I've always wanted to sail on a ship," Lydea says, and then arches her brow. "Maybe *now* you'll come with me?"

"Of course. And I won't even ask you to go to Skyllea." I grin. "Yet. I still want to see it someday, but I'm in no rush."

I still can't let go of that memory of my father, telling me of its beauty, and my desire to see it for his sake. But ever since I caught a glimpse of it through that magical window, I wouldn't mind seeing it for *me*.

We have time, though.

"We *should* be able to visit without trouble," Japha says, and then grumbles, "The queen better keep her promises, or I swear to the goddess I will *haunt* her."

I laugh. I'm just so *happy*, I could almost split with it.

"Across the sea, then?" Ivrilos asks, that boyish gleam of excitement in his eyes. It would be something new for him, I realize, in four hundred years of the same scenery. I want to give him all of that and more.

Speaking of scenery . . .

I drag whomever I can reach into a hug. Even Japha and I can touch now, because they're touching Lydea. I give them an extra-hard squeeze, like I couldn't earlier, pressing my forehead to theirs before pulling Lydea and Ivrilos into the huddle.

"Let's go," I breathe. "The world is ours." I withdraw a little sheepishly. "And I'm also hungry."

There's a wicked glint in Lydea's beautiful red eyes. It promises lifetimes of adventure. "Me too."

"What do we even eat, as shades?" Japha asks.

Ivrilos only laughs. The sound is delightful, even if edged in darkness.

Just like my family. I hope the world is ready for us.

"You'll see," I say.

Acknowledgments

Firstly, thanks to my amazing editor, John Morgan, for championing queer stories. Working with you is, as ever, a delight, and this year, it has been a solace. (Someday, we'll hang out for a much-needed drink.)

Thanks also to publisher Erin Stein and the team at Imprint for turning my manuscripts into beautiful books—especially Natalie C. Sousa for the most gorgeous cover ever.

Much appreciation to my indefatigable early readers: Deanna Birdsall, Chelsea Pitcher, Lukas Strickland, and Terran Williams. Your eyes on my first drafts are invaluable. I <3 you.

Thanks to Laia Jiménez i Danés and Alyssa Coll for making my non-writing time ridiculously fun, much enriched, and utterly unpredictable. It would have been a sad year without you both. Much love.

Thanks finally to my agent, Hannah Bowman, for joining me on this wild ride. Here's to working together on many more stories.